LEBENSTRAUM

ROYSTON MOORE

Order this book online at www.trafford.com
or email orders@trafford.com

Most Trafford titles are also available at major online book retailers.

Printed in Victoria, BC, Canada.

ISBN: 9780-1-4269-0313-7 (sc)

*Our mission is to efficiently provide the world's finest, most comprehensive
book publishing service, enabling every author to experience success.
To find out how to publish your book, your way, and have it available
worldwide, visit us online at www.trafford.com*

Trafford rev. 02/23/2010

 www.trafford.com

North America & international
toll-free: 1 888 232 4444 (USA & Canada)
phone: 250 383 6864 ♦ fax: 812 355 4082

LEBENSTRAUM

THE UNITED STATES CONTINUES TO EXPAND

HELPED BY FAMILIES LONG ESTABLISHED
AS WELL AS MANY NEW FAMILIES
COMING TO AMERICA FROM OVERSEAS

A CARROLL FAMILY SAGA

ROYSTON MOORE

READ OTHER BOOKS BY ROYSTON MOORE

FIVE BOOKS IN THE CARROLL FAMILY SAGA

FICTIONAL LOVE STORIES IN AMERICA FROM 1690 TO 1850

MARYLAND – a Rags to Riches love story around 1690 – Amelia Eliot and David Carroll begin the Carroll Family Saga

OHIO – The love stories of five couples during the "Seven Year War" – really British and French enemies who became friends

LIBERTY – Carroll descendents and other immigrants still survive and discover love during the American Revolution from Britain

GENESIS – The new United States struggles whilst chaos reigns in Europe. New immigrants helped by Carroll's to discover love.

LEBENSTRAUM – "Living-Dreams" - Later Carroll descendents also with others continue the expansion west looking for Living Space – Their part in River, Sea and now Railway transport for growing industry

LOVE 3000 YEARS AGO IN ANCIENT EGYPT

MAKERE – THE FEMALE PHAROAH – QUEEN OF SHEBA

Though written as fiction – It describes the actual life of MAKERE HATSHEPSUT –the only Female Pharaoh of Egypt – yet proves she was, also the mysterious Queen of Sheba – Her actual love for lowly web-priest, Senmut and Solomon, King of All Israel. – Her tempestuous life – so similar to British Tudor Queen Elizabeth.

PURCHASE ALL AT ANY BOOKSELLER OR ON LINE AT AMAZON.COM OR DIRECT AT TRAFFORD PUBLISHING

FOREWORD

A story of Romantic Love triumphing over all problems, as the new United States continues to expand westward towards the Pacific Ocean. Opening new lands beyond the Mississippi and Missouri Rivers, and into Mexico in Texas and California. Also continuing the Carroll Family Saga as descendents of Margaret Eliot of Ireland, but particularly those of Sir David and Amelia Carroll, who, still, continue to play a vital part in ensuring the rapid development of this expanding country.

Though both Michelle and Daniel Carroll are now deceased, their protégée, Mark and Estelle Carroll of Rockville, and their son Danton, now married to Claudia Albrecht, become part of the Diplomatic Legation in Mexico City. But, also, of the Downey, Eliot, and Reid families who were so greatly helped in the past by Daniel Carroll and Michelle to establish themselves. These were, also, aided by the other branch of the Carroll family, previously Roman Catholics, but who became Protestants when Edgar Carroll married into the rich New York, Dutch families. All fully described in the previous books covering the Carroll Family Saga.

This book "Lebenstraum" is the fifth in the series following the previous books "Maryland", "Ohio", "Liberty" and "Genesis". Though events in those books contributed to everything which happens in this current book, it contains sufficient information, necessary, to explain how important this was in deciding and contributing to their present lives.

Introducing Gordon Taylor from Manchester, Sheila McLean from Northern Ireland, and Rachael Gilbert forced to marry an evil Elder of the Mormon Sect. The escape of Otto Fallon from Germany bringing to this country his knowledge of banking and the investments made by the Ibsen family, coming from Scandinavia, and Otto's growing love for Freda Ibsen. Yet, how, the present long established residents of the United States, were to eventually, after many tribulations, to find love and a very happy future.

All historical references are accurately described, when required, in this book. How the expansion west was to add the Mexican lands of Texas and California to the map of the United States, until it became a country stretching from the Atlantic to the Pacific Oceans.

In spite of this, enjoy the many romantic love stories of life in this country from 1828 until after the U.S.A./Mexican War as late as 1850. Love stories, but which enabled the countries development in river, shipping and the advent of railways, adding to the agricultural wealth, the growing industrial, and economic richness. This, only possible because of the influx of so many new emigrants from Europe. Romance made all their troubles worthwhile, as they established themselves and added greatly to the future prosperity of the United States

ROYSTON MOORE

THE CARROL FAMILIES SAGAS IN AMERICA

MARYLAND – *Is the first of Five books set in America from colonial days in 1688 to 1694, and to the United States in 1850. This book introduces readers first, to the Protestant Carroll family going to America from Somerset to join the Roman Catholic Carroll family living there since they emigrated from Yorkshire. It is a Rags to Riches story of love in the late 17th. Century*

OHIO – *This second book covers the period from 1748 to 1763. the time of the Seven Years War between Britain and France – the first global war. It covers the life of five sets of partners, both British and French who, though should have been enemies, but due to their presence in this new land of Ohio, are drawn together and become friends. Continuing the Carroll Sagas, now with Daniel Carroll, grandson of Amelia and David Carroll.*

LIBERTY – *The period of 1770 to 1789 – The events leading to and the actual War of American Independence from Britain. Many characters from the previous books and the valuable assistance Daniel Carroll and his wife Michelle gave to George Washington during the bleak times of the war. Continuing the sagas of both branches of the Carroll families but introducing many new persons.*

GENESIS – *The New Country. The period from 1793 to 1803 when in a single day the size of the United States doubled with President Jefferson's 'Louisiana Purchase' from Spain. The problems besetting the United States - a country ruled by an elected President and not a king, attempting neutrality, whilst Europe descended into chaos with the French Revolution and the many European wars. Now we meet the numerous off springs of two Carroll families, and their love affairs, again concerning the life of Daniel Carroll, his wife Michelle and their children, and many new emigrants from Europe.*

LEBENSTRAUM– *"Living-Dreams " Covering the period from 1826 to 1850. The expansion Westwards – Texas and Mexico and events in California. The development of an industrial America and the vital* *part played by both Carroll families in both river and rail transport. Again dealing not only with their love affaires, but those of the many new emigrants coming to America and settling in love there.*

THE ENGLISH & AMERICAN CARROLL FAMILIES TO 1850

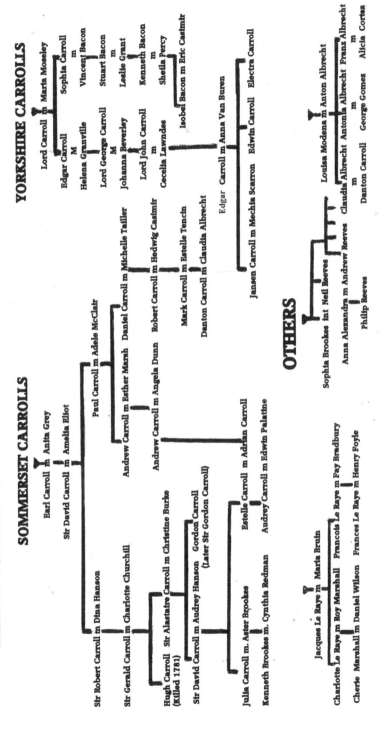

DESCENDENTS OF MARGARET ELIOT

John Eliot m Margaret Vine

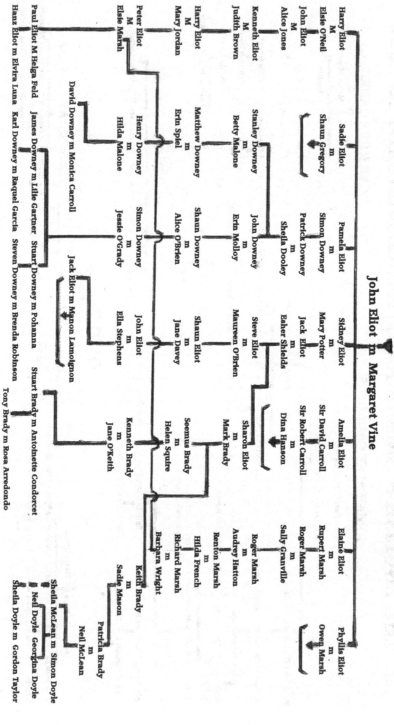

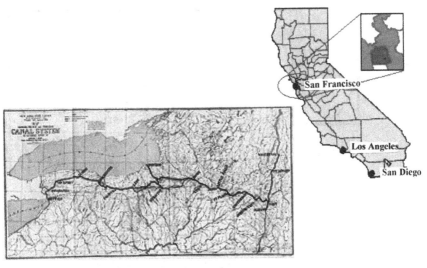

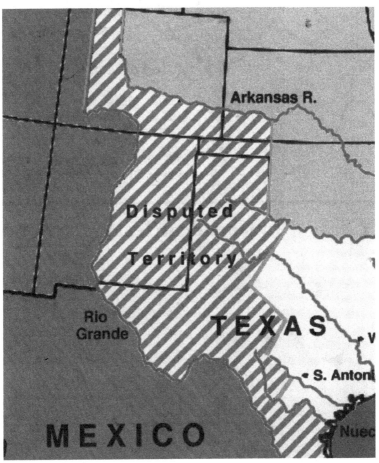

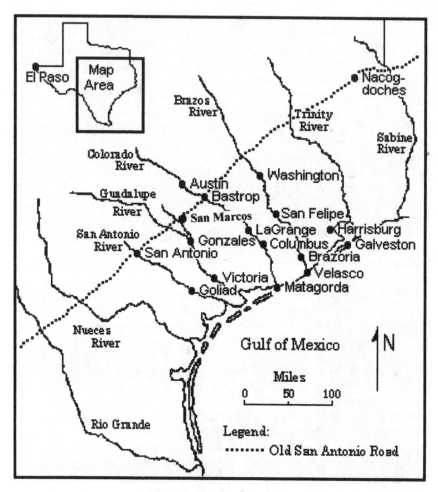

Independent Texas

CONTENTS

PART 1

AMBITION

LEBENSTRAUM PART 1
AMBITION

AMBITION

1.

Otto Fallen was twenty one years old, now conducting financial research into world economies of this time, having already received a Bachelors degree in Economics and Finance, at the University of Bremen in Germany. But Otto was a very worried man. That day his own professor had been arrested for actions against the state, being charged as being a member of a Secret Society which endangered the rulers of several countries.

It was January 1828 and due to violent student demonstrations the previous year resulting in the rulers of Brunswick, Saxony and Hanover having been forced to accept modifications in the constitutions of their countries. These actions had alerted both Prussia and Austria and had renewed the Carlsbad Decrees first instituted by Chancellor Metternich of Austria in 1819. They were decrees to subjugate the populace, which after the end of the Napoleonic Wars in 1815, had created a cry for freedom by many persons, particularly the students in Universities, who wished to remove the autocratic powers of both Kings, Emperors and unrepresentative governments.

The Carlsbad Decrees had followed the murder by Karl Sand, a student at the University of Jena, of a reactionary journalist, August von Kotzebue in March 1819. Metternich had persuaded the Central powers to institute these repressive powers, as the authority of their rulers were being challenged. Designed to control any rebellion in universities, it ruthlessly enforced its many provisions and prevented uprisings for almost ten years. But the student actions of the past year had renewed the repression, and even increased it.

Otto Follen was not, himself, an agitator. In fact because of his birth and his families prosperity, he should be one who would welcome these restrictions as it protected his fortunately happy life. His father was Senor Manager, and a Junior director of a large bank in Hanover living on an estate nearby. Otto had been sent to study at Bremen University and to graduate, being promised a lucrative position in the bank when qualified.

He had refused to take any part in any student societies as he studied for his degree, which had made him unpopular with his fellow students. However his course had awakened in him a realization that the present economic practices, particularly following the end of the war, had severely restricted the European countries economic progress. He saw that countries such as Austria and Prussia, and to a lesser extent, the smaller German states, spent so much on armaments, that it was greatly effecting their countries prosperity.

He was particularly surprised at the economic success of this new country, the United States of America, which had even acquired in a short time, the wealth to buy land to its west, now called the "Louisiana Purchase", which literately doubled its size in a single day. He had placed this in the thesis he was writing as part of his Master's Degree.

Only a week before he had been called before the University authorities, though really the security board which implemented the Carlsbad Decree, to explain his behaviour, denigrating the decisions being taken in most European Countries. He had not realised that has his submission was less than twenty pages in length, like any publication in the University it fell foul of the Carlsberg demands and was subjected to censorship.

The fact that this was a thesis to be published for submission to the University as an academic presentation, did nothing to absolve him from this crime. Yet, if it had been a scientific presentation refuting the very basis of the universe, no censorship would have accrued. He was told to rewrite his submission and remove any criticism to the countries economic methods. He had to submit a written apology, and was told his name would be noted in case theses actions were repeated. For the first time he realised why many of his fellow students, not having families with autocratic associations, were trying to rebel. However in deference to his family he had accepted his faults and apologised.

However today the security police had come, arrested, charged, and had taken away his own professor, under whose tutelage he had submitted his thesis. After his so recent accusations against the state, he realised he might be arrested as a co-conspirator with his professor, and possibly land in jail. Worse this would bring severe disgrace on his family, and particularly his father, so closely connected with the royal family.

Otto wasted no time, he quickly returned to his father in Hanover, and explained what had happened. His father, immediately saw the danger. It was imperative he left the country before any warrant could be served on him. Of course it might not happen as the true charges against his professor had not been stated, but it was a wise course of action.

Fortunately they were very rich. Otto could leave with considerable letters of credit negotiable in any civilized country, and with the means to travel anywhere in the world. His father had suggested Britain, but at present there had been some quite violent demands for the reform of their Parliament. After what his researches had shown him of the economic success of the United States, he felt it was there that he should go. As his father had for a long time done business with The Bank of Manhattan, in New York, his father agreed this was a better choice, and gave him a letter of introduction to that bank when he arrived, denoting his expertise in both banking and finance and his Honours degree of Bremen University.

After saying a sad and brief farewell to his parents, brothers and sisters he used the family coach to journey to Hamburg. After a stay of ten days, choosing to wait for any American boat, for if a warrant for his arrest was made and he travelled on a German ship, he might still be taken and returned for trial. He took a passage on the United States Ship "Boston Flyer" purchasing a very comfortable suite of cabins and set sail in February 1828 for New York.

His accommodation might have been comfortable, but crossing the Atlantic in February was not a pleasant journey. Even before it called at Harwich, Otto had been sea-sick several times. Then entering the English Channel and into the southern Atlantic approaches he was troubled several more times. However before they arrived and sailed up the Hudson to land a New York harbour, Otto had at last, obtained his sea-legs.

Once he disembarked, he took a cab to a large hotel and reserved a suite, as money was no obstacle. He felt he had made the right decision, first in leaving Germany very quickly, then choosing to come to New York. On the ship he had met many fellow travellers, a number like him travelling from European countries, to settle and start a new life in America. He had been particular pleased to meet a family coming from Scandinavia, who had sailed first to Harwich to join this ship. They came, with some money, hoping to start a business in either New York or Washington. They were particularly interested in investments, as the opportunities in the United States were much greater than at home. However Otto was more particularly pleased to meet their eldest daughter, Freda Ibsen.

He gave her his home address in Hanover, ensuring she knew he was quite rich, asking her to write there and inform him of wherever they decided to take habitation, as Otto made it very clear he would like to renew their acquaintance. However this must be sometime in the future. It was imperative that he first established himself in this new country, hoping to be given a reasonably important position in the Manhattan Bank and so ensure a profitable future for himself in the Untied States.

From his researches he felt certain there were many opportunities for him, and hoped he too would grow rich as did this country. The next day he went to the bank and produced his father's letter and shown them his qualifications. It seemed he would be offered a position, but must prove his capabilities, needing to learn how different were financial procedures here, compared with Europe. The salary was not great, but he, already, possessed sufficient wealth and knew his father could send him more.

So twenty one year old Otto Follen accept this position with a promise of advancement if he proved his worth. However it would not be the sinecure he would have enjoyed if he had taken up an employment in Hanover. He had told the bank he intended to purchase a small house, and they recommended the Bronx, then they suggested, once a property holder, he should, immediately apply, to become a United States Citizen. It seemed he must become part of this new country.

2.

Gordon Taylor was twenty years old and was at that moment both very sad and yet elated. Sad as he had just left the family he adored. Elated for he was going to America to start a new life there. He gasped as he thrust the leaver on the small truck up and down which, by his exertions, propelled him along the iron way, the one in which, in a small way, he had helped to construct. For he was travelling on what was to become the nearly the first Railway in Britain, and possibly in the world. The Liverpool-Manchester Railway.

It would not open, officially, for another eighteen months, though most of its length had been completed, at least as far as the outskirts of Liverpool. Only the one and half mile Wapping Tunnel, from Liverpool docks to Edge Hill and the seventy foot cutting was not yet finished. However as an engineer, who, through his father's firm 'Taylor Iron Smelters', he had fabricated and installed the iron structure demanded, so was allowed to use the Rail Truck to take him from Manchester to the beginning of the tunnel., and on that truck was the luggage he was taking to America.

The last six years had been exciting years for Gordon, and his father's business had been successful, trading in the construction of the line and the steam engines to be built to drive the coaches . Founded by his grandfather, they had much earlier helped in the construction of the canals now crossing Lancashire and Yorkshire. However since his father died in what was now called the 'Peterloo Massacre' in 1819, the business had been run by his elder brother James Taylor.

Like many industrious persons after the Napoleonic Wars ended. They wanted to reform Parliament, still the province of the rich and aristocrats, unable to vote to elect its members. At a demonstration outside St. Peters' Church and in the small square, his father William Taylor, along with other prosperous merchants had staged a demonstration. On the orders of the Prime Minister, the Duke of Wellington, all such demonstrations had to be curtailed. Exceeding their orders, the cavalry had charged the populace in the square, killing many. His father was one who died that day.

However his brother James, though only seventeen years old, had carried on the business, helped later by his two elder sisters, Elizabeth and Edna, who had married and whose husbands, also helped. The business had continued to prosper and they lived in some style in Ancoats, Manchester. Money was available for Gordon to attend the new Mechanics Institute in Moseley Street, where he qualified as a full engineer last year.

However the growing families of his brother and sisters and the younger members of his family, had placed a great strain on their wealth. The refusal to remove the Corn Laws was spreading poverty throughout the land. Even bread became a luxury few could afford. The situation of the Taylor family was not desperate but it would be helpful if some members of the family found other occupations. However unemployment was rampant through the land, making this very difficult.

Help had come from an unexpected quarter. Everyone knew their father William, had a brother, Silas Taylor, fourteen years younger than him. Again whilst working as a seventeen year old in Liverpool in 1812, Elias was seized and pressed into the British Navy when the 1812 war with the United States had begun. Everyone had lost touch with him until a year ago, when he had written to them telling them of his adventurous life.

It seemed he had been present in January 1815 at the Battle of New Orleans, which actually occurred just after a peace treaty had been signed. Due to the brilliance of militia leader, Andrew Jackson, and the incompetence of the British, the battle became a rout. So many soldiers died that the admiral, in desperation, sent many of his sailors ashore, to add to the numbers. In spite of this the British withdrew in panic. Silas Taylor, who had hated his conscription into the navy deserted, and made his way to the Mississippi waterway.

Within a few weeks he found employment on one of the many steam paddle cargo steamers which travelled the length of that river, going northwards into the Missouri and Ohio Rivers, even along the Monongahela River as far as Fort Pitt. However this old French Fort first called Duquesne, then after the Seven years was to become Fort Pitt. Now a town, fast becoming a city, had developed around the fort, which formed such a small part of it. Now it had been given a new name of Pittsburgh.

It seemed that for years Silas had travelled up and down those rivers, rising to become captains of the boats and even Master. Then having acquired sufficient wealth, in 1825 Silas had established on the water front at Pittsburgh, the Taylor Ship Cargo Company, with two steam ships of his own, and now lived in a house near the waterfront. At last settled he had decided to try to contact his brother's family and written to them, telling them of the wonderful opportunity for any shipbuilders, iron smelters and engineers in the expanding town,

It was one of the largest industrial towns in the Union. The Ship building Business called the Carroll/Marshall Boat Company, established in 1795, constructed many of the Steam ships which plied for trade on these rivers. Recently they had created and built luxury paddle ships which sailed the rivers, stopping on the banks at various ports, then opened them for entertainment such as gambling and dancing girls. They had been christened 'Show Boats'.

However with both bitumen and anthracite coal nearby, it was being mined in quantity. Now with the discovering of iron ore, iron smelting and casting had become established, essential when building these steam boats. Already there were some steel mills. So Silas had told them that the opportunities there were enormous. It awakened in Gordon a desire for adventure. He knew his families difficulties, perhaps it would be made more difficult once the railway was completed. With little chance of very profitable employment outside his firm, Gordon decided he would like to travel to America and join his uncle, who offered him employment.

This then, was why Gordon thrust his way from Manchester to the outskirts of Liverpool on the manually operated truck. His elation was due to the thought of starting a new life, a profitable life for himself in the United States. Provided he was careful, he had sufficient money to purchase a passage on a ship to New York. Silas had told him the easiest route to Pittsburgh was now to land at New York, sail up the Hudson River to Albany. Then travel by the newly constructed Erie Canal to Buffalo, Pennsylvania, then cross the few miles to Pittsburgh. That is what Gordon intended to do.

At last he reached the present end of the line, transferred to a canal boat and sailed down the docks to Liverpool. He purchased a berth on the "Atlantic Lady", sailing in two days time. Then found a inn for the night and during the next twenty four hours, as suggested by the shipping company, bought a stock of non-perishable food and some bottled wine, in case the boat was becalmed and food become restricted. This was still the practice which had been recommendation for passengers crossing the Atlantic for the last one hundred and fifty years.

In the past it had been a necessity. Now its use was unlikely, but it was sensible to take precautions, and Gordon knew he had to purchase this food, which even when suffering sea sickness, could easy the suffering. He knew he would be only one of many travelling on that ship as he had needed to queue for sometime to obtain his tickets, and there were still many others behind him, waiting to buy their tickets. Now he was ready to cross the great Atlantic Ocean with the dangers of severe storms always present.

3.

A twenty year old Donald Reid was returning with a large band of fur trappers from an exciting adventure where they had travelled as far as the Great Salt Lake in the Rockies. This was beyond the limit of land bought from the Spanish by the Louisiana Purchase. Yet it only proved the ever westward movements of settlers in the United States.

His party had left Independence, Missouri, almost a year ago in 1827. Thirsting for adventure. He had left his sister, Sharon, and her very rich husband, Charles Marshall. They were responsible for management of the Missouri Office, a very small part of the enormous Carroll/ Marshall Boat Company, just as his and Sharon's father and mother, Alan and Dora Reid, managed the main and very much bigger branch offices at St. Louis, where both he and his sister had been born.

In fact Independence was then a very small town with few buildings but was expanding, rapidly. Its important to the shipping company was its position at the junction of the Kansas and Missouri Rivers. This provided a setting off place for settlers daring to cross the river and settle in any of the western lands now available, but still likely to suffer from indian attack.

The history of the Carroll Marshall Boat Company was typical of the possibilities for riches in this new country, as its directors included a Frenchman and Frenchwoman, Francois and Charlotte Le Raye, brother and sister, aristocrats, who were assisted to escape from France at the height of the Terror there in 1793. Both had been trained as engineers, unusual for a woman at that time. Two other directors were Fay Bradbury and Roy Marshall escaping from Manchester after separately, they had helped to burn down Grimshaw's Mechanised Cotton Mill. Once in America they had met and pooled their expertise, with Roy adding steam power to the brilliant designs of Paddle Steamers of the Le Raye's.

Their business associations had matured leading to more intimate friendship. Firstly as their business prospered in Pittsburgh, Francois and Fay became intimate lovers leading to their birth of a daughter, Fiona in 1804, whilst in the same month, Charlotte bore Roy's son Charles. Eventually they both married in 1806, so legitimising their children. Of course many more children followed. However both partners would at times swap partners, as they had done before they married, and now they lived, close together, in a very large mansions where they often shared intimacy.

Alan Reid was the eldest son of Erin and Craig Reid and like Mary once married for many years to Brian Hobbs, both women had been for some years the indentured servants of both Brian and Craig, but after misuse by the men, eventually fell in love and married. This was not an unusual practice in America, whilst it was part of Britain. Many poor women who committed very small crimes were sent to the colonies as indentured servant, to act as virtual slaves for several years, whose master, the man who bought them, could use them for sexual purposes.

The four of them, now, ran a very rich arable farm to the south of Pittsburgh. It had led to them forming a friendship with the Le Raye's and Marshall's in the early days of the century. Alan had married a local girl Dora Conway and Dora bore both Sharon and Donald and several other children.

It was due to these friendships that the Ship building company, and later, becoming River boat owners, establishing a Shipping line, they had persuaded Alan and Dora to take charge of their important St. Louis Office, on the Mississippi River, as well as the repair facilities on that river. In due course Sharon had fallen in love with Charlotte and Roy's eldest son, Charles Marshall, married and then went to Independence to manage that office.

Though quite wealthy for a man of only twenty, Donald had craved for adventure. So when Andrew Henry and his partner William Ashley arrived at Independence willing to finance fur trading expeditions in the Rocky Mountains, Donald, against the wishes of his sister and brother-in-law, joined the large band recruited there. It proved to be an exciting and dangerous journey once they left the furthest settlements at the South Platte River. They were attacked by Sioux Indians, though they killed the entire party, one of their company was killed and two were wounded.

After staying at Fort Laramie and by then loaded with pelts, they took the south pass and eventually arrived at the Great Salt Lake. There Donald was to meet the famous Jedediah Smith, Mountain Man, who had travelled to the west coast and to the Pacific Ocean several times. He had just returned from tracking through California, travelling as far south as San Gabriel Mission, now being called Los Angeles, even to San Diego, as well as San Francisco and Sacramento, but now driven out by the Governor of California, who hated American 'invaders'.

The stories he told Donald installed in him a desire not only to see this land but perhaps learn to live there, for it seemed it was very poorly populated., mainly devoted to agriculture and farming with a few haciendas, with several miles between each habitation. This land of California, like the regions to the south of the United States had belonged to Spain for centuries. Then in 1821 a new state of Mexico had been established by force, and Spain vanquished. Now all these lands belonged to this new country of Mexico.

Donald believed this land should belong to the United States not Mexico. Then his country would extend from the Atlantic Ocean to the Pacific Ocean. Donald made a vow to himself, to devote part of his life to achieving that object, regretting now he was returning back to Independence, for his colleagues, rich with furs, refused to go further west. As once they returned and were sold, they would all reap considerable riches, including young Donald.

They returned the more southerly route via Pueblo and southern Kansas, seeing how rapidly homesteaders were arriving and settling these new lands. Kansas was still regarded as a Territory. In fact it would be another thirty years before it became a state, yet already many were arriving to settle here, as well as the Oklahoma Territory, to the south.

Missouri had become a state in 1821, only because of the 'Missouri Compromise' by which it declared that, in future, all states would be admitted in pairs. One for slavery and one against. Strangely Missouri became a slave state, though most of its inhabitants were against slavery. It was this compromise, which eventually led to the Civil War.

Although no indians actually attacked them on their return journey, many times war parties came to investigate them. Either because it was a large party, or because they were obviously leaving their territory, no hostilities occurred. They arrived back at Independence in the autumn of 1828.

Of course his sister and brother-in-law were delighted to welcome him back, unharmed, and after the pelts were sold Donald's share was quite large. However, useful as this was, Donald had inherited large assets from the family and was, already, quite rich. There was no doubt that Donald had enjoyed this adventure and craved for more. He was still young, he had no definite girl friends and not yet begun any real intimate adventures with any of them.

However he was now filled with a determination to visit, and possibly live in California, for it seemed there was so much space in which to live and the climate was very good. It should belong to the United States. He knew that many of his country men, even some friends of the family that lived in Kentucky and Tennessee, also believed the land to the south, especially north of the Rio Grande, should also belong to his country.

Mexico had no right to exist. Once they remove the Spanish Yolk, they should have joined the United States instead of forming a new country. Further more tales coming from that country told stories of oppression and dictatorship, with the people having no rights, dominated by rich aristocratic juntas, who robbed the country, taking its wealth for themselves.

Donald was determined to meet others who believed in his ideals. Perhaps sometime the United State might be strong enough and wish to possess these lands. He would help any who had this desire, but admitted his real love was for this land of California.

4.

Elvira Luna was terrified as she stood in front of the Governor of Vera Cruz, Antonio Lopez de Santa Anna. Barely sixteen she had been seized this evening by the aides of the Governor, from her parents town house in the city of Vera Cruz. Her father had stood powerless, holding her, equally, terrified mother, for no one dare challenge any decree of the Governor. Beside being Governor he was a General in the Army of Mexico, with a very distinguished reputation, though he frequently changed his allegiances.

Santa Anna had done this several times. An officer in the army of New Spain he had joined the rebellion which led to the independence of Mexico in1821. Then helped to remove the self declared new Emperor, Iturbide, and helped to establish a republic, at first fully supporting liberal ideals, until he found this unprofitable. Then he helped to establish the aristocratic landed gentry, in forming a conservative government, and repressing the masses.

Using arms, he had replaced the President installing Vicente Guerrero in its place with Anastasio Bustamante as Vice President. He had then won the affection of important persons in Mexico by defeating the attempted invasion of Spanish troops to re-conquer Mexico at the Battle of Tampico. This had established Santa Anna as Governor and ruler of the whole of Vera Cruz and land to the east including the Yucatan. Now he was one of the most important figures in the whole of Mexico and a man with extremely conservative views.

In 1826 at the age of thirty two he had married, eighteen year old, Ines Garcia, daughter of a rich Spanish landowner, who had recently born him their first child. However this was by no means his first child, being an inveterate womaniser. Like tonight, his aides were frequently requested to obtain a very young woman for his amusement. This then was how poor Elvira came to be standing terrified in front of this man.

At last he spoke to her. "Please, you have nothing to fear. Tonight I shall teach you how in future, you can enjoy your life. Provided your father is sensible I shall see he is sufficiently rewarded. I believe you have a large estate and a magnificent hacienda, in Coahuila Texas. I shall see the government confers on him a very wealthy and onerous position in that state. It will be his duty to stop the emigration of so many Americans from the United States there. I will see he receives this position in a few weeks time, and with a large salary, so then you can accompany your family there."

At this moment an older lady, dressed elegantly in a long black dress entered and bowed. Santa Anna spoke to her. "Ah! Isabel, thanking you for coming so quickly. Please take dear Elvira to the other room and prepare her. I want to show her my hospitality and a hope I can ensure she has a memorable and, I hope, a happy memory of tonight."

The lady bowed again then firmly gripped Elvira's arm, "Come dear with me, I shall ensure your pleasure tonight". However knowing the General's reputation, Elvira had already guessed what was his method of 'ensuring she received a memorable night'. She shivered in fear for she was still a virgin, but now feared she would not be one the following morning.

Nor was she wrong Isabel Galvano was forty two years of age, the mother of nine children, she knew how to prepare a young innocent girl for her bridal bed. However Isabel knew her master would not place a wedding ring on Elvira's finger, even though she would no longer be an innocent girl the next morning. Poor Elvira knew she had no escape. Sobbing in her despair as Isabel bathed her, adding cream to her body, paying particular attention to her lower quarters. Then covering her body in an almost transparent silk shift. Finally ensuring her cosmetics were perfect.

Then Elvira was lead to a four-poster bed next door and placed as a sacrificial offering to the general to await her fate. When he entered she begged him not to attack her. Once again Santa Anna showed he liked to dominate people. "Come Elvira you are quite old enough to become a woman. Think whilst you enjoy intimacy with me tonight how by doing so, you will also be improving the financial position and security of your family. I'm sure you would not want anything unpleasant to happen to them."

The threat had been made. Elvira knew, unless she surrendered her body to him, not only would she possibly have her life ended but a calamity of great proportions would land on her entire family. Elvira did not reply she merely lay back and accepted his attack on her body. At least he did not take her brutally, but the pain of her deflowering and her humiliation, the thought that she must conceive his child meant she was still consumed with terror.

When eventually, satisfied with the pleasures her young body had given him, he fell asleep, poor Elvira was unable to get that release. Only utter exhaustion and the impossibility of her position, now a dishonoured woman, possibly pregnant, soon to be an unmarried mother, eventually allowed her some respite. She was asleep when he awoke in the morning, alighted and he bathed and dressed in his uniform for the day, leaving a still sleeping young woman to awake and now realised, that for a time, it seems she was to become the mistress of this evil man.

Again she was not wrong. She was never allowed to leave his mansion at Jalapa very near the city of Vera Cruz. Poor Elvira spent nearly six weeks in this virtual prison. Santa Anna used her body whenever he came home, even during the day. Soon after a month of continued intercourse with him she was not surprised when her period failed to appear. When at last she returned to her home she was already six weeks pregnant by him, grateful to once again be received by her loving family, who did all which was possible to relieve her of any shame. She was the innocent victim of a very evil and very powerful man.

At least Santa Anna kept his word. Her father was installed by the government as State Lieutenant of the southern district of Coahuila Texas, with all its powers, and instructed to try to discourage the emigration of families coming across the unoccupied boarder, from the United States. It seemed, that soon there would be more Americans living there than Mexicans. Yet whatever the Mexican government thought of this invasion, there was little dislike of these incomers by the Mexicans living there. Soon their families were intermarrying for it seemed most of the Americans came with some wealth gained in the past.

As instructed Elvira and her family left their town house in Vera Cruz and returned to their estate near San Marcos, supposedly for her father to enforce his new position. However the dastardly treatment of his daughter had decided that her father would not attempt to impose restrictions on these emigrants, even believing like other Mexicans they should learn to live there in peace and not be subject to the dictates from Mexico City.

However even more than her father, Santa Anna's evil treatment of her had ensured that this man was now her principal enemy and decided to bring up their baby when it was born, to hate and learn to fight its evil father.

Meanwhile General Santa Anna was only concerned with improving his own position by again changing sides. In another two years he would help to remove Vicente Guerrero from his presidency and place the Vice-President and highly conservative Manuel Bustamante as President. Even then he deplored Bustamante's decision to execute Guerrero as he tried to flee the country. This was in time, to ensure the demise of the new president, from office.

All this meant great rewards from the persons in power. Even though they might distrust him, they would try hard not to make him their enemy. Santa Anna was smiling for he could see himself as the most powerful person in Mexico in a few years time, as well as an exceptionally rich one.

5.

"Danton, it's a great opportunity, but also a great responsibility, I was only able to get you appointed to the post, because as a Senator, following your grandfather's long period of office, my fellow Senator's felt it was a business which required a Carroll's experience. Remember, although you will have little power as Diplomatic Agent, you must with diligence and energy, support Anthony Butler, our Charge d'Affaires to the Republic of Mexico."

Mark Carroll, the United States Senator for Virginia, was informing his twenty-two year old son Danton Carroll that Congress had appointed him to the position of Diplomatic Agent, in Mexico City, to further the interests of the United States, in this new and somewhat chaotic Republic of Mexico.

Mark continued, "There is no doubt but that Mexico strongly dislikes how Stephen Austin has encouraged so many Americans to settle in their northern territory of Coahuila Texas. Very soon there will be ten times as many American's there as the native Mexicans. Somehow you will have to try ensure their safety, or a least, that they are not attacked. None of us can trust their General Santa Anna, who I believe will soon make an attempt to become President." Mark laid his hand on Danton's shoulder. "Remember your heritage and do nothing that might besmirch our famous name."

Mark Carroll was right for nearly two centuries various branches of the Carroll family had helped to ensure peace and prosperity, firstly in Virginia and Maryland, but later in both West Virginia and Pennsylvania, since the first Carroll's arrived in Maryland during the reign of King Charles I, when the king gave to Lord Baltimore, Maryland, for him to govern. Then a Roman Catholic branch of the Carroll family had arrived from Yorkshire, and though recently had changed their faith to protestant, now were extremely rich with lands along the Potomac, in West Virginia and estates and industrial mills in Philadelphia.

However Mark and Danton Carroll were descendents of Sir David and Lady Amelia Carroll. The protestant family branch which came from Somerset to Maryland when King James II persecuted them and when Edgar Carroll, David's Catholic cousin, persuaded him to come to America and work the profitable tobacco plantation of Rockville, alongside the River Potomac in Maryland.

From thereon, this branch enjoyed an unusually exciting lifestyle. Firstly David Carroll fell in love and married a pregnant indentured servant, Amelia Eliot, saving her from death, risking his life by refusing King William's III orders, to make all Marylanders, protestants, winning the right of freedom of worship. Then knighted and served for many years as Governor of Maryland. It was a real life Prince Charming and Cinderella story.

Later his grandson, and actually the grandfather of Mark, Daniel Carroll, led an equally adventurous life before he finally won the hand of Michelle, a refugee from France. Even later, this man played a very important part in helping George Washington during the American War of Independence, and helping to establish this new country. Then his son, Robert married to Hedwig Casimir, of Polish descent, became the Senator for Virginia for many years. Robert now sixty seven years old had retired and their eldest son, Mark, had taken his place as a Senator in Congress.

Mark's family all lived on the large Racoonsville Estate on the northern banks of the River Rappahannock whilst a cousin, of the brother of his grandfather, owned the equally large estate of Gordonsville, just to the south of the river. Finally a branch of that family had now inherited the extremely large and rich Rockville estate, given to be worked by the original David Carroll when he landed with his cousin Edgar, in Maryland in 1688.

So since that date long ago, this branch of the Carroll family had prospered and were now one of the largest and most famous families in both Virginia and Maryland. Thus it was inevitable that Mark Carroll should be elected Senator for Virginia, whilst Andrew Carroll, living at Rockville, might become Senator for Maryland. Again all the Carroll's had married women from equally important families. Mark had married the granddaughter of Anton Tencin, who was an illegitimate son of King Louis the Fourteenth of France, whilst his son Danton had recently married, Claudia Albrecht, the daughter of Louise and Anton Albrecht, both emigrant Princess and Princes of the Austrian Hapsburg family.

Both Mark and Danton were very proud of their ancestral past, and as children had sat on the knee of Robert Carroll, as he told them of the past lives of Sir David and then Robert's father, Daniel Carroll, and his wife Michelle. The insane way he, first went, to help Anton Tencin and Donald Wilson to rescue the two women they loved, Ruth Oldham and Kate Tavish, both indentured and misused servants, captured by the indians.

Even more astonishing it seemed Daniel and Donald, feeling they must repay a debt of honour to Major Jean Dumas, who at that time was, probably, an enemy of Britain, and had risked their lives several times to try to discover and free Jean's girlfriend, Madeleine Colet, captured and tortured by Mohawk indians. It was really a miracle that they survived and eventually discovered and freed Madeleine and another girl Cecile Bore, at present held in New England, brought them to Maryland and eventually Jean found and married Madeleine. This story in itself thrilled the young Mark and then Danton. It was all part of the Carroll Family Saga and told in the earlier books, "Maryland" and "Ohio"..

However, how Daniel, performed even greater miracles during the American War of Independence, helping George Washington, - even obtaining first French money and the French active support, when Washington, was in desperate straights, unable to both clothe and feed his troops. This was and is, a story in itself. Then after victory, to help to rescue French men and women from the Terror in France and later, invest his riches to enable the new country to survive and prosper. No wonder both Mark and Danton were proud of their ancestral past.

Only a short time later, Danton and his newly pregnant wife, Claudia, left their ancestral home at Racoonsville, to take up his new post as Diplomatic Agent, travelled to Annapolis, boarded a ship to the port of Vera Cruz in Mexico and then began, the tiresome journey to its capitol of Mexico City, high in the mountains. Accommodation was waiting for them. Very soon Danton was engaged in assisting both Anthony Butler, Charge d'Affaires, and Thompson, another Diplomatic Agent.

His poor pregnant wife Claudia was often left alone for considerable times, but did enjoy the many social occasions held in the capitol. She did enjoy writing long letters to her fifty two year old mother, Louisa Albrecht, now retired and living on one of their estates near La Falette, in Tennessee, describing the chaotic conditions in the country, wishing she could be with her in Tennessee.

They arrived soon after the republic was threatened by an invasion of the Spanish Army, determined to retake Mexico and make it again part of New Spain. The situation was dangerous. However due to the cleverness of General Santa Anna who outwitted and then final defeated the Spanish at the Battle of Tampico. It was this which lead to him becoming known as the 'Saviour of the Motherland'.

It is true that Santa Anna's victory was welcomed by all in Mexico City especially the president. However Danton, well remembered his father's fears that this man Santa Anna would soon become the most important power in Mexico. His father feared if he should become president, Santa Anna, would set himself up as a dictator and centralize all power in himself. Since they knew he wished to stop the invasion of the Texas area by Americans, he might then, use his powers to either forcibly remove them from Mexico, or even try to enslave them.

If this should occur it would become a diplomatic nightmare for Danton and his colleagues. These men and women were still United States citizens living in Mexico and must call on them for protection. Yet on no account must anything they do lead to a war with Mexico. With so many internal problems of their own, particularly with native indians, as the settlers pressed ever westwards, the United States army was already in great demand. On no account did Congress want a foreign war with Mexico on its hands. Yet their envoys in the capitol could not let these Americans in Texas be murdered.

6.

Louisa Albrecht had just received the second letter from her daughter, Claudia, now living as the wife of the United States Diplomatic Agent in Mexico City. She voiced her fears to her beloved fifty five year old husband, Anton. "I do hope she is safe. Claudia fears there is a possibility of civil war there, due to the ambitions of General Santa Anna. It seems he, also, dislikes Americans, and wants to prevent any more emigrating into his northern province of Texas."

Anton took hold of her hand and kissed it. "You know that area was far safer when it still belonged to Spain. The Mexican revolution has done little for the ordinary people in Mexico, only brought wealth and position to the nobility. You know it is a pity that when the Adams-Otis treaty which gave Spanish Florida to the United States in 1821, did not give all of Mexico to it as well."

This caused Louisa to smile, "Yes, both Eric Casimir and Robert Carroll were right so long ago in New Orleans, they forecast then our Spanish estate in Florida would one day be part of the United States. You know I liked living there when we escaped from Austria, but I prefer where we now live in Tennessee, though I am glad to visit Florida, and, all, our family, again."

Now Anton came and sat besides Louisa then kissed the side of her face. "You know it was fortunate we went to New Orleans after our escape to Florida, otherwise we would never have considered becoming a United States Citizen, nor buying land both in West Virginia and now here." The mention of their escape once again reminded them of their fleeing from Austria in 1793, with Louisa not married but pregnant by Anton, knowing in days the scandal would be discovered. Then she would be sent to a convent for life, her baby torn from her when born and adopted, and her beloved Anton executed for this crime.

Somehow they had managed to flee first to Spain and then Spanish Florida where they bought an estate, which they still owned and now, some of their married family lived there with their own families, yet they had rarely visited it since they left to settle for security on a small piece of forested land in West Virginia. This was purchased to give them United States citizenship and removed any danger of being returned to Austria for punishment.

Together they once again marvelled at there past adventurous life. There meeting with the United delegates meeting with Spanish government officers in New Orleans, their friendship and their coming to West Virginia. Then their acquired wealth when Anton father having, at last discovered where they were, deposited a fortune in Anton's European bank account. How then they had used this, first to invest in so many projects along with those families long since settled in that country.

Then the discovery of the adjacent neighbours, a man and his wife, Andrew and Anna Reeves, and that Anna was also a Princess of the Hapsburg family, again escaping from the same dangers as them, escaping from the scandal when Anna conceived by her young English tutors. Unlike them the Reeves were not rich but had set up a successful school for all the children of that area. Their similarities ensured that Louisa and Anton were happy to invest in their school, along with others who were their friends. This had enabled the school to expand employing other teachers and educating older students.

Today this was now a well established and large college, now preparing students for entering university. This had demanded extra space. Louisa and Anton came to their rescue. When they had joined the consortium investing money in the establishing of Dr. Crow's Bourbon Whiskey company, they had needed to travel to Paris, Kentucky to ascertain its value. Both had fallen in love with the area.

Then using their friends houses at Winchester, Kentucky, who raised and bred horses, they had spent many visits exploring the vast lands surrounding the area. Eventually further south in Tennessee, discovering on the edge of the Cumberland plateau, near the village of La Falette, a vista which delighted them. They purchased, bought and settled there on this estate building a magnificent mansion. Also as they always liked town living, they purchased a town house in the Nashville, the state capitol.

They had no longer any need for their small plantation in West Virginia so they gave the land to the Reeves, who moved into the mansion on that land and left the whole of the rest of the land and their own holding for educational development. So they became frequent visitors and stayed in their old mansion with Anna, Andrew and their family. Now the college was so large and prosperous that their only duties involved overseeing the management and helping to obtain places for their students in universities.

However, since 1805, Louisa and Anton had enjoyed their life on the Tennessee estates, and become part of its life. They had met Andrew Jackson many times especially after the War of 1812 to 1815 with Britain. Now Jackson, at the second attempt had just been elected as the seventh President to the United States. They had, also, come to know David Crockett, helping him to be elected to the House of Representatives both in 1826 and just recently. But now they had established for almost ten years a warm relationship with Samuel Houston.

It was because of this that they became so involved in politics in Tennessee. They helped Houston the be elected to Congress in both 1823 and 1825. Also they had helped to ensure Houston was elected with a large majority to become Governor of Tennessee in 1827 beating the present sitting Governor, Willie Blount. Then a tragedy had happened, there had been a scandal concerning his eighteen year old wife, Eliza

Allen, and Houston had resigned and left to live with the Cherokee indians.

Now having exhausted the information from Mexico they turned to the subject of Sam Houston. Anton said, "You know Sam was forced into his marriage to Eliza by her father, Colonel John Allen. I believe they never loved each other. It was simply that Sam was accused of dishonouring her."

Louisa replied, "Yes! Though I doubt if she was a virgin before Sam came to know her. She had a reputation with boys,. In fact, I don't think the present scandal is of Sam's making. I've been told she had, already, been unfaithful to him several times. – I wish I'd been in Nashville at the time. I would have stopped him resigning. – It's just he could not live there with her having her affairs and he, not knowing what to do. I believe Sam is a very honest man. We must try to help him and persuade him to return."

Anton replied, "Louisa, I've got an idea. You know the Carroll's, when at Congress, spoke highly about Sam in their debates when he was our congressman. He is also a very good lawyer, as well as being a war hero. – Although he was very friendly with Andrew Jackson, but I, also, know he hates Andrew's policy of forcibly removing indians from here and marching them to lands in the West. Many are dying on those journeys."

Now he smiled, "I must go to him on the Cherokee camp where he is at present living. He was their friend as a boy. I shall offer to establish him with a large salary in Washington, to petition Congress on all indian affairs, and help him to achieve better conditions for all the indian nations. I know how strongly he feels about them. I hope by doing this it will re-establish Sam in political matters. – Do you remember how strongly he felt in the past that northern Mexico, at least the Texas area and that Pacific coast area of California, should be part of the United States."

Louisa turned and kissed Anton on the cheek. "I think that would be a very good idea. You know it will mean we are, once again, attempting to increase the area of land belonging to this country, which gave us sanctuary, and now so many years of happiness. – Why Claudia, through Danton, may yet be able to help this to happen." Anton kissed her lovingly.

Louisa responded, "Which reminds me, Monica Downey wrote to me only a few days ago, giving me all the latest news about their five families growing wealth in horse breeding. It is, even more, successful than their parents holding in Virginia. Also the project we investigated for them, Bourbon Whiskey, as you know is rapidly becoming very profitable. – However it seems that Lilie and James Downey's twenty two year old son, Karl, along with Helga and Paul's son, Hanz, have both fled-the-nest, in Kentucky. They left a year ago each taking with them two of their trained horses. They travelled on one of the Carroll/ Marshall steam boats down the Mississippi to New Orleans. The last they heard from them told them they intended to cross Louisiana and enter Texas. – Perhaps, in time, we may learn first hand about life there."

7.

Hanz Eliot and Karl Downey had enjoyed their boat journey from Kentucky, along the River Ohio until it joined the massive Mississippi. Then down the river with the State of Tennessee on its left bank and the new State of Missouri on its right, passed the growing territory of Arkansas, then meandering for many miles with the levees, high banks on each side, as the river level was above the surrounding land. Then finally they arrived at the magnificent city of New Orleans, with its inherited Spanish ways, though also having a French influence.

So after stabling their four horses, they had brought with them on the boat, as they had a reasonable amount of money, they took accommodation in a small hotel and set out to see the sights. They found it a 'city of music' though as they had discovered on the southern part of the journey on the boat, the Negro music, seemed to have a sad tone with it. In fact locally it was called 'Soul Music'. It was very sad,, no doubt because of the hard lives these Negro slaves endured, but it was. also, very beautiful.

They stayed for a time there, not only in the city, managing to avoid the gambling in the many casinos, but enjoyed the heavy liquor, to which they had become accustomed back in Kentucky. However they used their horses to explore the surrounding land. In fact they found this disappointing, for the whole area was frequently disposed to flooding and very swampy. It seemed the southern part of Louisiana was, also very swampy and somewhat unhealthy, but they must cross it to get to Texas, about which they had heard so much, and which had engendered in them the wish to travel and see it for it for themselves.

They would never forget the difficult fight both had experienced with their parents when they had told them how much they wished to leave Kentucky and see other parts of this new country, as the United States was expanding, almost explosively. It was not for wealth that they wanted to leave. The whole of the area near Winchester that the five families had purchased over thirty year before in 1795, had become a vast ranch at Camargo, near Winchester, and now known as the Camargo Equestrian Establishment, rearing hundreds of horses, so much in demand by the many families travelling westward, past Kentucky and Tennessee and into that large, mainly unexplored region to the west of both the Mississippi and Missouri Rivers, rich relatively flat lands suitable for cattle raising or given over to wheat, in great demand in the east and Europe.

So both knew, if they stayed they could live in some wealth. Their work task would not be too great, and they could enjoy a very pleasant life as did so many of their growing families of their relatives, enjoyed at present. However each of them, were their parents fifth child. They knew their share of the family wealth would, naturally, be less than their elder brothers. However it was not this which had caused them to leave the security of Kentucky and now travel to far more dangerous regions, beset by indians and robbers. It was a spirit of adventure they had inherited from their own adventurous parents.

Perhaps also it was the Irish blood they had inherited. Like many others with the name Downey, Eliot, or Brady, they knew only too well, and were immensely proud of their ancestry. All in someway, were related to Margaret Eliot born and married and widowed, in Northern

Ireland, on the Calvert Roman Catholic estate. How her family, though many stayed and raised themselves out of poverty in Ireland, several had followed Margaret and her amazing daughter, Amelia, to America. To them Amelia Eliot had been a real life Cinderella, who somehow had met her Prince Charming, David Carroll, on a terrible journey across the Atlantic at the end of the Seventeenth Century.

Saved by this man, when as a convicted felon, pregnant and starving and about to drown herself. David Carroll, a rich aristocrat from Somerset, came to love, finding her 'glass slipper' – her undying love for him - and risking disinheritance from his father, married and freed Amelia, from her sentence of virtual sexual slavery, making Rockville a very successful tobacco estate. Eventually becoming Governor of Maryland, risking his life to persuade King William III to allow Maryland, unlike other areas, to still allow religious freedom, even becoming a Knight of the Bath and making his Amelia a Lady of quality.

This in itself, had made both Karl and Hanz proud of their ancestral past. However they both knew they owed even more to Sir David's, grandson, Daniel Carroll, who both brought so many of Amelia's family and relatives from Ireland to live a better life here in the United States, during the last one hundred and fifty years. With this inheritance, perhaps it was not exceptional that both of them felt the same need for excitement and adventure, to leave security in Kentucky and go into the wilderness. It was men like them who were ensuring the population, and the area of habitation in this new country, was growing so rapidly.

Although neither were looking forward to crossing the wet lands of Louisiana, having at last felt they had exhausted all the pleasures the city could offer them, and driven by this desire to see this vast land of Texas which they had heard about, they rode, each with their two horses across the flat-lands, avoiding the badly flooded area, in fact finding quite large areas were inhabited and being cultivated by new settlers, from every part of Europe, as well as from more eastern United States. Eventually they came to the unprotected border with the new Country of Mexico, marked only by a broken down sign. Travelling, north of a large bay which formed part of the large gulf beyond. Later they discovered this bay was named Galveston. The arrived at another river and met some Americans who had, already, settled there. They discovered this was called the River Brazos.

Though they were made very welcome and stayed with them for several days, the target of which they had heard a little, was the Mexican town of San Antonio, at least two hundred and fifty more miles to the west. So after enjoying their stay with these Americans, who had emigrated here from South Carolina over a year before, they felt they must leave. As they had heard in Kentucky, that these lands were mainly used for cattle breeding and several small ranches had been established, near to the few Mexican ranches, which had existed there for some years.

They travelled west, crossed the Colorado River. Eventually, having journeyed nearly two hundred miles from where they had enjoyed their stay on the Brazos, they reached the small but growing Mexican town of San Marcos, still fifty miles from San Antonio. They were tired, exhausted, and had no reason for reaching San Antonia quickly, they decided to stay here for a time. It was very Mexican with several very large ranches in its proximity.

They stayed at an Inn in the town and found local ranches belonged to branches of the Luna family. Victor Luna had recently been appointed as State Lieutenant of this province which was called Coahuila Texas. It was rumoured, but not confirmed, that he had obtained this high position in repayment for some service he had disliked, but been forced to accept. During their stay at the Brazos both Karl and Hanz had been told of the dislike of some Mexicans to Americans, - not the local ones, - but their government in Mexico City. It seemed that the same situation did not occur in San Marcos, the local Mexicans welcoming the Americans..

In fact they were told that now Victor Luna had been instructed to use force, if necessary, to prevent further encroachment of Mexican territory by Americans. Victor Luna himself, had placed a Poster on the wall of the Administration buildings declaring this fact. Then to everyone's surprise, especially the Americans, already settled near here, he had told them, that on no account would he enforce it, and hoped both American and the local Mexicans could live together in peace. This unexpected and unexplained explanation had ensured a continuance of the way they had existed, together, now for several years.

Both Karl and Hanz were intrigued with the situation. They were determined to meet his amazing man as soon as possible. It also meant that they had not any wish, at present, to resume their journey to San Antonio Certainly not until they had ascertained how a government official, having declared the government's order, then made known he had no intention of enforcing it. It seemed both Karl and Hanz felt they were going to enjoy their stay in this country.

It was then they received an even greater surprise. They were told to wait until a man called Senor Stephen Austin, an American visited the town, and then they should approach him. It seemed it was within his power to bestow on them a large stretch of land in the vicinity at a ridiculously low price per acre, which could be worked and used for any purpose they choose. This was why so many Americans had come to settle all over Coahuila Texas. This man Austin had been given the right to allocate this land many years before, though now it seemed the government wanted to take away this right.

It seemed there was an even greater reason for staying here. They knew the money they carried in their saddle bags would pay for a large portion of land. They would stay and become Mexican landowners. They might persuade other members of their families to come and join them here. Perhaps what they had believed was a visit to see this new land, might lead to a more permanent arrangement.

8.

The completion of the Erie Canal from Albany, on the river Hudson, to Buffalo, on Lake Erie, had resulted in the Port of New York becoming the most important, and most prosperous port, on the eastern seaboard of the United States. This route via the Hudson, the canal and then joining the Monongahela River at Pittsburgh, so onto the massive Ohio River, finally joining both the Mississippi and Missouri Rivers, it was the gateway to the developing West, or South, to New Orleans, and the Gulf of Mexico. Thousands of settlers wanting to acquire land

and future wealth, on the new lands opened to them by the Louisiana Purchase, - now having first arrived at New York, the settlers had made their way there.

Alternatively, there was another way, as the National Road, also called U.S. Route 40, had been constructed from Baltimore through Pennsylvania, Ohio, Indiana and had almost reached St. Louis, paid for by federal funds. As this could, easily, be accessed from Pittsburgh, the canal provided a wagon train route to the West. All this added to the ever growing economic prosperity of New York.

However all this was to disrupt the pleasant life of Otto Fallon. Having established himself at the bank, and settled in a small house in the Bronx, Otto had come to enjoy his life in New York City. Further more he had heard from Freda Ibsen, who he had met on the ship coming to America. Her letter had been forwarded by his father in Hanover, and told him they had settled in a house on the outskirts of Washington, however it seemed this would be only a temporary abode. Still he now had her address. Washington was only a short distance from New York and Otto planned to visit her.

Then the bombshell had landed. Though he had only done what was expected of him at the bank, being disappointed that he had not received a more important position, it seemed, unknown to him, he had greatly impressed his superiors with his ability. Perhaps this was not surprising, for apart from his German degree and research, banking had been ingrained in him by his father, since he was a boy. He had therefore applied himself, in a natural capacity, almost unconsciously, since he started his duties at the bank. It seemed he was to be promoted very rapidly. However it was not what he would have chosen.

As St. Louis was now an important economic centre on the Mississippi River, with access in all directions of the compass, it was essential a new bank of some size must be opened there., and Otto was to be given the task of both opening it and becoming manager of its operations. Though this meant, not only a very sudden promotion, and a great increase in his salary, it meant that Otto would be torn from his pleasures in the city, sent miles away, a long distance from his possible girlfriend, Freda, and what seemed to him a life in the wilderness, with only the veneer of civilization.

Further more, it was not to become a satellite of the Manhattan Bank but it was to operate under the name of its sister banking company, the Casimir/Holstein Bank, whose main office was in Pittsburgh. Michael Casimir, who had been the father of Robert Carroll's wife Hedwig and son Eric Casimir, already mentioned, and was a rich aristocrat who had come from Poland sixty years before and formed a friendship with William Holstein, who came there at the same time from Sweden. The two families had grown up together in the Potomac valley, both helping in America's war with Britain.

They were excessively rich with a joint enormous estate, near Fort Necessity and now Pittsburgh. Both invested heavily in the developing west and had, eventually, when nearly eighty years of age, had opened this bank in Pittsburgh. It had long since become the joint ownership of their sons, Eric Casimir and John Holstein, who also had grown up together as young men, with Eric, for a time being a Senator. However this banking adventure was more the result of the marriage of Michael Casimir's ward, Clare Collins to Philip Wycks. The previous life of Clare Collins was an adventure in itself, from being a Bristol prostitute to becoming Philip's second wife.

However Philip was a member of the large and wealthy Wycks family, who were the owners of the Bank of Manhattan, with several branches in the east and it had been the war which had made many of them leave New York and settle in the Potomac valley, and so had become the friends of the many families living there. So it was natural with Philip's close association with Michael Casimir after he married Clare, that he was instrumental in both advising and establishing the bank in Pittsburgh. In fact as the Manhattan Bank were shareholders in the Casimir/Holstein Bank, as were that bank shareholders in the Manhattan Bank, they were perhaps merely sister banking establishments.

This was why Otto was sent to establish and manage this new bank in St. Louis under the name of Casimir/Holstein, and not Manhattan. Never-the-less, it seemed that Otto Fallon must lose his pleasurable life in New York and forego the visit he was considering to call on Freda in

Washington. Instead he had to settle his affairs, place a agent to look after his city house, deciding to keep it and offer it for short term lets, as Otto wanted to return there as soon as possible. He, also, had to write to Freda explaining what had happened, promising to inform her of his address in St. Louis.

He was in a miserable mood as he took his few belongs on the boat to Albany, then traveled the canal to Pittsburgh, for there he was to first call at the bank for instructions and the necessary credits to purchase and then commence business at this new bank at St. Louis. Although the day to day running of the Bank had long since been given over to their eldest sons, Otto was pleased to meet the mid seventy old Eric Casimir and John Holstein, and entertained to dinner at their Pittsburgh mansion.

Otto was introduced to Eric's wife, Isabel and John's wife, Hilary. Though only a little younger than their husbands, they were still quite attractive women. Again Otto, himself a Roman Catholic was to learn of the unusual happenings in this part of America. It seemed both Eric and John were staunch protestants yet their wives were equally staunch Catholics, having married twice in both churches. He was intrigued when he learned their convoluted history, and again heard of the mysterious Daniel Carroll, who had helped to make this possible, against the desires of their wives parents, extremely strong Catholics. Again Otto marveled how different the United states was to any country in Europe.

After a stay of three days, whilst Otto was fully informed of what would be expected of him, he left on this new National Road in two coaches accompanied by the grandson of the Eric Casimir, Michel Casimir along with Philip Holstein, grandson of John Holstein, junior directors of the Pittsburgh bank, who came with him to assist but also supervise Otto. At twenty three they were only slightly older than Otto, but he was determined to make a success of his appointment. Otto, though he felt he knew more about banking than his fellow travelers, he still tried to steer a peaceful solution. However Otto hoped their presence in St. Louis would be short lived, hoping they would return to Pittsburgh once the bank had been established.

Although the road had nearly reached St. Louis and was a metalled road of good quality except for the last twenty miles, never-the-less, it was a long and tiring journey, and they were all glad when at last they could rest in reasonable hotel in the town. The banks agents had already found what they considered was a suitable building in a good location. After viewing the choice, and deciding after a few minor structural modifications, it would suffice, they all set about laying the foundations for a successful bank. They each called on the many businesses, now occurring, and some being established in this growing town. They finally called on the imposing offices and workshops of the Carroll/Marshall Shipbuilding and Shipping Company and met Alan Reid the manager of this complex.

Here Otto had to admit, the presence of both Michel and Philip helped, for it seemed both of them knew of Alan's employers, having met both Francois Le Raye and Roy Marshall many times in Pittsburgh. Alan Reid, consequently was pleased to change his bank from the local small bank which had found difficulty in dealing with Alan's considerable and extremely valuable assets, now agreeing to bank with their new one as soon as it started to operate.

So by the summer of 1829 the new bank of Casimir/Holstein Bank of St. Louis had become operating. At last Michel and Philip retuned to Pittsburgh and Otto was left to run and manage this new business. He admitted he felt proud now to be given the opportunity to make this branch a success. He felt sure it would be.

However, as yet he had not heard form Freda Ibsen, although he had sent her the address of the new house he had bought, on a beautiful stretch of land, near the banks of the Mississippi River, but well above the expected flood line. He was becoming desperate for feminine company and had even considered using the local brothel, but feared the scandal, if it was discovered he managed the large new bank. So it was a very dissatisfied Otto who sat in his extremely hot office as the summer approached.

9.

Gordon Taylor quickly settled down in his small cabin on the "Atlantic Lady", as did the many other passengers joining him as they travelled to America. Only a few were visiting relatives or friends, or returning to their homes there, in which they lived. The vast majority were persons wanting to settle in America for many reasons, or just to own a small pact of land they could develop and call their own. Gordon quickly made the acquaintance of many of them before they were beset by Atlantic storms. Even then, there were several periods between each gale, with pleasant sunny days, if boisterous winds, but which, still, enable him to communicate with them.

It seemed that the city of New York or sites along the Hudson River were the final destinations of a number of them. Some who had, already, been offered employment in the industrial regions of New York State and Pennsylvania. Many were individual men, though a few had brought their wives or lovers. However the vast majority were entire families determined the start a new life there.

Though Gordon found it fascinating to hear the various reasons for being on the boat, he was very quick to discover and enter in conversation with an attractive young girl, and so had needed to accept the presence of her family. Her name was Sheila McLean, and she was travelling with her mother and father, an elder brother and two younger sisters. It seemed they had joined the ship after first travelling from Dublin, in Northern Ireland, to Liverpool, having sold their small farm north of Belfast believing life in America would be preferable to eking out an existence in Ireland, though they were not poor, they only possessed a little wealth.

From Sheila's father, Neil McLean, Gordon learned a little of their families history. They were known as Scottish-Irish. It seemed that his great, great grandfather, though not taking part in the Rebellion of the Young Pretender, had been persecuted and gone south to live in Glasgow. There he and his son, Neil's great grandfather had eked out an existence. Then in 1770 the family having gained a little money left Glasgow and went to Northern Ireland and hired a farm. It was this farm which his grandfather had, eventually, purchased, which Neil McLean had sold prior to coming to Liverpool.

It seemed they hoped to be able to find a way to travel to Cole County, and to near a small town, but which had, already, been named Jefferson City, in the new state of Missouri. It seemed a near neighbour of them in Ireland, the Doyle family, had emigrated there over two years before, and had written to them telling them of the wonderful opportunities awaiting them there. Relatively flat land, suitable for any form of agriculture. They were not quite certain how to get there, but had been told that from New York they could travel there, almost, entirely by boat, using a new creation the Eire Canal. In view of the information Silas Taylor had sent to Manchester when he invited Gordon to come to live with him, Gordon was able to add to their knowledge.

"Mr. McLean," Gordon offered, "Yes! I can set your mind at rest. In fact I shall be traveling with you for part of the way. Once we arrive at New York we can book passage on a boat which will travel north, up the River Hudson, to Albany. There we can get a boat along this new canal all the way to Buffalo, on Lake Erie. Then a short drive will take us to Pittsburgh .That is my destination, and where my uncle lives."

Suddenly Gordon had an idea which might extend the time he had to enjoy with Sheila McLean, with whom he had become intrigued, as she seemed to enjoy talking with him. "Mr. McLean, I know uncle owns a number of Steam boats which sail on those rivers from Pittsburgh to the Mississippi and Missouri Rivers. They travel vast distances, as far south as New Orleans on the Gulf of Mexico and as far west as Independence, Missouri. I'm sure your destination will lie on that route. I will take you to meet him when we arrive at Pittsburgh. I'm certain he will know how to get your there."

There was no doubt but that the entire McLean family were very relieved and grateful to Gordon for his offer, and told him so. He was more gratified when, later, as he spoke to Sheila she said, "Mr. Taylor, I believe you are very kind to offer to help my family this way. I know my father was a little afraid that we might find it difficult to discover how to get to Cole County."

Now for the first time Gordon had the courage to take hold of her hand and kiss it gently, causing Sheila to smile as he replied, "Miss McLean, I would feel fully rewarded, if you would call me by my first name, Gordon, instead of Mr. Taylor, and I would hope I might call you Sheila. – I hope I do not offend you – but surely you have guessed that I enjoy being with you. This voyage would be very unpleasant and boring but for the fact I have met you, and I admire your family for risking so much by leaving Ireland and coming to America. – I hope to make my own name there, when we arrive."

Sheila was delighted to accept his offer and soon, when she asked him about his past life, she was astonished at the part he and his family had played, for so many years now, in helping to build both the Leeds-Liverpool and Rochdale Canals, and so recently this new railway from Manchester to Liverpool, which, when soon, it would be completed, would be the first operating Railway Track in the World. Naturally, he ensured she knew he was a fully qualified engineer who hoped to use his knowledge to good advantage and become rich in this new country.

After that Gordon was able to court this lovely sixteen year old girl. There was no doubt but that Sheila felt flattered that this man, who was, obviously, very intelligent, and considered it worth while to monopolise her company. She had little experience with men, not having any boy friends back in Ireland, so his felicitations to some extent frightened her. However, she already knew she liked him, so did not try to discourage him when he took the liberty of placing his arm around her small waist. Shelia knew she wanted their association to continue. Like Gordon, she was very pleased that it would not end when they arrived at New York and would continue, at least to this mysterious town of Pittsburgh.

It did not take long for her parents to notice this growing association between them. However they had been impressed with Gordon, especially, after his offer to assist them on their journey, and more so when Sheila was able to tell them of his accomplishments, and ambitions. So they made no attempt to discourage their liaison, in any case, they believed it would be short lived, and unlikely to continue after they left Pittsburgh, for they guessed Jefferson City would be very many miles from that town. So it was unlikely to become a full love affair, and on the ship they could ensure Sheila did not enter into any dangerous relationships.

So this continued, and at last the reached New York, disembarked and Gordon, acting on his uncle's instructions, led them to where they could book passage on boats, first to Albany and then from Albany to Buffalo, on Lake Erie. It was a long journey and somewhat slow, as on the Canal they had to use so many locks. However to Gordon, it became a boon. It extended the time he had to improve his courtship of this lovely young girl.

He knew he was smitten with her and his feelings were, already, more than a causal courtship. It pleased him that she seemed to reciprocate, though he was unsure of the depth of her emotions, for she seemed to keep them very much under control. In any case her parents appeared to limit the time he had alone with her. However another idea was arising in his head.

Suppose he could persuade his uncle to give them a passage on one of his own boats. Before he took up any employment under his uncle, he still had some money. He might just manage to extend the time with his lovely, Sheila, and perhaps ensure their relationship continued, even after the McLean's arrived at their destinations. He would ask his uncle for permission to accompany them the whole way to their projected land in Missouri, even help them settle there. By then he might have been able to develop more intimate relationships with his now, beloved, Sheila. Though at present, he had not the recourses to consider offering her marriage. Perhaps she might still be willing to yield herself to him. He would try

However all such plans would have to wait until they arrived at Pittsburgh and then would depend on how amenable, would be his uncle, to his plans to remain with the McLean's to the very end of their journey. After changing boats at Albany, they eventually arrived at Buffalo. Then they hired a coach to take them the short journey to Pittsburgh, and found where his uncle Silas lived. The first part of their long journey from Liverpool had been completed. Now so much depended on whether Silas Taylor was willing to assist them with a passage on one of this boats.

10.

When early in the voyage across the Atlantic Gordon Taylor had made, for a short time, the acquaintance of brother and sister, Edwin and Joan Palatine, Gordon did not know they were closely related to both the British and French Royalty. After Gordon had discovered his beautiful Sheila McLean, he rarely spoke to them again. However he had learned that their final destination was New York City.

For both Edwin and Joan were the illegitimate children of Eliza Palatine and Louis Philippe, the result of their six year love affair from 1802 when Louise lived, for a time, at Twickenham, outside London. Louise Philippe, Duc d'Orleans, a descendent of King Louis XIV of France, joined the early years of the French Revolution. He often appeared to advocate a French Republic, but also, a times sided with the Royalists. This attitude resulted in him going into exile in Switzerland, as the Terror mounted in 1793, going with his sister Louise Adelaide d'Orleans.

After moving constantly from country to country, he and his two brothers went to the United States, for over four years. Settled temporary there, he persuaded his sister, Louise Adelaide to join him. In fact on the journey Adelaide, was ship-wrecked on Guadeloupe, in the West Indies. There she met, fell in love and married George Schroeppel, a Prussian tea-exporter, but now a naturalized American. Only then did she continue with her husband to New York to meet her brother. Adelaide lived with her husband in New York until he died in 1825 and, bore him four children.

However Louis Philippe moved to England to live at Twickenham in 1801 and it was during his stay there that he developed a relationship with Eliza Palatine, whose grandfather was the Duke of Cumberland, second son of King George II of Great Britain, so was still part of the British Royal family. Eliza bore him a son, Edwin in 1804 and a daughter, Joan Palatine in 1806. Then in 1807, Louis virtually deserted Eliza, returned to France.

Then invited to Italy, he was befriend by, and married the daughter of King Ferdinand I of the Two Scicilies, Maria Amelie de Bourbon, in 1809. After many further adventures, cleverly changing as required from being a Republican to a Royalist, by 1828 though he seemed to support King Charles X of France, he became more popular and was planning to depose him and assume the kingship himself.

After the death of her husband Louise Adelaide, at Louis request, had returned to France, leaving her four children in New York, to act as Louis' advisor, his 'Egerir'. Adelaide had known for many years the number of illegitimate children Louis had sired during his years of exile. In most cases this did not prove a problem, however when she intercepted a letter to him from Edwin and Joan Palatine, explaining that their mother had died recently and now, parentless, would like to come and live with him in France.

Adelaide quickly realised the danger of Louis scandalous past life becoming public, just as he was attempting to make himself King of France, especially as it, also, involved a member of the British Royal family. Adelaide immediately went to England and met both Edwin and Joan. She was very direct in her approach. Warning them she would never allow them to join their father in France, she offered instead, to place a large sum of money in trust in a bank in New York. Then she would pay and send them to live with her daughter, Marie Eugenie, and her husband, John Hinman, now Mayor of Utica, New York State. Adelaide promised both of them a very happy and prosperous life there, quite impossible if they went to France.

A sad Edwin and Joan now realised that their father had no love for them, and was only interested in his own ambition, so reluctantly they had no option but to accept the alternative offer. So they made their way to Liverpool and boarded the "Atlantic Lady" bound for New York. This was how Gordon Taylor came to meet and know them. However they too made several friends on that voyage.

The most interesting was Adrian and Estelle Carroll, a married couple both over fifty years of age. They were returning from a long visit to meet a branch of their ancestors in England. It seemed they both had a common ancestor, Robert, Earl Carroll of Wookey in Somerset, who it seemed welcomed and helped to place King William III on the throne in 1688.

Adrian Carroll had told them that he and Estelle were distant cousins. "I am the great, great, great grandson of Earl Robert Carroll and Estelle is 'a further great' of him. In fact we both have another common ancestor in Sir David Carroll, Earl Carroll's son, who came to take possession of the large enormous Rockville estate in Maryland about that time. Our side of the family have remained in America ever since, but Estelle's forbearers went back to England for a time. "

Adrian had smiled, "I would never have met and fallen in love with Estelle but for the fact that when forced into an engagement with a Scottish Earl's son. On her way to marry him, her ship was attacked by French Privateer during the Revolutionary war with France. Her mother was killed as they held hands in great fear. However she was rescued by a United States Naval Ship and brought to Annapolis. It was where my father met her and brought her to Rockville that I first met her. I can tell you I fell in love with her that day."

Now Estelle took up the tale, "Yes! At that time I hated all the American Carroll's, I believed Adrian's uncle, Daniel Carroll, was a brigand who stole Rockville from my parent's ownership, but this was changed by the wonderful and kind consideration I received from Adrian's father and mother. Later I learned from this Daniel Carroll, the reason why this had to be. Perhaps it was because they removed my father's debts, saving him from a debtor's prison, then bringing him and my sister to live here, or simply because I had to admit Daniel's reasons were completely justified."

Still holding Adrian's hands and smiling at him, "In fact these wonderful people not only removed by father's debts in England, just as he was about to be committed to a debtor's prison. In 1802, they paid to bring him and my sister, Julie, to come to America and live with us. They never returned. In fact Julia married here, to Aster Brookes, the son of Sophia Chalmers and her first husband, Keith Brookes. Again you see the importance of this man Daniel Carroll, for Sophia is Daniel's step-daughter."

Now Adrian intervened, "You must not forget to tell them that your father was named Sir David Carroll, and again was a direct descendent of the first Sir David, who established our family in Maryland in 1688."

Now she laughed. "Well, in a sense I got my way. I married Adrian and when Adrian's parents die, they are in their seventies, I shall become Mistress of Rockville. However I love both his parents as much as my own father, I only hope they live many more years, for they have given me this wonderful life I now enjoy."

Estelle squeezed Adrian's hands as both Edward and Joan listened, fascinated by the story. Estelle concluded, "Well last year, at Rockville, Julia's son Kenneth, now a Lieutenent in the United States navy, married Sarah Du Pont, daughter of an important Naval family. It seems he will soon be promoted. So all my family prospered by coming to America."

It was a remarkable tale which intrigued both Edwin and Joan. They told them they had twice met the present Earl Carroll of Wookey, explaining that their mother was the great, great granddaughter of King George II of Britain. So it seemed that in a way, they were all part of British Aristocracy. They learned why they were sailing to New York and not Annapolis. It seemed that their eldest son, Peter Carroll had married Amy Vanderbilt, a daughter of that large family.

They now lived in New York and Peter and invested in his brother-in-laws steamship venture on the River Hudson and hoped soon to be able to build steam driven ocean-going steamers. Peter was already rich, as were all the Carroll's, but he wanted with his wife to establish, not only further riches, but to promote this new and exciting inventions. Adrian and Estelle could hardly wait to learn how successful was this new business. Like them they would be staying in New York for a time.

Estelle, now enlarged, saying, "Also whilst we are in New York, I want to meet again Muriel Alexander, daughter of Sir Robert Alexander, to try to discover what happened to Blanche Carroll, Lady Amelia's daughter, the result of her raping by Edward Calvert, in Ireland, before she met Sir David Carroll, who adopted Blanche as his daughter. Manon

Eliot, who explored the Carroll families descendents, found little about Blanche, except she married a Felix Backhouse and went to live with him in New York."

However, on the boat, they gave them not only their New York address but also that of their mansion of Rockville in Maryland, on the banks of the River Potomac. However poor Edwin and Joan wondered what would be their own future. In spite of the welcome Louise Adelaide had guaranteed them on their arrival it was with some trepidation that they walked down the gangway and on to the quay at New York harbour. For good or bad they had arrived to start a completely new life in the United States of America.

Like Gordon Taylor, the McLean's, Otto Follen, Donald Reid, Hanz Eliot and Karl Downey, Edwin and Joan Palatine, they all hoped to make a success of their life here, That was the ambition of all of them. However the man with the greatest ambition, and one which would greatly affect the lives of all of them was General Santa Anna of Mexico. This man was to become an enemy and a very great danger to the United States of America, and yet, in time would, also, enable it to become a still larger country.

PART 2

NEW LANDS

Lebenstraum Part 2
New Lands

NEW LANDS

1.

Senora Nora Delgado, seeing at last Santa Anna had fallen asleep, exhausted, having so passionately used her body, creped silently out of bed and raced, completely naked to the bathroom. Senora Delgado was desperate to remove as quickly as possible all traces of their recent encounter, hoping by doing so she would not suffer the consequences of their recent intimacies. Nora Delgado had been the mistress of General Santa Anna for nearly a year. It was the death of her husband in battle which had forced her into a life as a courtesan, as she had been left with little wealth.

Though Santa Anna was not the only man she accepted intimacy, he was the most regular. She knew he only used her body when his aides had not found a young girl substitute for her. He was not a violent lover but extremely demanding. Further more it was the length of his possession each night which spelled danger to Nora, as it had done this evening, beginning over six hours ago. Already Nora had needed to result in an abortion to remove his child, it was painful but he paid for it to be done.

It seemed in spite of the careful way she had exited from his bed, she had, still, managed to awake him, and he was calling for her again. Quickly completing her essential toilet she returned to the bedroom and no option but to climb back and lay alongside him. She feared he would want to possess once again, and was relieved when he merely grasped rather painfully, both her large breasts with his two hands., making her scream with pain and shout out, "You brute."

He merely laughed, kissed the side of her face and released his painful holding of her mammary. "You should not complain of me doing that to you. I might yet insist I filled them to suckle our baby. Ines has already born me two children, and I've just got Senora Isabel Galvano at forty five into the family way for the second time. Isabel knows I shall probably want another from her before she's too old."

Now he actually smacked both her breasts with his hand causing her to scream out her agony. Then he continued, "You must consider yourself lucky I agreed to your abortion hast time. I may not, if it happens again. You know I always watch my women give birth, as I would watch yours. I should enjoy the agony you would suffer during labour. I hope a long one, as Ines always endures. You should be very willing to please me that way after the valuable gifts I bestow on you. Why, if it were not for men like me, you might had had to spend your life in a brothel."

Unfortunately Nora knew he was right. However distasteful was his attentions she still lived the opulent life she had enjoyed with her dead husband and knew her own extravagance had contributed to her parlous monetary position. However, Santa Anna's words had reminded her, how in her seven years of marriage she had endured three ten hour periods of labour, as she delivered her husbands children

Suddenly she smiled which confused her present lover, for she remembered she could not be sure, who actually fathered those three children. Even during marriage she was unfaithful, having very strong sexual desires. Like tonight, no woman could be sure she had removed all those deadly seeds from inside her – and then - if in time------!!. However it seemed he now wanted to talk to her.

He began, "You know you should actually be desperately trying to conceive my children. – Nora it won't be long before I am head of the country. Then you might be the mother of the children of the President. I did support President Guerrero, he may be a good soldier but he made a poor administrator and worst had liberal ideas. I believe his Vice President Bustamante, will soon tire of him and oust him. This will cause trouble and rebellion throughout the land. That is when I shall come into my own.

Now he once again started to use his hands to explore her still lovely naked body. "Think what your position would be in Mexico City when everyone knows your last child was by me. What does a few hours of pain matter, provided your get your reward, afterwards. If so you must take your chance soon. You have only to ask and I shall try to oblige."

Nora felt annoyed at his attitude and replied accordingly. "Unfortunately Antonio, I know your real preference is not for mature women like me but your young girl conquests who you aides provide. "

He quickly retaliated, "Yes! But you forget, I might get them started but it is unwise for me to keep them for very long. This means I cannot watch and enjoy their antics as they deliver my child. - I tell you a year ago I did thoroughly enjoy one Senorita Elvira Luna. She was a beautiful young girl with an exquisite body. Unfortunately affairs of state prevented me from keeping her and she had returned to her family home in Coahuila before it happened. I trust she still remembers me."

Now just as abruptly he ordered her out of his bed. "Come I've much work to do. Come back this evening, I will take my pleasure of you again. Perhaps by then you might have considered if my proposition might interest you." She obeyed him and as he always expected, Nora had to dress herself completely in front of him as he watched. Suddenly when almost fully dressed he stopped her. "Nora dear, please lift up your skirt again and remove those horrible long knickers. You must keep your love nest uncovered all day and come to me that way tonight."

Poor Nora had no option but to obey. Thankful that it was not an awkward time in the month, like the last time he demanded this. Still she gratefully grasped the tiny box with the three diamonds set in it, her payment for his pleasure last night. After she left, Santa Anna still felt very tired. They had not slept much that evening. However his mind raced again at what he had said to Nora about the future. He did believe his star was waiting to arise.

He never had any compunction in changing sides. Since his defeat of the Spanish invasion he had become the hero of his country. He knew President Guerrero's liberal ideas would never work in this country, it needed a strong hand. Soon Bustamante would displace him and introduce severe conservative attrition. However this would cause rebellion. He then would save the country again, in the cause of liberalism. He would be crowned President but would let his Vice President attempt to introduce liberal ideas. Again it would fail. Then once again he would take control. However this time he would make his control, a sheer dictatorship.

Since his victory two years ago he had been carefully extending his control of the whole of the region, including the Yucatan. He was gradually building up his forces ready for the necessary confrontation. He was still young, only thirty six years old, he could afford to wait. Meantime, as last night, he could enjoy life with almost an unlimited bevy of women who knew they must submit to him.

However, once President, he knew what he must do. First he must stop any further excursion of these families from the United States. How foolish was their past policies of encouraging that man Stephen Austin to bring them into the Coahuila-Texas region. He hoped that his new State Lieutenant, Senor Luna was already ensuring it was being curtailed, if not stopped, again he thought of his daughter's lovely body and wondered about the child he had given her. He knew he would like to repeat this and add to her family. Still he felt sure his aides would soon find another young girl to satisfy his desires. Once President he knew he would add considerably to the population in Mexico City.

He arose as he had much work to do before Nora Delgado came to him again that evening. Then he must be fair and find the time to send for Isabel Galvano. After all, she was already seven months pregnant again with his second child. He always thought pregnant women very ugly. However she was suffering this for him and the generous gifts he gave him. He admitted he enjoyed her eleven hours of suffering last time and hoped it would be at least as long again this next time. By now she had endured eleven births and two miscarriages. Isabel was used to pain, and he knew she would not mind him watching, for her pain was inevitable. Yes, he thought, 'I must get Isabel going again very quickly, after she bears this child.'

Then he smiled and thought, 'I wonder if I can seduce my dear Nora to conceive my child. She told me she had a painfully delivery her previous times, that was why she asked me to pay for abortion.- If it happens – I don't think I will agree next time. At least with my women obliging me, it means I can make less demands on my dear wife, Ines." With that feeling of generosity he dressed and applied himself to a full day of work.

2.

It seemed Santa Anna would have enjoyed watching poor Elvira Luna as she went into labour. For it took almost nine very painful hours before she was delivered of a seven pound baby girl she name Adela. Of course all her family knew the name of the father of her child, but even in San Macros it was rumoured that the daughter of Victor Luna had given birth to a child, yet they knew she was not married. Her family feared repercussions, were they to let it be known that she was the victim of the evil Santa Anna. However if this information came from someone outside the family, then no blame would be attached to them.

It was fortunate that Victor Luna, had many years before, befriended Stephen Austin when he first came, following his father Moses Austin, and continuing his work of settling citizens of the United States on this land. This had been allocated to him by Emperor Iturbide, when Mexico obtained its independence from Spain, but who was then removed when it became a Republic. Austin was a frequent visitor to his hacienda, so had been informed of Elvira's pregnancy, and the man responsible, almost as soon as they had returned here from Vera Cruz. It was easy for Stephen Austin to speak to the people of San Marcos, to remove any shame from Elvira, by ensuring they knew she was a victim of General Santa Anna, who they detested but, also, feared.

Now whenever Elvira ventured into the town, she and her baby daughter received great sympathy. Adela was now nine months old and Elvira had brought her into town to purchase some necessary things for her baby. She had just learned that Stephen Austin was in town, so she decided she would call on him at his office, where he conducted his business when in San Marcos. She entered just as Stephen was explaining to two new young American men, what land was available for purchase nearby, and it seemed there were still several tracts of land on offer between the Colorado River and to the east of the town.

"I think Karl we should buy that tract next to the river, it will ensure we have sufficient water were we to raise horses or cattle." Hanz Eliot was suggesting this course of action to Karl Downey. Karl replied, "I agree, but I think our first venture should be to raise horses. It is what in which, we are proficient. Why we might get other members in Kentucky to come here and drive stock for breeding from our farms there." Karl then turned to Stephen Austin, "I assume there is the usual demand for new horses around here?"

Elvira who had just entered carrying her daughter had heard his inquiry. She had to admit both these young men looked quite attractive. Also their dress indicated they had some wealth and probably came from a slightly higher class than the usual new American's coming here, desperate to obtain land, and rest a hard living from it. She felt obliged to intervene. "It seemed you have just arrived here and intend to settle. – Your assumption is right. Like my father most American's coming here, if in the south raise cotton, but here breed cattle on their land, though we all, also, breed the horses we need. – However we can never have too many. If you have knowledge of horse breeding, then I feel sure your venture would be successful."

Perhaps the fact that this lady had addressed them in English, if with a Spanish accent, whereas so far all the locals had used the latter language, even though they often could understand English. There was no doubt that when they turned and saw what an attractive women she was, it intrigued them. Elvira saw at once her suspicions that they were well educated, for both removed their hats and bowed to her in greeting, and she inclined her head to them as they would any lady of quality. Stephen Austin noticed this.

"Please let me introduce to you Senorita Elvira Luna, the daughter of the State Lieutenant of this area, and who owns large stretches of lands in this area. As I do not remember the names you have just given me, perhaps you would introduce yourself to the Senorita." Both, immediately realised she was introduced as Senorita, yet she was carrying a small baby in her arms. However their training ensured they did not show their surprise and both hastened to acquaint her of their names, adding they both had come here from Kentucky, and belonged to two of five families, who had established a very successful and prosperous horse breeding business near Winchester.

Once again Elvira was delighted when they showed their good manners by bringing a spare chair and placed it near the two chairs from which they had arisen as they were first introduced to her, and helped her to sit in it, still holding baby Adela. Now she smiled at both of them.

Then again in English asked, "Then it seems you have not come here in desperate need of succour, anxious to obtain cheap land and obtain a living from it?"

Karl replied, "No we are fortunate, all our five families in Kentucky are reasonably wealthy. Sometime, I hope I may have the opportunity of explaining how thirty years ago our five families who had come to know each other and were in fact related, then settled in Kentucky, coming from an equally prosperous horse breeding family in West Virginia. We have pooled our resources and this has been the reason for our success."

He continued, "Naturally we are now all part of five large families, who are continuing our profession. We came here, simply, because we had heard so much about your country and knew many Americans had settled here. – Actually we only came for a visit. – However once we heard how easy it was to purchase land, we have today come to see Stephen Austin, for that purpose."

Elvira asked, "If so, do you intend to stay here." Karl smile, "Of course, this has changed our intentions. We shall see if any more of our relatives would like to come and settle here. In fact, should we decided on horse breeding, we will need to ask some family members to bring stock here for that purpose. Yes, we shall stay, and try to make this land a success." Now he smiled bent over taking hold of her one free hand an kissed it casing Elvira to react in some panic. Then he said "Dear lady, now we know there are such beautiful young ladies, like you are living here, it seems we have added reasons for staying." Then he released her hand.

Stephen Austin had listened and been entertained by the quick repartee between them. Now at last he intervened. "Senorita Luna, I must apologise for the behaviour of my countrymen. I'm afraid too many of them are impetuous and coming here fail to understand that Spanish ladies do not expect, nor desire, such uncouth behaviour as these present gentleman have displayed this day. I feel both of you should apologise."

Once again they stood up and both bowed to her. This time it was Hanz who spoke. "I too apologise for the behaviour of my cousin. However I think there are extenuating circumstances. Please believe me, it is a long time since we have been privileged with the company of such a beautiful young lady. We both hope that somehow you will forgive us for our behaviour, and beg that we may be blest with the added privilege, of being able to meet you again in the not too distant future."

Now it was Elvira's turn to respond and she stood up, "Stephen I fear I must leave you but hope you may call on us in the near future. I know my father wishes to speak with you, as he fears for the future." Then she turned to the two men, "I accept your apologises. Neither do I think ill of you. Impetuous you may be. But you seem to know how to conduct yourself as gentlemen, not something I can say of many of your compatriots. Perhaps if you do decide to stay and purchase land here, we may meet again in the future. I can add, I would like that to happen."

She turned, still carrying her baby and left. This meeting had made up their minds. Very quickly they finished their business with Stephen Austin and purchased that land near the river, paying him the money, and receiving deeds giving them ownership. However before they left they felt bound to question him on the ambiguity that he called her Senorita yet she was carrying a child.

Austin was not willing to give them the full information. However he did tell them she was the victim of the evil desires of General Santa Anna, being, virtually, raped pregnant by him, then discarded. The baby Adela was his child and had caused her downfall. There was no doubt but that both Karl and Hanz were extremely sorry for her. It certainly, did nothing to detract from their, already, good opinion of the lady, and increased further their desire to soon, again, make her acquaintance.

3.

"So you really do know how to shape and construct this engine?", Silas Taylor asked his nephew, Gordon Taylor.

Gordon replied, "Yes! Once I dismantle it, I could fabricate any part of it in iron, provide I had a workshop with the necessary machinery. It seems to me that this steam engine is very similar to the ones we are constructing, which we called Locomotives, and will draw the coaches on the new iron way, we call railways, from Liverpool to Manchester. In fact I believe it is even more like the engines we fit into what we call Tractors which run on large wheels and pull other trucks with cargoes."

Now he smiled, "But where could I find the necessary machinery to smelt and mould these parts? I doubt if you could afford to set up a workshop similar to what we had at Ancoats."

Silas placed his hand on his shoulder. "For several years I captained and ran several of the River Boats belonging to the Carroll/Marshall Company. When I, eventually purchased my own ships - I bought them from them – they agreed they could be maintained in any of their workshops. They have a very big one close by, and another large one at St. Louis, with a maintenance one at New Orleans. At present I pay them quite large sums of money to maintain my boats, but I'm certain I could, for a price, let you work in any of their shops. I'll take you to the one down the road."

Gordon Taylor had arrived two days before bringing with him the entire McLean family. They were all made very welcome by both Silas and his thirty one year old Spanish wife, Gloria. Gloria had heard so much about Gordon from her husband and felt she had known him, even before he arrived. She was, also, delighted to meet the new family which had arrived with Gordon, happy to have a young woman nearly her own age to talk with. It was she who insisted they stayed as their guests for several days, and rested from their long journey.

Gloria had married Silas in New Orleans in 1817, nine years before Patricia had married Neil McLean, and so had born one more child than had Patricia, though both women had a baby now over a year old. Later Gordon was to learn that Silas had met and fallen in love with Gloria soon after he deserted and became a sailor on the Mississippi Steam boats. Of course he could only be with Gloria whenever his boat returned to New Orleans.

It seemed their love making got out of hand and Gloria conceived his child. It was a very difficult time for both of them, and Gloria was six months pregnant before they married. By then he had managed to buy a very small house near the docks in Pittsburgh, and persuaded his captain to let him bring Gloria on his boat from New Orleans. So his eldest son, Hector was born there in 1817. Silas had told Gordon, he owed so much to his wife, who stopped him drinking, shepherded his finances and enabled him, finally, to buy two boats of his own. They now lived in a large house in the well to do area of the city. Since then Gloria had born him four more children.

Silas took Gordon to the Ship building yards of the Carroll/Marshall Shipping Lines and introduced him to the manager of the repair shop. By chance at that moment one of the owners and senior directors of the Line was visiting, - fifty five year old Roy Marshall. Silas had met him once or twice before, and so lost no time in introducing Gordon to him, telling him he had just arrived from Manchester in England. Gordon had proudly informed him that he was a fully qualified engineer and had so recently been involved in the construction of the new Liverpool to Manchester Railway and the construction of steam locomotives to pull coaches on that line.

At once Roy Marshall had asked him from what part of Manchester he had come. When Gordon told him he was born and bred in Ancoats, Roy had smiled and informed him he was born, not far away in Gorton, and his family had been Hand Loom weavers until Grimshaw's Mill had closed them down and into poverty, adding that he was delighted that the mob had burnt down the mill just as he came to America.

Of course like everyone in Manchester, Gordon knew about the demise of the mill, and how it had been rebuilt and destroyed all hope for the hand loom weavers. When Gordon told him as much, Roy had smiled, "I will now confess my evil past, for I was one of the mob who destroyed the mill that day. Yet, it seems I was destined to meet another, and together we came here. Ironically, I then became prosperous by helping to found the first steam powered Cotton Mill here in Philadelphia, learning all about steam power. It was this knowledge which led to four of us establishing this steam boat building company, now diversifying into steam transportation."

"Then, like me, you are a trained engineer?" Gordon asked.

Roy Marshall laughed, "Indeed I am not and only gained my proficiency by experimenting on the site. In fact my wonderful wife Charlotte, is a qualified engineer and a brilliant draughtswoman and designer. My company owes so much to her and her brother, Francois Le Raye, both refugees escaping from the Terror in France in 1793, and who married Fay Bradbury, who I meet at that fire, when her lover had been killed by the soldiers. I brought her to America and now the four of us live close by in Pittsburgh, friends, as well as the founders of this firm., with the help of the investments made by Edgar Carroll, whose family have lived in America since King Charles I was on the throne."

Gordon Taylor was astounded, "Sir, I do hope I do not annoy you. As an engineer myself, I am first amazed that you could mechanise and add steam power to a cotton mill, then apply this to steam power in a boat, yet without any engineering training. Even more perplexed that your wife, a woman, was fully trained as both an engineer and a draughtswoman and designer. Could you please enlighten me on this amazing fact?"

Roy, smiled, "No I'm not annoyed. In my case, it is probably that I have an excellent memory. Perhaps because I so hated that mill in Manchester I remembered in detail every way the power was connected to the looms. By simple experimentation I applied this in Philadelphia and won the respect of the father of the owner of the mill. Then I met, and realised the wonderful ability of both Francois and Charlotte, who had been trained by their father, who was killed in France. Together we established not just a prosperous company, but a life long friendship. We are virtually one large family."

Gordon hastened to thank him for taking him into his confidence. Then adding he had come here today to see if he would be allowed to use their own machinery, for which they would pay, to enable him to maintain and improve his uncle's own two steam ships. "If so, " he added, "I would hope I might someday meet your remarkable partners and especially meet your wonderful and brilliant wife. I can understand how proud you must be of her achievements."

Roy now turned to his uncle. "Silas Taylor I respect you for the years you served my Shipping Line. I am pleased you have brought this man from Manchester to act as your own engineer. For your past service, I will ensure my managers provided him with everything he needs. We shall only charge you for the use of our basic materials, however I would like to ask your permission for him, in a short time, to visit all our maintenance yards in both St. Louis and New Orleans, and report on their efficiency, whenever he sails there on your boats."

Of course Silas gladly accented and Gordon confirmed he would be delighted to do this, but asked if so that he might be given authorisation to do so, as he feared his presence would not be welcomed when they knew the reason for his visit. Roy had laughed and promised to do so, "It seems you are a very enterprising young man. You remind me so much of what I was like at your age. I am glad I've met you today, and hope to hear from you again, in due course."

After that neither of them had any difficulty with the management of the maintenance and building works. Gordon saw at once that their equipment, was if anything, even better that that he had worked on in their own works in Ancoats. He told Silas he was sure he could, if necessary construct entirely new Steam Engines for his ships. It was two very happy men who returned to the house.

For Gordon. It meant even more. It would not be necessary for him to persuade his uncle to let him accompany the McLean family, but more importantly, Sheila McLean, on the river journey to Missouri, for St. Louis was on that route, and he would ensure they arrived safely and settled down before returning to St. Louis and then descending south to New Orleans to report for Roy Marshall on the efficiency of their maintenance shops for his company.

Gordon smiled, he knew his uncle had already agreed to employ him as the company engineer, so he would receive his salary the whole time. But now would receive a retainer from Roy Marshal. Also, as he returned north again he would make a small detour to call again on the McLean's, to ensure they were all safe and had managed to establish themselves in his absence. Finally paying a second visit to St. Louis on his return to Pittsburgh.

4.

Meanwhile in New York, Estelle and Adrian Carroll, had been staying with their daughter, Ann and her husband, Peter Vanderbilt. They were delighted to find that their business association with Cornelius Vanderbilt was progressing favourably. Earlier trials with propeller driven boats had been successful, and they were now trying to introduce similar means of propulsion into ocean going ships. However they still had not overcome the difficulties experienced when such new ships encountered the savage waves of the Atlantic Ocean.

However Estelle had renewed her friendship with Muriel Alexander, daughter of Sir Richard Alexander, a lady now over forty years of age. Estelle already knew that Sir Richard had sided with his father, Sir William Alexander, supporting George Washington during the American Revolution, and at that time in New York was considered a rebel.

The majority of British aristocratic families in New York, were loyalists and supported General Clinton and King George III. The chief supporters were Sir John Johnson and his brother, Sir Richard Johnson, along with several branches of the Livingston families. It seemed, however when the Americans won the war and established the new United States of America, many of these families were forced, for safety, to emigrate to Canada. Many, especially the Johnston's, going to live near Montreal.

Muriel as a young girl had been fascinated by her own father, Richard Alexander's tales of how his father, Sir William, with inferior forces, was able to beat the British forces, lead by Sir William Johnson. And that man's close relationships with the Mohawk indians, this man even taking several Mohawk women to their delight, as his mistresses. It seemed she had learned of the various descendents of Blanche Carroll after she married Felix Backhouse, eventually coming to know both Daniel and Danton Backhouse, now living in Montreal, in Canada. From them Muriel had managed to learn about Daniel's ancestors and how his family had prospered whilst living in New York.

Estelle, from Manon Eliot, had learned of a scandal years ago. This was the scandal involving Blanche Carroll. How during a visit from New York of Sir William Hyde and his son, Edward Hyde, when entertained by Sir David Carroll, whilst David was Governor of Maryland. It seemed that a step-son of Sir William, Felix Backhouse had seduced sixteen year old Blanche, who conceived, resulting in her having to marry Felix and return with him to New York.

Again there was some, unconfirmed suspicions, concerning Felix's parents. It was even suggested that Felix Backhouse and Edward Hyde's daughter, Catherine Hyde, born in the same year, were possibly incestuous children of, first, Sir William's wife, Flower, and his son, Edward, whilst Catherine might be the daughter of Edward's fiancée to, Kathleen O'Brien, and may have been responsible for Edward's hurried marriage to Kathleen. The fact was that Blanche bore Felix a son, Bruce Backhouse in 1705, having then settled in New York.

Muriel over time, and during her visits to the Backhouse family in Montreal, had managed to construct a life line, joining Bruce Backhouse to his great, great grandson, Daniel Backhouse. All descended through five generations from Bruce Backhouse, and it seemed in Montreal, many future husbands and wives were related to many high born families previously living in New York. They had been forced after the War of Independence, to emigrate to Montreal This especially was the case of those who married the decedents of Sir William Robinson, a famous general who had lived in New England in the past

Both Muriel and Estelle were fascinated by this close relationship with the original Sir William Robinson, an eminent British General of the Seven Years War against France, and how it had affected the future descendents of Blanche Carroll.

Manon's book described the events concerning the Carroll family during the Seven Years war. Estelle could inform Muriel that this same Sir William Robinson had saved both Daniel Carroll and Donald Wilson's life when imprisoned as traitors at Stillwater during that war. Estelle knew that Manon Eliot would be delighted to have this information which she could add to her own account of the period.

The full facts concerning Daniel Carroll, Donald Wilson and Sir William Johnson are accurately described in the Book 'Ohio, Author Royston Moore'. See the Carroll Family Saga, explained at the beginning of this book.

Finally, it seemed Danton and Rachael had born a son, aptly named David Backhouse, bearing the name of his famous predecessor Sir David Carroll. He was now nineteen years old.

Thirsting for adventure, David had now, gone west to the Oregon country, believing this area should belong to Canada, and not to the United States, who were claiming it. He also wished to free the area south, from its present ownership by Mexico.

Estelle felt this was wrong and that it should really belong to the United States, and neither Canada nor Mexico. However she knew that both Danton and Rachel were concerned for the safety of their son, which she could appreciate. So Estelle returned to Rockville a very satisfied woman.

5.

Gordon Taylor had his arm around Sheila McLean's small waist as they stood leaning over the handrail enthralled as they watched the heavy planks of the large paddle wheel as it churned up the water in the river, thrusting the boat ever forward. Sheila inclined her head to look at him and her face showed she was very happy.

"You know I think it is wonderful that you decided to join us on this boat and accompany us to our new home. I really thought I would have to say goodbye to you once we left Pittsburgh.". Still smiling she added, "You know my parents are very grateful to you, first for ensuring we arrived safely at Pittsburgh and then persuading your uncle to help us and then, you, coming so far with us, but I am not certain they approve of your friendship with me."

Gordon now released her and turned her round so that she faced him. Then he replied. "Oh! Sheila surely that's not true. I thought, even long ago, when we were on the ship coming to New York, you knew how much I appreciated your company. I confess, everything I have done since then has been to give me a longer period to be with you and for us to get to know each other. You must know you are very special to me."

Now a Sheila's face turned sadly away. "Yes, dear Gordon, I've hoped you felt that way about me. But at Jefferson, we shall have to say goodbye. After you leave us, it is unlikely we shall ever see each other again." Just for a moment Gordon was tempted to press his lips on her lovely lips for he saw a few tears were appearing in her eyes. However he knew her parents were watching them. He felt they feared his intentions might not be sincere. Instead he took hold of her hand and kissed it.

Again he smiled, "If you think that, then you are very mistaken. It seems as I work for my uncle I shall have to travel far on our ships. You know Roy Marshall, the senior director of the Carroll/Marshall Shipping Line has hired me to assess the efficiency of his ship maintenance yards, because of my past history in helping to build machinery for our Railway line in Lancashire. Soon I will have money. Believe me – I shall use every opportunity to use these facilities to call and visit you. – That is if it is what you want."

Now to his disappointment she turned aside. "Dear Gordon, of course I want and would love that. I confess I like you very much but father believes I must look to a future near our new home. – I don't think he dislikes you. – It's just that he fears our relationship is only a temporary one, and that I should find a man near where we shall live, rather than believe I could have a future with you."

Now Gordon did hold her tightly against him, "Dear Sheila, I must know. Would you like – would you consider a future with me, if it were possible." Shelia blushed and before she spoke Gordon guessed her answer. "Dear, dear Gordon, I would love to spend my life with you. – I have never had a boyfriend – I have never had the chance to flirt with men. So this is why my times with you have been so wonderful. Please, please try to come and visit me. Prove father is wrong."

In spite of them watching Gordon now threw caution to the wind, bent and very briefly kissed her on her offered lips. "Now I know how you feel, I promise I will come to you. – Try to believe me when I say a hope our friendship can continue – but hope it may mean more than that for us." After that Gordon felt that her parents were ever present whenever he was near her. There was no doubt she was being chaperoned. However he did not let that prevent him meeting Sheila whenever possible.

After the boat called at St. Louis it took the northern route entering the River Missouri, tracing the river westwards until it came to the landing stage at Jefferson. A sign proclaimed it as 'Jefferson City' in honour of the past president. However it was really only a very small one street town. The McLean's destination was some ten miles inland of what was becoming known as Cole County.

The Doyle family who had been their neighbours in Northern Island had prepared for their arrival, having purchased the land, at a very small price, and had built for them a four roomed wooden logged cabin, built by slaves, from the money the McLean's had sent them in advance. So after hiring a wagon they had travelled to meet them and given a good welcome. Gordon had accompanied them and was delighted that the Doyle family had done so much to ensure they had no difficulty in establishing themselves.

Kevin Doyle had married Mary O'Brien in 1806, when Kevin was eight years older than Neil McLean. They now had seven children, four daughters and three sons. Gordon, at once noticed that their eldest son, Simon Doyle, though two years older than Sheila seemed to try to monopolise her attention and Gordon realised he might soon become a rival for Shelia's friendship. It made him even more determined to call on her fairly regularly.

Gordon stayed a week with them. He had to head back to Jefferson for the boat having proceeded after they left, as far as Independence. Then it had discharged its cargo and taken on new stores and Gordon needed to be on the quay when it returned. However the night before he left, with difficulty he managed to take Sheila outside to talk to her.

He possibly frightened her a little by taking her into his arms and kissing her lips for a minute or two. However as he released her, he smiled and said, "I apologise for this, but I just wanted you to know, I shall be thinking of you the whole time I am away. As I promised on the boat, it won't be long before I call on you again. – Please try not to forget me. It was a Thursday when we first met on the ship after Liverpool. Before I go to sleep each Thursday night in future, I shall remember again the wonderful moments I have had with you since that first day."

Now having lost her fear she gently kissed his lips again, "That is my promise that, I too, will think of you each Thursday evening.". He left the next day and her father took him on his wagon to the quay. As they parted her said, "Thank you Gordon, we are very much indebted to you for helping us so much in coming here. "

Then Neil looked firmly at him, "Gordon, I know you think a lot about my daughter, Sheila. – I assure you, I have nothing against you. – but I want Sheila to have a good and happy life. Your work must take you far away from Jefferson City, and I feel it would be better if she was to eventually find a permanent partner near to where we live."

Gordon smiled as he shook hands with Neil. "I understand. However I like Sheila very much. I warn you I intend to call on you very regularly. Then it will be up to Sheila to decide the man she should like." He said no more and turned away, not giving Neil a chance to reply, as they could see the boat was rapidly approaching the quay.

Gordon joined it and was allocated a good cabin, being a relative of the owner of the vessel. However it was with sadness that Gordon sailed back along the river, joining again the Mississippi and eventually drawing alongside the quay at St. Louis. Here he disembarked. The boat was not going down river to New Orleans but was returning via Kentucky to Pittsburgh. Now Gordon had the task of first finding an hotel for accommodation and then to discover the whereabouts of the Carroll/Marshall Maintenance shop. He knew this would not be difficult, for at the quay he saw the headquarters of that large company standing in spacious apartments nearby. It seemed the company held a very special place in the town.

Taking his few belongings with him he found a suitable hotel and registered, having to fill up a special form as a foreigner, for he was not a citizen of the United States and Britain was a foreign country. This made Gordon consider he must soon apply to become a citizen, but his uncle told him he should first need to own a house or land in this country, though he could apply quoting his uncle's address.

He realised it was Thursday night, and true to his promise he knelt down at the side of his bed, said a little pray for Sheila remembering the very many happy hours he had spent with her. He could not be sure he was yet falling in love with her. He had never done that with any of his girlfriends in the past. However he knew how much he now missed her and wanted to met her again, as soon as possible, no matter what her father would think. Now there was work for him to do.

6.

The next day Gordon had to call at the headquarters of the Carroll/ Marshall Shipping Line at their magnificent building near the quay in St. Louis. Handing the receptionist the letter Roy Marshall had given him as an introduction. After a short wait he was lead into the spacious office of the man, who was head of the St. Louis operations, Alan Reid, a man about fifty years of age, and asked to sit down.

"Mr. Taylor, Roy Marshall has written to me telling me you would be arriving. It seems, in spite of your age, you are a qualified engineer, even helping to establish a Railway to convey passengers by a steam train from two towns in England many miles apart. I have heard that such things are being attempted in the eastern United States. Please tell me truthfully, is this possible." It seemed Roy Marshall had informed his man very fully.

Gordon replied, "Quite possible and though it was not fully completed when I left England, I have seen it happening, with a steam locomotive pulling wagons. However my engineering training is far broader than that. I am qualified to cast and perform metal into any shape. I can build any steam machinery necessary, and many other useful engineering objects. That is why I believe I am well qualified to assess the present efficiency of either your ship building or maintenance yards, and then suggest possible changes. I do hope my presence does not constitute a threat to your management in any way, I will do my best not to embarrass you."

Alan Reid laughed, "At least you are honest. I can set your mind at rest. I doubt if Roy would castigate me, even if you should show our weaknesses. You see Roy's eldest son, Charles is married to my eldest daughter, Sharon, and together manage our small office in Independence, Missouri., so we are all part of the family and been friends for many years."

Now he stood up and came to him and as Gordon arose he said, "Come I will take you to the Marshalling yards, you can see the extent of our ship building, although it is nothing as large as the works in Pittsburgh, - then to the building near to it - where we maintain our vessels and many of other rival companies. Please feel free to spend as much time as possible examining them. I shall be delighted to receive your report in due course, which I will gladly send to Roy."

The ice was broken. Gordon had feared this man would look upon him as a possible danger to his future. Now it seemed Alan Reid was as anxious as Roy Marshall for him to perform his task. They chatted together as they walked to the two buildings. Alan telling him he came from a family which had established a very large arable farm, a few miles south of Pittsburgh.

Then he surprised Gordon, "In England, have you ever heard of indentured servants, for that country was responsible for sending so many poor women here to America into a virtual life of both domestic, and sexual slavery for a number of years, to be misused and bare children out of wedlock, simply for some minor crime of thieving in the old country. Well my mother Erin was one of these women sent this way from Ireland, and my father purchased her at the fort. – It is fortunate for them and for me that, they fell in love with each other and, eventually, married."

He could see the bitterness in Alan's voice as he spoke, so Gordon replied cautiously. "I have heard of this for it seems we still do these things and send poor women and men as indentured servants, though we now called it transportation to Australia. Few in Britain know what happens there, perhaps it is as well. I would appreciate it, if before I leave, you could enlarge on what happened to your mother, if it did not offend you to tell me." Alan's spirit seemed to rise again, "You shall hear that, before you leave us I will invite you to our house for an evening, and you can meet my wife, Dora." He said no more and soon they reached the buildings and went inside.

For the next month Gordon, spent virtually every day in those two buildings watching the operations and noting any faults in his book. Alan was true to his promise and Gordon was invited to his house three times during his stay and made very welcome. There he learned the difficult life of his mother sent to Pittsburgh as an indentured servant with another young girl Mary Malloy, to work for a very cruel and lecherous Fur Merchant, both frequently used sexually. Then after he died, two young men Brian Hobbs and Craig Reid bought them, again enjoying intimacy with them, however not demanding pregnancy.

Eventually all four had fallen in love and Brian had married Mary, while his father Craig had married Erin.

It seemed it was this partnership, all four still living almost as one large family, even still swapping partners, occasionally, which had resulted in their now great prosperity . Then, how being so near to Pittsburgh they had become very friendly with Francois Le Raye, his sister, Charlotte and Fay Bradbury who Francois married and Roy Marshall, who married his sister, Charlotte. It seemed their four families all prospered together, hence the inter marrying and Alan and Sharon's positions in management of the Carroll-Marshall Shipping Line.

Gordon was intrigued by Alan's story and over the three nights, also, learned a lot about other persons who had lived in that area of West Virginia. Again Gordon was to learn of another branch of the Carroll family, who lived in Virginia and Maryland, and especially about a certain Daniel Carroll who during the last century had done so much for many families there. His own father, Craig, owed his success to the investment Daniel had made to enable both Craig and Brian to purchase and work the original holding. It, also, seemed that this Daniel Carroll had played an important part in supporting George Washington during the War of independence, when help was desperately needed.

At the end of two months Gordon had concluded his examination and written a detailed report, given it to Alan, for forwarding to Roy Marshall in Pittsburgh. Alan was very impressed by it and was able to institute several changes very quickly finding how more efficient was the result. During his stay, Alan had given him several letters of credit to cash at the new local Casimir/Holstein Bank, to cover his expenses whilst in the town. It was there he was to meet the manager, Otto Fallon, who had recently established the bank on behalf of the Manhattan Bank of New York. A man Gordon was to meet again in different circumstances in the future.

His first task completed, Gordon, now had to travel down the river to New Orleans to perform a similar task on the maintenance workshops there. Naturally he was anxious to conclude this task as quickly as possible so that he could return north again to renew his acquaintance with Sheila McLean. In fact having told Alan Reid of his desire, Alan had smiled and helped to make this possible. Alan suggested when he returned from New Orleans he should visit their smaller office at Independence and perhaps suggest minimum changes to their repair workshops, necessary for frequent breakdowns, and so save them from having to reach St. Louis.

Alan had smiled, pointing out his journey would still be covered by his companies expenses, and he could easily break his journey at Jefferson, if it was his wish. Of course Gordon was grateful and told Alan so, however Alan admitted he had been impressed with his report. The company would gain financially as a result. Alan also planned the quickest way of getting to New Orleans. Some of their boats made the quick journey from Pittsburgh straight down the Ohio and Mississippi Rivers to New Orleans without coming north to call at St. Louis. This meant that Gordon must travel on a boat first to Cairo where the Ohio joined the Mississippi. Stay there and then board the fast boat after a wait of three days. This is what he did, staying at a small hotel for two nights.

Joining the boat, he was fortunate that Alan had arranged a cabin for his journey as the ship was very loaded with both goods, animals and passengers. Of course the boat called at many towns on the way and Gordon had plenty of time to enter into conversation with many of the passengers. Knowing very little about horses he was intrigued by two men who it seemed were transporting several mares and stallions down river from Kentucky. However he discovered that when they arrived at New Orleans, these two men intended to drive this horses across Louisiana to Texas in Mexico, as two of their relatives had purchased land there. Now the idea was to use it for horse breeding, as was their successful practice in Kentucky. The whole idea intrigued Gordon and so naturally he tried to find out as much as possible about this project.

He learned they came from a very large horse breeding estate, called the Camargo Equestrian Establishment, near Winchester, Kentucky, where five families had settled thirty years ago coming from West Virginia. They had pooled their resources and this had lead to their financial success. Now two sons, Karl Downey and Hanz Eliot, had decided, purely for adventure, to go to Mexico. There they found many

Americans were settling, swamping the smaller Mexican population, which was creating a problem to the government of Mexico in Mexico City.

However Karl and Hanz found good land was available for purchase, for a pittance, and so had purchased a large area near San Marcos. Now they had written to them begging some of them to travel down to Mexico and to bring a selection of horses for breeding purposes, so to establish another farm to run in conjunction with the one in Kentucky.

This was what the two men were doing with the full approval of everyone. One of these men was called Steven Downey, but was a cousin, not a brother of Karl Downey. The other was Tony Brady. The name Brady rang a bell in Gordon's mind. He remembered Shelia's mother telling him she was Patricia Brady before she married Neil McLean and lived on part of the Calvert estate in Northern Island. Patricia did not know the circumstances but was sure that some branches of the Brady family had come from Northern Island, near to where she had been born. They had settled in America nearly fifty years before. However that was all he knew. Gordon wished to discover if this man Tony Brady, was in any way, connected to the Brady family to which Sheila's mother had belonged.

He asked, "By any chance do any of your ancestors come from Northern Ireland?" Tony Brady answered immediately, "Why yes, my father came from there after he rescued a number of aristocratic people from France at the height of the Terror there, in1793. In fact my mother was one of the persons he rescued. Her name was Antoinette Condorcet, and her father was one of King Louis XV's Ministers, executed before my father rescued her. It seemed they fell in love and then later married. I am their fourth child."

He continued, "You see my father, with two other relatives David Downey and Stuart Downey, who is Steven's father, were the three men who rescued all these people. After that they accompanied them, - really at the instigation of Daniel Carroll, - and they came to live in America. However James Downey and Peter Eliot are part of families

68

who came from the same place in Ireland, the Calvert Estate, twenty years before we came."

Seeing Gordon was perplexed, he laughed, "It really is a very complicated story, since in a way we are all descendents of Margaret Eliot, also born on the Calvert Estate in Ireland, whose daughter, Amelia, herself an indentured servant, came to America, married a David Carroll, who came from illustrious parents in Wookey in Somerset. He then became Governor of Maryland and was knighted. The Daniel Carroll who helped my father, was the grandson of this man. "

Over time both Tony and Steven were able to show on paper the life lines which led back to this Margaret Eliot, living in the reign of King James II of England. Gordon thanked them, telling why he was interested and knew now when he returned to see Sheila, he could inform her mother of her relatives living in both Kentucky and West Virginia.

In fact before they arrived at New Orleans, they had begged Gordon to ask this Patricia McLean to contact both their parents in Kentucky as well as the older families in West Virginia, giving Gordon the address for him to give to her. Finding that his work would mean him travelling often near to Winchester, they asked him to call on their families, and gave him a letter of introduction. When they parted, Gordon felt his journey south had been very important, apart from his duty now to Roy Marshall.

They shook hands on the quay and Gordon wished them luck in their new venture.

7.

Edwin and Joan Palatine were met by Louise Adelaide d'Orleans' daughter Marie Eugenie von Schroeppel. Almost to their surprise she made them very welcome, taking them to her home in Utica. It seemed her husband John Hinman was Mayor of that town. No sooner had they settled there, each given a spacious rooms of their own, before Marie made her position very clear.

"Dear Edwin and Joan, I hope I can make you both happy here. I will try. It seems that neither your father nor my mother have any time for you and certainly do not love you. Both are very ambitious people, only interested in bettering themselves. I have no doubt but within weeks your father will be crowned King of France. Frankly, you both are liability to them, that is why they have sent you here."

Now a little sadly she continued, "I'm afraid her past actions have placed me and my brothers and sisters far apart from her. I no longer love her, neither do they. I believe her persistent quarrelling with my father, George, was, eventually, responsible for his death. My father met and fell in love with my mother in Guadeloupe, where my mother had been wrecked. It was a hasty courtship and the married there. I believe she conceived my eldest brother even before she married. Then they came and settled here in New York."

Now she smiled happily, "My father though much older than my mother was a fine man, and very prosperous, providing all of us with much wealth. Frankly I was glad when, after my father's sad death five years ago, she deserted us and returned to France. I believe that even her strong love for her brother, your father, Louis Philippe, is a little stronger than as a sister and brother."

She stood up and came and laid a hand on each of their shoulders, "I tell you this so you will not blame me for what my mother has forced you to accept. She has set up a very large trust fund for both of you. However, I want you to save that until you find partners with whom you would like to spend your lives. We are rich, my husband and I will see to all your needs, and ensure you have a pleasant life with us."

Of course both Edwin and Joan were gratified at Marie's offer. Very quickly they settled into their new life in their new home. Gone were the fears they had felt as they crossed the Atlantic. They both had much free time and they told Marie of the Carroll's they had meet on the ship and their unusual ancestry and relationship. They explained how they would like to meet their son Peter and his wife, Amy, a member of the Vanderbilt family. Of course Marie knew of them and their endevours to develop ocean going Steam Ships. So she arranged for them to go and meet them quoting the introduction they had been given on the ship.

They were well received, and both Peter and Amy Carroll had been fully informed of their ancestry by Peter's mother and father whilst they stayed with them. In fact they were told that his mother and father, hoped they would be able to come and stay with them at Rockville in Maryland, before Easter. Edwin was particularly curious to know how successful they had been about their steam ship inventions. Once again they were to learn of the intricate relationships of the various branches of the Carroll family, for the basis for the steam engine in their ships, was their right to use the copy right of the Carroll branch in Pennsylvania and belonged to the Carroll/Marshall Ship Building Company, used on their Ohio and Mississippi Steam boats.

However the steam power on those boats drove paddle wheels for motivation. Peter with his brother-in-law, Cornelius Vanderbilt were endeavouring to use the steam power to drive propeller screws at the stern of the ship. They considered paddle wheels were too vulnerable when beset with the fierce Atlantic storms. So far they had enjoyed limited success on ships tested at the mouth of the River Hudson, but still not stable enough for full Atlantic use. They enjoyed a entertaining day and evening with them and were invited to call on them again anytime.

Now they were anxious to meet again Adrian and Estelle Carroll, who they had met on the ship and wrote to them informing them of their visit to their son and daughter-in-law, and expressed the wish they might call on them at Rockville. They received a reply immediately, telling them, they would send a coach to bring them to stay with them for a few days. The coach arrived as promised and travelling through Philadelphia and the growing city of Baltimore, named after George Calvert, First Lord Baltimore and for a long time the owner of what was now the State of Maryland. They were astounded at the magnificence of the mansion of Rockville, unlike any they had known in England.

Though met by Estelle and Adrian, they were quickly introduced to Adrian's mother and father, Andrew and Angela Carroll, both in their late seventies and a little infirm but still in quite good health. It was from Andrew Carroll they learned the long history of Rockville and the two original branches of the Carroll family, the Roman Catholic branch from Yorkshire and the Protestant branch from Somerset. How when persecuted by King James II, Roman Catholic Edgar Carroll had persuaded his Protestant cousin, David Carroll to come with him to Maryland on the promise of being given the Rockville estate, to work as a Tobacco farm.

A some length Andrew was to tell them of the incredible meeting of this David Carroll on this small ship with Amelia Eliot, raped pregnant by an Irish lord, condemned to go to America and then to conceive three more children by the American branch of her despoiler. David's saving of her life, his use of her, then accepting responsibility for her, falling in love and marrying her. When David was made Governor, risking his life to win religious freedom for Maryland, made a Knight of the Bath, giving peasant girl Amelia the title of Lady Amelia.

Andrew explained, "Everything stems from that incredible meeting on that ship, as she was nearly dying from starvation. I am descended from Sir David through my father, Anthony Carroll, the son of Paul Carroll, who was Amelia's second son. Estelle is descended from her eldest son, Sir Robert. Though his son, Sir Gerald, was a great disappointment to him. Gerald's son, Hugh, was even worse and when he became the owner of Rockville, tried first to sell it, then during the War of Independence so fiercely supported the British, executing several men who sided with the revolution."

Now Andrew smiled, "This is where my story of events may differ from my daughter-in-law, who I love as much as my own son. At the end the mob caught Hugh as he tried to escape and killed him. The possession of Rockville was taken away from Sir Gerald and the Carroll family in Britain by Congress, and given for disposal to my uncle, Daniel Carroll. We each had a common ancestor, Paul, Amelia's second son. Well Daniel believing his uncle Sir Robert would not have wanted his family to own Rockville, gave it to me, as the eldest son, of Anthony the eldest son of Paul and therefore after Sir Gerald the direct descendent of Sir David and Amelia. That if how I inherited it."

Now he came an put a loving arm around Estelle's waist. "You see this wonderful woman who had given my son, children, and nearly thirty years of continuous love, is the great granddaughter of that Sir

Gerald Carroll. Since the descendent of Amelia's eldest son, Rockville technically belonged to her. – However a miracle happened. I was to meet, come to love and even more delighted when my son, Adrian, fell in love with her, almost as soon as she arrived here. This was when a French Privateer attacked the British ship she was travelling on to the Bahamas, destined to marry a man she disliked, to save her family from ruin. Fate in the shape of a U.S. Naval vessel saved her life but not before her mother died beside her. Estelle landed at Annapolis, I met her, brought her here, to make me a very happy father-in-law."

Now he kissed Estelle, as she threw her arms around him and kissed him in return before adding, "I could never have hoped to meet a more wonderful couple than my father-in-law and mother-in-law." Hugging her, Andrew concluded, "So at length justice will be done. Adrian and Estelle will become Master and Mistress of Rockville, as was intended, though the route was not the one planned."

Of course both Edwin and Joan were intrigued with this complicated story of events in the past, and whilst there met Estelle's sister, Julia, and her husband, Aster Brookes. Once again Daniel Carroll's ghost appeared when Aster told her of his mother Sophia Chalmers. However they still had to wait to learn what happened to the Roman Catholic branch of the Carroll family, which it seemed, some time before chose to live in Pennsylvania and West Virginia. But that is another story they would hear about as the enjoyed their prolonged stay at Rockville.

8.

Donald Reid wishes to visit and possibly settle in California, had developed during the last two years. He was disappointed to learn that the area to the north of Mexican California, on the Pacific coast, called the Oregon Territory, to which several fur traders had travelled, had not led to any real settlements. Worse the area was savagely disputed by the British from Canada. Even those people who landed from ships, which had sailed around Cape Horn, had not resulted in many permanent settlements. Both invasions had done little but to bring disease, which decimated the native indian population. These include measles, malaria, influenza and small pox.

At least this meant few natives were left and reduced the dangers of indian attacks upon any white settlements. Donald had known of this area when he was at the Great Salt Lake. In fact the journey to the territory was roughly the route they had taken to get there. It did not have the same attraction as California, being so far to the north, but it would have provided a foothold on which to drive south into Mexican territory.

Donald had considered retracing his steps or taking the route to Santa Fe, but now the land to the south west of Independence would soon become official indian territory as Congress had past the 'Indian Removal Bill'. This gave the government power to use pressure and intimidation to force the Seminoles, Chickasaws and several other indian nations to leave their home land, and move hundreds of miles further west, to this new territory. The area was in almost permanent upheaval, and not a place to journey to, at present.

However it would not prevent Donald attempting to travel west towards California, in land to the south of this new indian territory, and he knew several rivers rose in the western hills and flowed eastwards to join the mighty Mississippi River. Donald remembered viewing the mouth of these rivers when he travelled on the Carroll/Marshall Steamers to New Orleans. This gave him an idea, and he went to visit his parents at St. Louis.

"Please mother and dad, we must try to explore routes to California. Eventually it must become our possession on the Pacific coast. We have the means to pioneer a possible route. Give me 'Little Nellie', its small, has a low draft and is very powerful. That is why it is so useful in towing our boats which break down. On it I could explore those rivers which join the Mississippi near to New Orleans". Donald's idea did not find immediate acceptance, for it would remove it from its presence use, which might by lost and would cost the company in providing the sailors for it.

It began a long period of acrimony but at last Donald got his way. His mother and father, Alan and Dora Reid got approval from their head office in Pittsburgh for its use for this purpose. Meantime Donald had been studying the known maps of these rivers, though not necessarily accurate, they gave him some guidance. He had considered the large Arkansas River which entered the Mississippi through the Arkansas territory, rapidly growing in seize and might soon become a state. However after it flowed to the west of this state, it appeared to move north west into the new Indian Territory.

The so called Red River did not seem to have this fault, though it joined the Mississippi only north of Baton Rouge, and not far from New Orleans, So the journey would be much longer. At last Donald decided to take this route, and at the end of 1830 sailed on the 'Little Nellie', down from St. Louis to the mouth of the Red River, then entered it and sailed upstream. Although it meandered considerably and when he tried some westward tributaries, they quickly became too shallow, and he had to reverse downstream.

Gradually he was being driven ever further north, which he feared might end in Indian Territory, then mercifully it suddenly turned due west and ran that way for two hundred miles. It passed the last settlement of Fort Denison and was navigable to a shallow draft boat as theirs for another fifty miles. Only then did they have to accept this was the furthest they could sail by boat.

They landed the supply wagon and horses and Donald with three sailors drove over relatively flat land to the west but were not equipped for a long land journey. Instead, they turned south, travelling over a hundred miles, when they were surprised to discover a small settlement. It was populated by Mexicans so without realising it they had invaded Mexico. It was the northern most limit of Coahuila-Texas, where much further south many Americans were now settling. The Mexican families made them very welcome, as Donald had learned a little Spanish on his journey to the Great Salt Lake.

The land was extensive with at present, few hostile indians and like the present settlements was an area for raising large herds of cattle. Donald and his sailors would take back with them, the news that it was

75

possible for many Americans to use the Red River for transportation and then by driving south could enjoy vast areas of land suitable for development. After staying for a time and even exploring further south, they did find a few Americans who had driven north from southern Texas, but not yet fully settled there. Finally they returned to the boat and slowly made their way down river to the Mississippi and back northwards to home at St. Louis.

Donald had not found an alternative way to California but discovered areas waiting to be settled by the multitudes still arriving from Europe and wanting lands to settle. However this, also applied, to the children of many families in the eastern states, with a lack of land near their homes, but who could come and colonise this new area.

Donald had emphasised to his parents, the journey had not been wasted, nor the expense. Now the Carroll/Marshall Steam Ship Company could provide suitable transport for families wishing to make their way to settle there. Donald still believed that where their boat had needed to stop, it might still provide a better route to California than the way he had travelled two years before. On his parents suggestion Donald took a boat to their head office in Pittsburgh, ostensively to meet his grandparents, but then to convince them to advertise the opportunity awaiting families in this new area, for Pittsburgh was still the place where much westward migration began..

He was delighted to meet again his now seventy year old grandmother, Erin and grandfather, Craig Read, and of course their intimate friends and partners, Mary and Brian Hobbs. Of course he knew all about their turbulent history, how misuse had turned to true love and a partnership of four people, who together had established this extremely rich arable farm, on which they still chose to live. He also called on his brother-in-laws parents, Charlotte and Roy Marshall, one of the four original directors of the Shipping and Building Company. They congratulated him on the economic success of his journey in the 'Little Nellie'

Donald, again saw the number of would be settlers who now used the Erie Canal to get to Pittsburgh and from there to chose one of many opportunities of settling in the lands to the west. The State of Missouri was a favourite destination. Though for some it would only be a staging area. Travelling to Independence and then joining wagon trains to travel further west.

One matter which both intrigued and puzzled Donald was the news that Joseph Smith and the Mormon families were now arriving there, escaping from persecution in both New York State and Ohio. It seemed their Messiah, Joseph Smith, had decreed that land near his home at Independence was the land chosen by the Lord on which Mormons must settle and establish their community. Donald wondered how his local community would take to these 'heathens' arrival..

The idea of multiple marriages was not one which appealed to many. It certainly made Donald think about the subject. Could he ever consider marrying more than one woman, if it should ever become the normal custom. He smiled to himself. He realised his thirst for adventure during the last three and a half years had left him without even a girlfriend, not even one to take to a local dance, let alone the thought of marrying more then just one wife. Donald wondered if he could ever contemplate marrying two, three or more women. Again why should they want to do this.

Donald made up his mind that if the Mormons did establish a settlement near to his home he would make it his business to try to discover the answer. Why should any woman tie herself to a man who already had an existing wife. He smiled, now it seemed that his desire to find a route to California was on hold, he might not have the time to explore this matter. At twenty two, he knew it was high time he considered a possible partner for life. At least he should try to find a girl who might, sometime, perform this task. It was with anticipation Donald returned home to Independence in early 1831.

9.

Once they had decided to buy the land and stay to work it, the Downey and Eliot's set about improving the area. Firstly they sent the note to their home in Kentucky which was the reason why Gordon Taylor had met Steven Downey and Tony Brady, bringing breeding horses to

Mexico for Hanz and Karl. However they also received letters of credit, for their keep but, also, to prepare for their cousins' arrival.

They had visited the dwelling places of several American settlers in the area, and decided to construct a very much more elaborate hacienda, with several rooms and bedrooms, using the money sent to them. So everything would be ready and in order for when the horses arrived. However this meant, that at present, they had much time on their hands and decided to put it to good use.

Using the good offices of Stephen Austin they were able to invite most of the Luna family, but more particularly, Elvira Luna, along with some of their relatives to a 'house warming' party, declaring their new home ready. They had managed to appoint several Mexicans to staff and act as servants, including quite able cooks. There is no doubt but the Luna family and their friends quickly realised that Hanz Eliot and Karl Downey, were of a different category than most Americans who arrived searching for cheap land on which to settle.

Elvira made this clear only a short time after they arrived and as they circulated during pre-meal drinks. "It seems I was right on that first day I met both of you. You are indeed gentlemen and well versed in social behaviour. The investment you have made here, indicates you are not short of money, so it seems your family in Kentucky must, also, be wealthy." Now she smiled at them, "However money does not necessary mean you are truly the gentlemen you first appear to be.- I believe I must watch my step, in case you prove to have more vices."

Both Hanz and Karl laughed quite loudly at her remarks, and Hanz said, "It seems you are already suspicious of our motives. – Perhaps you may be right to do so, for I fear, much as we wish to get to know all your family, being honoured by the presence of your father, such an important man here working for the government --- However we both confess, the real reason for this evening was to once again have the blessing of your company. – We both will always remember that brief, but wonderful moments, we enjoyed in Stephen Austin's office. – Again, we confess, that we now hope we may have the pleasure of your company more frequently in future."

To their surprise they saw Elvira blush. She seemed unsure of herself. Then more hesitantly, "Perhaps it I my fault – but in Mexico before a man even tells a lady he would like to get to know her, he is supposed to call at her house and meet her father and possibly her brothers, to see if he is suitable. I think----"

There was no doubt she was shocked at their familiarity and was about to turn away. Hanz quickly caught her arm, "Please do not go. We apologise if we have offended you. – It is simply that as Americans, when we meet an attractive lady – and please believe me – you are very beautiful – then it is our practice to try and make her acquaintance, if only to let her know, how much we like to be with her. – Elvira, we both do really like you, and wish to get to know you better."

Now she replied more forcibly, "As gentleman, - just because I may have a child and are unmarried – as you learned on that first day – does not mean I bestow my favours very freely, as it seems you think I do." Now Hanz forced her hand upwards and kissed it, "Dear Elvira, you wrong both of us. I assure you we do not think that of you. Indeed, now, knowing a little of you past, we truly believe you are a very courageous woman – a true lady, who we admire. – Please, we beg you, not to blame us. We have no friends here but would be honoured if you could consider letting us try to see if you would like us that way. "

Before she could reply a lady to whom they had been introduced as Gloria Garcia, the sister of Elvira's mother, Elsa Luna, and her husband Julio Garcia, both came to speak to them, bringing with them their daughter, Raquel, who seemed to be the same age as Elvira. "I hope we do not disturb you, it seemed as if the three of you were engaged in some discussion," Gloria stated. "We wish to say that we are grateful for inviting us this evening. I'm sorry to say, not many of your countrymen who come here enjoy the same social graces which we Mexican's enjoy. It seems my daughter, Raquel, is anxious to make your acquaintance."

Karl, very pleased to be introduced to another very beautiful girl, and did the honours. Taking her hand gracefully, he placed it to his mouth and kissed it, then said, "It seems the ladies of this land are all very beautiful. I assure you, it is with the greatest of pleasure that greet you. Like Elvira here, we both hope that you will both want to become our friends, for since we come from so long away, in Kentucky, we have not been fortunate that way up to now."

It seemed his speech had pleased her mother, as Elvira's mother and father came to them, Gloria Garcia spoke to them. "I, also, hope we can become friends. Next Saturday, we will send our coach and you must come to dinner with us, so we can all get to know you better." Not to be outdone, it seemed Elvira's mother did not want her sister to better her. "Quite so, in fact my husband and I would like to reciprocate the offer and in a fortnight you must come and have dinner with us."

Then turning to her sister, "I think we should repeat the pleasant arrangements of this evening. Let us all meet again each Saturday, as we have met this evening." Both Karl and Hanz hurried to accept their invitations. Then, especially for Elvira's benefit, Hanz said, "Senior Luna, if it were possible I would like to discuss with you Mexico's future. You see a relative of mine is a member of the United States Congress, as a Senator. I also know his son Danton Carroll and his wife Claudia are now part of the Diplomatic Embassy in Mexico City. Before we came here they both informed me that they were concerned at Mexico's evident dislike of people such as we, in deciding to buy land and settle here. I wondered if you could enlighten us in this matter."

Hanz saw the surprised look on Victor Luna's face so he continued, "My reason is entirely selfish. We were both telling your lovely daughter a few moments ago, how much we would value her friendship. You must forgive us, for it seems, unknowingly, we trespassed on the correct procedures in this land. It seems, we should first have asked your permission to do so. Now, belatedly I am doing so, trusting you can excuse our behaviour, for we would consider it an honour if we could all be friends."

It seemed his last request had removed the concern on Victor Luna's face, for his earlier statement now became no more than an indirect request to be accepted. However, in truth, Hanz Eliot, really did want to learn about the intriguing dichotomy of a government official who promulgated orders on the notice boards and then told everyone to ignore them. Also.- If possible to learn of why his daughter, Elvira had needed to submit to this evil man Santa Anna.

10.

There were very good reasons why both Hanz Eliot and Karl Downey should concern themselves concerning their future in this country, Santa Anna was gradually ensuring that he soon would be the man controlling this country. Already there were many in the Mexican Congress who were suspicions about him. President Vicente Guerrero had been a gallant soldier but was incompetent in running the country. Most people of importance were totally dissatisfied with him and the states were in perpetual uproar.

As Santa Anna had forecast, General Bustamante revolted, deposed Guerrero, then captured him as he attempted to flee by sea from Acapulco, then had him executed at Cuilapa, before becoming president. As planed Santa Anna stayed at Vera Cruz enjoying his women's bodies and not taking part. But there were constant revolts and he seemed to be supporting them. Bustamante sent General Calderon and the army to capture him, even besieging him in Vera Cruz. However this was his chance. Reinforced Santa Anna claimed to place himself at the country's disposal and defeated Calderon, forcing the present President Bustamante to quit the country.

With no President present, Congress declared that Pedraza, originally elected in 1828, then deposed, still held that post but his term expired in March 1833 and Santa Anna, knowing he intended to stand for office when this happened, so he would seem to accept Congress' decision. He knew now it would not be long before he assumed full control of Mexico, then he would alter matters and ensure his orders were obeyed. However to all the persons that mattered it seemed Santa Anna was not being selfish but trying to bring peace to the country.

Meantime his aides had found two young aristocratic girls about fifteen to assuage his sexual desires and both were soon carrying his child. This time he kept them as virtual prisoners until they delivered their babies, then enjoyed watching their painful labours. Meanwhile he had made forty six year old Senora Isabel Galvano pregnant again only five months after she delivered his last child. Isabel had not wanted this and pleaded with him not to do it as she had endure so much pain delivering their son. In fact Santa Anna hoped it would be just as painful and as entertaining this next time. However none of his mistresses dare disobey him. Now Senora Nora Delgado, also, feared she soon would have to conceive his child.

This then was the situation when Hanz and Karl went to discuss matters with Victor Luna, even before they attended the dinner arranged by the Garcia families. They had arranged what to say before they came and Hanz was to be the spokesman. "Senor Luna, we have learned that you were sent here to stop Americans such as we invading Mexico and settling here, even though Senor Austin has a right given in the past to encourage this. You proclaimed that this must be done, yet you then told us we could stay, and you and your daughter welcomed us. Why is this?"

Victor had smiled, "Simply because I believe that order is wrong. For many years both Mexicans and Americans have lived here together in peace. The land is vast and too few Mexican families choose to come and live here. Also there is no real government in Mexico. I come from a long aristocratic family but too many families like mine jockey for position, for control, in Mexico City, even kill each other. The ordinary peasant has no rights. It is so different to your country. I believe when we won our independence from Spain we should have become part of your country, like Florida has done."

Now he paused, "What I now say is treason. I trust you will not tell other of your countrymen, for it could mean not only my death but all my family." They immediately interjected telling him anything he said would be in confidence. Then he continued, "I have no doubt but that within two or three years, that evil man General Santa Anna, will seize power. If so he will dispense with Congress and rule as if he was Emperor, a dictator. I believe you should know the facts, for I would be blind if I did not see your interest in my daughter, Elvira."

Tears now came into his eyes, "Do you know that Elvira's baby daughter, Adela, is Santa Anna's child. His aides took her forcibly from my house. Then he raped her repeatedly for a month until she conceived his child, then the monster sent her back to me, a fallen women, though no fault of her own. That is why she has a baby but is unmarried."

Hanz now placing his hands on Victor's shoulders. "Senor Luna we learned a little of this from Senor Austin that first day when we met Elvira. If it may help we both can say we not only admire your daughter, for her fortitude, but we both would like to see if we could make her life a little better. We both have strong feelings for her, yet I fear she believes our admiration is not honest, because of her past. I, - and I know Karl, -believed you have a truly wonderful daughter, and hope to prove to you we mean this."

At last Victor smiled, "Thank you. I fear since this happened she does not trust any man. I will do my best to try make her think differently about you, for I now admire you both. Your social position in the United States is very similar to ours. Should your friendship progress, I can say I would welcome it."

Now he spoke angrily but not against them, "The irony is, that my present position given me by the government as State Lieutenant, is undoubtedly due to Santa Anna's demand of Congress. It is suppose to be my reward for the use he made of my daughter's body. However distasteful this is to me, I had no option but to accept. However I knew the real reason was to ensure poor Elvira was miles away from him when she bore his child. – Gentlemen, I have only one wish in life and that is to reek my revenge on that man and I may die in doing so."

Now, at last, he broke down and sobbed violently. Hanz once again place his hand on his shoulder then added, "Senor Luna. Now you have told us what happened I can assure you, irrespective of any dangers to us, we will stand side by side with you. I believe this world would be a better place if we were to rid it of this evil man. – I assure you, we will, with very great care, let our relatives, who have considerable power, know a little of what this man does. It seems to me that if he should become President, as you forecast, there will come a time when the might of the United States will be in collision with his own powerful position."

It seemed that that afternoon spent in discussion with Senor Luna, had given the latter, some hope that others too would eventually stand up against this evil Santa Anna. He had no doubt of their sincerity. He even smiled to himself. If they were to find his daughter sufficiently attractive to want to establish a permanent relationship, he knew they would have his blessing. Meantime he would ensure that Elvira knew their intentions were honourable.

So it seemed that for the Downey's, the Eliot's and soon the Brady's, Mexico was to provide them with new lands. However that also applied to Gordon Taylor and Donald Reid. Again this also applied to the invasion of the West, by not only those fleeing from Europe, but also the sons and daughters of many families born in the eastern states where land was no longer available. Texas, California and lands to the west of the Mississippi were waiting to be colonised and become part of the new country, the United States.

PART 3

CONFLICT

LEBENSTRAUM PART 3
CONFLICT

CONFLICT

1.

Andrew Jackson had replaced John Quincy Adams as President of the United States in 1828, having just failed to do so four years earlier. He was the first 'backwoods man' to become President. However tragedy occurred as his wife Rachael died almost immediately after his election. It is said her death was hastened by the scandalous reporting of their earlier life.

It seemed that Jackson and Rachael due entirely to a misunderstanding, committed bigamy when they married before Rachael's first marriage had ended in divorce. Ever afterwards Andrew Jackson had to defend her honour in duels receiving countless wounds, even killing one man, and leaving himself with bleeding lungs. He was a man with very definite views. In fact ex-President Thomas Jefferson publicably stated 'He is the most unfit man I know for such a place'.

He hated the British, blaming them for the death of most of his family whilst he was their prisoner in the War of Independence. It was these views which made Senator Mark Carroll of Virginia and Senator Keith Casimir of West Virginia, both following in the footsteps of their illustrious fathers, who had previously, held these posts, severe opponents of much of his plans. They also fought him, but failed, on his introduction of the 'spoils policy', whereby he removed from office any official not of his party, often receiving payment from the incoming holder of the post. Perhaps, even, more important, was his hatred of indians.

He believed no indian should be allowed to possess lands to the east of the Mississippi. Believing that the United States should be an 'agricultural republic' also believing the industrial north and the banks were evil He managed to destroy the Bank of the United States in 1832 replacing it with state banks. However perhaps his most controversial and unjust act was the 'Indian Removal Act' of 1830, resulting in the forced removal of 45,000 Native Americans from eastern lands to the new 'Indian Territory' west of the Mississippi, though in fact this, also, restricted settlers wanting to colonise this area of Kansas.

It was this decision which lead to over four thousand deaths of the Cherokee nation in moving there from Tennessee on what was called the 'Trail of Tears'.

It was this which led to Samuel Huston's severance from the President, as he was a long time friend of Andrew Jackson. Jackson was the man he had adored as a younger man and faithfully served as a soldier to Jackson, as his senior officer. Sam Houston had been brought up amongst the Cherokee's. After his marriage to Eliza Allen failed due to her unfaithfulness which, also resulted in him resigning as Governor of Tennessee, he had gone to live with the Cherokee's and married one of their widows, Tiana Rogers Gentry, set up a trading post and drank very heavily.

However when Anton and Louisa Albrecht had gone to him, he willing accepted their offer and money to go to Washington, to petition on behalf of the indian communities. He did succeed in taking the Cherokee case to the Supreme Court and winning. However Jackson cleverly nullified its decision using pressure to divide their leaders and leading to the Treaty of New Echota, even though the vast majority of Cherokee's opposed its signing.

It was a very disillusioned Houston who soon afterwards, got into a fight with a Congressman William Stanbery, who he considered had attacked his name in Congress, and beat him with a cane. Although Stanbery had placed a pistol at Houston's chest and pulled the trigger, though it fortunately misfired, this was ignored, and Houston, taken to court, and was found guilty. However his friends supported him and it became a civil case and a fine of five hundred dollars. In fact Houston never paid the fine.

Actually the publicity restored Houston's political reputation. Friends who had emigrated to Texas begged him to go there. As Sam Houston had always believed that most of Mexico and certainly California, belonged to the United States, Houston readily accepted. Once again both Louisa and Anton Albrecht, willingly provided the means and gave him a substantial sum of money. His Cherokee wife, Tania Rodgers did not want to leave her tribe, so Houston left her and made his way to Texas. Tania never forgave him for going and severed all communication with him.

Arriving there, his friends and his political reputation, ensured he was quickly swept into Mexican politics. In fact it seemed this was supported by President Jackson for two reasons. Firstly he had been a severe opponent with his pro-indian petitions. Jackson was pleased to see him go. However, secondly, both strongly supported the annexation of at least Texas and other parts of Mexico into the United States. So it was not surprising that now, Houston publicably supported the complete independence of Texas, gaining further popularity amongst American settlers there.

This did in fact bring him into conflict with Hanz Eliot and Karl Downey as well as Steven Downey and Tony Brady who had now arrived at the hacienda with their stock of horses, and breeding was already in operation. It was not that they did not like the idea of independence, but now having established very good relations with both Victor Luna and Julio Garcia, they knew only too well the growing power of General Santa Anna. Soon he would gain control of not only his own forces from Vera Cruz, but the entire Mexican Army. They feared that these forces were too strong, as the Texans, both Mexican and American, had few trained men to fight.

They knew and respected Sam Houston's past Military accomplishments, but believed he should not have stated their desire for independence until he had been able to raise and train a comparable force. Houston was calling for a convention with representatives of both Mexico and America should sit, to plan a course for independence.

Through Victor Luna whose name had been submitted, Hanz Eliot's name was, also, submitted. His inclusion as opposed to his friend Karl, was undoubtedly because of the ripening relationship between Hanz and Elvira Luna. It seemed each men had their preferences. Hanz had very strong feelings for Elvira whilst Karl Downey's preference was for Elvira's cousin, Raquel Garcia.

All these relationships had matured during the last two years as they had met frequently at the various dinners arranged between the families. Perhaps Elvira had found a preference for Hanz over Karl, as her father, after that meeting between Victor and Hanz concerning Santa Anna, had done everything possible to assure his daughter, that Hanz motives were both sincere and genuine. He convinced her that Hanz completely understood how, and why, she conceived her daughter, and was not considering her as an easy sexual capture. She stopped challenging him and responded happily to Hanz' sincere flirtations. She even overcame her Spanish reservations to unmarried men, possibly because Hanz made no unpleasant advances to her when they were alone, though he did try to kiss her when possible.

Karl Downey had quickly seen what was happening. Though he liked, and no doubt, would have made advances himself to Elvira, seeing her preference for Hanz, had quickly responded to Raquel's desire for a flirtation. Again, Karl realising the reservation it seemed all Spanish women had, so different from the way the girls at home behaved, he ensured his flirtation was slow and did not cause her any alarm.

However after their relationship had developed for over a year, both girls now made it clear by their actions that they would accept more intimate pleasures. The two men quickly accepted their offer and so now both relationships had become serious. It seemed to the four of them that it might soon become more formal and even the possibility of engagements.

Perhaps it was because, if Sam Houston's remarks encouraged Santa Anna to attack and invade, and military insurgency resulted, not only would the whole of Texas be subjected to war, but their present delightful and enjoyable lives with Elvira and Raquel would be in jeopardy. This was the real reason why both of them and their two recent arrivals, were strongly opposed to what Houston was creating.

There was no doubt but that both Victor and Hanz would do everything in their power to prevent Houston convincing this Convention, whenever it was formed, against trying to impose independence from Mexico by force of arms. They now liked Texas and wished to live in peace there. However they knew that many new arrivals from the United States would support Houston.

All that was needed to light the touch paper for an explosion, was for the government, and now that was coming to mean, for either the president or Santa Anna, to attempt to enforce the order he had given Victor Luna, when he made him State Lieutenant three years before. Should the government send troops to enforce it then, however impossible it might seem, it would lead to open rebellion, and as Hanz believed, absolute disaster.

2.

"I'm sorry Gordon, I'm afraid we can never have a future together," Sheila confronted him. Gordon, having finished his business in New Orleans, had hurried north again to Cole County to call on Sheila and the McLean family. Now she continued, "Father, knows your intentions are honourable, however he believes your work will take you away for so long, it is better that I have a future here." Gordon was stunned by her remarks only an hour after he arrived. Now, almost ashamed, she looked away. "I am being courted by Simon Doyle, Kevin and Mary's son. Father believes he is a fine man, and he lives here so close to us."

In spite of what she had said, Gordon seized her and turned her round, holding her firmly. "Tell me Sheila, - tell me – do you love Simon, I must know." She fought him and broke away. Then very quietly she replied, "Father believes Simon would make me a good husband, his family are very prosperous, as we hope soon to be."

He caught hold of her again, "You did not say you loved Simon --- do you – tell me it is so." He saw tears appeared in her eyes then almost in a whisper she answered, "I like Simon, very much, and I know my father approves." Now Gordon felt angry and told her so, "Sheila, your life is your own, it does not belong to your father. – I do not believe you love Simon, I warn you, whatever your father decides, I will not surrender the chance that I may still win you. I had intended to stay, but I will leave again today – but I shall be back – many times. You will not be free of me that easily. Then I shall see whether it is Simon or I with whom you would like to spend your life."

At this moment both heard her mother and father approaching, so he said no more. Then when they appeared he looked fearlessly at her father and said, "Mr. McLean, in spite of what you may think of me, I intend to still call upon you in the future. However I shall leave again today but before I do so, I need to speak to Mrs. McLean. I have need to inform her of the existence of the American branch of the Brady family who came from Northern Island many years before."

Before Neil could reply, Gordon turned to Patricia and told him of his fortuitous meeting on the boat with Steven Downey and Tony Brady. "It seems you both have a rather famous common ancestor, Margaret Eliot, who lived on the Calvert Estate in Northern Ireland when King James II ruled Britain. One of her daughters, Amelia Eliot had a very courageous life and married into British aristocracy, to David Carroll, who was knighted and became Governor of Maryland."

He now smiled at an astonished woman. "It seemed the Carroll's, Eliot's, Downey's and Brady's are all related to this Margaret Eliot, just as you are. Now I am instructed to give you some addresses of your American relatives who would hope you would write to them and establish good relationships as quickly as possible. They are all important and very prosperous families. – Mrs. McLean, in spite of what has happened today, I wish you well, and now bid all of you farewell."

After handing her the list of addresses he turned to Sheila, "Miss McLean, I shall endeavour to call on you frequently when I journey to this area.", then took her hand and kissed it, turned and left without bidding her parents goodbye. As he climbed back onto the wagon, tears were streaming down his face and he felt his heart was breaking. He had been expecting a wonderful welcome from Sheila, after being parted for several months. Today she had told him she was being courted by another. He knew it was not her choice, but she feared she dare not disobey her father.

It seemed his world was crumbling around him as he drove back to Jefferson City, there to wait for a boat to take him to Independence. All the time he had worked in New Orleans, and writing the report for Roy Marshall about the maintenance depot, he had been thinking of Sheila. Even though he had enjoyed flirting with Carlotta Lebron, a cousin of Silas' wife Gloria, a very attractive girl about his own age. She was a very passionate woman and their courting had been a little intimate, though not as fully as he had hoped. She had made him promise to call again the next time he came to New Orleans.

However throughout those weeks Gordon had been waiting in anticipation of again calling and being with Sheila McLean. He was even becoming to believe that it might become serious, at least as soon as he had acquired a reasonable amount of money. Now in a few hours, all this had been dashed. Yet even now he felt it was not what Sheila wanted, but she dare not confront her father. He felt her parents were more concerned at wanting to retain the near proximity of their daughter, then even her true happiness. He now regretted he had told her mother about her past, and introduced her to others in America.

Now Gordon had to wait for a boat to take him up river to Independence, where he called on Charles and Sharon Marshall. Sharon was Alan and Dora Reid's daughter, who he had met at St. Louis and he knew Charles was Roy Marshall's son. They were expecting him and made him welcome. Of course their maintenance depot was very small and it took Gordon only three days to write his report. However he was entertained very well by the Marshall's. As they knew he was now returning to Pittsburgh to report to Charles father, Sharon, explained her younger brother had just travelled there to report on his exploration of the Red River and northern Texas, and asked him to make contact with him when he arrived.

On the journey from Jefferson to Independence Gordon had found the boat was carrying a large number of Mormons coming from Ohio to settle there and Gordon had mentioned this to both Sharon and Charles. They told him many were arriving daily, and seemed to be monopolising an area barely ten miles way. However their presence was not welcomed by the local people and they feared a confrontation would occur. Of course Gordon knew of their multiple marriages, even wondering if this might be what he might like.

Having finished his business at Independence he waited for a boat which would take him directly to Pittsburgh and joined it. All his expenses were being paid by the Carroll/Marshall company, and his salary was being banked regularly. Gordon was quickly acquiring quite a lot of money very quickly, yet he had not yet started working for his uncle Silas, which had been his intention when he came to America.

When he arrived back at Pittsburgh it was almost a year since his ship from England had docked at New York and was pitifully reminded of the happy days he had spent with Sheila as they waited at Silas' house. He was very sad. However when he reported to the Carroll/Marshall Company that he had arrived back, he was almost immediately invited to attend at Roy Marshall's house and a carriage was sent for him. Gordon was delighted, for at last he was able to meet Roy's still attractive fifty six year old wife Charlotte, this woman who, was amazingly a fully trained engineer.

In a few moments he realised she was as competent as himself, but more in the theoretical field, and was both a qualified draughtswoman and designer. Very quickly a professional bond was established between them. It seemed she had read, carefully, all his reports and questioned him on it. In fact he was both gratified and proud when eventually she complimented him on his findings.

She spoke, still with a little French accent, "Mr. Taylor, I believe your findings will greatly effect the efficiency of our work places and will save us considerable money. I have asked my husband to offer you employment in our company with a salary three times what he has paid you to date."

Now Roy Marshall smiled and intervened. "I trust you will accept, I would not want to separate you from any duties to your uncle and will accept that some of your time must be given to him. However, I respect my wife's better understanding in these matters and I may add I have had excellent reports from our relatives both in St. Louis and Independence."

Then at last Gordon was introduced to a man, about his own age, who had been sitting with them the whole time. Roy said, "Please meet Donald Reid, you met his sister at Independence. Donald here, had the mad ambition to not only finding an easy route to California but actually believes we should annex it from Mexico. In this process, accidentally, he has found what may become a very lucrative extra route for our shipping lines, up the Red River and into northern Texas. Perhaps we might acquire Texas, even before he manages to win us California."

Gordon was very pleased to meet Donald, telling him his sister had asked him to call on him when he arrived at Pittsburgh. However Gordon was even more delighted when he was introduced to Cherie Marshall, the third child and daughter of both Charlotte and Roy Marshall. It seemed that from her mother she had learned of the long distances Gordon had travelled in helping their company and like her mother congratulated him.

Gordon felt even more pleased when he was seated next to Cherie over dinner, and could hardly fail to notice that she wished to captivate his attention the whole time. It was a very delightful evening. Before he left Roy Marshall asked him to call on him at their headquarters where together they could best decide, the best use of his talents, and was even more surprised but delighted when Cheri Marshall asked her father to invite Gordon to dinner again the following weekend adding, "It seems Gordon Taylor comes from a similar stock as yours, father. Since I have heard so much of your terrible crime in burning down that mill in Manchester, I would like to know what Manchester is like today some forty years later."

Gordon could still hear Sheila's words ringing in his brain, "I'm sorry Gordon, I'm afraid we can never have a future together" Gordon, after this potential loss of the woman he might soon had married, was only too delighted to accept the dual invitation and wondered just how sincere was Cherie Marshall's offered friendship, but feared she was already a woman of the world, and had to admit he was a beginner in the land of amorous or sexual associations. However, only time would tell.

3.

Otto Fallon had now settled in his bank in St. Louis for almost two years. It had now been successfully established. Eventually he had heard from Freda Ibsen still living in Washington but was disappointed that he did not receive a invitation to visit them. Granted it would have been a long journey, but he was given reasonable lengths of holidays. Otto would definitely have gone to Washington if requested.

Freda did comment on what was her father's occupation, enlarging on the little he had learned on the ship coming to America. It seemed her family had experience in financially supporting small hotels in Northern Germany. Now anxious to gain profits from investing in United State businesses, her father, had decided to use his knowledge of hotels to start, or at least help to establish, hotels in the United States growing cities, especially west of the Allegheny mountains.

Freda informed him that they had, already, founded two hotels in Kentucky, one in Ohio and one in Albany. They had used the United Bank of Washington for investment purposes. This gave Otto an idea. At present there was only one reasonable hotel in St. Louis. It was the one Gordon Taylor had used during his stay. Now Otto controlled all investments in the town and around, as well as the major investments of the Carroll-Marshall Company. He wrote to Freda's father suggesting he used his bank and supported the building of another and more superior hotel in St. Louis.

Otto knew if the idea was accepted her father must come, first, to St. Louis to assess its potential. He considered if so it was very probable that Freda would accompany her father, knowing he was there and doing business with her father. The idea was successful. Kansan Ibsen replied explaining he was coming and bringing his family to discuss the hotel's establishment. As Otto's house in St. Louis was large and fully staffed with servants, he immediately replied, inviting them to come and stay with him. The invitation was accepted.

Remembering the severe difficulties of his own journey by coach, in spite of a good metalled road, but principally because of the distance. Though it would be much slower he advised them to travel by coach to Pittsburgh, then take a boat all the way, coming north from Cairo, where the Ohio joined the Mississippi, and thus onto St. Louis. This was what they did and found they enjoyed the time on the rivers, and the places they visited. Otto met them and took them in his coach to his house on the river bank.

Kanson Ibsen wanted to begin right away to see the possibilities offered. Otto again used his coach, to first point out a site above the river and on the outskirts of town, but also, easily reached from the quay where the boats landed. Kanson, seemed satisfied. On visiting the present hotel he realised that his site suggested was superior and he intended the accommodation would be first class. Then Otto took him to the bank.

Only then did he discover just how rich was this man. Most of his wealth had come from inheritance as it seemed his family and his wife's were extremely rich ones, their wealth resulting from the time when Sweden controlled Denmark and Finland, besides Scandinavia. Although Otto's family were rich, it was nothing compared with the resources which the Ibsen family had to invest in projects in the United States. Apart from his desire to enjoy Freda's company, Otto realised his superiors would be delighted if he could persuade Kanson Ibsen to invest through his bank. However this would mean weaning Kanson from the United Bank of Washington, to his bank, or the Manhattan Bank of New York.

It seemed that Kanson had been in touch with parties which would set up and run the hotel, before he left Washington, so, now they had to wait until these gentlemen appeared. Fortunately this did give Otto, at last a chance, to renew his acquaintance with Freda, continuing where they had parted when the ship had reached New York. However she was very strongly chaperoned by her mother. Otto had to be contented with taking both of them in his coach to view the surrounding area.

However when her father explained he must spend over a week with the would be hoteliers, Otto decided to take a little vacation. Leaving Kanson to entertain these men by using his house, he persuaded Freda and her mother to sail up river as far as Independence, telling them this was the very edge of the civilized areas. This was possible because of his good relationship with Alan Reid and his company, Alan arranged for his daughter and son-in-law to entertain and house the three of them, when they reached that town. Further more, it was possible, on the boat to arrange a little more privacy and for Otto to engage Freda in conversation, out of earshot of her mother.

Then Otto received a shock. Firstly it seemed that Freda appeared to have discovered a possible boy-friend, much nearer to where they lived in Washington. His name was Pieter Wycks. Pieter was the son of Carl and Aleida Wycks and Otto knew from his time at the Bank of Manhattan that Carl Wycks was the Managing Director of that bank. It would seem that Pieter's wealth would be very attractive to the Ibsen family.

Further more what Freda told him destroyed any hope of him being able to wean the Ibsen family from the United Bank of Washington to his own bank. She informed him that the Wycks family owned the United Bank, the same as the Manhattan Bank. Otto's happy world seemed to be crashing at his feet. The only comfort was that in spite of her relationship with Pieter, as they leaned over the hand rail of the boat, she kissed him lightly on the cheek and said, "You must excuse the way my mother so closely chaperones me when I'm with you. She does it the same when I'm with Pieter."

Now she kissed him again. "I like you – I enjoyed being with you on the ship coming over. – But you are living so far from me. – I don't think my father wants me to marry anybody yet, and frankly I'm not anxious to be tied down. Actually father has heard very good reports about you from Pieter's father, Carl, and your reputation in the Bank of Manhattan is very great. I believe you will soon be promoted much higher than at present. It was your reputation which convinced father to come here to see about an hotel."

So disconsolate as Otto felt, it seemed there still might be a possibility of a future with Freda, in spite of the opposition living in Washington. Neither did she withdraw from him when he took the liberty of placing his arm around her, though he disengaged when he saw he mother coming up on deck. Soon they reached Independence and went to stay with Sharon and Charles Marshall, who made them all very welcome.

Freda's mother Isolda, was extremely anxious to learn from Charles of his father's shipping company. Otto was to learn that Kanson Ibsen, when investing in an hotel complex in Albany, met Cornelius Vanderbilt, who ran a flotilla of steam boats between New York and Albany transporting the many persons who wanted to journey west on the Eire Canal. Now it seemed Vanderbilt, in conjunction with a Peter Carroll, in New York, were experimenting in trying to construct steam boats sufficiently robust, to be driven by screw propellers instead of Paddle wheels, and capable of withstanding Atlantic waves. It seemed Freda's father was contemplating, investing in this project.

Both Freda and her mother had been thrilled when Peter Carroll and his wife Amy, a sister of Cornelius Vanderbilt, had invited them to spend a weekend on his grand father's estate on the River Potomac called Rockville. It seemed they had learned from the families of the history that Rockville when it was the ancient home of Sir David and Amelia Carroll, once Governor of Maryland in Colonial days, and responsible for so many Carroll families in various parts of the United States. The Ibsen's had found these histories very fascinating. How Daniel Carroll, one of Amelia's descendents had greatly assisted his friend George Washington during the War for Independence.

After staying a few days and cautiously visiting the Mormon settlement which was growing rapidly very close to the town, but whose existence was challenged by the local population, being opposed to their beliefs in multi marriages and polygamy. The Marshall's feared this might soon lead to open warfare between the Mormons and the locals. Eventually they all took the boat down river, and back to St. Louis.

It seemed Kanson Ibsen had completed his business during their absence and the hoteliers had agreed to build where Otto had suggested so Kanson had invested in it. Otto was pleased when Kanson

99

complimented him on his choice of the locality and the need for it, and therefore the certain success of the project. One thing which, especially, pleased Otto was Kanson's final remark.

He said, "Mr. Fallon it only confirms what I was told about your business acumen before I came here. Carl Wycks has had very good reports about you from his directors in the Manhattan Bank. It seems you have inherited your father's expertise in banking. – I shall not be surprised if you soon should receive promotion from this small bank. It seems the Managership of the Annapolis Bank will soon become vacant, after the present man retires. I believe they have you in mind as his successor. I shall certainly let Carl know I would support this."

So as he saw their entire family on the boat to take them back to Pittsburgh, and then onto Washington, Otto, in private spoke to Freda. "My dear Freda, if I come to Annapolis I shall call upon you frequently. Then we shall see whether I might interest you, more than Pieter Wycks." She just smiled as he kissed her hand but made no reply.

4.

It seemed to Donald Reid that Cheri Marshall was very fickle in her acquisition of lovers. Until Gordon Taylor had arrived Donald had been the centre of her attention, now Donald knew he took second place. This was true of her cousin, Frances Le Raye, the same age as Donald. This was only one disappointment Donald suffered. It, also, seemed his discovery of a slow, but easy route to northern Texas, promising to be lucrative to Carroll-Marshall shipping, as it provided the boats for the journey up the Red River, might not materialise.

When Donald had called on the settlers to the south of the river at its highest navigable point, although they told him of indian presence, they had not been attacked. It seemed it was the Comanche Tribe on whose land they had settled. The Comanche race were very large but they extended over a very large area, most of it desert, or semi-desert, So there were only small bands in each of there areas they claimed as their own. When the number of settler were small the Comanche's did not see them as invaders. However as the boats began bringing many new settlers to the same area, the Comanches feared their lands would be stolen. So large groups had banded together and now often attacked. These dangers were greatly reducing the numbers using the Carroll/Marshall boats.

In fact this had led to a third disappointment for Donald. A wagon trail had been discovered by William Becknell in 1821, including signing a treaty with Osage indians for a right of way through their lands. The route was further surveyed and accepted as a wagon route, called the Santa Fe trial, by George Sibley in 1827, starting from Independence, Missouri, through the indian lands to Santa Fe over seven hundred miles in length. Santa Fe was important as the staging post for trade with Mexican California. Donald had studied the existing maps and believed the journey could be eased by sailing to his discovered navigable limit on the Red River, as this seemed by about two hundred miles from Bicknell and Sibley's end of the Santa Fe route, very close to the town.

Donald had obtained a promise from Roy Marshall to finance an exploration of this land journey which would be far less tiresome than the complete land route. Now Donald knew any such attempt would be through the centre of Comanche territory and with their numbers, the attempt would end in disaster. Donald liked adventure but did not want to throw away his life for so little. So Donald had abandoned risking it. At least for the present.

It seemed Donald had no reason for staying longer in Pittsburgh and decided to return home to his family at Independence. He might break his journey at St. Louis, even considering sailing down to New Orleans, perhaps even visiting south Texas. He was a rich free man with no serious attachments. At least Gordon Taylor had told him the type of people now making their homes there. Of course he was well aware of the Downey, Eliot and Brady families successful horse breeding establishment in Kentucky, who frequently used their ships to export their horses, elsewhere. In fact he had wondered if he might break his journey and call on them. So saying farewell to everyone in Pittsburgh, Donald joined a boat leaving for Independence but passing through St. Louis. There he would decide whether to disembark and take a boat down to New Orleans later.

Once on board Donald discovered the passengers included a very large number of Mormons, leaving Ohio to settle in what they claim to be Zion, a settlement of which his family, and recently Gordon, had told him so recently, that they had established just outside Independence, and which was apposed by those already living there. They appeared to be very pious men and women, often kneeling and praying. There was no avoiding knowing they were polygamous as each man appeared to have at least two, three or four woman who walked close to him.

It seemed they had to obey their husband implicitly. If he left them they had to obey him and stay where they were until he returned, however long this was. This practice intrigued Donald and he spent hours watching their behaviour. Again, Donald noticed, that each of their wives appeared to conceive and bare their husband's child in strict rotation. As many had three wives, Donald could see one wife supervising a child not quite two years old, another breast feeding baby and the third with a swelling denoting she was then carrying her husband's unborn child. Thus, if so, each wife must conceive about every three years.

Most wives appeared to accept their position without questioning the fact that their husband completely controlled their lives, though he did notice that a few appeared to be very happy. Donald quickly discovered this did not apply to a very pretty girl about nineteen or twenty, who seemed to have tear stained eyes, many days. This further intrigued Donald, and ensuring they did not suspect his interest, he tended to follow them, particularly when their husband left them. Though he tried, it was difficult to hear their conversations, though snippets, again indicated either their fear or complete submission to their men.

Whilst still on the Ohio River and some way from Cairo where they would join the Mississippi, a rare occasion happened, as it was possible, this time, for Donald to hear clearly, their conversion. It happened after a man in his middle thirties took one of this wives, who Donald thought was the eldest, by the arm, and he heard him say, "Nancy I want to have sacred communication with you. It is time God visited you again, and begat our child."

Donald gasped as Nancy bowed low to him and replied, "Lord, if it is your wish, I will try to please you and our god, though I thought you might wait until Rachael bares your child." Donald knew this man was ordering one of his wives to conceive his child, not even considering her own desires. He heard her husband reply, But now he included his other two wives in this conversation. "Constance and Rachael you should know, God spoke to me last night. He scolded me. He told me as we were going to Zion, the population must increase more frequently. From now on I shall try to ensure you are blessed with a child about every eighteen months to two years. I hope Nancy will be with child before we reach Zion and you, Constance and then Rachael will begin when the last wife is less than six months pregnant."

He saw all three women gasped but this particularly applied to the two named Constance and Rachael. Then the man left with Nancy, and though in public, Constance unfastened the top of her dress exposing her large and heavy breasts, bent down and took her baby from the crib. Placed it to her nipple and commenced to feed it. Now her husband had left it seemed that the youngest wife was daring to challenge what her husband had decreed.

Even as she began to speak Constance prevented it, "Rachael, I forbid you to say anything against what Lord Sidney says. It seems god has visited him. However much we may not like it, it would be blasphemy not to obey. Rachael we are fortunate to be married to a man like Sidney, and that he has chosen each of us. If we had married a gentile, why we should probably have conceived a baby almost every year. Two years is a reasonable time between pregnancies."

There was no doubt that Rachel did not agree. "Sister, I only married Sidney because he told you he would not marry you, even though you had conceived his child, unless I too married him. I had no choice. Father was so disgusted at you having carnal love with Sidney before marriage, he forced both of us to marry Sidney. You know mother was very upset when father became a Mormon."

So it seemed Rachael was Constance's younger sister, and was forced into marriage with Sidney by her father, as Sidney had got his daughter pregnant and wanted to enjoy Rachael's younger body, demanding she too married him. Constance now suddenly appeared to show fear as she responded, "Rachael, I beg you say no more, our souls may be in danger. Not only have you shown protest at your own husband. Remember, your body is his to do with it what he wants, but you have dared to criticise our own father, an elder of the church. God will punish us if we oppose what is planned for us."

Her words did not stop Rachael's angry reply. "Sister you may want to spend your life in this way. I do not believe as you do. I do not believe a man has the right to do the things Sidney demands of us. You know I did not want this baby. I fought him when he tried. I failed, he raped me. I do not think I deserved the punishment he gave me saying God had ordered him to make me conceive. – I tell you sister, if I had the chance I would run away and leave all of you, but I know that is impossible. Where could I go, and hide before the church elders found me and dragged me back. I must consider if life is worth living in this way."

Then she walked away as Constance shouted after her saying, "You must not leave me here, Sidney demanded we stayed right here until he comes for us." If so Rachel did not seem to hear, and this gave Donald a chance to follow and meet her. He came up behind her and heard her sobbing violently her unhappiness. Very quietly and carefully he placed his hands on her arms from behind. Poor Rachael almost fainted with fear, as no one was near, and feared she was being attacked.

Then she was astounded when this man who it seemed wanted to possess her simply said, "Rachael, my dear, please do not be afraid. I promise I do not want to hurt you. – I heard your conversation with your sister – I want to help you. – I know you are very unhappy. – Somehow I want to gain your trust – I know it won't be easy, but I swear I will not do anything to you, for I believe if I can win your trust, I may be able to free you from the dominance of the man you call your husband. The United States gives all of us the right of freedom. Your husband is refusing you this right, and claiming God has ordained him to do this to you. – Please let me try to help you."

Rachel now turned and faced him though her body was trembling and still in fear. Then he smiled at her before continuing, "Please, my dear, try to trust me. I may be able to suggest a way out of your unhappiness, but for it to happen, I must, - even as a complete stranger, - gain your trust." At last she relaxed and a wistful smile appeared on her tear stained face. "I do not know who you are – or why I should trust you – but I will stay and listen to what you have to offer. In any case my husband will punish me from leaving Constance without his permission. – It cannot be worse if he finds I have spoken and listened to you. – I will stay."

<h2 style="text-align:center">5.</h2>

He lead her to the rail of the boat and then stood by her side. Then he asked, "Are you willing to leave your husband, as you said you would like to do?" Now Rachael looked at him. "Yes! I hate him. I never wanted to marry him. My father forced me to accept to save my sister from her disgrace. – But where could I go. I have no means to support myself. Until we reach Independence, I'm watched night and day. – Then when we reach Zion, I would be a prisoner there, all our brothers would watch me and bring me back for punishment, if I attempted to escape."

Now carefully Donald took hold of her hand, so as not to frighten her before replying, "I think I could find a way of taking you from this boat. Then I could take you to safety." Donald felt her jerk in fear as she almost shouted, "You want me to run away with you. – Then you want to posses me, since you know I'm pregnant. You want to use me." Donald now pulled her hand to his lips, even as she struggled, and kissed it, "Rachael, this is what I meant, when I said you must be willing to trust me, I have no intention of hurting – or as you say – using you, as you fear. Frankly, I just feel sorry for you and want to help. – However for me to do so, you would have to trust me and believe I would not molest you."

Very unsure she took her hand from him saying, "I must get back before my husband returns. – I will think of what you have said." Now Donald knew he had to find a way of speaking to her in private, if he was able to plan her escape and asked her how this might happen. At last she smiled, "My husband usually leaves us just before noon each day to pray with all our male brothers. We are supposed to meet with our sisters, however I could always creep away for as long as half an hour. I don't think anyone would miss me, if I was careful."

Now she at last smiling at him before adding, "I will trust you this much. I will come to this very place tomorrow as soon a Sidney leaves us. Then if you want you can explain what you meant by helping me to escape." Now she even gave a short laugh, "You know my name – I would like to know yours." It was Donald's turn to laugh at the absurdity that he had told her he wanted to help her leave her husband and not even told her his name.

Very quickly he apologised and told her he was called Donald, then before he could say more she, quickly turned away, and ran back to where her sister was sitting, still feeding her baby. Now Donald realised what he had just done. Promising he would set her free from her domineering husband, yet had not even considered how he could do this. It was simply that he had felt so very sorry for her as she poured out her unhappiness to her sister, and realised she had been forced to conceive by a husband she never wanted to marry. Now he knew he must think of a plan, one she would be willing to accept, provided he could ensure she could trust him.

He pondered on the question for the rest of the day. He knew if the plan was to be successful, it must operate before they reached Independence. So he could not wait till then and then take her to his home. Yet he knew she would be too afraid to just leave with him, not knowing where he was taking her. Then he smiled to himself. He thought he had found a solution of where they should leave the ship, also remembering his family virtually owned this boat and he could expect the full cooperation of the captain. That night in bed he refined his ideas and felt sure of his plan when he, at last, fell asleep.

The next day he waited, once again leaning over the rail, for her to join him. Even wondering if she would come, for there was no doubt that she had been in fear, the whole time the day before. Then to his delight he saw he approaching and turned to meet her.

She smiled but he could see she was still unsure wondering if she should have come. Donald tried to reassure her by taking her hand and kissing it as he would do to any lady of quality. He smiled, "First let me truly introduce myself. I am Donald Reid and I am part of a large family of relatives who are very rich. My family owns this boat, on which we sail, and many more. We also build many boats, including the Show Boats we sail on the Mississippi . Now please tell me your full name and where you come from."

At least she was still smiling, "I'm called Rachael Gilbert and like my sister I belonged to the Donelson family and we lived in New York State before my father became a Mormon and made all our family join with him. He has now taken two more wives. --- However, I do hope that you do not think you can buy me, simply because you are rich."

Again Donald smiled, "Rachael, I do not want to purchase you. I don't even expect you to like me, - though if we are successful – I would hope we might become friends. Perhaps if so, you would not believe all men are wicked. --- It's just that when I heard yesterday, the way you had been treated – my heart went out to you. – Perhaps it's because I've had a very happy and contented life so far. But I realise, that in some way, I must earn your trust. – Now please listen to my plan, then you can consider if it is what you would like to happen."

Now Donald told her of his family. How his home was really in Independence but that for the last few years he had explored new lands. Then he told her of his parents house in St. Louis. It was there he would like to take her once they escaped from the ship. They could leave the ship immediately it docked at St. Louis, but they must be careful not to attract attention on the long journey up to then.

It was then that Rachael told him that her husband and all Mormon families, locked their wives in their cabins when they reached a port. "I would not be available for you to take me from the boat. Even with your power, you could not free me, for I am my husband's possession – and that is the law." Donald though surprised told her he thought he could overcome this but it would mean she had to trust him even more. Then he said he would explain this another day. In the little remaining time available he tried to win her confidence by explaining a little of his families history. Then it was time for her to return, but she agreed to meet him again, two days later, as they would reach Cairo the next day and she would be locked in her cabin.

Meantime Donald had spoken at length to the captain and won his full support. At Cairo he sent an urgent message to their office at St. Louis, demanding their cooperation. It was fortunate that his importance ensured they would do this. Then at last he was able to outline the plan to Rachael. Eventually he obtained her agreement, and it would require very accurate timing.

As they approached St. Louis and the passengers watched, knowing soon, several of them would alight, they saw a smaller but very manoeuvrable boat approach, signal the captain to stop the ship and pulled alongside. Then the crews of both boats were very busy apparently transferring cargoes from one boat to the other. This included two large boxes which almost looked like coffins. The work finished, both boats resumed their journey. Soon they were a long way apart. Only then, on the new boat, did a man and a woman surface and come on deck.

Donald Reid spoke to a bemused Rachael Gilbert, "Welcome on board the 'Little Nellie'. Last year I sailed in her right up the Red River in the south and entered the northern part of Texas, in Mexico. It severed my purpose then as it has done today. Soon we shall go about and then return to St. Louis, but not until the boat on which your husband sails has left the port."

His plan had been successful, but it had required accurate timing. As all the passengers, including Sidney Gilbert and his wives had watched the approach of 'Little Nellie' intrigued at the hooting of the two horns, as arranged Rachael, in the confusion had detached herself. Then a crew member had seized her as planned, taken her below, where Donald was waiting. Then placed each of them in two long boxes and closed the lid, but with holes punctured into them to give them air. After this it was easy for the boxes to be transferred by the crew, along with other boxes, so both were on board 'Little Nellie' before the two ships parted.

Now, though very flushed, and still in some fear, for what awaited her in the future, Rachael let Donald place his arm around her waist

Then he said, "You will like mother and father, and I know they will like you. As I said, you must trust me for a little longer, then you will really believe you are free."

Rachael turned and faced him. "Donald I am now truly in your power. I may have let you kidnap me so you could enjoy me, as Sidney did for so long. Yet somehow, I believe you really do have a loving mother and father in St. Louis, but will they or you, be willing to keep me – remember in less then six months I shall have a baby to feed. – and in any case – how do you want me to reward you?"

Now Donald again took hold of her hand, "I know mother, particularly, will be pleased to welcome you, especially when she finds you are soon to become a mother. – As for reward. You owe me nothing. When I heard how you were being treated, I believe I would have done the same for any woman – though I will confess your beauty attracted me, for you are a very beautiful woman. – All I hope is that, as you come to know me, perhaps even learn to trust me, I hope that we could become friends. – I know I would like that."

Suddenly Donald was shocked for Rachael lent forward and pressed her lips on his, "Donald, I do trust you. I have ever since that second day when we met. On the first occasion I was not sure. That night I wondered if I should come to you the next day. – I now confess, I was so unhappy, I knew even if your plan was to kidnap and use me, I was already pregnant, at least you were handsome. It could not be any worse than the life I was living. Then when I met you again, I really convinced myself, that your approach was honourable. I too want you to become my friend – perhaps even more than that. Only time will tell. – Now I simply want to meet your wonderful mother. She must be wonderful to bring up a son like you."

6.

Edwin and Joan Palatine had been delighted to extend their visit to Rockville when both Andrew and Angela Carroll as well as Adrian and Estelle, asked them to stay, equally delighted, due to their interest in the past life of the Carroll's. There was no doubt by that Edwin was quickly smitten with the Adrian and Estelle's eldest daughter, Audrey Carroll, just two years his junior. It seemed that she too felt an interest in this handsome young man, particularly, as like her mother, he was of English descent. Both Adrian and Estelle quickly noticed this and certainly approved.

It took them some time to understand the life-lines of the various branches of the Carroll family. The convoluted way Adrian's wife, Estelle, was a descendent, like him, from the original David and Amelia Carroll. Estelle via Amelia's eldest son, Robert and descendants in England, Adrian, descendant of her second son, Paul, always living in America.

Angela increased their confusion, but even more their desire to learn an understand, when she placed a well worn book titled, "The Carroll family from Yorkshire and Gloucestershire 1630 to 1800", by Manon Lamoignon. Angela explained that Manon was the legitimate daughter of Comte de Malesherbes Lamoignon, who after his execution was saved and brought to America from France at the height of the Terror in 1793, by three Irish men. Eventually Manon had learned to love and marry one of them, Jack Eliot, then settle in Pittsburgh, when he became the accountant of the Carroll/Marshall Ship building and Shipping Company. So Manon and Jack were now immensely rich.

However Manon, when she lived in France was both a successful artist and author. Intrigued when she first lived in America, with the complicated relationships, especially of the two Carroll branches, that she had diligently researched their histories, having so much time to herself. Then she had produced this explanation, though in its preface, Manon readily accepted it was incomplete, though accurate in its present content.

Both Edwin and Joan were fascinated as they virtually, devoured the tome, awakening in them a desire to explore and question its contents. Since all at Rockville were very proud of their past to that branch of the Carroll's, who came first from Gloucester, before moving to Somerset, being the protestant branch. They had been able, at times to enlarge on what Manon had written in her book.

Although every part of this branch resulted from David Carroll emigrating from Somerset when King James II ruled Britain, and his meeting with the peasant and then indentured servant, Irish Amelia Eliot, learning perhaps, an even more important man was David's grandson, via his second son, Paul. This man was Daniel Carroll, who it seemed had played such an important part in Maryland, Virginia and West Virginia, during the latter part of the eighteenth century. This especially applied to his assistance to his long and childhood friend, George Washington, during the American Revolution.

They remembered how Estelle had told them her intense hatred which turned to love and acceptance. How Daniel at the end of the war, had torn Rockville from the Carroll branch in England for their support of England in the war, and given it to both Andrew and Angela. However Estelle had learned how wrong she was, and how Daniel had saved her father from a debtors prison, and brought her family to live at Rockville.

Estelle even told them of her friendship with Muriel Alexander, and how she had, added to Manon's book, by discovering what happened to Blanche Carroll, the daughter Amelia conceived when she was raped by Edward Calvert, and who Sir David had adopted after their marriage. It seemed Blanche's descendents, after her marriage to Felix Backhouse, now lived in Montreal. One of the youngest sons was David Backhouse, who was now enjoying an adventurous life in the Oregon country, disputed between the United States, Britain and Mexico.

It seemed they must learn of this first hand from Daniel's successors, who lived on the Racoonsville Estate in Virginia. Arrangements were made to take them there. Here they were introduced to Robert and Hedwig Carroll, both in their late sixties, Robert being the eldest son of Daniel and Michelle Carroll, a past Senator for Virginia. Now this position was held by their eldest son, Mark Carroll married to Estelle Tencin, who they learned was the granddaughter of the infamous Claudine Tencin, Mistress of King Louis XIV of France.

Both Robert and Hedwig were delighted to tell Edwin and Joan about both Daniel and his remarkable wife Michelle, who they had adored. It seemed Daniel had grown up on the nearby Gordonsville estate, owned by his brother and Andrew's father. His boyhood friend was George Washington. How for adventure both had joined the Ohio Company, and found the French had settled there claiming it for New France. Then with difficulty Robert tried to explain Daniel's relationship with two French Officers, Louis Scarron and Jean Dumas, technically their enemy, but soon to become their friends. How Daniel meantime, met Michelle Tailier, a Frenchwoman, who Donald Wilson, a smuggler, had rescued from France and brought to America, living together for almost ten years, before Daniel, eventually won her as his wife. This, after Donald and Daniel had risked their lives to free another Frenchwoman, Madeleine Colet, due to his friendship and debt to Jean Dumas. All this happened during the Seven Years war.

It seemed this unselfish act won Daniel the estate of Racoonsville from Sir David's eldest son, Sir Robert Carroll, the present Robert's namesake, as well as the undying love of Michelle for Daniel. How the two of them had helped so many people, many relatives and descendants of Amelia Eliot. The considerable help to George Washington during the War for Independence, and the use of their wealth to invest and help to establish the young United States.

It seemed that Daniel's love for Michelle was so great that when at last, an exhausted Michelle died in 1806 when seventy eight years of age, Daniel had no wish to live and died less than a year later, though he was only seventy six years old. Now both Edwin and Joan realised why these two names had appeared so often in different ways throughout Manon's history of the Carroll family. It was from Robert's wife Hedwig that they learned of the part her father, Michael Casimir and his friend, William Holstein had helped Daniel during the last war, coming as rich emigrants from Poland and Sweden.

However there were so many little episodes related to all these families. The history of the Reid and Hobbs family, the Scott's and of course the Wycks but especially Clare Wycks, earlier a Bristol prostitute, Clare Collins, who it seemed Hedwig's father, considered her to be a reincarnation of his first lover, who committed suicide. They enjoyed hearing about this but became even more confused. Still it did make them promise to research further, and particular to meet Manon Eliot, as she was now called.

They fully enjoyed their stay at Racoonsville before returning to Rockville to complete their visit. Now, Robert's son, Mark Carroll and his wife, Estelle, and Mark was now Senator for Virginia had arrived with news just received from his son, now living in what was virtually the United States Embassy to Mexico, that General Santa Anna had been elected as the new President of Mexico. They all knew of his dislike of all Americans. Years ago he had demanded those American settlers in Texas should be removed and new emigrants refused entry.

It seemed to both Mark and his father Robert, well used to decision making in Congress, able to assess quickly any political question, soon the United States might become involved in delicate, if perhaps even military, relations with Mexico, as they might be called upon to defend their countrymen living in this foreign country. However War with Mexico was something they all felt should be avoided, if possible.

Edwin and Joan were yet to learn how this might effect them. However at that moment Edwin's only desire was to develop further his interest in Audrey Carroll. They would in time learn how other families, who had been helped in the past by Daniel and Michelle to establish themselves in America, branches of which had gone to Mexico. Soon the lives of these families would be in danger.

7.

General Santa Anna was a very happy man. He felt sure that in only a few more weeks he would be President of Mexico. He congratulated himself on the brilliant way he had ensured his coming success. Though it was the behaviour of other powerful men who were making it a certainty. He had let others make the mistakes, and at the right time he would 'save the country' and come to its rescue.

He had supported Guerrero, a very competent general, to become president. However Santa Anna knew he would be a incompetent administrator. Very quickly he proved this and rebellion occurred.

So then Santa Anna had supported General Bustamante's rebellion to displace the very unpopular Guerrero, though he made clear his disapproval, when Bustamante captured the fleeing Guerrero at Acapulco, he had him executed.

Santa Anna knew that Bustamante was an extreme conservative, believing the right of the aristocratic families to rule Mexico. He was one himself although in his youth he had been a liberal, supporting the independence of Mexico from Spain. He quickly learned and later in life espoused, that the ordinary people, especially the peasants had no capacity to rule and required strong discipline to maintain order. However knowing Bustamante would very quickly pass and impose restrictive laws, which again would cause revolution, Santa Anna waited whilst he made these mistakes, and then would seem to support more liberal attitudes. This would give him popularity.

However Santa Anna had not changed his views. He would bide his time. Then once secure he would impose dictatorial control and not like Bustamante, still govern through Congress. He would seem to be the saviour of the people and thereby gain control. To his satisfaction this was beginning to happen. For Bustamante was a centralist, whilst most of Mexico whished to be Federalists, with each region having some element of control. So his declaration and act of 1830, immediately created revolt.

Many parts of the act were sensible, but firstly all taxes collected came to Mexico City, none to the provinces. It had incorporated Santa Anna's own views and Foreign immigration was to be eliminated, and prevented any further introduction of slaves. This was to cause revolts in the provinces of Zecatecas, Vera Cruz but especially in Coahuila y Texas. The Americans in the latter considered this a direct attack on their liberty, whereas the rest felt the act was trying to remove their own powers and it was opposed to the 1824 act of Federalism.

It was the situation both Karl Downey and Hanz Eliot had feared and which with the help of Victor Luna and his Mexican friends, they had been furiously trying to avoid, as Sam Houston speeches inflamed the resident American settlers to action. The action of the Mexican commander, Juan Bradburn, sent by Bustamante to ensure these decrees, with his soldiers mainly convicted convicts, led to a dangerous confrontation at Anahuac, in June 1832 and the so called Battle of Velasco, at the mouth of the Brazos River. It was here that a Texas lawyer and supporter of Houston established himself as Colonel William Travis, who was to become famous later at the Battle of the Alamo, but he was now captured and imprisoned by Bradburn.

It was on this day that the so called Turtle Bayou resolutions were first propagated. These resolution later became the basis for the Texas demand for independence. The Battle of Velasco at the end of June resulted from the earlier conflict, when the subordinate Mexican officer Domingo Ugartechea attempt to stop the Texans assembling cannons on the Brazos River, led by John Austin and Henry Smith. His force was much smaller than the Texan militia and eventually were forced to surrender causing greater reprisals by Command Bradburn.

Helped by Karl, Hanz and Victor Luna, Stephen Austin did everything possible to calm the situation as they all realised that politically this was playing into the hands of Santa Anna, who they all feared. However to their horror Santa Anna used this to his advantage sailing to the mouth of the river, and who promised to restore the republican principles. As they feared, most Texans, were completely fooled by his oration and considered that Santa Anna was their friend against the dictatorial President Bustamante.

As a result of this Sam Houston, who had settled at Nacogdoches to the north of the present battles, in August with John Henry Brown and three hundred men, attacked and stormed the Mexican Colonel Piedras' position, who though he attempted to retreat, was eventually forced to surrender and then sent to Velasco, and made to declare allegiance not just to General Santa Anna, but to the Constitution of 1824. A certain Mexican Texan Colonel James Bowie, who had invented a special type of knife, and again would become famous at the Battle of the Alamo, played an important part in this conflict.

Hearing that Santa Anna had declared against him, President Bustamante sent General Calderon to attack him. This failed, as demonstration against the president increased. As Santa Anna reinforced this attack, Bustamante resigned and agreed to leave the country. Now

Santa Anna played his trump card. He got congress to agree that Pedraza who had been elected as President in 1828 and then removed, should be reinstated. However everyone knew that his term of office ended in March 1833. Santa Anna was now considered by the people, including many American Settlers in Texas, as the saviour of the country.

So he was very popular man. It seemed he was a Federalist and seem to support liberalism. Just as he had planned some two years before, he would stand for election as President at that time, and achieve his ambition to rule Mexico. To further support him as a liberal minded man, he persuaded a very strong liberal Gomez Farias to stand for the position of Vice-President. Now Santa Anna waited with his many women at Vera Cruz for that day to arrive.

Santa Anna had enjoyed a very interesting sexual life during the last two years. Besides giving his wife another child, at her request, he had sired no less than six more illegitimate children, though two were still yet unborn. In fact the one in which he was most interested, was because he had forced this on her, then found she was experiencing a very painful pregnancy. As a result he showed his cruelty by not caring what it cost her but demanded intercourse with her each day.

Senora Nora Delgado was holding her swollen abdomen and sobbing in pain as at last Santa Anna rolled over one the bed beside her having just completed his intercourse. She tried to remonstrate with him as she gasped out her pain "You are – a – monster. Why must – you use me – so – when you know – I'm in agony." But Santa Anna just laughed.

He even turned back, taking her nipple in his mouth and bit it, causing her to squeal, then replied, "You are such a baby. Isabel never minds what I do to her. You should be proud that I think you are worthy of bearing me a child. At least it will ensure your finances are in good order for the time being. – You must get used to pain – I may start you again after it is born, as I did to Isabel."

There was no doubt that Nora was suffering. She felt she must protest at his attitude. She might well be a courtesan but she felt she had some rights. Deciding her attack would concern others she retorted,

"Yes! It's obvious you like your women to be pregnant or lactating. I think it was bestially of you to give your fifteen year old abductees, Diane Corila and Rosa Rechi two babies one after another. Though now only seventeen years old."

Again Santa Anna laughed. "Well neither of them has made the same fuss you have made. In fact I've told Diane's father I want another baby from his daughter before she's twenty one, whilst Rosa though seven months gone, actually asked me if I wanted her to start again after her baby is born. I have always believed the lot of any woman is to be pregnant as frequently as possible."

Poor Nora realised whatever she said would not change him. As the soreness in her genitals increased she did everything she knew to ease it, drinking the drugged water by the side of the bed. Then she thought, 'My God! If I survive this one – could I endure another pregnancy again so soon. – Yet how could I stop him – He knows I need his gifts, I am in his power. It is this domination he enjoys, not minding what we women suffer."

8.

The first convention met in San Felipe de Austin in October 1832 following the uprisings and battles of June and August, called to frame and state the Texan response to the illegalities, believed to be against the Federalist Constitution of 1824. Victor Luna with Hanz Eliot attending as did Sam Houston. Stephen Austin was elected President of the Convention, though William Wharton became chairman of the committees, and wielded the chief power. However representatives from San Antonio and La Bahia did not attend.

It had been a very difficult time for Victor Luna during the last two years as the Jefe-Politico Don Jose de La Garrza had arrived at San Antonio to implement the Bustamante decrees in the act of 1830. Luna, now, had no option but the attempt to enforce the laws, and which Santa Anna had previously instructed him, in stopping further emigration from the United States. Fortunately his past refusal to do so had shown he was now acting under duress, and he still retained the sympathy of American Texans.

It had also effected both Karl Downey and Hanz Eliot in their relationships with their girlfriends. Elvira's hatred of Santa Anna for raping her, was so great that she could not understand her father and Hanz' determination to oppose Sam Houston, as he attempted to raise a rebellion. Elvira felt that such a rebellion might mean the end of this evil man. As Elvira obtained support from Raquel Garcia, it meant both Karl and Hanz had a difficult time trying to explain, that the people in Texas were not strong enough to fight the trained Mexican army.

The Convention eventually agreed on a Memorial by which they should submit their objections to the Mexican Congress, whilst not, at this stage, asking for independence. They stated their belief in the 1824 Mexican Constitution, and wishing to be part of a Federal Government of Mexico, but wanting separation from Coahuila and being granted full State Government like the others, with representatives on Congress.

They protested at the new taxes on imported goods, which could not be obtained in Mexico, yet were essential for their livelihood, stating that prohibition of slaves spelled disaster to their economy. Lastly, asking why, - whilst emigration from any part of the world, especially Europe was granted, it was not allowed from the United States, the home of republicanism whilst Europe was mainly a monarchy.

Whilst both Victor and Hanz agreed with most of these statements and applauded the consolatory language in which the Memorial was framed, they opposed and did not support it, as it seemed to give complete approval to General Santa Anna. Though they had vigorously opposed Sam Houston's attempts to increase belligerency into the document, they were surprised when he, like them, derided the obvious belief of most Americans that Santa Anna supported their cause. Even when Victor read out his directive from Santa Anna given to him four years before, ordering him to stop Americans coming, it had no impact and he was still considered their friend.

Once agreed William Wharton and Don Rafael were deputised to take this Memorial and place it before the commissioners at Saltillo.

Don La Garza appeared to accept it as an expression of their views, but very quickly wrote to the Governor warning him that he might soon have to take military opposition. As it happened Don La Garza was soon superseded by Ramon Musquiz who wrote, accusing Stephen Austin as President of the Convention, of interference in the affairs of the Mexican Government and reminded him that such assemblies were forbidden. Again it was clear that another dislike of the Americans was because they were, in the main, Protestants, whilst all educated Mexicans holding any office, were strong Roman Catholics.

It seemed the Convention had achieved little, and was to play into the hands of Sam Houston. At least Victor and Karl returned, believing the Convention had not yet spoken of independence and only asked for the separation of Texas as a separate state from Coahuila. They felt they had neutralised Sam Houston's fiery demands for independence, even obtaining his support that Santa Anna was not a friend, but a real danger to Texans.

Meantime the love affairs of Hanz with Elvira and Karl with Raquel were progressing. In spite of their Spanish reticence, both girls were allowing some quite intimate lovemaking, and both men felt they would soon ask their hands in marriage and make it quite legal. Elvira during one of these sessions, after he returned from the convention, had asked Hanz directly what were his intentions.

She had said, "Hanz, I'm a woman of twenty, in Mexico most women such as I are married. Of course I have an illegitimate child, born out of wedlock, so there are few men who would want me. – I'm sure - you – know this is a fact. I long since lost my fear that your attentions were not honourable. – I believe you really do have some affection for me, which pleases me. – However could there ever be anything more between us – and if so – what would be the position of Adela, for she is my daughter, and I love her, in spite of how it happened."

Hanz had been considering their position very carefully since he had returned. Now he took her into his arms and pressed her body to his. She did not resist, though it not often had happened, in the past. Then gently he pressed his lips on hers. Again she did not object. Now he smiled assuring at her, "Please tell me Elvira, honestly, would you like there to be anything between us. – Anything strong enough to enable us to spend our lives together?"

A few tears came into her eyes, "Oh! Yes! Dear Hanz, I would love that. I do admire you – I wonder what you really think of me for letting you take liberties with me. As a Spanish girl, and as my church has taught me, I know it is wrong. Yet I cannot help myself – and – well I'm surprised you even want to associate with me a fallen woman. – That was why I so mistrusted you at the beginning. It was father who spoke up for you – and so far you have proved to be a gentleman. – However I am an unmarried woman with a child – a child I love. – Please, I would not wish to hurry you – but is there any chance of me having any future with you?"

Now he shocked her. He pulled her body tightly to his crushing her curves into his strong body. Then he passionately pressed his lips on her so she could hardly breath and she was gasping with fear and lack of breath when he broke apart. Then he said the words she longed to hear. "Oh! Dear! Dear! Elvira, cannot you see, I am desperately in love with you. – I think I have been since that day we met in Stephen Austin's office and when he explained how terribly you had been treated. – How can I convince you – you are not a fallen woman. It is your church and your Spanish Conventions which make you think so.- Really I do believe you are a wonderful woman. – I've felt honoured that you considered me more than a friend. --- Today I think you have been trying to tell me you loved me, but your foolish ideas on morality made you fearful of saying so, possibly believing it might end our relationship."

Now to her delight, though he broke free, but he sank on bended knee. Then taking hold of her hands he looked into her face and said, "Dear! Dear! Elvira! Will you marry me, become my wife and spend your life with me - and if so – would you let me adopt your equally wonderful daughter, Adela, who I love. Then perhaps in time you might even give me one of our own."

Hanz saw the look of astonishment and yet happiness on her face as she used her hands to pull him onto his feet, Then it was her turn to pull him to her, press her body, into his giving him three quick kisses, then said, "Oh! Yes! Please! I will – Hanz I've loved you since that day. – Then you were so demonstrative and so kind. It was foolish but I thought your liking for me, was that I was a fallen woman, and would easily yield to you. I nearly drove you away. - Even today, I could not believe you could love me enough to marry you. – I had decided after you went to the convention that when you returned I would offer to become your mistress – in every way. -- I wanted your children. Despoiled by an evil man, I might as well offer myself in that way. – Oh! Hanz! I knew you liked me, you've shown me that many times, but I could not believe you actually loved me – yes – and my daughter. – Darling, I want to spend the rest of my life making you happy, as happy as you have just made me."

They continued to embrace for a long time, happy that they could bring joy and pleasure to both of them. Then they went to meet her father, and Hanz told Victor he had proposed marriage to Elvira, and now came to ask his permission for the hand of his daughter.

Victor had taken both their hands and joined them together. Then he said, "Hanz, I could never have hoped for a better son-in-law. I've admired you since we first met and ever since you've proved to me the kind man you are. – However though I knew you liked Elvira, and did not blame her for the past – I still could not believe you would ask her to marry you. I just hoped you might take her as your mistress, for I knew if so you would still treat her kindly. Today you have made me as happy as I know Elvira is. It is a miracle which I thought would never happen, after what that evil man did to her."

Hanz just smiled as he looked at a deliriously happy Elvira then said, "Victor, it is I who is so fortunate that this wonderful and courageous woman could love me, as I love her. – Now somehow we must find a way to keep peace in this wonderful land." Victor just replied, "Amen."

9.

Gordon Taylor made rapid progress with both Cherie Marshall and Frances Le Raye after Donald Reid had left, but it was entirely the work of the two women. He quickly realised his inability to control the situation. He was putty in their hands. He knew they entirely dominated him. The truth was they were both far more sexually mature than he was, and he admitted he had little experience that way. He felt sure this was why he had failed to win the complete love of Sheila McLean.

He surrendered to their victory over him, at least enjoying the somewhat intimate pleasures they gave him, though he knew they were merely using him to achieve their own desires. Meantime he immersed himself in proving to Silas Taylor his worth as an engineer. He personally oversaw the maintenance of every one of Silas' boats when they arrived at Pittsburgh, vigorously driving the workmen to complete their tasks, and using Roy Marshall's workshops to manufacture any parts of machinery necessary. However, at the same time he made himself available to Roy for anything work he might require.

Actually his relationships with Cherie and Frances resulted in him being invited, many times, to their house for dinners, though he, also, realised that it was Charlotte Marshall who monopolised him whenever he came. Every time she involved him in conversation about some engineering problem, as if she was desperately trying to refresh again, her extensive knowledge in this field. In fact Gordon felt proud she considered him worthy of her attention.

This evening at dinner the Marshall's were entertaining a number of old friends who had come to stay with them. Besides their neighbours who Gordon had known of but not met before, were Francois and his wife, Fay le Raye, the parents of Frances who he had only met with Cherie at her house. However Gordon had been informed of their past, several times. It seemed Roy and Fay, then Fay Bradbury, had met as the mob burnt down Grimshaw's Cotton Mill in Manchester, as she sobbed over the dead body of her lover Trevor Reynolds whose child she was then carrying. It was Roy who brought Fay to America after meeting and establishing friendship, with Linda and Hugh Foyle, at Liverpool, all four had travelled to Philadelphia to set up a mechanised Cotton Mill there, for Jansen Carroll, the son of Edgar Carroll, a descendent of the original Roman Catholic branch of the Carroll family, who came from Yorkshire in King Charles I time. Though Edgar's family had become protestants after he married Anna van Buren, a rich Dutch family from New York.

In fact the other four guests, staying with Marshall's were Edgar's son, Jansen Carroll and his wife, Mechia and Hugh Foyle and his wife Ellia. That night he was to learn all their histories which he found fascinating, and knowing now, such things could only happen in America. Of course Gordon had learned everything about Roy Marshall and Fay Bradbury and the burning to the mill at Knot Mill. It was part of the history of Manchester of which Gordon had learned as a boy. How Hugh Foyle had brought his murdered father's knowledge of the 'flying shuttle' which enabled Roy and he, to set up a similar mechanised cotton mill in Philadelphia, for Jansen Carroll, becoming partners in the lucrative business.

However it was when Charlotte had told him how her husband Roy, even before they met, though not a trained engineer, working from memory of how it worked in Grimshaw's Mill, had devised steam power to run the looms. His ability to do this made Gordon proud to know this man. Gordon had learned of these facts years before, marvelling at Roy's ability, by sheer persistence, of not only doing this but also devising the much smaller steam boiler to drive the paddle wheels of the boats they commenced building, which had made them so rich

It was Fay who said, "Really, I have no right to be part of this enormous company, Roy acquired his engineering abilities but both Charlotte and Francois are the only trained engineers." Charlotte very generously retorted. "We might be engineers but it was Fay, who until we acquired our accountant, Jack Eliot saw to our finances and stopped us from going broke. Without her help we would not now have such a rich company."

Now for the first time Jansen Carroll spoke. "I suppose – but for me – neither Fay, Roy nor Hugh would be sitting here tonight. – I wrote to Hugh's father begging him to come with his invention of the 'flying shuttle', when my father gave me the money to build the mill. – It seemed his father had been murdered by a mob in Lancashire and Hugh and his sister, Linda, came to escape a similar fate. However we would all admit there would not have been the success we now enjoy, but for the fortunate meeting with Roy and Fay in Liverpool. – Gordon, - Hugh and I, are now partners along with Roy in an enormous number of cotton mills driven by steam, which has made us prosperous and very rich. But like Roy and Francois, we are also blessed with wives who have given us the real happiness in our lives."

Gordon felt he must respond. There was no doubt that Mechia Carroll and Ellia Foyle, each with an unusual name, both about fifty five years of age, but still very beautiful, yet who in truth, were quite different in appearance to either Fay or Charlotte. He said, "It is a privilege to be here tonight to meet all of you, especially so many very beautiful women. I must complement all your husbands in winning the hands of four beautiful wives. Pray Mechia and Ellia your names fascinate me, please tell me how did you acquire them."

To his surprise both women broke into uncontrollable laughter and it was Mechia who replied. "Mr Taylor we two are in fact cousins. In fact we each have a grandfather, Checcokee, who was the chief of the Chickasaw Indian Tribe, whose lands are in fact near where we now sit, and who allied themselves with the French when they came and built a fort, then called Fort Duquesne, renamed much latter as Fort Pitt. These events were just before the beginning of the Seven Years War."

Now Ellia took up the story. "Actually we are both illegitimate, our fathers never married our mothers, though he treated them as equals to his legal wives, who he married many years after he lived with our mothers. We are both proud of our indian blood. My father, Jean Dumas, was a French soldier who came to serve France in New France just as Mechia's father, Louis Scarron, a French aristocrat, did the same. In fact they were virtually forced to choose our mothers and undergo an Indian wedding, not valid in France, to cement and ensure that the Chickasaw Tribe became their allies and friends, in their coming struggle with the English. "

Now Mechia concluded the tale. "Though this was how it began, in fact our fathers came to love our mothers, and was possibly the reason why they surrendered to fort to the British as New France fell, for if not and they resisted, they knew our mothers would have died with them. – It is a very complicated story, too long to tell you tonight, but eventually when our fathers found and legally married the two women they had wanted, but separated from them, for ten years, it seemed their wives came to love our mothers as much as their husbands. – So we became civilized and given a life of luxury which enabled us to ensnare our two handsome husbands."

Gordon thanked them for the story but contradicted them. "I believe your ending is very wrong. It seemed that Jansen and Hugh are very fortunate men to come to know and eventually win you as their wives." So ended the introductions began some time before as they consumed their after dinner drinks.

Now Charlotte changed the conversation. "Gordon, last week after you left we were quite taken by your belief in the future of Railways as a preferred method of transportation, and your belief we should invest in its future. We should be very pleased if you would, once again, explain your reasons, and the knowledge you have of them. For all four of us are quite rich enough, to subsidise their future, provide it will bring worth while dividends later. Frankly I don't think what has happened here in America, warrants this interest."

Gordon smiled, "I can understand your doubts. So far the iron ways are really only metal tracks and all the wagons are horse drawn. This can have a very small future. However, I and my family, have been privileged to see the creation of that magnificent Liverpool of Manchester Railway in Lancashire. We have worked on it and I even used it travel the many miles to Liverpool from my home in Manchester, when I came here to America."

Now elated at being given the chance to speak of his past involvement he continued, "It is a remarkable achievement almost forty miles in length, overcoming enormous engineering problems, such as crossing Chat Moss, which could not be drained and rails laid on virtually a mattress to prevent the lines sinking. However the most important part is the steam locomotive, which pulls the coaches in which passengers sit. Of course these can only pull coaches and themselves up a reasonable gradient, never more than one in one hundred and often only one in a thousand.--"

At this point Jansen interrupted, "Then it could never but used where mountains existed only on flat plains."

Gordon smiled, "No you are wrong. It only means you have to plan your route and circle the lines to rise more slowly, even tunnel if necessary. This has been done in England. However as I said, the important part is the locomotive. – Roy, at the moment you know of the horse drawn track form Buffalo to Jacksonville. If this was extended to Pittsburgh and a steam locomotive used instead of horses you could transport those hundred of persons arriving by the Erie Canal to Buffalo to your boats at Pittsburgh as they make their way west."

Now Roy was interested. "But how could we build a steam locomotive?" Now Gordon laughed, "If you are willing to squander a little of your wealth. My family have, on license, the plans of George Stephenson's 'Rocket' Locomotive. They are copyright, but if you are willing to pay the price I could get my family to send you the blue prints. Then I'm certain Roy, Charlotte or Francois, could understand and I would be able to build one in your works by the river. Once that line was built it would greatly added to the wealth of your Boat company."

Charlotte at once saw its value. "Roy, at least let us purchase those blue prints. Then see if we should invest further." As Roy nodded Francois, Jansen and Hugh stated they would at least like to contribute so far. Only when they had received these need they consider further expenditure. Gordon was delighted at their offer and even more so when Charlotte leant over to him and said quietly, "Gordon, we are going to need your expertise. I believe in your future of railways for the United States.

He left tonight believing he might well have a future in this new form of transport. However America was a very different place to England. Where they had met that evening was little different to Lancashire, but all the news was of growing conflict in the western lands.

The indian attacks in northern Texas which was detracting from settlement there. Even actual small battles further south in Texas, possibly leading to war with the United States. Even smaller battles near Independence, not too far from where his beloved Sheila lived as the locals fought the incursion of so many Mormons who the locals considered irreligious . This might become very serious.

Again what future was there westward now land to the west of Missouri was being settled by indian tribes forcibly removed from their own lands in the west. Gordon thought, 'It would be a very long time before they built any railways there, in the midst of conflict. – However this one line from Buffalo to Pittsburgh might prove his belief that this was their future means of transport from one part of the country to another.' Gordon was now, determined to play a part in its development and now knew he would have Charlotte's assistance in making this possible.

PART 4

RESOLUTION

LEBENSTRAUM PART 4 RESOLUTION

RESOLUTION

1.

Donald Reid was very worried, fearing Rachael Gilbert might die. It was less than three weeks since the 'Little Nellie' had landed both of them at the dock at St. Louis. To Donald's joy he found both his parents awaiting his arrival, with one of their coaches. Having quickly introduced Rachael to them, they joined the coach and were taken to their house. His mother, Dora, made sure Rachael knew they were pleased to help her, which quickly removed the fear she had when on the boat.

Of course his mother had known little about Rachel until she arrived, only that her son had needed to free her from some form of captivity. Now she inquired fully from Rachael what this meant. In fact Dora was very concerned when she learned that Rachael was married, as a Mormon wife, to a fifteen year older man, Sidney Gilbert, who had two other wives, one of which was Rachael's elder sister. Also that it was Sidney Gilbert's child she carried inside her.

However as soon as she undressed Rachael and helped her to bathe, Dora was even more concerned when she found how, terribly, thin was her body. It seemed her husband had not been very rich and all his wives never received sufficient food, considering their frequent pregnancies, though her husband had deliberately robbed Rachael of food as a punishment for not, freely, yielding herself to him. Dora, immediately, called their local doctor who was equally fearful of her condition, starved of essential food whilst trying to nurture an unborn baby inside her. In fact as it seemed the foetus was about four months old, the doctor wondered if her near starvation might of robbed her child the nutriments required to unsure a happy future.

Of course everyone now ensured Rachael obtained considerably increased feasts but it seemed this was not very successful. Rachael's recent experiences had taken its toll on her body. Suddenly increasing her food consumption only caused her often to vomit it soon afterwards, as her body was not used to digesting so much so quickly. Again poor Rachael had been so misused by her husband ever since they married, she had lived perpetually in fear of his sexual attacks. This undoubtedly had weakened her constitution. Then the adrenaline caused by fear, of what Donald might do to her, when she placed herself in his control, had produced even greater stress on her.

At the end of ten days, everyone knew Rachael was very unwell and finally she collapsed unconscious, and had to be carried to her bed. At last she regained consciousness, and was delighted to find that not only Dora was watching her but also Donald. For a moment it seemed the worst was over, however suddenly she went into labour and miscarried. For over a week it seemed that Rachael would not survive. However today as Donald sat next to her bed, holding one of her hands, as she knew he had done for sometime, when she became ill, Rachael, at last began to feel stronger. Even Donald believed she was recovering, even if slowly. At least now she could speak without tiring herself.

She even managed to smile a little, as she spoke. "Dear! Donald! You know I probably owe my life to you. If you had left me on the boat. This would have happened before we reached Independence. There would have been no one to look after me as both you and your family have done."

Donald was very pleased at her words so replied, "However I believe it was your belief I could be trusted, which is the real reason. I knew from the start what you must fear by surrendering yourself to a man you did not know and had never met until a week before you came away with me. We would not have been able to help you if you had not trusted me. It makes me proud to think you were willing to do that."

Rachael managed a little laugh. "I think I told you at the time but I will do so again. I was so unhappy that I convinced myself, that even if you proved to be unreliable – yes, even if you possessed me – it would be no worse than what Sidney did to me when I conceived my baby. –" Now another laugh before continuing – "and Donald you are far more handsome than Sidney. – Life with you, even if you possessed me, could not be worse than the life I had lived, ever since I was married."

Donald gently kissed the hand he was holding, "And, now, what do you think of me. – Is it possible you might consider me your friend – for I would like that?" She answered by pulling his hand, as he held hers, to her mouth an kissed it. Then she replied, "Dear! Donald! You have given me a new life – I somehow hope I can sometime repay you for bringing me here." Then a few tears appeared in her eyes then continued, "I'm heartbroken I lost my baby – even though it was Sidney's, and I did not want to conceive it – I knew I would love it when it was born. – Now it is gone."

Now Donald kissed her hand, "I understand. But to me your life is far more important. You will have others, mother asked doctor and he told her it was only your fearful treatment and lack of food which caused the miscarriage. – it seemed your baby was not properly formed and was why your body discarded it. Doctor says there are no reasons why you should not bare babies in future."

Now Rachael smiled, "Yes! Your kind mother has already told me. I'm so sorry I've caused her so much trouble. Now I can see why you are such a wonderful man. I can hardly believed that it is only about six weeks since you scared me so much on the boat, when you first touched me. Now I'm here, free from my horrible husband, living in this luxurious house – and with a very handsome man, my Prince Charming, who has saved me and taken me from an evil monster, and now is holding my hand. Please do not let this fairy story end."

Donald could see she was tired, so excused himself, but now felt sure she would recover. He spent many hours talking to her as today. Then she was strong enough to get out of bed and sit in a chair. By then they had spent many hours talking to each other. Donald had told her of his family in Independence. All about his earlier life. His adventurous journey the Great Salt Lake and his wish for this wonderful western land bordering the Pacific Ocean, the land of California, which he wanted to see, but which he hoped someday would be part of the United States. Then it would stretch from the Pacific to the Atlantic Oceans. Again he told her of his journey up the rivers to northern Texas, hoping to discover an easier route to California.

She had surprised him when she said, "Donald, I would like to come with you, if you ever again try to discover a route – or any place you want to visit. Could you possibly accept me – a woman – to come with you. I know I could withstand any dangers. – After all you've saved my life, already, I know I would be safe with you – and Donald, I do understand, but do not fear the dangers."

He thought of her offer but considered such a life was not one for a woman to endure. Then again he thought he was silly as many women, wives or lovers of men had for many years followed their men into the wilderness. At least he knew he would like her to be with him, at such times.

During these weeks they learned from Sharon and Charles Marshall in Independence of the growing hostility of the local inhabitants of Jackson County, in which Independence was situated, to the ever increasing Mormon population now settling only twelve miles from the town as they established their Zion-on-Earth in Missouri. They had called it 'Big Blue'. It developed so quickly that before 1833 its population was almost one third of the entire population of Jackson County.

As it seemed Mormons as a whole, nearly always voted together, as one, this represented an enormous voting power and the locals, referred to by Mormons, as the gentiles, feared they would soon swamp the county, and begin to rule everyone, forcing themselves into their faith. As they were considered irreligious, and blasphemed God, the locals felt they must stop further Mormons from arriving and the drive the others out of the county. Already small battles and attacks were being made.

There was no doubt but that Sharon and Charles feared their battles might place their own house and Shipping office in danger. They had started hiring men to act as defenders, were it to happen. It was this which had prevented them informing Donald and everyone of any news about the Gilbert family. Of course Rachael was worried about her elders sister, Constance, and her baby.

When Donald had asked her why her sister stayed with Sidney, even seeming to like him, Rachael had explained, "Father and Sidney are very dominating people. However it was not just this, but the fear they placed in my mother and Constance minds, that they must conform to the Commandments in the Mormon Bible, or they would never have a future life and be thrown down into hell. They never convinced me – though I admit I was afraid, even thinking I might be wrong. All Mormon women may seem to want the life their husbands and elders demand of them. Though it is often fear or uncontrollable sexual desires. However they do believe their afterlife will be one of paradise, and do not want to lose it – as I must have done."

To her amazement Donald now seized her and gently kissed he lips. "Don't ever think of such stupid ideas, believing you have sinned. Believe only in my promises – not demands like you husband made – just believe in me and that I will ensure you have a happy life on this earth and will do everything in my power to ensue it will continued – Yes, even after you die."

This was the very words Rachael had been hoping to hear from Donald, ever since she had recovered. For she knew by then, she had fallen desperately in love with him, yet, though he was especially kind to her, he had never shown any stronger feelings for her, than genuine friendship. It was the reason she had told him how much she would like to go exploring with him, telling him she wanted to be part of him. However the most he ever did was to hold her hands, as he had done for so long whilst she was ill, and sometimes kissed the side of her face.

Now today, for the first time, he had seized her and planted that solitary kiss on her lips. How much she would have loved him to grasp her body tightly to his and almost choke herself with long passionate kisses. It was her resolution to someday, somehow, persuade him to do this to her. However those few words had, at last, given her hope. Perhaps, after all his feeling for her were far more intense than his actions. She wondered, was it his promise he made on the boat, not to molest her, which restricted him. – Perhaps, somehow, she should encourage him, try to let him know she wanted to free him from that promise. Now she knew she must begin to attempt it.

2.

Rachael knew Donald had recently contemplated taking the fearful Oregon Trail to the north west, as he knew this area, which was claimed by both British Canada and the United States. He wanted to do this, not to stay there, but travel south, from there, possibly by ship to Mexican California. He had even considered repeating his journey of four years before to the Great Salt Lake and then find the trail to California. However both these journeys must start from Independence and he knew it was dangerous to consider this at present. Even his family there, required many paid men to defend their possessions. Such a journey would have to wait.

Rachael had informed him she would like to accompany him should he decide to go to Independence and attempt the task. She felt hurt when he said such an idea was silly. It was not something for a woman to attempt. She even felt annoyed when she had retorted that many women with families had accepted these risks, for he had replied but these women were the wives of the men going there. Still she feared she dare not tell him she would like to accompany him like these other women, especially as his wife, as she feared it would destroy the good relationship with him, she was enjoying and wanted to develop.

Donald had just received the large dividends from his financial investment in Andrew Henry and William Ashley Fur Trading Company. It was the company which had sponsored the journey of which Donald had joined for adventure in 1827. This time Donald was contented to invest his previous gains from that journey and more from his annual allowance sponsoring further fur trading projects. It was the returns from these which now had made him quite rich, apart from the large allowance he received from the Carroll /Marshall Company.

Denied the chance to go to California for the moment, this recent windfall gave Donald an idea. He knew his elder cousin, Ryan Hobbs, and part owner of the very large Hobbs-Reid ranch, the original home of the both the Reid and Hobbs family, was a Congressman as a Representative for Ohio. He would be able to tell him fully, what was the United States present attitude to Mexico and whether the government had any desire to acquire the lands of either Texas or California. He had heard of the most recent developments in Texas and the attacks made on American residents there.

In the last few weeks he had learned from Rachael of her early life, and how her family had become Mormons. It seemed they lived in Palmyra, on the Erie Canal near Rochester when Joseph Smith and his early band of Mormons descended on the town. Her father James Donelson had married her mother Sarah Brown in the Baptist chapel in the town and he completely dominated her. She bore Constance when only eighteen and then had two miscarriages before Rachael was born in 1813. Bearing a still born son in 1817, she miscarried late in pregnancy in 1821, almost dying and was then infertile.

Soon after that her father became very interested in his wife's niece, Jessie Brown, already twenty years of age. Rachael knew their affair became intimate. In fact her father had considered divorcing her mother. Meantime it seemed he partially abused, first Constance and then herself, sometimes coming behind them and placing both hands on their covered breasts, or placing one on the lower part of their abdomen. Rachael hated this but it seemed her sister, Constance, enjoyed these attacks, even wishing he did more to her. Perhaps this was why she fell to the wiles of Sidney Gilbert and transgressed.

In fact the descent of the Mormons on Palmyra probably prevented scandals being discovered in the Donelson family. It seemed, in spite of her use of preventatives, Jessie Brown had conceived. James Donelson was, immediately, converted to the Mormon faith, took Jessie as his second wife and married her in the Mormon Church. His strength of conversion soon lead to him becoming an elder of the church before Jessie's baby was born in 1829. Soon James had a third wife only sixteen years old, who he seduced, then married this daughter of another Mormon elder.

It was then that Constance met and was seduced by Sidney Gilbert already married to his first wife, Nancy, as both believed that god told them when they should conceive a child. It seemed this resulted in Constance conceiving and their father forcing both Constance and Rachael to marry Sidney. So began two years of purgatory and the unwanted raped pregnancy. However when Joseph Smith, virtually driven out of Palmyra, decided to set up a Church in Kirkland near Lake Erie and another in Missouri. Sidney Gilbert, believing everything the Mormon Bible stated, considered Missouri was the new Zion, and wanted to be part of it, hence their journey on the boat.

Fascinated by the history of the Donelson family, Donald decided to offer to take Rachael back east to meet his family and many associated with them in the past. Of course Rachael was delighted, as she had feared losing contact with him if he left alone. Both his father and mother considered it was time he either devoted himself to the family business, or set up one of his own, as he was now rich enough. Though she did not tell him, his mother, wondered if his taking Rachael with him denoted a possible sexual interest in her, for up to now he did not seem to be attracted to any woman. She knew his reason for befriending Rachael at the time was simply one of pity, at an attractive girl being so badly treated. His mother, Dora, liked Rachael and hoped he might become interested in her. However she did not speak to him about it.

Of course Donald was free to use any of their River boats to travel anywhere he desired. He decide he would take her first back to Pittsburgh and introduce her to Charlotte and Roy Marshall. On the boat Donald met Otto Fallon, who he knew as the Manager of the St. Louis Bank, and introduced Rachael to him. It seemed Otto was no longer Manager at St. Louis and had received a very welcomed promotion . He was travelling back east to take up the now vacant Managership of the Bank of Annapolis. Donald had wished him well in his new appointment. He liked Otto very much having learned of his past and his family's importance in the banking world of Germany. Before they arrived at Pittsburgh, Otto had given him his new address in Annapolis.

There was another reason for returning to the Marshall household. He believed bringing Rachael would give him some satisfaction in parading her before Cheri Marshall, and this would be revenge her for changing her affections to Gordon Taylor. In fact they arrived at the Marshall mansion before Jenson Carroll and Mechia and Hugh Foyle and Ellia had left. It so happened that Fay and Francois Le Raye had called that day.

Very quickly poor Rachael had to digest the very complicated relationships of the Carroll's, Foyle's, La Raye's and Marshall's including British and French births and learning that both Mechia and Ellia were in fact illegitimate daughters of two indian wives of French officers. Perhaps it was fortunate that later that week Rachael was to meet Manon and Jack Eliot and Manon presented her with her own researched history of the two branches of the Carroll family. Again Rachael became intrigued by the two original Roman Catholic and Protestant families.

It seemed to Rachael that many women in those past days had suffered far more distress and humiliation than even she had suffered, women condemned to a life as indentured servants becoming often the sexual slaves of the men who purchased them. It was after this and before Donald took her to meet his family on the nearby ranch that she learned that he, and the man who she was to be introduced to as Ryan Hobbs, were in fact descendants of two Irish indentured servants, Erin O'Neil and Mary Malloy who were purchased as indentured servants by Donald's grandfather, Craig Reid and Ryan's father, Brian Hobbs. It seemed for some time these two men misused them, each enjoying their bodies, before discovering their love for them, and marrying them. However it seemed, all four, even after marriage continued to swap partners occasionally.

However Rachael was delighted to meet Ryan Hobbs and his large family, but especially Donald's eighty year old grandmother, Erin Reid, as well as other branches of the Reid family, descendents of Erin and Craig Reid. There was no doubting how magnificent was the combined Hobbs-Reid ranch. This had only been possible due to the unselfish devotion of the two original women to their men folk, helped by loans from two men Daniel Carroll and Michel Casimir. Now Donald wished to learn from Ryan as much as possible about Mexico and was fortunate that he had only recently returned from Washington and was therefore able to give him the most up to date information.

3.

Unfortunately Ryan knew little more than Donald had, already, discovered. Ryan disliked the President, Andrew Jackson and had affiliated instead to Senator Henry Clay, a vigorous opponent of the president and his party, and was helping Henry in the formation of an opposition Whig Party to try to unseat Jackson when he came up for re-election. He was sure that the president would have liked to incorporate part of northern Mexico into the United States, especially the area of Texas. He even considered he had helped to persuade Sam Houston to leave Tennessee and go to Mexico for this purpose. Ryan felt sure Houston was trying to stir up rebellion by Americans there, to sever relations with Mexico.

Ryan did suggest that Donald went quickly down the Potomac to Racoonsville where Senator Mark Carroll lived, particularly as his son Danton and his wife, Claudia had recently returned on vacation from Mexico where Danton had been an accredited representative of the United States in Mexico, and would soon be returning. Danton could tell Donald the latest position of the various factions trying to obtain control of the country. Donald agreed to do this and again, would take Rachael with him.

Meantime Rachael had felt privileged to meet privately, Donald's grandmother, Erin Reid. Even daring to raise the question of Erin's time as an indentured servant. Erin had smiled and was not offended, explaining how both she and Mary Malloy had been sent to America for minor crimes they had committed in Ireland. Their terrible life to a past fur trader, who had set up a shop in Fort Pitt, who had misused them. His murder and then purchased by two young men, Craig Reid and Brian Hobbs who had started to cultivate this land. She freely admitted both men used them, alternating in their attacks. How in spite of this both Erin and Mary came to like, even love them.

Now Erin explained, "We wanted to conceive their children but they fervently refused. We felt sure they did not love us but we wanted their babies in any case. However we know, and owe our happiness, to Michelle and Daniel Carroll, whose descendants you will meet at Racoonsville. It seemed they did love us, but had promised their family not to marry until they were prosperous. A loan to be returned in ten years made this possible and they came to apologise and beg us to marry them. They loved us both, but I preferred Craig whilst Mary liked Brian. So we married but the large house we built, which is part of this mansion today, had shared reception and dining rooms. – We still continued to swap partners for the rest of our lives. – However we were careful that all our children were by our husbands."

Now a few tears came into Erin's eyes. "Now I'm the only one of the four left. It makes me so very sad, for we know our considerable wealth was because the four of us worked as one large family, all so very happy that we had found each other. – Actually we were never misused, even in the past. We did enjoy our sexual lives with them, they were so kind. Only the fact they would not give us those babies we wanted for so long, hurt us. They told us later, it was because they did love us, but felt they could not marry us. They felt the could not make us unmarried mothers."

Erin saw a few tears had appeared in Rachael's eyes, then surprised her. "Rachael dear, you are in love with Donald, aren't you? Do not be afraid you can tell me." Now Rachael did break down and stared sobbing so Erin bent over and held her face close to hers. "Does he know how you feel – Have you told him?"

Now her sobbing became greater. "No. I dare not. I'm afraid of losing him. Erin I want to lie with him – give him the child I lost recently. Perhaps I should tell you my past." Then Rachael explained in full her forced Mormon marriage her husband's rape of her to make her conceive. How Donald had taken pity on her and finally managed to free her and take her to his home and Erin's son's home. Her miscarriage and near death. She concluded, "So you see I believe Donald saved my life, for I would have died on that boat before we reached Independence. – Oh! Erin, what am I to do. We have slept apart since we left St. Louis, yet I would willingly have slept with him. – I do not expect him to marry me – just give me a little happiness that way. – Yet Erin, he is so kind to me, yet does not realise he also hurts me."

Erin smiled a little, "Dear Rachael, I only know too well, what you are suffering. It was the same between Craig and me, so long ago. I promise I will speak to Donald before you leave – no – not to tell him to love you or even take you, but I will prepare the ground. I will, also, write to Hedwig, Robert's wife. She has inherited Michelle's, her mother-in-laws, ways. I know she will want to help and will know what to do. – Dear Rachael you must be patient. – It seems Donald has never had a girl of his own. You must even consider he may not want intimacy with any woman. – Some men are like that.- However keep being patient and keep trying, for what I've seen of you, makes me feel Donald would be a lucky man to have a girl like you to love."

Erin kept her promise. She spoke to Donald but quite causally, telling him how fortunate he was to discover a girl like Rachael and knew she was both grateful to him but had come to like him. She concluded, "Try not to loose her and please value her friendship. I think she likes you." It was enough to make him think a little differently about her. However Erin also wrote a long letter to Hedwig Carroll imploring her to try to foster Donald's interest in Rachael. Then they both left in one of their Surrey's and drove the long journey down the gap and then across the river to this magnificent mansion of Racoonsville.

Rachel had been told its history. Being Daniel Carroll's reward from Sir Robert Carroll of Rockville on his marriage to Michelle Tailler, for his and Donald Wilson's insane, but courageous act of risking their lives to find and save Madeleine Colet, to repay a debt to a French Officer Jean Dumas, then virtually his enemy. Again Rachael was to learn how these lives were intertwined, for Jean was the father of Mechia Carroll, she had met in Pittsburgh.

She was told the Master of Racoonsville was still Robert Carroll, eldest son of Michelle and Daniel Carroll, assisted by his wife Hedwig, daughter of Michael Casimir, who was a rich man who had come to

America from Poland.. However they were both now seventy years old, and somewhat infirm, so the house was now run by Robert's son, Mark Carroll now replacing his father, as Senator for Virginia, along with his wife Estelle Tencin, granddaughter of Anton Tencin, an illegitimate son of King Louis XIV and his mistress Claudine Tencin.

However the persons Donald wished to meet were their son, Danton Carroll and his wife Claudia, recently returned from duty in Mexico. Very quickly Hedwig took Rachael away to talk to her leaving Donald to question Danton alone. Donald explained his interest in California and why and how it had developed, gaining Danton's admiration for him.

Danton had told him that, at the moment, his work in Mexico was almost entirely concerned with trying to protect, in some unofficial way, the large number of American settlers in Texas and that neither the United States, nor Mexico, seemed particularly interested in those areas of California. The latter area was very sparsely populated and large areas mainly controlled by Catholic Priests, from their missions. The only areas of contention there, were in the north, where settlers in Oregon, but mainly fur trappers, were illegally crossed the border driving south. This invasion was strongly opposed, as now was any further settlement by Americans in Texas. However Danton feared that very soon this latter area would be threatened with fierce battles, far more serious than the recent outbreaks.

Donald learned that General Santa Anna, a long time opponent of Americans settling in Mexico, particularly Texas, had manipulated matters ensuring he was to be elected President of Mexico. Danton considered him to be both a clever, and a very evil man, as well as a womaniser, particularly with young girls. The General was courting approval as a liberal after the very conservative President Bustamante, had been removed from office. However Danton felt sure this was a act. He believed Santa Anna had a plan for complete dictatorial power. Once elected he would let his true liberal Vice President rule, knowing this would be a disaster. Then, at the right time, Santa Anna would intervene, take up office and install himself as Dictator to 'save the country'. Danton felt sure it would work.

From that moment on he would become oppressive, probably dissolve and remove Congress, then attempt to ensure the future greatness of Mexico. The first act of which would be, to persecute all American's in Texas to drive them out. Danton feared for them for he knew, at the moment, with the forced transportation of the indian tribes across the Mississippi, the United States were not willing to go to war, and the Texans would have to fight alone. He feared his position in Mexico City could be threatened.

Donald felt very disappointed for it seemed that with the growing problems in Texas, there was little chance of getting the government to consider, possibly annexing, California. Yet he knew that here were excellent lands bordering the Pacific Ocean just waiting for Americans to colonise and live in. However the Carroll's had implored him to stay, and to use their coaches to show Rachael the beautiful countryside. The Blue Ridge mountains to the west and possibly visit the Rockville estate, even Annapolis.

When he asked Rachael if she would like this, she not only gladly assented, but began to put into action the advice Hedwig Carroll had given her for winning a more a romantic relationship with Donald. Rachael used the very words in which Hedwig had instructed her. "Dear! Donald! I would love to accompany you to all these wonderful places. You know, now I've heard so much of this fantastic family the Carroll's and now come to meet them. Realising how your own families are interconnected. – Donald – I really would like to come to know you better. I feel I too I would like to become connected, and I'm sure you could show me how."

Rachael concluded by saying, "You know we have now known each other for many months – yet – Donald, I still do not seem to really know you. You often seem to me to be some distance apart. After the wonderful way you freed me from hell, I want to reward you, if you would let me." Then she lightly kissed his cheek before excusing herself saying that Hedwig wished to converse with her before they left. Her words and attitude left Donald very perplexed, particularly her reference for him appearing to be a distance apart from her. What did this mean?

4.

Danton Carroll had been right in his prophesies. General Santa Anna had been elected as President to succeed Pedraza after the latter's term of office ended in March 1833 however, feigning illness, he authorised his Vice President Gomez Farias to run the country, retiring temporarily to Vera Cruz to enjoy the bodies of his four mistresses as well as that of his wife. Farias was a liberal and this had given everyone the impression, including many Americans in Texas, that Santa Anna held similar views, gaining him electoral support. However he knew that as soon as Farias attempted to introduce laws of a liberal nature there would be trouble.

It happened very quickly when Farias attacked the wholesale corruption in the country involving the military, and wealthy landowners, also incurring the wrath of the Roman Catholic Church. It created chaos. At this point, in May 1834, claiming to save the country from misrule Santa Anna returned to Mexico City and dismissed Farias, receiving public approval. However to everyone's dismay, certain of military support, due to his past support of many high ranking officers, he now dismissed Congress, claiming it was their indecision which had been the root of the trouble. In a few days Santa Anna became the Dictator of Mexico obtaining powers no previous president had enjoyed.

Since this threatened the liberal principles enjoyed by the states since 1824 this caused open rebellion in many areas particularly in Zecatecas and Texas At that moment the most serious rebellion was in Zecatecas where a well armed militia, led by Francisco Garcia, a distant cousin of Julio Garcia of San Marcos, stood against the Mexican Army. However after two hours they were comprehensively defeated and three thousand prisoners were taken. Santa Anna then ransacked the city for forty eight hours, his army raping and pillaging, with many dead.

He intended this as a demonstration of what any other rebellious state may expect, and this was, particularly, directed at Texas, especially the many Americans who had settled there. He was determined, not only to stop any more Americans coming there, but wanted to displace

Lebenstraum

all who had been there for some time. It seemed by 1834 most Texans, had at last realised, that he was their enemy, and soon would attack them, so rather late, they prepared for this.

However many things had happened in San Marcos, since the first convention in San Felipe in 1832. Victor Luna had been delighted when they had come to him and Hanz asked his permission to marry Elvira. Not only did he agree but ensured they were made husband and wife very quickly and only six weeks later Elvira knew she had conceived Karl's child, but was even more delighted at his loving treatment of her four year old daughter, Adela. Hanz had legally adopted her, for she knew that her daughter had never known or met her true father, but had come to regarded Hanz in that capacity for some time, and loved him just as much as her mother did.

In fact this had caused a series of marriages and engagements. It was hardly surprising that Karl Downey had followed Hanz lead and married Raquel Garcia soon afterwards. Then Steven Downey much older than either of them, once he had decided to stay in Texas had courted Joel Robinson's daughter, Brenda Robinson, a widow almost the same age. Brenda's husband had died of small pox less than a year after they had married and before she could conceive his child. The Robinson family ran a large farm and had lived in Mexico for over ten years.

Now the only remaining man to come to join them and bring the original strain of horse, Tony Brady, was courting Rosa Arredondo, six years younger than him, and whose family had lived on their ranch, not far from the Luna ranch, for over thirty years, so were a very settled Mexican family. So now it seemed all four men who had come from Kentucky has decided to make Texas there permanent home, and risk what all four felt was the coming conflict.

As the government had ignored the Memorial sent after the Convention in 1832, pleading for Texas to be given separate statehood under the 1824 manifesto. In fact it seemed all it had done was to created suspicion in Mexico City. It was decided to call a second convention in April 1833 and once again both Victor and Hanz were representatives. Against a number of delegates wishes, a vote decided that they must draft a constitution and to both Victor and Hanz disgust

Sam Houston was elected Chairman of the committee. So powerful was his personality, that Houston virtually wrote this constitution, and he based its principles on the United States Constitution but included a number of Andrew Jackson's more radical articles.

Then the convention accepted this draft and incorporated this into a Memorandum to be sent to Mexico City now, demanding, acceptance of this constitution, a repeal of the decree of 1830 and to allow American immigration into Texas, as well as lowering the tariff's imposed at that time. They once again demanding Statehood for Texas under the 1824 manifesto. It appended to this its reasons, - the total differences in land and background between Coahuila and Texas, the indian treatise signed by the government but not acted upon, causing dangerous dissention, leading to indian attacks on their ranches. This then was sent to the Mexican government at the very time when Santa Anna was assuming control.

Both Victor Luna and Hanz Eliot with many others, opposed the strong language in the Memorandum but, unfortunately, they were in the minority, and it was passed so they returned to San Macros very disillusioned and feared now for their future and that of the women they now loved.

Their fears were confirmed for when Stephen Austin presented the memorandum, it was at the very time when Vice President Ferias was under attack and just before Santa Anna removed him from office. He declared the Federal Government policies of 1824 were now completely removed, and he would establish a fully centralist government. So neither Coahuila nor Texas would have any powers of government but must obey dictates from Mexico City. So Stephen Austin was arrested without trial and denied contact with anyone. He was held a prisoner for nearly a year and a half, during which time the demand for rebellion was growing in Texas, enflamed by Sam Houston, who now demanded complete independence for Texas from Mexico.

Just as Victor and Hanz had prophesied, they had given Santa Anna a perfect reason to attack them. They knew that, they were still ill prepared to deal with the Mexican Army, even though Houston had now introduced a training camp, using his past military experience in Tennessee, whilst fighting alongside Andrew Jackson. Very soon Santa Anna had attacked Zecatecas, destroyed their militia and then ransacked and pillaged their people. It would not be long before he descended on them.

Now everyone near San Marcos were living in fear of this attack. Not only did they fear for the very successful ranches, but even more for the lives of the women they had come to know and learned to love. San Antonio was not far away, it was the centre of government for that area, and militarily controlled. They felt sure it would be there that the Mexican Army would first make its appearance. It would establish its base there, and then carefully, even if slowly, press eastwards both towards San Marcos as well as south wards, to the gulf coast. They were all well aware of the military abilities of General Santa Anna.

In fact Hanz became even more alarmed when Elvira has come to him one day, saying she hoped he would come. If so, he must not try to stop her, for she intended to go to Santa Anna, infiltrated his base, apparently offering him her body again. But this time she would ensure she held a knife and would plunge it into his heart killing him, and saving them all. Her final words before she left him dumbfounded were, "Dear Hanz, I must leave you then. Please take care of our children. However please do not try to stop me."

Poor Hanz did not know what to do. However much, after that, he tried to dissuade her she only smiled and told him she could not go on living, if Santa Anna now controlled all their lives. If he tried to stop her she would kill herself rather than live in that way. He told Victor, but he told him that Elvira would not listen to any of them, and thirsted for revenge for what he had done to her.

5.

"Cherie, dear, you do not fool me," Gordon Taylor was lying on the day couch with Cheri Marshall half lying at his side. She had allowed Gordon some intimacy, which she had recently enjoyed. "I confess my lack of experience as a lover, and may disappoint you. – In fact I seem to enjoy little success with my girl friends. – But I know both you and

Frances are merely playing with my affections. Neither of you have any strong feelings for me. You both just use me for your amusements."

Cherie laughed and gave the side of his cheek a peck with her lips. "But of course, we are women and enjoy and encourage a little intimacy with you. – But that is all. – Why should it be different. Neither of us at present want to settle down and marry, but we both have the same strong feelings, which both you and me have. So let us sublimate them without the need for any permanent attentions. – Don't tell me you are like Donald Reid – It was obvious he wanted us to take him seriously."

Now Gordon had to smile as he replied. "No I'm not demanding a serious liaison between us. – I confess my heart still longs for another girl I met and who seemed to show a strong liking for me. However her parents seemed to think I was unsuitable for her. – No! Cherie, I'm grateful for the liberties you grant me. But tell me truthfully. – Do you not have any wishes to have children?"

Cherie laughed again. "Yes! I am a woman and want a family – but not yet. You see I'm half French, and like my mother I want to enjoy affairs with men before I'm ready to become serious. – I confess you fascinate both Frances and I. I really am proud of my mother and her knowledge of engineering. I love the way both you and mother discuss these things, of which both of you know far more than father. – Again you should know the real reason for my friendship with Frances. – Do you know, father lived with Frances' mother Fay, for several years before either met Charlotte or Francois. Fay was pregnant by another man but father befriended her and brought her to America. I know they still like each other and I'm surprised they never married each other. That is why both our families are so close."

Gordon was impressed as he had not known of this. Before he could inquire further, Cherie was continuing. "Yes! I like to hear you and mother discussing matters. I wish mother had taught me to become an engineer. I suppose it was my fault for I'm lazy. However tell me about your progress on building railways. It fascinated me when you first described how you and your family managed to build that first railway

149

in England. – Truthfully do you think we can build them here and will it be profitable?"

"Oh! Yes! I'm certain of that and so evidently are the banks. " Gordon replied. "You know Charlotte, Roy and I went to place our proposals to the Casimir/Holstein Bank in Pittsburgh. Eric Casimir and John Holstein received us happily conceding lines must be built. It seemed that our original idea of a line from Buffalo to Pittsburgh must wait. Already there a number of persons investing in a line from Baltimore. They want to eventually provide a quicker alternative to the west from the coast at Baltimore or Annapolis, to compete with the slow Erie Canal route. – It seemed that our arrival was particularly fortunate."

Now delighted to find someone so interested in his scheme, he did his best to make his explanation as simple as possible. "What the original investors needed was a workable locomotive to drive the coaches. This was where we could oblige. Since your father paid my family in Manchester to sell us the blue prints of the successful "Rocket" which powers the Liverpool to Manchester Line, and we built "Tom Thumb" as a replica in America, we could offer this to the consortium building the Baltimore line, and guaranteed positions as directors in the company. We are investing along with several others. One important one is a Scandinavian family, called Ibsen, who came to America, primary to invest in the building of hotels, but then became interested in Cornelius Vanderbilt's attempts to use steam power to drive ocean going ships using a propeller at its stern, as paddle wheels are often destroyed in heavy seas. "

Now he paused, merely to give an effect, then smiled and continued. "However realising the location of any hotel made it essential to have good communications for people to be able to reach it, Ibsen realised a quick rail connection would be the answer. He invested, as a trail, in a line to join Baltimore to Washington. Later, if successful to join this and drive north east to eventually reach the Ohio River. Since we realised that this, if built, might injure our profitable river traffic, it is sensible we invest in its construction, so at least to profit from it if our shipping profits were to decrease. Cherie that line to Washington, and a possible extension to Annapolis, will exist within the next five years."

Cherie had been fascinated by Gordon' description. "So you think railways will displace river and canal transportation?" Now Gordon risked gently kissing her lips. "No! Not entirely. I firmly believe there is a future for both. The slower water transport for heavy machinery, and people not in a hurry, and at a cheaper rate. Railways for mainly passenger transportation, and those willing to pay to arrive far more quickly. – It simply means we must set up anther company alongside our present, investing in railway construction, possibly leaving others to actually run it."

Now Cherie asked, "And will you be part of that. Have you the money to invest?"

Gordon replied, "Indeed not! However your father, the bank and now the other investors are willing to include me as a junior director. I am one of the few persons at present living in America who has had experience and helped to build a railway. They realise its success may well depend on my expertise. – I am grateful for your father including me in his schemes, though I believe I probably owe more to your mother. She fully understands the problems, particularly the difficulty of gradients, for there is a limit after which no locomotive could drive a coach. I shall try to train her to understand all these new problems which did not exist in her previous life. I would like to take her to England to see railways working there, but Roy is not very keen."

"And would you be willing to take me?" Cherie now asked. Gordon was astounded. He had never considered she would ask such a question. "Yes! If your father approved and was willing to finance the trip. But why would you want to do it. – Also, what would you be willing to do to recompense me for my trouble?"

She laughed, "It seems you have a desire for even more intimate relationships with me. – I might not mind that – but if so you must not think it would lead to any permanent relationships. – As I said, I'm not ready to settle down and raise a family."

It did seem to Gordon that perhaps Cheri's feelings for him were possibly more intense than he had believed earlier that day, but her idea was too far fetched. Why should her father allow it happen and finance it. He knew he could not afford such a journey. However he did ask, "If in some way it became possible – would you be willing to accept risking coming with me." At least Cherie smiled and did not laugh at him, "Yes! Gordon! I would – and allow those little extra things which we both might enjoy. – However if so – remember – it would only last for the visit."

This completed their conversation. However that night in bed he had to admit he would enjoy such a journey. It would certainly shake his family that a single girl would travel alone with a man not her husband and compromise herself. Such things did not happen in England, but then they did not know how different were these conventions in America. However he could see no reason why Roy Marshall should consider such a project. It would make far more sense if it was Charlotte who came to England with him.

Gordon, could not be sure of his true feelings were for Cherie. Of course he liked her and enjoyed the intimate fondling she allowed him, but as he said that day, he was not stupid and knew she was only playing with him for her own amusement. But would he want a more permanent and not a temporary liaison with her. What really did he think of her. He knew his feelings for Sheila McLean was as strong as ever. However he, also, knew that there was very little chance of him being able to win her and marry her. In fact she soon would marry the man her father had chosen for her – or might have already married him.. It seemed, in spite of what he had told her, Sheila was probably lost to him.

But would he want Cherie as a replacement even if it was possible. Even today, though she had, so blatantly, offered him the use of her body, she had made it abundancely clear, there liaison, however intimate, would only be temporary. As she said, 'to give each other pleasure'. Yes! He would enjoy it but then it seemed she would be no substitute for his Sheila.

Now Gordon had to become a realist. His future was in applying his engineering experience. Now besides ships engines, it was railways which were his future. He had arrived virtually penniless, now it seemed in a very few years he might have become a very rich man. He knew with money he would have the choice of many women. He decided to wait and see what the future had to offer him.

6.

Sixteen and fourteen year old Gloria and Elsa Regio stood completely naked, nearly fainting with fear as they were led into the bedroom of Santa Anna by his fifty five year old mistress Senora Isabel Galvano. They were followed by another of his mistresses Senora Nora Delgado carrying her six month old daughter, Cecilia, her second child conceived by Santa Anna, which like her first, her son, Arturo, now nearly three years old, had caused her to endure a very painful pregnancy and delivery last November. But it was this which pleased her cruel possessor. At least the jewels he gave her were some recompense for her suffering, and she was becoming quite rich,.

She hoped that these two young girls being led into the bedchamber might save her from his threat a week ago to make her conceive his third child. She was now thirty eight years old, but knew he might force her to endure many more painful pregnancies. Perhaps like Senora Galvano who had born him four children in five years starting when she was already forty three years of age. This after bearing nine children and enduring two miscarriages to her late husband. Her last child born in 1831 was when she was amazingly fifty years of age. However, Nora knew, Isabel Galvano was grateful to Santa Anna for not discarding her now she could no longer conceive his children.

The presence of these two naked young girls soon to become the possession of this cruel man, might well at least delay the day Nora Delgado conceived again, for both his mistresses were well aware of his delight in enjoying the bodies of very young women. At his home near Vera Cruz, two previous young girls who became his mistresses Dianne Corila, and Rosa Rechi, now twenty one years of age were both nearly seven months pregnant with his third child, and Santa Anna would soon return to watch them deliver his children.

Now poor Gloria and Elsa stood in front of Santa Anna, seated on a chair, as, desperately, they were trying to hide the nakedness of their most intimate parts with their tiny hands. It was the fourteenth of May 1835. This bedroom was one of several in this large mansion in the better part of Zecatecas, and was actually both Gloria and Elsa home. However this mansion now belonged to the general who was responsible for their father's death two days before, in the two hour battle on the twelfth of May. It was when the General's Army had completely defeated the large army of militia led by Francisco Garcia, trying to retain the privileges given to the State of Zecatecas by the 1824 constitution. But Santa Anna had repudiated this when he dismissed Congress and imposed himself as dictator eighteen months before establishing a centralist system of Government, and removing all power from the states.

Then to teach the remainder of Mexico to conform to his demands he had turned his army on to the streets killing hundreds of people and raping many females. Perhaps Gloria and Elsa were fortunate for his aides had prevented the soldiers taking them away, as they did their mother. They were not to know, but feared their mother would have been raped, as they saw other females suffering, and was now probably dead. That was two days ago and since then both girls had lived in fear.

Now this morning Senora Galvano had come to them with servants, ensured they were bathed and perfumed and now led this little column into he bedroom, but were not allowed to dress. So they stood as sacrificial victims to his sensuous pleasures. They already knew their fate. As they bathed and were perfumed under Isabel's instructions, Nora had appeared carrying her baby daughter, which she was feeding at her bare breasts.

She had laughed cynically, saying, "You are very privileged women. You were saved two days ago from falling into the clutches of the rampaging soldiers. Today you will begin to repay your master, General Santa Anna, by freely offering your bodies to him to give him pleasure. He may take you back to Mexico City but I am sure before he does that he will make sure you have both been given the gift of one of his children, just like baby Cecelia is. He has blessed me with two children and Senora Galvano has been blessed with four of his children.

Of course they were traumatised with the idea of conceiving so young and out of wedlock but knew there was no escape. Now they stood before him knowing he would soon take one or both of them and force intercourse on them. They well knew the consequences, and Nora had told them how many times he would be able to repeat this in the next few days.

At last he arose and came towards them. Both squealed in fear, shouting in panic, "Please Lord Master spare us. Neither of us have known a man before. Please do not do those things Senora Delgado says you may do. We are too young to have children and are not married."

However he merely smiled at them before replying, "Dear girls you are very fortunate women. I will do my best to give you pleasure and in doing so, give you the gift of my child. You will become very privileged women. You need have no fear you will be well looked after, as will be any babies you bear me. I shall give you very valuable gifts. Then later when you find a man to marry, he will be very pleased to make you his wife for you will be very rich. Fear not, forget the things your parents taught you. Instead you will soon learn to enjoy a life very different from that which you would have endured if you had stayed with your parents."

Now still smiling he told them both to come to his bed that night, and that his mistresses would look after them and prepare them during the day, for he had much work to do before evening. Finally he added, "Please do not fear what will happen tonight. I will be very kind to you, more than if you were the new bride of your husband. I know how to give a woman pleasure. Nora and Isabel take them – explain what I expect of them and show them how they can reward me for my trouble."

Without saying more he left them in the bedroom and went downstairs where the officers of his army were waiting for further instructions. He asked them first if the savagery was over and had they restrained any further deprivations and made sure their soldiers were again ready for action. He was assured this was so, though there was still much work to be done in burying the many people who had been murdered.

He called for his scribe so he could issue orders and have them written and signed. First the whole of Mexico should be told what they must expect should they foolishly rebel against him. However Zecatecas punishment was only beginning. No longer would it remain a single state. It must be divided, so it would never be strong enough to rise again. The rich agricultural territory must be separated, given the name Aguascalientes. This was the rich part of the state and so the rest of the state would suffer by its loss.

Finally the rich silver mines at Fresnicco must be acquired as the property of the state, to help pay for the cost of the rebellion but to add to the much need finances of the country. As it seemed the ring leaders including Francisco Garcia and their families had all perished in ransacking of the city, it seemed there were no other important people to be brought before him for punishment. So as a warning, once again, the whole of Mexico must be told the fate of those who caused a rebellion.

Now he gave a special order. "I want all the inhabitants of the State of Coahuila Texas to know immediately what fate awaits them, should they foolishly not comply to my orders. Those Americans living there must realise it would be foolish to try to rebel and I would advise them, as quickly as possible to leave their homes and return to the United States. Their foolish requests for statehood and any attempt to resurrect the Act of 1824, will lead to the same results as has happened in Zecatecas."

Now smiling he continued, "Never-the-less we should be prepared for any possibilities and emergencies. I want the army to be ready soon to march into Texas. Establish our base at San Antonio. My brother-in-law Martin Perfecta Cos will take part of my army and establish himself there. I believe when they see the might of my power and learn what happened here, I shall have no further trouble from these Americans. I know, at present they could not receive any support from the United

States, which is at present, is fully involved in displacing the indians from the land they want for their own people. Come let us enjoy our victory."

It was certain, whatever the others present in that room intended to do that day, Santa Anna was going to enjoy the very youthful bodies of those two women, Gloria and Elsa. Nor was he wrong. There was no doubt but that he was a very virile man. That night both Gloria and Elsa shared his bed and suffered as he took his pleasure of their bodies. Perhaps it was worse for them as they had received a very strict upbringing. It seemed that they had become fallen women, fearing what their church would do to them, for they feared the must expect no forgiveness from their god. It mattered little that their possession was not of their choosing. What future could they have after what this terrible man had done to them that night.

7.

Donald Reid and Rachael Gilbert had travelled from Racoonsville to Rockville so Donald could introduce Rachael to the family directly related to Sir David and Amelia Carroll, who received this estate in 1688, the protestant branch of the Carroll family from Somerset. Rachael had read so much of this from the book Manon Eliot had given her. They received wonderful welcome from both Andrew and Angela Carroll and their son and daughter-in-law, Adrian and Estelle Carroll. Of course they had been expected.

It was fortunate that Edwin and his sister Joan Palatine had once again come to stay with them from New York, though this was now a frequent event. In fact both Adrian and Estelle were delighted that Edwin had taken a keen interest in their daughter Audrey. As her mother Estelle, with her British birth, welcomed a possible association of her daughter with a man of royal descent.

Again poor Rachael had to quickly try to assimilate more complicated relationships. She was told Edwin and Joan were related to the British Royal Family and they were the illegitimate children of Louis Philippe, now King of France, but who had disowned them fearing the scandal would have injured his chance to gain the throne.

Rachael was introduced to Estelle's sister, Julia, married to Aster Brookes. In fact as they stayed, they were fortunate to meet their son, Kenneth, now a captain in the United States Navy. Donald was particularly interested when Kenneth told him that he hoped in the not to distant future to sail into the Pacific, visit South America and even call on the sea ports along the coast of California. The mention of California, once again caused Donald to tell Kenneth, how he hoped soon to visit that area. Little did he know that in future years they were both to meet in that country.

But then there were several other visitors to Rockville. Jean and Kitty Condorset were frequent guests. Kitty was the daughter of Sophia and Keith Brookes and Sophia was the daughter of the famous Michelle Carroll. Unfortunately Keith had died early and after a period when Sophia, to her mother's distress, had tried to ease her sorrow using her wealth to live a somewhat desolate life, before, fortunately, finding another man she could love in Colin Chalmers, and marry, combining his and her estates. Today Kitty and Jean were accompanied by their eldest son, Keith Condorcet.

However soon after they arrived Adrian and Estelle's son Peter Carroll and his wife Amy had joined them. They were accompanied by a Kanson and Isolda Ibsen and their daughter Freda and so to their surprise, was Otto Fallen, who they had met on the boat from St. Louis. It seemed they had all come to discuss the financial proposals of Peter Carroll and his brother-in-law Cornelius Vanderbilt, concerning investment in the Vanderbilt's projected development, of using Steam driven propellers to drive large ships across oceans. If successful it would quickly replace the attempts already made to drive ships propelled by paddle wheels, for these were so easily damaged during storms.

They learned that Ibsen's were rich investors who had come to America, originally, to invest in hotels being established on routes of communication, but had learned of the Vanderbilt project. Since Peter Carroll and the Carroll family at Rockville were already investing, they had persuaded Otto Fallen, now Manager of the Annapolis Bank, with a wealth of family experience in banking in Germany, to join them to advise them on its possibilities.

Donald had known Otto, when he was manager of the local St. Louis Bank, and when he was separated for a long time from Freda. who lived mainly in Washington and New York. He had told Donald that his concern for Freda, for whilst he was isolated from her in St. Louis, she seemed to have found a possible lover in Washington. Now, at last, he had returned close to Washington in Annapolis, and had been desperately trying to re-establish the good relationship begun on the ship. This meeting at Rockville had given Otto a new opportunity to develop this.

Of course neither Donald nor Rachael were in any way involved in these projected investments in the Vanderbilt's propulsion methods, but were delighted to meet so many new people. It did give both eighty year old Andrew and Angela Carroll, a chance to further acquaint poor Rachael of the convoluted histories of the Carroll families. The history of Rockville itself was worth many years of research. However Rachael quickly remembered the facts she had been told, that David Carroll, and the protestant branch, might never have come to America, but for his friendship with Edgar Carroll of the Roman Catholic branch. Edgar had then, offered to bring him to America to work the Rockville Estate. Also, to remember that the other Carroll's, had been living in America for nearly seventy years before this had happened.

From Angela, Donald and Rachel learned of Estelle's recent discoveries, adding to what Manon Eliot had known, about the life and descendents of the original Blanche Carroll, the daughter Amelia had conceived when raped by Edward Calvert in Ireland, before she met Sir David and who he adopted after he married Amelia.

How Blanche, pregnant by Felix Backhouse, had needed to marry Felix and went to live with his family in New York. Donald and Rachael were fascinated to learn of the five further generations of the Backhouse family, now, forced as loyalist, after the United States were victorious, to flee to Montreal. That day they learned of a certain David Backhouse, who they were told had gone west seeking adventure in the Oregon country. At the time it was merely a name they remembered. Yet a few years later they were to remember, when they lived in California, though at that time it was merely of historical interest.

Both Donald and Rachael saw that Joan Palatine had soon stolen away with Keith Condorcet. Angela and Andrew Carroll had smiled as they told both of them that this often occurred when Keith came to visit and no doubt was the reason why he had joined his parents in visiting today.

However during the first few days after they had arrived at Rockville, Rachael had been putting into practice the plan Hedwig Carroll had suggested to her at Racoonsville. This was to adopt a far more intimate approach, whenever they were alone together. Whilst Donald took her on the many short walks around the vast estate, or came to sit of the banks of the river Potomac, Rachael would take the liberty of placing her arm around Donald's waist and sometimes enabled her to take his arm and place it around her waist.

She could see he liked this for, though he never initiated this movement, Donald never attempted to stop her doing so. She knew he must like it, but he never spoke to her about it. In fact he barely offered any conversation except to discuss or describe the beautiful vista. His attitude exasperated poor Rachael. She even began to wonder if he was one of those men who it seemed had no interest in a woman, except as a companion. It seemed he had never developed a loving relationship with another female. After a few days of trying, she decided, even if it harmed the warm friendship she at least enjoyed, she must take the lead to make clear her affection for him.

It was a warm afternoon and they had left the mansion where very complicated discussions on finance were taking place, and walked to its rear where the beautiful gardens were laid out leading to the landing stage on the river bank. Rachael had succeeded in placing both their arms around their waists, but now Donald had broken away and sat on the ground at the beginning of the quay. This was so that they still sit side-by-side. Almost as if to avoid any further closeness, he was speaking, pointing out that on the opposite bank of the river lay both the extremities of both the Gordonsville and Racoonsville estates which they had both previously visited. He told her how much he wished he had his own vast estate like these. It was too much for poor Rachel.

She turned round and attempted to sit in front of him. Though she feared what would be the result, she knew she must make the attempt. "Donald as I said to you at Racoonsville, I still feel I have not been able to come to know you. You always seem to be so far away from me. – Surely by now you must know I think a lot about you. – I do value your friendship – but I must tell you – I really want more. You know you saved my life by enabling me to escape from that boat and go to your mother's - but Donald – it's not to reward you for what you did. - I've found what a truly wonderful man you are. Yet, though you are kind to me, even seem you want to be with and near me – you still treat me as if I were your sister."

She saw the startled look on his face and feared the more she said might destroy the friendship he had given her. But her intimate feelings for him meant she could not endure much longer, the distance he seemed to place between them. "Please tell me, truthfully. – Do I interest you as woman. – I need to know. –If you already have in mind some other woman you might want as a more permanent partner. – Please tell me . – I will understand. – Because if not – I want you to know – I would like to begin a more intimate life with you. – I may be a married woman but I have never known what love was until I came to know you."

Suddenly she saw his face tense and feared the worse. - But it was not to be and very quickly a pleasant smile appeared. "Oh! Dear Rachael! You misjudge me. – I had promised you on the boat I would not take any advantage of you, for I was genuinely sorry for you.. Then you nearly died. You told me I had saved your life. – Dear Rachael since I sat by your bed as you recovered, you kept telling me how grateful you were to me. Ever since then I believed you felt you owed me a debt. One you wanted to repay. – But I never wanted repayment."

Now at last he took hold of both her hands, "Dearest Rachael, you may find it difficult to believe but I have never had a girl friend. – I never felt I needed one. I will tell you now I was smitten by your beauty on that boat – then appalled at what you had to endure. I realised I had to gain your trust – I tried hard not to frighten you. Frankly I did not know what to do. As a result you did trust me, and that meant a lot to me."

Now to her delight Donald, bent forward, and kissed the side of her face before continuing. "Perhaps if you had not nearly died as you came to live with my family, I might have tried to achieve a more intimate friendship. But then I could see you felt in debt to me for saving your life. – Perhaps its because I have never known what it is like to have a girl friend and did not know what to do. – I suppose I thought two things. - If I made any unwelcome approaches you might accept as a reward for the past. – The other was worse – It might be you would wanted to end our friendship. – Rachael I could not bear that. I do believe I've been in love with you since those days on the boat but knowing what you had to endure I did not want to make you suffer more. – Rachael – I do love you – However I feel we should begin to really get to know each other. Please now tell me your true feelings for me."

It seemed to Rachael that in those few wonderful words a new world had suddenly opened to her.

Now she did take the initiative . She virtually threw herself on him knocking him backwards to the floor and before he could stop her buried her lips on his. "Oh! Donald! You must forgive me. I love you! I love you! I have done so for months. I've craved for you to hold me in your arms and passionately kiss me -- and do to me what always happens between men and women who love each other. – Please! Please! Donald show me what love is like, for my husband never tried to do this."

Donald hugged her to him and returned her kisses as fervently as she did hers. Then she broke a little apart and spoke again. "Dear, dear Donald, though I fear what type of woman you may think of me. I want to spend my life with you. There is no need for you to marry me, but I do want to live with you and go wherever you go. – I am not afraid - I will never be afraid when I'm with you. Let us go to Oregon or California or Texas, I shall love it, provided I am with you. Any where so long as we are together."

Donald responded by taking hold of her and pressing her soft body against his. It lasted for some time and it had never happened before. Then he pressed his lips on hers nearly suffocating her. Rachael felt she must have arrived at heaven.

At last she broke away. Then smiling said, "Donald,, whatever you may think of me. - I really do want you – Please let us go to see Angela and see if she would mind if I came and slept in your room tonight – Donald, dear, I want this – and have wanted it for several weeks."

Donald now clasped her to him again, then added. "But if so you must be protected. I do not want you to risk your life again – however much it might be that you feel you want another child. – I want you first to learn if I truly are the man you want – particularly after what Sydney did to you. – You may find you do not like it"

8.

Gordon Taylor and Cherie Marshall had been discussing a possibly more intimate life including a visit to Britain. Yet Gordon felt this was unlikely to become a permanent partnership, for it seemed Cherie still was not yet considering settling down. In any case, though Gordon, now liked Cherie very much and enjoyed his somewhat intimate liaison with her, he still could not forget his still strong affection for Shelia McLean. He wondered if her father had succeeded in further developing her relationship with Simon Doyle. He was not to know that his Sheila was now in Kentucky visiting the Brady family who like her mother were the decedents of Sydney Eliot and Sydney's mother Margaret Eliot, who also were related to so many descendents in America, including the famous Sir David and Amelia Carroll.

Sheila's mother Patricia, had accepted the invitation which Gordon had conveyed to her, the very last time he called on the McLean's. Gordon still relived that very unhappy event which had decreed his separation from his beloved Sheila. Many were the times he had regretted informing her mother of the existence of her relatives from Ireland now living in wealth in Kentucky.

However Patricia had been fascinated by the knowledge that she had relatives living in America, and very soon had written to them at the addresses Gordon had given her. Very quickly she had received replies, not just from the Brady family but the other descendents of Margaret Eliot, and the Downey's who had set up a consortium at Winchester, Kentucky, called the Camargo Equestrian Establishment, establishing a very successful horse breeding business which had resulted in them becoming very rich.

Of course they had often invited her to come to stay with them, but the McLean family had little time for any pleasures as they established themselves on the farm in Cole County, next to the Doyle's, so Patricia had never been able to accept their offer. Their son, Alfred, then twenty one had quickly formed a friendship with, Ester, the daughter of Molloy family on another nearly farm and had married in 1831. Alfred now helped his father to run the large holding, and it was very hard work.

However life for Sheila left much to be desired. Like Gordon, she still, sadly, remembers that day when he called and quickly left again, virtually ejected by her father. She had known her feelings for him were very different to any other men. – In fact he was, virtually, was the only man she had really known, until that day. It is true that since she arrived and Gordon had left, Simon Doyle had called frequently on her, and she knew he liked her. She had responded – but knew this was, mainly, because she knew her father wanted it to develop. It was true that Simon lived most of the time nearby and Gordon had admitted his life must take him away for many months.

It was not that her father disliked Gordon and he knew Gordon had helped them on the journey. Sheila knew it was because her father still wanted her to live close bye. America, unlike Ireland, was a very big place. If she found a life with Simon, she would still live near her father, for at least that would be where they would stay.

Simon, very quickly, showed he liked her very much and she was, almost overwhelmed by his courtship. But then, apart from those few days with Gordon, Sheila had never known what it was like to have a man's attention. Even then she had hoped that Gordon might suddenly appear again. Soon she knew this wish was hopeless, for her father had made it clear he would never have sanctioned her marrying Gordon. Now she realised that her future must be with Simon and to please her family, began to respond to his ministrations.

It developed further during 1831 and on her twenty first birthday in 1832, Sheila and Simon became engaged to marry, and their affair became more intimate, which was a new emotion for Sheila. Perhaps it might have been different, if Gordon had kept his promise and returned. However it progressed and, eventually, Sheila married Simon in September 1833 in the small church in Cole County.

Very quickly she found Simon was a very different man as her husband, than as he had been as he had courted her. She had known that when he went frequently into Jefferson City, he drank very heavily. He would come home, still worse for wear and at times even frightened Sheila. When she told her mother and father, neither of them were very supportive, saying as a newly married man, he had not yet fully surrendered his independence. He did certainly claim his rights and enjoyed his wife's body. Poor Sheila was pregnant within eight weeks of their wedding.

In late July 1834 Sheila gave birth to a baby boy, they named Neil after her father. For a time it did seem to steady Simon, and for a few months he was quite supportive. Then it began again. Worse as it was now necessary on behalf of his family to go to St. Louis for agricultural machinery, he would be away from Sheila for more than a fortnight at a time. She felt sure he was paralytically drunk for many days. When he returned he was sometimes quite ill and completely exhausted. It was hardly a very happy married life for Sheila, but she idolised her baby.

She knew her mother continued to write to her relatives in Kentucky, and her mother now realised the unhappy life Sheila had to live. Patricia blamed her husband Neil for Sheila's unhappiness. Unlike Neil she had liked Gordon Taylor very much. Also she had not felt as possessive of her daughter, as Neil had done. Patricia now knew Gordon would have made her daughter a much better husband than Simon – but it was too late. Patricia was determined to give her daughter a little break from her unhappiness.

When it was time for Simon to once again go to St. Louis, to Simon's horror, Patricia told him she would take Sheila with her and him on the boat. Her father and son would look after his farm. She told him when he disembarked at St. Louis, she and Sheila would continue onto the new town of Cincinnati, which was developing next to the old Fort Washington. She had written to Kentucky and they had promised to meet her with a coach at the quay and then take them to stay at Camargo, near Winchester.

Of course Patricia has insisted Sheila brought as well, her now almost one year old son. So when they arrived they were met by sixty year old Stuart Brady and his wife, Antoinette and travelled in their large coach, over the rough road down to their estate to be introduced to the other four couples, - again descendents of Margaret Eliot, these couples who almost forty years ago had settled there, established their joint business, and became rich in horse breeding and rearing.

Now each had large families of their own. They had become immensely rich and no longer need attend greatly to the days labours, having many employees to see to their needs. To Patricia and Sheila and her baby it seemed they had landed in paradise and knew they would enjoy the full month as their guests.

On the journey Sheila could not but realise she was travelling on a Carroll/Marshall steam boat, and remembered that Gordon Taylor had started employment with that company as he had escorted them to Jefferson City. She wondered as she lay in a lovely bed on the estate, waited on by negro slaves, what Gordon was now doing. Was he still with that company. Had he found another girlfriend – even married, and where was he.

She little knew that Gordon was now lying in his bed in the Marshall household, having enjoyed a rather intimate and enjoyable time with Cherie. She little knew that, even then, Gordon was also thinking of her, wondering if she had married Simon, and still hoped he might yet meet her again. He little knew that Sheila now broke down and cried in her bed, realising the hopelessness of her future life with Simon, and that she was heartbroken that her father had robbed her, of a probably much more happy life with Gordon Taylor.

9.

After his victory and the rape of Zecatecas, Santa Anna retired to his Presidential Palace in Mexico City claiming exhaustion. In fact he wished to enjoy the harem he had installed there as soon as he became President. Now taking sixteen Gloria Regio and her fourteen year old sister, Elsa, now both feared were carrying his child, as he had used them daily since the night he had deflowered them.

Again he wanted to be present and enjoy watching twenty one year old Diana Corila as she bore his third child in six years. Then just three weeks later enjoy again watching twenty one year old Rosa Rechi's delivery. Also as Isabel Galvano was now fifty two years of age, and after dutifully bearing Santa Anna five children in nine years, could not oblige him that way, though was pleased he would still invite her into his bed. Now he was enjoying trying to get Senora Nora Delgado pregnant again, for the third time only a year after she bore his last child. Only thirty eight years of age, she wondered how many more bastard children she must conceive by him.

After the example of Zecatecas of what could happen, should anyone challenge him, the small rebellions in the other states, very quickly ceased and the new centralist constitution for Mexico was voted on and accepted. This established Santa Anna, not only as President, but a virtual military dictator of the country. Though he had heard of some protestations from Coahuila y Texas, they seemed to him as insignificant. He would wait and watch, but little feared any real trouble as their numbers, though a nuisance to him, and were the ones he wanted to be sent back to the United States, they could never hope to better his military might.

In fact he would order his officers to try not to produce confrontations but if they should occur to deal with them ruthlessly. He hoped soon he would be able to drive them back over the border. He could not tolerate Protestants in a Roman Catholic country. But this could wait and he wished to enjoy his presidential rewards to the full. His wife Ines fully understood and approved his infidelities. She was willing to perform her duties as his wife, but was grateful, as with so many other women's bodies to enjoy, he only occasionally demanded she conceived his child. In fact she thoroughly enjoyed the esteem she received as she accompanied her husband at state functions.

But perhaps his over confidence in his power might lead to eventual problems. He failed to realise that the strong sentiments expressed on paper after the 1832 an 1833 conventions in San Felipe were a direct threat to his overall power. It is true, to begin with, they did not call for independence only full statehood under the 1824 agreement. However with men like Sam Houston, thirsting for full freedom, in spite of the opposition of men like Victor Luna and Hanz Eliot, ordinary Texians and even Mexican Tejanos, now would risk imprisonment and even death in demanding their freedom.

It happened soon after Santa Anna returned to his capitol. It originated when Captain Andre Briscoe and his partner Clinton Harris complained about unfair port taxes, to the government commander Captain Antonio Tenorio which resulted in them being arrested. As soon as it happened a local lawyer, William B. Travis, soon to become very famous after his defence of the Alamo, commandeered the vessel Ohio, sailed into Anahuac with twenty five men, and using cannon, forced Tenorio's surrender and freed their prisoners. This was referred to as the Anahuac disturbance. This was June 1835.

During that summer there was an attempt at cooperation, but during September due to a senseless dispute by Lieutenant Castaneda from San Antonio demanding the Texans, deliver to him a fairly useless cannon given to them years before for defence against indian attack. This had resulted in October in a military confrontation on the banks of the Guadalupe River, and so two hundred Texans defeated Casteneda's smaller forces causing his withdrawing to San Antonia. This was referred as the battle of Gonzales.

In December 1835 a far more serious altercation occurred at the Mexican base in San Antonio. The base was under the control of the Mexican General Cos who had almost one thousand two hundred soldiers. However attempting to impose severe restrictions on the movement of Texans, it created a very strong opposition and many camped outside the base for two months, virtually creating a siege.

Just as they believed it was not having any effect, Ben Milam and Frank Johnson arrived and demanded the siege continued, rising their volunteers to over three hundred.

This lead to several confrontations and minor skirmishes. One was called the Grass battle, when Cos' soldiers came out to find and cut grass to feed their hungry horses, but with General Cos still retiring back into his base as they were threatened. Eventually on December 9th after five days of fighting, Cos asked for a truce. Ben Milam was killed in the fighting. After long discussions Cos agreed to withdraw and take his soldiers back into Mexico surrendering his base to the Texans. So now San Antonio, supposedly the chief Mexican base in Texas fell to the Texan irregulars.

It would be months before it returned into Mexican control. It took the massive army brought by Santa Anna to defeat the two hundred odd volunteers, including David Crockett, James Bowie under the direction of Colonel William B. Travis in the Battle for the Alamo, before Santa Anna could once again establish his base there. A fight which raised the call of 'Remember the Alamo'.

So in spite of Santa Anna's superiority in military might, with Sam Huston only now trying to train his volunteers into an army to face the General, Mexico was gradually drifting into a war of annihilation with Texas. A war, which in 1836, after Texas, at last declared their independence, appeared to be one they could never hope to win.

Yet it was a confrontation many Texians and Tejanos wished to avoid. For most feared the strength and ruthlessness of General Santa Anna. They all knew what had happened in Zecatecas and wished to avoid it happening here. But, again, men like Sam Houston were thirsting for a fight, believing that with independence, eventually Texas might become part of the United States.

Now Victor Luna, Hanz Eliot and his beloved wife, Elvira and their children feared for their future. Just as Karl Downey, his wife Raquel and her children, as well as others who had joined them to establish their horse breeding business. Now their world was going to be torn apart, as Santa Anna's massive military machine descended upon them to crush them. All they had worked so hard to avoid, now it seemed inevitable they must lose. It seemed that after 1836 none of them would have a future there. Yet none of them intended to leave, and escape by returning to Kentucky. Texas was now their home, it was their resolution that this place was where they would live or die.

———————————

PART 5

OPTIONS

Lebenstraum Part 5 Options

OPTIONS

1.

The next two years were to provide everyone with many possibilities or options which if taken would result in either success or defeat. They were challenges which had to be faced, and that applied to everyone in the United States and Mexico, who ever had settled there. It applied to the Carroll's, Reid's, Downey's, Eliot's, as it did to Marshall's and others residing near the River Potomac.

Cherie Marshall had failed completely in persuading her father to finance a trip for both her and Gordon to travel to Britain, supposedly to see how successful was the Liverpool to Manchester Railway. Gordon was not surprised, Undoubtedly if anyone should make that journey it should be Charlotte Marshall. Gordon did, however, regret he would not be able to enjoy much more intimate hours with this delightful daughter.

In fact when he meet Charlotte again, a few days later, she had smiled at him. "I'm sorry that Roy has dashed Cherie's dream of taking you to Britain. As her mother I, know only too well, what plan she had, that also involved you, on that long journey. – please tell me, Gordon, what are your true feelings for my daughter."

Actually Gordon was taken aback. He had not expected to be questioned on his relationship with Cherie. He was not sure how he should reply. In fact it was not necessary. Charlotte had laughed, "Dear Gordon don't be bashful – I know how my daughter encourages somewhat intimate relations with all her boy friends. – I do not mind – Remember I'm French and my youth was spent in that licentious court of Versailles. I suppose it is in Cherie's genes. She is so like me at her age. You have nothing of which to be ashamed. – But tell me you do like Cherie – don't you?"

Now Gordon smiled relieved that Charlotte already knew of his and her daughter's escapades. He could reply, "I do like Cherie – but I'm not a fool. – I realise she is only playing - only toying with me. I'm accepted, as I give her some pleasures."

Now Charlotte roared, "Yes. Gordon and I know only to well what are those pleasures. You have no need to worry. I don't believe, as yet, she has not found any man with whom she would wish to spend her life. – Actually I am pleased. – It seems whilst ensuring she does not miss the intimate pleasures any girl needs, she is taking her time – hoping to make certain that the man she eventually chooses is really the one for eternity. Meantime, whilst she offers it, please enjoy my daughter and try to reward her a little."

Now Charlotte changed the subject. "I do appreciate the way you have increased my knowledge in engineering, now to include steam trains and railways. You know my husband is grateful for providing him with this new challenge of the Baltimore to Washington line. I fully support him. He accepts your point. Railways if constructed will challenge our present supremacy on water, so I agree with Roy we must invest in railway construction, as a parallel means of transport."

Now she place her hand on Gordon's shoulder, "Gordon enjoy your relationship with Cherie but the real reason I wanted to see you today, was Roy wants you to be with us when we discuss with our chief accountant, Jack Eliot, to decide how great should be our investment. You know Jack and I are very old friends. It was Jack, with two of his colleagues, David Downey and Stuart Brady, who saved our lives, risking their own, and enabled eight of us to escape death in France during the Terror in 1793. I expect Manon, his wife will come too, for Manon, also owes her life to him."

Charlotte now rang for afternoon tea and as the maid appeared as she was telling Gordon, how much they now relied on his knowledge. "It will have to be you to persuade Jack we should make these large investments. Jack believes it is far too early to risk investment in something which has not yet been proven. That's why Roy wanted you to come today." They talked for some time, and Charlotte once again requested him to help her to increase her engineering knowledge in this new form of motion.

About half an hour later Jack Eliot arrived and as Charlotte had expected, he had brought his wife, Manon, with him. However to Charlotte's surprise but delight, they were accompanied by Stuart Brady and his wife Antoinette who were introduced to Gordon. Again Charlotte had to explain to Gordon that all four who had come, were amongst those who had forty years ago escaped death in France.

However, it was Gordon who was surprised for Stuart Brady told him how delighted he was to meet him. "You see it was fortunate that on that boat sailing to New Orleans, you met our son, Tony Brady and his friend, Steven Downey, as they took those horses to our relatives ranch in Texas. You told us about a friend you had met and her mother's name before marriage was Patricia Brady. Steven and Tony were certain that she was a distant relation – for we are all in someway, related to that wonderful Margaret Eliot, who lived so long ago in Ireland, and why so many of us are now, here, living in America."

Still perplexing Gordon, he continued, "Gordon Taylor I'm so delighted and we owe you so much for informing Patricia about us living in Kentucky. It was because of this that she wrote to us. – Very soon we established communication and invited her to come and visit us and stay for a time. – However it seemed her family were so involved in establishing their new farm near Jefferson City that this was impossible."

Then Gordon's heart leaped, for Stuart went on to add, "Well, eventually, just over six weeks ago, Patricia McLean, as she is now called, accepted our invitation and she came with her daughter Sheila and her one year old son, Neil to stay with us for a month. We all had a wonderful time, and they have only just returned home." From feeling ecstatic Gordon's heart now sank into oblivion. It seemed his beloved Sheila had now born a son, and so his worse fears had happened. It seemed she had married.

Charlotte had been watching Gordon and seen the look of recognition on his face, now seeing, instead a complete look of dejection. "Gordon, I do not wish to pry – but you are unhappy. Did you know this girl Sheila. If so please tell us for it seems to me that the news is not good?"

Tears fell down his cheek and he explained. "Yes! I met Sheila McLean on the ship as I travelled from Liverpool to New York and got to know, and liked her very much. I was able to help her family.- Actually with Roy's employment of me to review your maintenance workshops, I was able to accompany them when they went to live in Cole County, Missouri."

He turned to Charlotte as he continued, "Charlotte, she was the first girl for whom I had any real feelings – I liked her – perhaps I loved her – I know she liked me – but it seemed her father, Neil McLean did not think I was a suitable man for his daughter. He wanted to Sheila to live close to them and he felt my life meant, I must travel extensively. There is no doubt in my mind he wanted her to marry a man on a farm near to them. It seems this is what has happened."

Now a rather sombre Stuart confirmed Gordon's worst fears, "I'm sorry Gordon, I told you about Patricia. I had no idea of your feelings for Sheila. You are right she married Simon Doyle two years ago. Neil is their first child."

Now Stuart came an placed his hand on Gordon's shoulders, "Now I feel I should tell you, and Antoinette will confirm, I don't believe it is a very happy marriage. In fact Patricia confessed to Antoinette that she considered that she now felt it was very wrong that she supported her husband and virtually forced Sheila into Simon's hands. The truth is he is drunkard and uses every opportunity to go into Jefferson City but also St. Louis, and drinks heavily."

Stuart continued, "It seems he must visit St. Louis frequently buying machinery and other things for both their farms. When he returns drunk and exhausted he gives his wife a very bad time. This was why Patricia had brought both Sheila and young Neil with her, leaving Simon at St. Louis – just to give her a time away from her husband."

Now Antoinette came to commiserate with Gordon, "I'm sorry to bring such bad news. – I suppose I should have guessed – We knew it was you who told Patricia about us, and were even more pleased that she brought Sheila to stay. – I had the chance, in private, to carefully question her. She broke down and told me how unhappy she was. She even told me of another man she had met, but never mentioned his name – but she told me how much she would have liked to live a life with him – Now I realise you are that man. "

She gently kissed the side of Gordon's face, "If it is any consolation to you – I really believe she is still, very much in love with you. – However impossible it must seem to you – as I can see you still have the very strong feelings to her, as she has to you. – Gordon, do not give up hope."

Now turning to her husband she said, "I don't believe it would be wise for Gordon to go to Missouri to see her.- I fact I fear the outcome. – Now we know, we must play a part. – We must ask Patricia to bring Sheila to stay again with us again. – I'm certain she will oblige, if only to get her away from her cruel husband. – If so Gordon, we will let you know when she is coming, then Charlotte or Roy can find an excuse for you to 'accidentally' visit us whilst she is there. – Gordon – if you still really have strong feelings for Sheila - then it will be up to you to see if you still might have a future with her."

At least all this sympathy for him restored his feelings a little and he managed to thank Antoinette for her offer. However they rose further when now Charlotte came and hugged him, just as a mother would do. She smiled at him, "Roy and I owe so much to you. I will tell him of your predicament – Together, I feel we shall be able to help. Sadly I fear Cherie is not the woman for you – For that I'm sorry. But we both owe you a happy future – you must trust us."

Gordon stayed and in spite of his sadness joined Charlotte and Roy in discussing with Jack Eliot a future in railways and persuaded Jack that their investment was not only justified but necessary. He stayed there the night. However once again alone in bed, poor Gordon, could not dispel his despondency. He now knew he really did love Sheila – but it seemed she was no longer his to win.

2.

After Donald and Rachael had at last discovered, and affirmed, their love for each other, Rachael practically pulled him to his feet. Now it was his turn to clasp her body to his and smoother her lips with his kisses, so that poor Rachael found it difficult to breathe. At last, though still tightly holding her body close to his, his lips broke apart to say. "You said we should go to Angela to see if she would agree to you sleeping with me. – You now know I want this, just as much as you do. – You said you would like to come with me wherever I went – to live intimately with me and for me to show you what love really was like. – But Rachael I want more than this before this happens."

Just for a moment Rachael feared he did not want to make a commitment, but might want to enjoy her sexually – if so she knew she would agree. An hour ago she had feared what she was to say to him, might lead to him severing their present relationship. It was only her desperate love and longing for him to possess her, which had made her take the risk of losing him. Perhaps now it was what she had feared. - Then he astounded her.

Still holding her close he said, "Yes! I do want to sleep with you tonight. But instead of what you have proposed – Let us go to Angela and tell her we both want to marry. If you could forgo a large wedding with my family and everyone – If you would have me – I would like to marry you this week – tomorrow if possible – for, you may be surprised, I do not want to sleep with you until we are man and wife – Dear, dear, Rachael. – Will you marry me?"

All Rachael could do was to once again sink her lips in his in a very long and breathless kiss, then broke apart and gasped, "Oh! – Yes! – Dear – Dear - Donald - I want you – I want – to be your wife. – Lets tell Angela." Now she spoke with some conviction, "but only dear, Donald, - provided you take me with you wherever you go. – I shall never be afraid – if you are there."

They almost ran back to the mansion and sort for Angela to whom they unburdened their hearts. Angela had smiled, "What marry so soon – don't you want a large magnificent wedding. If you were to wait I would be very pleased to arrange it." They looked at each other, smiled and then replied, together, "No! We just want to become husband and wife – tomorrow if possible – but as soon after, if not."

Rachael knew this moment could never have happened, if Sydney had not forced her and his family to take the boat to Independence. Then in her darkest hour she found the man with whom she could now spend her life. Then she smiled to herself. She remembered Manon Eliot's tale of Amelia Eliot, forced to board a ship to sail for sexual purposes in Maryland. Her meeting with David Carroll and how he saved her life, and his lust turned to love and later marriage. Like Amelia, she had met Donald on a boat. Was this not exactly what had happened to her. However, condemned to a life of sheer hell, Donald had found her on that boat, taking to his home, and so saving her life. Like Amelia it had taken some time, but now, it had happened. Donald had proposed marriage to her. She prayed she might be blessed with the same ever lasting happiness she knew Amelia enjoyed.

They got their wish. Angela and her husband arranged for their local minister to marry them at the little church, where all weddings from Rockville had been held since that day, over one hundred and forty years ago, that Amelia Eliot married her beloved David Carroll. A marriage which released Amelia from sexual servitude as an indentured servant to the Calvert family.

Though it was quickly arranged, far too soon for Donald's family to attended, all the many persons who had come to Rockville so recently for many different reasons, came to the nuptials. They were even more delighted that Mark and Estelle Carroll had come with their son, Danton and his wife Claudia, as Danton and Claudia were returning to Mexico City and intended sailing from Annapolis in four days time. So the four of them were happy to help the newly married couple enjoy their wedding.

In spite of their haste to get married, they had discussed just where and in what way they would spend their honeymoon, yet could not decide on a solution. In fact it was the coming of the four from Racoonsville which provided the answer. Once again Donald had asked how he might be able to journey to California, which had now, almost, become an obsession to him.

Almost jokingly Danton had said, there was one easy way. Since Donald held quite rich resources in letters of credit, Donald could sail back with him to Vera Cruz, then he could take him in the Diplomatic coach which would be waiting for him, to Mexico City. After that his diplomatic position would enable him, to provide a coach for the long, but well used road, to the port of Acapulco. From there, provided he waited, Donald could board one of the many ships that called there, and then travelling north to San Diego, Los Angeles or even further north. Donald could decide which part of California he would first want to sample. Danton doubted if there would be any restrictions if they landed from a ship.

Donald's new bride pulled her new husband to her and said, "Please Donald – Let this be our honeymoon. Let us both go together to California – You must decide where we should first land – though you might, later, want to continue to another place. Let me, as your wife, help you to establish a presence in this land, you have for so long wanted to see. I don't mind how hard life may be, so long as I am by your side.

Donald's answer was to once again to kiss her passionately and then replied, "As a dutiful husband, I must listen carefully to my wife's requests. I have the necessary funds. I will willing accept, your proposals Danton. – Let us join you – Let us go to California in the way you has suggested. – You know Dear, Rachael, we might, yet, set up our first home together there."

Rachael smiled and questioned, "And there, start a family – for I do want a baby to replace the one I lost." Donald only smiled back – but did not reply. So it was decided. The newly weds would spend their honeymoon in California the place the bridegroom had wanted to see for over eight years. Now with a willing wife, it seemed it might be possible.

First Donald had to write two letters, one to his mother and father in St. Louis, and the other to his sister and brother-in-law at Independence, telling them Rachael and he were married. Also that they both now intended to travel, first to Mexico, and then to California. So it may be a very long time before they saw them again. Donald knew they first would be perplexed at his sudden marriage, but then no doubt, would be a little worried for their future.

Meantime Rachael wrote two letters, one to Erin and the other to Helga telling them how well their advice had worked and that Donald and she had married. She thanked them profusely for helping to make this possible, knowing they would be just as pleased as she was. It was time for them to leave Rockville and travel with the Carroll's to Annapolis. There, Donald purchased a completely new wardrobe for both of them, one suitable to their coming journey.

However Claudia took Rachael into town and to a chemist. There to purchase something far more precious for both of them. It was something which might ensure they only increased their family when it was what they wanted. Claudia told her they must purchase a large supply as they were both going to Roman Catholic countries where such things were not easily available. Having learned of their use from Donald's mother, Rachael was very grateful to Claudia for seeing to her needs.

Now they all boarded the ship and spent a enjoyable cruise past the Carolinas and Georgia, across the Gulf and to land a Vera Cruz. They were fortunate that the passage was so peaceful and without any storms or high winds. A coach was waiting to take all of them to the United States Diplomatic buildings in Mexico City. Donald and Rachael had been invited to stay with them until they commenced their extended journey to the Pacific coast and then onto California.

Danton supplied them with a very detailed map of the Californian coast as far a the Oregon country which was still disputed with Great Britain. The mention of the Oregon country, reminded him suddenly of what Angela Carroll had told them of a descendent of Blanche Carroll – a young David Backhouse, - who had gone there searching for adventure.

Now Donald and Rachael had to decide where they should first call on that long Pacific coast. Both knew it would be a difficult journey. However Donald was extremely happy that Rachael would travel at his side. He knew that not only was she unafraid of the hardships and dangers. He knew that she was just as anxious as he was to see California and that she wished to help him achieve his wish to make this land part of the United States.

3.

"Dear Freda, You know how I feel about you, and have, ever since we met on the ship. – Please tell me is there any chance you might have any similar feelings for me." Otto Fallon had managed to separate Freda Ibsen from the others, the day after they had returned from Donald's marriage to Rachael. It was the first time he had been able to talk to Freda in private.

Freda smiled and took hold of his offered hands. "I've known this for sometime, especially after the wonderful time we had together at St, Louis and Independence." Now she raised his hands to her mouth and gently kissed them. "But as I said then, I am not anxious, yet, to think seriously of a life with any man."

She could see the, look of disappointment on Otto's face. He spoke again, "Is it that, or have you discovered, stronger feelings for Pieter Wycks. – I know he is far richer than me, but that will not be for long. I know I shall make a great success at my bank in Annapolis. In any case, my father is just as rich. I know he would help me if ever I should need money. I only left Germany because, I might have been imprisoned if I had stayed. Otherwise I would now enjoy, a position in my father's bank, just as important as Pieter."

Now Freda could not avoid emitting a little laugh, but it was not a cruel one. "Otto, I believe you are jealous. – You have no need to be – I like you very much – I, also, like Pieter. – But as I said then, I don't feel, yet, I can make a commitment – not a permanent one. You know my father relies on me, and mother. Together we decide what is best for our investments."

Now she gently kissed his hands again. "From being a child, father taught me about finance and trained me to be able to understand financial matters. You see he relies on my advice. Before we came to St. Louis he asked my advice about investing in that hotel – just as a few days ago he sort my opinion, again, over this investment in steam propulsion in ships. – Really, I enjoy my work – as I said it is too early for me to look for a man to spend my life with. – But I do like you – yes! – even more than Pieter – but that is all. – I am sorry if that is not enough – for I enjoy being with you."

She could see the look of disappointment on his face as he asked, "Freda, I do not want to lose you, but I need to know, if I have any chance of winning you."

Now even a few tears appeared in her eyes. "I wish I could answer more positively. If it is any consolation, I will say, I do enjoy being with you. – Now you may think I am not the type of woman you might want, someday, to marry – You see I would like to begin a more intimate relationship with you, and this may disgust you. – But I am a woman, I'm twenty six years old, and have the same desires as any woman of my age. You see my mother lived with my father for over two years before she married Kanson."

It was true Otto was a little shocked at her admission. Though he did not consider himself very religious. He had been brought up a Roman Catholic, and up to now had never had any seriously intimate affairs with any woman. Now it seemed Freda was offering him some. He felt even more downcast, "Then it seems I must have disappointed you. But I have always believed I should respect a woman."

Now Freda gently kissed the side of his face. "No, in fact I admit I respect you more for not trying to take liberties with me. – I was merely telling you, that if you felt you would like a more intimate relationship with me, I would not think ill of you. – In Scandinavia, we women have never considered it wrong to enjoy a more amorous flirtation than you do in Germany and Austria. But we were shown how to take precautions. That was why my mother could live with father, virtually as his wife, for so long before she married."

"My mother told me when I was only fourteen that I should never marry any man, until I had truly found if I would want to give my life to him. – It seems, unlike Europe – the same things happen in America." Now tears did stream down her face as she continued, "Now you know the type of woman I am, perhaps you will not want to get to know me better."

Whether it was her tears, or whether her voice betrayed a fear that he would find her wanting, Otto heart leaped. It seemed Freda did care for him and now feared she might loose him for her admission. He could not help himself. She was virtually pleading for him to understand her way of life. Now he took her into his arms, and to his delight, not only did she not object, but gently surrendered her body to his embrace.

Now Otto buried his lips on hers before breaking free and telling her. "Oh! Freda, I'm sorry, I did not understand. Please forgive me. You must think I am a very foolish man. – If you would allow me. If you could forgive me. I would love to accept your offer – an offer with no guarantees of permanency. Let me try to see if I am the type of man your mother told you to sample, to see if it might be the one to spend your life with. Then you can tell me if I really am that man."

Freda hugged him close and again buried her lips on his. It was a very long embrace. At last they broke apart but both were looking at each other smiling. Then Freda took him by his hand and led him upstairs, passed his own room but into her own. Then closed the door behind them – but gently led him to her bed and they both collapsed upon it.

*   *   *   *   *   *   *   *   *   *   *   *   *   *   *

It was obvious to everyone that Edwin Palatine, completely monopolised the attention of Audrey Carroll during the reception celebrating the wedding, and that it seemed Audrey appeared to like this. So it was not surprising that both Andrew and Angela Carroll could see that there was a growing affinity between both of them. They also knew that their son and their beloved daughter-in-law, were pleased and wished to develop their relationship.

However, though like their daughter-in-law, they felt proud of Edwin's royal ancestry, they were aware that he was illegitimate, and that his father, now King of France, had deserted him. So it would seem that Edwin had little resources and would find it difficult to provide for a family. So the next day they asked him to come to see them in their private apartments, which he did.

It was Angela who opened the conversation, "You do like Audrey, don't you – also we could see that Audrey appears to like you. You should know we think greatly about her future and wish her to have a happy life. – For that reason we feel we should ask you what are your resources. Does your father help to finance you?"

Edwin was quite unprepared for this line of questioning but he replied honestly. "No! My father has completely dissociated himself from both my sister and I. You know he never married my wonderful mother, and virtually deserted her after we were born. It seems he fears a scandal might injure his political future. However though he has not, nor will not, see to our future, his sister has deposited with her daughter, - who has so kindly looked after us since we arrived here – a very large amount of money which, divided, will be ours when we marry or reach the age of thirty." Now he smiled, "Though I know and understand your fears – we are not penniless- though I would, very much, like to have a permanent, paid, occupation. You see I do possess a degree."

Both Andrew and Angela showed their surprise. Andrew responded, "No! We did not know. That is a great accomplishment, please tell us about it."

"I graduated with an honours degree in Natural Sciences of Cambridge University. I specialised in Mathematics and this led me to my love of Astronomy – After all Sir Isaac Newton established this faculty so long ago after his treatise on Gravitation."

Now Edwin laughed as he saw he had confounded the other two. "I have particularly made my research into eclipses, and spent most of my free time since I landed in America in calculating them for this neighbourhood. – Would you be surprised if I were to tell you that in five days time there will be a partial eclipse of the moon which will be visible here, and you can see it?"

They were certainly surprised, particularly Andrew. "Do you think you might be able to teach these subjects, particularly higher mathematics?" "Oh! Yes, for a time I lectured at the university after completing my degree. – I would love to expand on these subjects.", Edwin replied. Now Andrew turned to Angela.

Then smiled and said, "Considering the money I have donated to the Annapolis University, now it has been re-established at College Park and renamed the University of Maryland, I can insist that Edwin was appointed to their staff. – Why I believe they have no school of Mathematics, though they have a Professor of Physics – Edwin if you would agree, we might install you as Professor of Mathematics. – I would gladly contribute a little to this formation. If you would accept this I can assure, you would receive quite a substantial salary. Please tell me would like to do this?"

In fact Edwin was astounded. It was an offer he could never have hoped to achieve. Now it seemed to be a possibility. Immediately he stood up and clasped Andrew's hands. "Sir! No only would I agree. It would be a task which I would enjoy. Why, I might even introduce there a school of Astronomy – my hobby would become my future." Then he thought perhaps then I might consider a more permanent relationship with Audrey Carroll. He was in a dream when Andrew Carroll told him he would ensure this happen with the next eight weeks, and smiling added, "Then you will truly have resources of your own."

4.

Danton Carroll had informed Donald Reid before they left Annapolis that he had heard from his superior, Anthony Butler, Charge d'Affaires of the worsening situation in northern Mexico. It seemed small rebellions were breaking out everywhere. They knew of the disturbance at Anahuac and the amazing capture of the Mexican base at San Antonio, which Danton feared would force Santa Anna to retaliate.

It seemed that Stephen Austin had been elected as Commander of the Volunteer army. So this would soon begin further forays against the Mexican Government. Yet it was not just the Americans who were leading this but also important Mexicans. now called Tejanos. Jose Mexia had travelled to New Orleans and obtained large financial support, raising some volunteers and had sailed to Tampico, intending to take it as a port but failed. Thirty one prisoners were executed on Santa Anna's orders.

In fact Danton told Donald that whilst Santa Anna, to his surprise, had retained Congress. In fact its powers were impotent, and had to obey what ever measures he imposed. One was that any one who rebelled must be considered as pirates, no mercy should be given, and they were to be executed. But then there was foolish dissention in Texas General Council. There was the peace party and in November 1836 they had disowned the idea of complete independence, only demanding the re-introduction of the Proclamation of 1824 which gave power to the states.

Yet the newly elected Texan Governor Henry Smith demanded complete independence and tried to dismiss the Council, before he was, himself impeached for doing this. Surely this could not be countenanced, when Texas might be invaded at any time by Santa Anna, and unity was essential.

Danton had told Donald that, now, he felt full confrontation between The Texan people and Santa Anna was inevitable. Also he feared that their small Diplomatic unit in Mexico City could do little to help them if it occurred. It seemed that the President, Andrew Jackson, though, at present avoiding military involvement, had, never-the-less reinforced the number of soldiers along the Sabine River border, ready to help any Texans, driven eastwards trying to escape any conflict.

Donald was both appalled and annoyed that the government were doing so little to help their own countrymen, as he felt that Texas, like California, should be part of the United States. He asked how this might effect this own journey. He was relieved that Danton, felt sure that as he was not trying to get to Texas and in fact travelling west to Acapulco, he would not be affected. However, Danton had told him it would be wise to leave Mexico and travel to California as soon as possible.

*   *   *   *   *   *   *   *   *   *   *   *   *   *

Meantime all the families at San Marcos were very concerned at what was happening. Though they still hoped that a full confrontation might be avoided. They had been delighted to support the election of Stephen Austin as Commander of the volunteer force. But both Victor Luna and Hanz Eliot were regarded as members of the 'peace party'. They still hoped by not demanding independence and supporting the desire to revert back to the 1824 federal system of states and make Texas one of these, it might yet prevent full scale invasion by Santa Anna.

Realising that the so called victory over General Cos in taking possession of the Mexican base at San Antonio must bring retribution from Santa Anna, for Cos was his brother-in-law. Yet most Texans did not seem to see the dangers They had tried to gain support for attempts to call together aid from other nearby states who liked themselves believed in federation. So they had been pleased of the attempt to take Tampico, though felt it had failed due to poor leadership. Again in January they learned of another similar attempt on Matamoras. Yet again this failed.

However, although unknown to them, they felt the same as Danton Carroll, when their newly elected Governor, Henry Smith, defied the resolution of the General Council on which they served. Smith demanded, everyone, including the Council, at once déclassé independence from Mexico, threatening to dismiss the entire council, unless they agreed. In return the Council now wanted to impeach their governor for not obeying its elected decision.

Like Danton, they considered it insane to have two factions fighting each other, when the lives of everyone in Texas was threatened It seemed this infighting continued. Although they completely disapproved of Sam Houston and his strong belief in independence, they knew he understood warfare better than anyone else. So when first he was appointed general of the Voluntary Army and then Commander–in-

Chief, in place of Steven Austin, they did not oppose this for two reasons. Firstly Stephen Austin was to head a commission to the United States for financial and active support, which would necessitating him standing down, in any case. Also, much as they disapproved of the way he had lead Texas towards confrontation and independence, since now it seemed battles were inevitable, both Hanz and Victor knew Houston's military ability. In any fight he was their man.

Yet as soon as Austin left to go to New Orleans, moves were made to limit Houston's powers of decision by appointing James Fanning, as the Council's agent. Then between them Fanning, Francis Johnson and James Grant, along with others interfered and doomed the attack on Matamoras, to eventual failure. Worse this led eight weeks later to the failure of Grant and those at the Battle of San Patricio, defeated by General Jose de Urrea. Of the thirty four competents, twenty one were killed, or later captured and executed.

Much as they disliked Huston's determination to confront Santa Anna and win independence, he must be able to take control of the present volunteer army which was growing. For many more Americans were coming to help the Texans in their coming battle. Besides James Bowie who had, already helped in several ways, very famous David Crockett came with his contingent of Kentuckians and those from Tennessee, and were to become even more famous at the Battle of the Alamo. They now did everything they could to ensure Huston gained full control, in spite of the many who were either jealous of him, or stupidly considered they had more ability.

However all the Luna, Garcia, Eliot. Downey and Brady families at San Marcos knew they must make plans as they feared Santa Anna would soon invade Texas and attempt to destroy all of them. Victor Luna and Hanz Eliot, as members of the council must be willing to make themselves available for soldering under Sam Houston, but they all wished, as far as possible to retain their own lands in productivity, for as long as possible.

So far it seemed all the fighting, with the exception at San Antonio, had been in the south, very near the Gulf of Mexico. Such as Goliad, San Patricio and even Gonzales.. San Marcos was fifty miles to the north-east on a tributary of the River Guadalupe and near to the high ground. It was possible that the battles might yet miss them. They should plan on this assumption, though an attack to retake San Antonio might spread eastwards to engulf them. The sensible thing was to raise their own militia to guard their area, and their estates, after Hanz and Victor left. Of course things may change and they must be prepared to flee eastwards, even as far as the Sabine River and into the United States.

In any case, even if they had been spared the early conflict. If Santa Anna's forces won, they were sure they all would either be killed imprisoned - or at the best driven into the United States. Victor Luna's sons and those of Julio Garcia, along with Karl and Steven Downey and Tony Brady, could organise their defences. In fact they agreed that when Victor and Hanz left, they should take with them several horses to help mount the volunteer army.

But to Hanz the problem was not this, - not even the danger to himself or the possible loss of his lands. The real problem was his wife, Elvira, who he now loved more than life itself. Since her amazing utterance that if it became to invasion she would use her past detestable relationship with Antonio Santa Anna, infiltrating where he stayed and then choose the moment to kill him. Not just to revenge what he had done to her but also for she felt she did not want to live in a country where she must obey everyone of his demands.

In spite of both her father and Hanz' protestations, both telling her how much they loved her, with Hanz saying if she died, he no longer had any wish to go on living. Yet in spite of all they said and begged, Elvira would reply by smiling and saying she understood, but no one would change her mind, only begging them to see to her children. The thought of losing Elvira was far more terrible to Hanz than anything Santa Anna could do to them., yet he felt so helpless and feared it would come about. So the winter of 1836 continued from January into February and now into March.

5.

When Sheila returned from Kentucky with her mother it seemed she had returned to hell. Her husband Simon, was furious at her long stay away. After spending a week in St. Louis drinking heavily and visiting the large brothel in the town, he returned to the farm in Cole County expecting Sheila would return very soon. When he received a letter from her at the end of a further ten days, telling him she was staying away for a full month, he virtually went berserk. So much so that his mother, Mary, and father, Kevin Doyle, were very concerned at his behaviour.

Then he vanished again. It seemed, furious at his wife's long absence, he left and went into Jefferson City, to drink and use the women of low repute. In fact he had not returned when Sheila and Patricia, at last returned. Since no one could tell them the whereabouts of Simon, and in their absence since they left to go to Kentucky, her father Neil and brother Alfred had been looking after the farm, on which Simon had settled on his marriage to Sheila. They felt it unwise for Sheila to remain to await her husbands return, especially with her young son, so Sheila went to live with her mother and father.

Almost a week after this Simon suddenly appeared, still in a half drunken state and came and demanded Sheila returned with him to their own farm. Patricia was loathe to let Sheila go, but her father reluctantly had to agree, when Simon claimed they had no right to keep Sheila, as she was his lawful wife. Now even Neil began to realise and accept, what Patricia had been saying for some time, that it had been a serious mistake to encourage the early relationship of Sheila with Simon and, virtually, persuading her that Simon would make her a good husband.

As soon as they returned to the farm, Sheila life of hell began. It was far worse than it had been before. Not only did he dominate her and caused her to live each day in fear, he would sometimes strike, her when she annoyed him, or failed to react immediately to his bidding. His drinking became worse and then would force her to have intercourse with him, almost raping her. Though she had brought back from Kentucky a large supply of contraceptives, these eventually were

191

exhausted, yet she was not allowed into town to purchase more. Soon she feared she must conceive again by him, however much she did not want this.

Now he would even use his belt on her when drunk and in temper. Even his family began to realise their son was now a viscous bully. Though ashamed, they were not able to alter and change his attitudes. Together they went to see Neil and Patricia to find what could be done. Because in the State of Missouri, a wife, virtually, became the chattel of her husband, and although divorce did happen, it was a very long and lengthy process. Even then it often failed unless the wife was in danger of being killed.. Even if the husband resulted to corporal punishment, the body of the wife had to show extensive scarring before this was accepted as a reason for separation.

Neil and Patricia now feared for Sheila's life and realised they must, somehow remove Sheila from the farm. It would be no use bringing her to the family home as, once again, Simon would demand his conjugal rights. Fortunately their local doctor could see what was happening, and was willing to help. He made a, supposedly, routine visit to see how her son was progressing. He saw immediately Sheila had recently been attacked, as she had a black eye and bruises on both her lips. Cleverly, without referring to her wounds, he demanded to examine her, and told Simon she had some genital problem and must go to St. Louis for medical treatment. Although Simon protested, the doctor insisted, explaining that if Simon did not accede, and Sheila died, he would be charged with manslaughter.

The doctor took both Sheila and her son to her parents house, as he said she needed the attention of a woman, namely her mother, to accompany her to St. Louis. Only when they arrived there did the doctor tell them. Sheila's problems were not truly genital, though he feared she might have recently conceived, but her body was severely beaten. He recommended that, for her safety she should be taken completely away from Cole County, for a time, to stay in St. Louis or somewhere else where she could recover in safety.

Patricia knew she must take both Sheila and young Neil back to Kentucky but if so she had to make arrangements there for their visit. Fortunately on their last visit the families their had told them of their friendship with Alan and Dora Reid and their importance in St. Louis where they lived, as they superintended the work of the Carroll/ Marshall steam boat company. If ever they had wanted to visit them again, quickly, they should go to St. Louis and call on the Reid's, who could very quickly let them know they wanted to come and stay with them.

Since this, also, meant they were actually travelling to St. Louis, it would remove any doubt Simon might have laboured if they were to stay in Cole County, waiting for an invitation. Now very concerned about his daughter's future, and at last realised he was responsible for her unhappy life, Neil, very quickly took them to Jefferson City and waited there with them until they could board a boat to St. Louis. They had already written to the Reid's explaining they would be arriving as they wanted to stay with them until they went onto Kentucky

They had written, also, to Kentucky begging them to allow them to come and stay with them for a time, admitting they were now concerned at Sheila's health, telling them they were taking their advice and going to stay with the Reid's until arrangements could be made, asking them to communicate with them there. So at last Sheila and her mother sailed once again on the steam boat to the quay at St. Louis, and to their delight were met by both Dora and Alan Reid, taken to their mansion near the river and made very welcome.

As to be expected, as they waited Dora asked Patricia, "How did you come to know the five families, and so came to stay with them last time."

Patricia, only a little embarrassed by Dora's question, had replied, "It's a long story. On the ship coming from Liverpool to America we met a very nice man, Gordon Taylor, who helped us greatly, in ensuring we arrived, safely, and with the least difficulty, at Cole County. He then had to travel to Independence – and I believe St. Louis – and down to New Orleans – something to do with your steam boat line."

Now she smiled, "Amazingly on the boat, travelling to New Orleans, he meet two of the sons, of the Kentucky family, taking horses for breading, to a ranch in Texas. One man was called Tony Brady, and Gordon knew my maiden name, was Brady. – Well amazingly it seemed Tony was a distant relative of mine. Evidently we all came from Northern Ireland the decedents of an amazing woman, Margaret Eliot, who lived at the end of the seventh century."

Now for the first time Patricia realised some real embarrassment as she continued. "Well Gordon returned from New Orleans to visit us again. It seemed he had developed an affection for Sheila, whilst on the ship, and afterwards. However, now to my regret, my husband Neil, had considered Gordon was not a suitable future partner for Sheila. Firstly his work would require much travelling and that would mean Sheila was either left alone, or worse if she accompanied him, we should lose the close relationship we enjoyed with our children. Also, though evidently a trained engineer, it seemed he had few resources – certainly not enough to keep a wife. Now I doubt if we were wise and I have many times wondered what happened to Gordon, for after telling me of my relations he left, and we have not heard from him since that day. – still I am very grateful he gave me my relatives address in Kentucky which enable me to contact them, and why we visited them a few months ago."

As she finished her explanation Dora could see Patricia was unhappy and her head had dropped, as she concluded her tale. Of course Dora knew Gordon very well, and now remembered him saying something about a girl he liked but whose parents disapproved of him being with her. So it seemed Sheila now staying with them and with her baby son, was evidently, Gordon's lost girl friend. With some conviction she replied to Patricia, "I do believe you probably were wrong in misjudging Gordon Taylor. He is a fine man. It must have been about that time that he inspected all our maintenance shops. His criticisms and suggestions now operating, have saved our company thousands of dollars. – Well now I think he is gradually becoming a rich man. "

Dora could see the consternation on both Patricia's and Sheila's faces and then saw tears start to roll down from Sheila's eyes. Still she continued, considering they should know the truth. "Well both Roy and Charlotte Marshall think very highly of Gordon Taylor. You see Charlotte is like Gordon, a trained engineer, very strange for a woman, and she saw his value immediately. – We know, he was in someway responsible for building the first railway in Great Britain, so he has persuaded them to invest in a company building railroads near Baltimore and Washington. He persuade them it was necessary for once built, they would greatly reduce our monopoly of persons travelling westwards on our boats. So we are now going to build railroads, and this we owe to Gordon. Oh! Yes! Soon Gordon will become very rich and I believe he deserves it."

Neither Patricia nor Sheila commented on what she had said but Dora believed that poor Sheila, now, felt her present desperate position, was due to her parents wrong decision several years before. However Dora did not press them for an answer.

They stayed there for nearly a week until one of the ships brought a letter telling them that someone would be waiting for them at Cincinnati, with a coach to take them to their large estate. During their stay, Patricia and Sheila learned of the very involved relationships which had resulted in the Reid's becoming friendly with all on the Kentucky estate, also, it was difficult to understand the equally complicated relationships with, the owners of the Carroll/Marshall company in Pittsburgh and the large joint farm of the Hobbs and the Reid's by the river, not far from that town. Neither could, say anything, but these tales completely intrigued them.

Once the letter had arrived Dora and Allan saw them onto the boat, refusing to let them pay any fares and let them sail downstream to Cairo and then onto Cincinnati, where sixty year old Stuart Downey, and his wife Pohanna, waited to greet them and take them on their coach to once again settle on the ranch. Of course they both knew Stuart and Pohanna from their previous visit.

By now Sheila was recovering a little from the terrible treatment meted on her by he cruel husband. She was extremely pleased to be visiting again, having, enjoyed so much her previous time. However when she arrived she was quite unprepared for what awaited her as she descended from the coach and as their luggage was off loaded. Sheila entered the mansion, and saw the many persons waiting to greet her.

Then her surprise was complete, for she saw who was amongst those people, and who were so kind, and anxious to welcome her, for she saw one she knew but never expected to see..

6.

"For over eight years I've dreamed of visiting California, and now it seems it may be possible. I had expected I would have to make this journey alone, now by a miracle I shall be accompanied by my lovely, beautiful, Rachael and has become my wife, - who I love as much as my own life." Donald Reid was looking out of the window in Mexico City, planning his next moves and waiting for the coach to take them, cross country to the port of Acapulco.

Now Rachael came up behind him, place her hands about his waist, pulled him to her, as she forced his body close to hers. Unashamedly she pressed her soft feminine body against his hard masculine back, before burying her lips on his neck She turned him round. Only after a long kiss did their lips part. Now it was her turn to speak.

"Oh! Dear! Donald. I love you. I love you. I do so want to be with you as we both go to explore this new land. – I believe I am your life – the one you gave me – when you rescued me from hell on that boat. You know, only too well, I should have died, if you had not done so. – so by right I am yours for the rest of your life. Never fear for me. I shall be beside you, no matter the difficulties we shall face."

She kissed him again and then said, "You know I really did think you were one of those men who do not want to be with a girl. I tried so hard but you never responded. Then when, at last, fearfully, believing I might loose the wonderful friendship you had given me – when I virtually begged you to take my body and use me – in one wonderful moment – not only did you take me in your arms – and though I offered you my possession, amazingly you would not accept it until we married. – I doubt if many women – suddenly find a man who can love them – accept and marry them in less than a week. – Yet you did this and that is why I am here, beside you, waiting to discover this new land."

Donald delighted pressed his body even closer to hers knowing this was what she wanted. Then a little frown appeared on his brow. "Dear! Dear! Rachael. It was wonderful for me to discover you loved me and your friendship was not simply a reward for what I had done in taking you from that evil man."

Now it seemed he was finding difficulty in what he was to say. "Dearest, I heard what you said, just before we left Rockville, and after we agreed to try to visit California. I remember, almost your plea, for us to start a family. – Rachael, I do want one, - I know how much you want a baby to replace the one you lost. – But – er – well – can you love me enough to agree to wait for this. – You see – I just do not want to visit just one place in California – I crave for adventure there – I want first to explore the whole coast – then probably go inland to the mountains. – Dearest! I want you with me. It would be both difficult and dangerous if you were pregnant at the same time."

Immediately Donald could see the disappointment on Rachael's face. Of course he knew how much she wanted that child. Then he was more than gratified as she replied, "Donald- I've told you – just how much I love you – how I believe my life is now yours – and now will always be. – Donald I do want your child – many if you love me enough – but I am now your wife. I want to be with you. Go wherever you go. – I can see if I was pregnant, not only would that be difficult and dangerous – it might rob you of your chance to do the things you want. – It will hurt – but, after what you have done for me, I will agree. I shall do everything possible not to conceive – if it occurs – it will be an accident – for I still want to enjoy the wonderfully intimate life you have given me. One I had never known in my years with Sydney."

Donald kissed her again and simply said, "Thank you. I shall remember your sacrifice today. I promise, sometime, not to far in the future, to reward you for your patience."

Now it was time to say goodbye to Danton and Claudia, the coach arrived and they loaded their luggage and departed. It was a hard and long journey over a very poor road, but the weather was good, even if a little hot.. It was a journey of over two hundred and fifty miles and they could travel little more than thirty miles each day. Fortunately there were taverns where they could eat and rest. So it took them eight hard days before they arrived at Acapulco, tired and exhausted.

However they found it a delightful place. Small but with good port facilities and they took up residence at a small hotel near the waterfront The coach, belonging to the Diplomatic corps returned immediately to Mexico City as soon as they were accommodated. Now it was time to look and wait for a boat which did trade with the various ports along the California coast. The main trade was for furs, also importing hides, and soft goods, but there was considerable trade across the Pacific to China and Asia. So they had to wait some time.

After some weeks at last a Brig 'Catalino' whose master was Joseph Snook docked at the port. As was the norm, he intended to sail north up the coast calling at ports on the way to purchase goods, readily available from Californians or Californios as they were usually called. It seemed these hides were especially valuable and brought good prices on the east coast of America. Captain Snook was delighted to give both Donald and Rachael passage on his ship, for which he was well paid.

Neither had sailed before and as the early part of their journey was very rough, they did not enjoy their new domain. However as they drifted slowly along the coast of which Snook, called Baja California, the weather improved and soon they came to enjoy the sunny if windy days. They were never far from land. It seemed that this coast was called Baja California but where they were heading was referred to as Alta or Upper California.

As the captain had travelled this coast before, Donald spent several hours absorbing the wealth of knowledge Snook retained. Donald found the first important port they would meet was that of San Diego, then further up was the growing village port of Los Angeles. Still further north was the already settled port of San Francisco. This port interested Donald and was told the Presidia in charge was doing everything possible to prevent the incursion of so many people of different nationalities. These included Russians, British but ever more Americans, coming south from Oregon.

Donald discussed with Rachael what they should do. She suggested they first founded a base, even buying a small house in one of the ports. Then after discovering what happened in every day life in the town and the area around they might take another ship and travel to both Los Angeles and San Francisco. After all Donald had told her that he had many letters of credit, so had the resources, but both, also, knew they must husband these, and if possible add to them.

Finally they both agreed they should land at San Diego when the ship sailed into the port. There they should disembark, first find a small inn, as Snook told them there were few hotels existed. Then as soon as possible they should purchase a house, if any were available, and set up a home. This could become their base. From here they would first discover what San Diego and the surrounding land had to offer. They now knew of the Missions, though they had been told they were now, being dismantled and the land was available for purchase. Only after this should they proceed further up north, though Rachael could see that Donald was fascinated about what he had heard about San Francisco and the mixed population there. Rachael knew it would not be long before Donald wanted to visit that area.

Soon their ship was entering the La Playa, the old Spanish Anchorage in the vast Bay of San Diego. At last they drew alongside the quay and tied up. As the Catalino was to stay here a few days whilst Joseph Snook purchased a large consignment of hides, available at a very low price, which would make a good profit in the United States. Donald and Rachael stayed on board but ventured into the town. They found the place was very small with only a little over five hundred people living there.

In fact they were fortunate and had no need to find an inn to stay, as they discovered a small, but four roomed stone house vacant, as the previous owner had left and so far no one had come to purchase it. Donald was able to buy it at a ridiculously low price, though he had to lie, as he had to swear they were both Roman Catholics, a provision demanded by the law there. However it seemed this was not enforced very strongly, and they might not, even, need to attend church.

Both Rachael and Donald, strong protestants were amused at this foolish demand. However, even if they were eventually forced to attend mass, they knew their obligations would be insincere. Having bought the house they left the ship and brought with them their belongings. Now using Donald's credits Rachael enjoyed her wifely duties of creating a home in those four rooms. It was their first home of their wedded life, but Rachael now knew Donald so well. She would have to be able to plan many more in future. Still they had achieved their first desire. They had arrived in California and established a home there. It was March 1836.

7.

Now with investments occurring regularly in railway construction, as a working junior director of the company, Gordon Taylor had to spend weeks away, as the Railway line joining Baltimore to Washington was taking shape. Although he had other engineers to help him, his knowledge far exceeded these men. In fact, at her request, though she was now over sixty years of age, Charlotte Marshall was very fit, so Gordon had gladly agreed to take her to south Maryland and learn from him, as he surveyed the best route.

They were also, investing in another lines planned from New Jersey, via New Brunswick and Trenton to Philadelphia. So Gordon took Charlotte on an investigation trip to survey possible routes. Here he found her help invaluable, for he found she could quickly translate his measurements into a scale drawing for the proposed line, including, graphically, showing the gradients. There was no doubt but that Charlotte was a very accomplished draughts woman, and it pleased her that Gordon considered her so invaluable to his own work. They had formed a team.

As they retired at night to live and eat in the camp, food brought to them by the many persons employed for this purpose, she showed him, in return, how much they needed his expertise, and it pleased him that she, with her own excellent engineering background, seemed to consider him her equal – even her tutor.

As they ate she said, "I know Roy has given you a reasonable salary, but you still have few resources. Yet you are now vital to our financial future. Just making you a junior director is not enough. I know you are loyal and feel you owe us respect for helping you in the past. I know you would not desert us and join a rival company – but you could, and no one could blame you."

Now she smiled at him, "When I return I shall ask Roy to more than double your present salary. We are very rich, we can afford it, and it is you who will ensure we get good returns from our investments." Now she laughed, but not unkindly and continued, "In any case if you are to pursue your quest for the hand of Sheila Doyle, if she should think kindly of you, eventually leading to you setting up home together – yes – and starting a family - besides what she already has.- Then you really will need extra resources. – I'm sorry if I seem to pry – but will you tell me how this liaison with Sheila happened."

Gordon looked at her and tears welled up in his eyes, "I don't mind telling you everything – but now Sheila is legally married to another and has born him a son. I really cannot see that I have any chance with her. Of course I want to meet her again, but she could not possibly leave her husband, even if she wanted. – Anyway let me tell you the whole story – and how it happened."

Then explaining for the first time why he left his family in Manchester – though not poor – it growing size made life difficult. How he had propelled himself and his luggage on the nearly finished railway to Liverpool, having accepted his uncle, Silas, suggestion to come to live and work for him. Meeting the McLean's on the ship, their lack of knowledge of how to get to Missouri, his help, bringing them to stay with his uncle, and then as Roy had asked him to test the efficiency of their maintenance shops, was able to accompany Sheila as far as Jefferson City.

Now he continue, "Charlotte I knew very soon Sheila liked me. I doubt if she had ever had a real boy-friend before, for she was very shy. – I promise I did not take any liberties with her, but knew I wanted to continue to be with her. I'm sure then this was, also, her wish. Well everything seemed right. I knew the McLean's were grateful to me for helping them arrive safely. I left and did the work for Roy, looking forward to returning to perhaps commit myself more firmly to Sheila."

Now he broke down sobbing and Charlotte had to comfort him as she asked, "Then what happened?" It was a little time before he could reply and his answer was broken with his sobbing. "Neil McLean made it very clear - that he would never approve of Sheila - ever considering - marriage to me. – I could see he wanted to - dominate his daughter, - and keep her living near him. He virtually told me - he felt Simon Doyle would make Sheila a better partner."

Again Gordon broke down but then appeared to recover, "I asked Sheila if she loved Simon. – There was no doubt in my mind - she did not love him – but respected her father's wishes. – I was devastated, for some five months I had been living just to return to Sheila, now in a few minutes all hopes for me were dashed. – I did speak to her mother Patricia, telling her of her relations in Kentucky who wanted to get to know her."

Now he laughed very cynically, "Afterwards, until just recently, I regretted doing this – yet now it has provided me of news of Sheila after her visit to Kentucky. - I told Neil McLean, I would not give up seeking a life with Sheila and would be back – Now I regret I never kept my promise. I suppose your husband was so kind to me and seemed to believe in me, I wanted to devote myself to helping him, but more to become successful. – Perhaps it's my fault – I became too absorbed in my own future and now it is too late."

Now Charlotte put her arms around him, hugged her to him, just as a mother would do, kissing the side of his face. "Then it seems we must take the blame. – By helping us you denied yourself this opportunity. Now we truly have a responsibly to help you. I agree with Stuart, you must not go to Cole County – It might even lead to a duel, but if Sheila ever comes to Kentucky again, and Stuart informs us – Gordon you must go to her – Whatever you think – you must tell her what you've just told me. You both deserve a life together."

She kissed the side of his face again. "Gordon, we are very rich, and we have many powerful friends – Together we can do things to help you. Marriages are not in dissolvable. – But it will take time. I can see that our first task is to separate Sheila from her cruel husband. – If you can ascertain, however much she may believe, she must remain with her husband – if you can discover whether she still would have liked, - even now, a - life with you. Then you must tell us. Only then can we try to help and make it happen."

Now Charlotte laughed, "You know, now, I'm really sorry that your relationship with Cherie has not matured to a happy conclusion. - I know you would make me a very good son-in-law – and more important make my wild and sometimes irresponsible daughter – a very good and loveable husband. It is strange how little we can plan our lives, however much we think we are doing. – Sometime I will tell you in detail how Roy and I came to live together, before we felt we could commit ourselves to a permanent partnership. – In fact I owe a lot to Fay for my present happiness, for she lived with Roy for a long time, before I knew them. So I was delighted she found she could love my brother, Francois."

After that evenings conversation with Charlotte, Gordon began to feel less sad. Perhaps he might yet have a future with Sheila – but if so what about Cheri. However much she might be using him, there was no doubt, but that she had strong feelings about him. Possibly, like her mother, she might want to start a fully intimate life with him – at least for a time. – Oh! Why did he feel so strongly for Sheila. Whatever Charlotte had said, he still believed he had no future life with her. Again, he was not a cruel man, he did not want to hurt Cheri, who had kept him sane in those first weeks when he had arrived at Pittsburgh from Cole County.

Now, it was with even greater energy, he threw himself in surveying the routes for their projected railways, happy that he could see Charlotte was enjoying her work, just as much as him. Eventually, it was time for them to return to Pittsburgh to report of their successes. However when he arrived he found a letter waiting for him, which once again, tore his life in two, but knew he must act upon it.

8.

Poor Sheila could not believe her eyes, for she had just arrived at Camargo and entered their magnificent mansion, now she saw amongst those many persons, waiting to greet her, was none other than an immaculately dressed, Gordon Taylor, who she had last, sadly, said goodbye, over five years before. Poor Sheila was devastated as she then remembered her farewell words to him as he had arrived from New Orleans, 'I am afraid, Gordon, we can never have a future together.'

Now as she saw this handsome man standing in front of her smiling kindly at her, how very much she regretted having said those words to him. It had been her rejection of him which had resulted in her, now, very unhappy life. Again she knew she had been foolish, for even then she had harboured strong romantic feelings about him. The man who had become her first boy-friend after they met on that boat sailing from Liverpool. She knew it was only because her father had forbidden any relationship with him, that she had made her say those cruel words, and sent him away. It had been her father who had encouraged her to develop a romantic friendship with Simon Doyle.

Sheila was almost in a dream as Gordon, still smiling, came forward from all the others waiting there, took hold of her right hand, raised it to his lips and gently kissed it. Then still holding her hand he said, "My Dear Sheila, it is wonderful to once again meet you and welcome you to your holiday here. I feel fortunate that I chose to come for a visit to Camargo, just at the very moment you, also, came to visit."

Still in a dream she heard him say, "I do hope during our stay here, I might enjoy the pleasure of your company, for I'm sure you will remember those happy days we had, first on the ship, and then on you long journey to Missouri. It would be wonderful to renew again our past acquaintance." Poor Sheila could not find the words to reply, for her head was swimming and her heart was overflowing, at once again meeting this man, who had meant so much to her. All she could do was the nod her agreement, as he released the hold on her hand.

Now it was time for all the other persons to come hold her hand, kiss and even hug her to show their welcome. As Pohanna who had followed behind her, into the house, now leading a hardly conscious Sheila and her mother upstairs to their room, with the luggage carried by servants following. Sheila was further embarrassed when Pohanna said, "I did not know you knew Gordon Taylor. We think he is a very kind man, and are very pleased when he decides to call upon us. For you should know. He is a very busy man, becoming extremely rich. He is now an essential member of the Carroll/Marshall Steam Boat Company and several of their subsidiaries." Once again both Patricia and Sheila learned of Gordon's, financial success.

Of course Pohanna was only one of the players in the magnificent charade, organised so brilliantly by Charlotte Marshall, and why that letter had been awaiting Gordon, on his return from Maryland. Its members were very numerous, not only all those at Camargo, as well as those in the Potomac valley, but this extended to all branches of their steam boat company. Both Alan and Dora Reid were part of the scheme. So it was Dora who alerted Charlotte, to what was happening, as soon as Patricia had written to her to tell them they were coming to stay.

Once Patricia and Sheila had descended on them, and learned of the plight in which Sheila was placed, realising that Simon Doyle would soon become suspicious of his wife's departure, and feared he would soon come to St. Louis to the hospital to see his wife, Alan set in motion an elaborate spy system, which would alert him of the moment Simon appeared in St. Louis, but also to try to discover his reaction when he found his wife was missing from the hospital, where she was supposed to have gone.

They were all well aware of the laws of Missouri and the conjugal rights of husbands over their wives. Charlotte had guessed that, even if he could not get Neil McLean to inform him of where his wife now resided. He must remember her last long visit to Kentucky and would, almost certainly descend on the ranch, possibly with a Missouri's law officer, to demand his wife's return. Though their power might not be upheld when on Kentucky soil. It would almost certainly meant Sheila being, even if temporary, held in a jail in Lexington.

Assuming that Sheila could be persuaded to challenge her husband and not capitulate to his demands. Then it was essential that Sheila should be moved to a place of safety before Simon arrived with his demands. It was those in Kentucky who were able to assure Charlotte this was possible, as, for many years they had been friendly with another family, who had helped them in the past and even, for a time lived near them. So too, these persons had been alerted and promised to help them when necessary.

Now the key to any success would depend on the attitude of both Patricia and Sheila, should the occasion occur. Dora felt sure that Patricia would respond favourably as she had, carefully, questioned her as they had stayed with her. Patricia had told her she now feared for the life of her daughter with Simon, and would do anything to try to keep them apart.

However it seemed they could not be so sure of Sheila. Though she had now lost all of her love for Simon and was terrified of him. She had given her vows in church, and still felt, as he was her husband, he still had justifiable rights because of this. They all knew it must be Gordon, who somehow, must change her mind. Even Gordon felt there was no chance of him persuading her to elope with him, though he told Charlotte when in Maryland, if Sheila had been free, he would now, have willing proposed marriage to her.

This then was the position as Pohanna left both Patricia and Sheila to settle in their allocated suite, asking them to refresh themselves and then come down to sit for a meal with the entire family. This they did.

There was little opportunity for any private conversation between Sheila and Gordon that evening, as the ate together and then indulged happily in after dinner drinks. Something neither Patricia nor Sheila usually enjoyed at home. But then Sheila's mind was still in a state of shock, of once again being thrown into the company of Gordon Taylor. As she lay in bed, unable to sleep, she wondered, first what Gordon, now thought of her, and knew the next day she must discover if he had married. She did want to converse with him, though she feared there could never be a future with him.

In another part of the house Sheila was unaware that Gordon was thinking similar thoughts. Meeting her again today was like opening a new page of his life. He thought her so beautiful as she ascended the steps into the house and his reactions were such that as he had taken hold of her hands, he knew he wanted, there and then, to take her into his arms and cover her lips with his kisses. He knew then, what he had, now, believed for some time. Gone were any doubts. Gone were his pleasure in his affair with Cheri Marshall. He knew now that he did truly love Sheila and must have loved her, unknowingly, for some time.

Charlotte had instructed him before he left her to come to Kentucky, not to rush matters, however much were his desires. Sheila was not Cherie. There was no chance, however much seeing him again affected her, that she would respond as Cherie so willingly did. He must remember she was a married woman, of some three years, married with a son by her husband, and now, possibility pregnant by him again. Sheila, however much she might want it, could not yield herself to him, however much he tried.

Charlotte had told him he must woo her very carefully, not raise any fears in her mind that he might be trying to seduce her away from her husband. He must show his concern to her and to impress on her that if she returned to live with Simon, she might not live much longer. Sometime soon, Simon in a drunken rage might attack and kill her, even if he had not wanted this to happen.

In virtually a few days, Gordon, must try to impress on her mind, that she must get away from Simon, certainly before he might find her. Reminding her of her responsibilities as a mother to her son, Neil. However she might feel about her duties as a wife, her first duties as a mother was to her son. She must ensure she lived and why to return to Simon was far less important, than of ensuring a happy future for her son. Charlotte felt he must decide how strongly he told her of his feelings for her, but on no account should he propose, or she left Simon to come and live with him.

Gordon knew what was his most difficult task during the next few days. To gain her trust, and yet somehow submerge his strong desires to persuade her to come and live with him, especially, as he could not make her his wife, however much he desired this. The only important thing was to convince her to let these people, she now recognised as her friends, spirit her away to somewhere where Simon could never find her. What happened later would depend on the plans, already in Charlotte's mind of how she could obtain a divorce for Sheila from Simon. She thought she knew how this might be achieved but she had not, as yet, told anyone of these plans.

So Gordon before at last, his mind still in turmoil, fell asleep, very tired and the night almost over, Gordon knew so much depended on him, and how Sheila responded to him the next day.

9.

At San Marcos, everything had been done to prepare for a possible attack by Santa Anna's Mexican troops. Several places for defence with the possibility of retreating eastward, if necessary, to a new defence points had been planned and instituted. It was February 1836 and news had arrived that Santa Anna had left Mexico City with his army, and had now reached Guerrero, then proceeded and crossed the Rio Grande so, already, had entered territory claimed by Texians. However there was still foolish dissention within Congress and both Victor Luna, Hanz Eliot and several others decided they must try to stop this.

So they left San Marcos and went south to where Congress had set up its base. It seemed that Colonel Fannin was still attempting to gain control of the Volunteer Army over Sam Houston. Together, with others they forced a meeting of the General Council, and demanding the presence of both Fannin and Houston. In fact Fannin was away in the south west and could not attend..

Houston of course was well aware of how, particularly, Victor and Hanz, had for so long opposed him, and the way he seemly wanted confrontation with the government, and seeking complete independence. So now Houston believed they had demanded this meeting to remove him from control of the army, possibly favouring Fannin. But he was ready to fight them. Within a few minutes he was disarmed.

His supposed enemies were demanding that Congress gave Houston, not only complete control of the army, with powers over any of his subordinates. He must be given, complete, powers in deploying and controlling the army, if necessary, without the first approval of Congress. Although there was much opposition, as Fannin and others had good friends, who considered they were better qualified in military matters, a vote was passed which gave Houston overall control. Though he realised, that later, they might still attempt to interfere, especially if things were not going well.

Still he could not understand that, particularly, Victor and Hanz had given him such strong support. As the meeting broke up, he came to address them, "Frankly gentlemen, I have never considered either of you my friends or supporters. Since the Convention in 1832, you seem to have opposed me in every way, often winning points against me. – Pray tell me, why today, you took such a radically different line?"

As an American Hanz considered he should reply. "Sam Houston, from the start, possibly even acting on behalf of Andrew Jackson, who you knew, - you did everything possible to cause confrontation, and seemed to hope we should demand independence. – We did not oppose you because we did not want independence, but considered that our numbers in Texas, and our lack of training, meant complete disaster for all of us and the life we enjoy, for, frankly, we are no match for Santa Anna's military machine."

Now Houston smiled cynically and asked, "And have you now changed your opinions and believe we can win?"

Hanz smiled in return, "Of course not. Unfortunately I believe that within six weeks or less Santa Anna will have routed us and gained complete control. Many of us will be dead, our homes destroyed, at the best still alive, but forced back to the United States."

Houston raised his hands not comprehending what they said and asked, "With such defeatist attitudes, why support me today. Is it because you believe I must fail, you want your revenge and make sure the blame falls on me?"

Still smiling Hanz replied, "No! Just the opposite. Both Victor Luna and I believe that, however small is our chance of success, you above any other man, is the only one, who miraculously might achieve the impossible. – You have proved your abilities in the United States, and as a young man I learned of your brilliant campaigns. - From today we will support you in very way. We will stand beside you, and if necessary, die, in the attempt. – Now the die is cast. – We must fight – It is death or Independence. Further more I'm certain we can get you the support of many who think like us and who have been your opponents in the past. – Now! Are you willing to forget the past."

Now Sam Houston laughed outright held out his hand and took Hanz and Victor's in turn, "Glad I am to do this. In fact, now, I admire you more for your attitudes. I believe I at last understand you past opposition – but today you have shown me, that you believe – all that matters, is that we have the best chance of success. I hope I can rely on you during the next momentous weeks, for you know, even after today, I shall still have strong opposition from many members of Congress and their friends."

So an unusual alliance was forged between them that day, and one, born in adversity which would last for many years. However matters were developing rapidly, even before Houston could exert his authority. Victor and Hanz made a rapid return to San Marcos, knowing they must soon go back to join Houston and the army, But before that, both wanted to receive the love of their families, believing that it might be the last time they saw them.

Hanz took his beloved Elvira in his arms after she had laid down to sleep, their one and a half year old son, Juan. Both knew that Elvira had conceived their second child, but it was the early months. "Dearest Elvira, I cannot honestly tell you that I can believe we can win. Santa Anna has too large an army and they are well trained. "

Now she gently kissed him, "Yet you are going with Houston to fight – perhaps die." He kissed her, replying, "Yes! Dear, it is a possibility – both your father and I may die, but so could so many of us even if we stay here. Perhaps it is wishful thinking, but I believe Houston could do it – he's faced impossible odds before in the United States. – I know he will wait, retreat, until he discovers a place, an event, which might just give him a chance of success. My task, being with him, is to try to prevent those fools in Congress trying to force his action too quickly."

But now he hugged her even more closely, "My only worry is you – and your insane desire to revenge yourself on Santa Anna, and to destroy yourself as well as him. – What then will I do?"

She just kissed him and replied, "Dearest, cannot you see that I too fear for your life. – What life is there for me if both you and father are dead. – At least I shall be trying to do something which might produce a victory. Without Santa Anna to lead them – Houston, might have a chance."

Hanz was devastated, "So you do this as a sacrifice of your life to help Texas."

Now her voice dropped as she replied, "Yes! I only hope that is my reason. But dearest, no man can possibly imagine what it means to a woman, when she is taken and raped, raped repeatedly, just to ensure she conceives his child. – Perhaps it may destroy my soul, but I must avenge myself on this monster, who not only debased me, but many other young women." She looked hard at Hanz as she concluded, "However you try to stop me, I shall find a way. Please, Dear, dear, Hanz forgive me. Even your wonderful love for me, is not enough to prevent me doing this."

Hanz said no more, though he had made and continued to make plans, to prevent Elvira leaving San Marcos and going to Santa Anna, but he knew they could not watch her night and day. So Hanz tried to ascertain what was the true position of Texas at the moment. Events were happening so fast.

Before they had ensured Sam Houston's undisputed command of the army, Governor Henry Smith had given orders of his own, without consulting anyone. Liking the man, he commanded Colonel William Travis to go to San Antonio, and take charge there, to build up the defences of the Alamo, the original Mexican base, and try to prevent it falling, back, into Mexican hands.

Travis did this and besides his own militia, received support from James Bowie and his men and a larger consignment from Kentucky and Tennessee from David Crocket and the New Orleans' Greys. Travis had sent a request to Colonel Fannin for reinforcements. Here Fannin showed his incompetence, in spite of his bravery. In control of five hundred trained soldiers he set out for San Antonio. But it was ill prepared, his carriages broke down before he reached the River San Antonio, and by then Santa Anna had arrived at the town and his soldiers fanned out preventing Fannin joining Travis, so had to retire back to Goliad.

So it seemed Travis with Bowie, Crocket and some two hundred and fifty Texans and Tejanos must defend the Alamo on their own against the full Mexican Army which was slowly gathering and pouring into the town to destroy the bastion, defended by so few men. They were fully prepared for the fate now decreed on them on March 3rd. 1836. Just one day after Texas, on March 2nd. declared its Independence from Mexico and David G. Burnett was installed as their first interim President. – Now the battle had begun. The fate of so many American and Mexicans in Texas now depended on what happened in the next few days, and there were few options,

It really began with the Battle of the Alamo, and the battle for San Antonio.

PART 6

DEVELOPMENT

LEBENSTRAUM PART 6
DEVELOPMENT

DEVELOPMENT

1.

The future of Texas trembled in the balance. Santa Anna had entered San Antonio with some five thousand soldiers, surrounding the Alamo with its mixed contingent of defenders of about two hundred and fifty men, some, still, with their wives and children around them. They knew, now, that no further reinforcements would reach them. Now Santa Anna raised the red flag, and the defenders, well knew its meaning. Surrender now without a fight or no prisoners would be taken, and all would die.

Whether they could believe they had a future, even if they surrended, knowing all who took up arms were to be killed, no one could be sure. But Colonel Travis answer was to order them to fire the cannon, signalling they would fight. The unequal, battle began and lasted thirteen days before the Alamo was overrun and every man inside, except for two slaves, were massacred. However its resistance had done three things. Firstly, it showed that only a few could hold up a superior army for a time. Two, it gave Sam Houston and the Texas army of volunteers time to prepare and train. Of greatest importance it raised in the hearts of those fighting, in spite of the odds, a spirit, and gave them a slogan –'Remember the Alamo'.

However, it also created panic among ordinary Texan people, American or Mexican. With Santa Anna's army now free to move eastward, both to the north or south, men quickly collected their families together, placed them in wagons and fled eastwards, as quickly as possible towards the Sabine River and the United States border. This was to become known as the 'Runaway Scrape'. In fact this did not apply to the Luna, Garcia, Eliot or Downey families at San Marcos. Though every precaution was taken, if evacuation became imperative, they decided it wise to proceed as they had planed.

However San Houston had now established his army at Gonzales and that was where both Victor Luna and Hanz Eliot went to join him, leaving the others to defend their estates. Houston, as Commander–in–chief, ordered James Fannin, and his five hundred me, now returned to Goliad, after his abortive effort to help Travis at the Alamo, to join him, with his trained men, quickly at Gonzales. However, still believing he should be in charge, and considered he could stand against the Mexican Army, in the good fort at Goliad, and would prevent them gaining supplies from the sea. So he refused the order and stayed.

General Urrea very quickly defeated three Texian forces at San Patricio, Agua Dulce and Refugio. Again Fannin was responsible for the massacre at Refugio sending Captain King to defend Refugio who found himself surrounded. Sending William Ward and the Georgia battalion, to assist, they were caught in open ground surrendered only to be executed. At last Fannin realised his predicament, and hoping to escape before Urrea's superior forces surrounded Goliad, at last decided to join Houston.

However like Ward, weighed down by cannon, he was caught in open prairie. No one could criticize Fannin's bravery. He stood his ground and killed at least two hundred Mexicans with only nine dead and sixty injured but were encircled. Urrea received large reinforcements and Fanning realised his condition was critical discussed terms and surrendered. Urrea might have agreed to them being taken prisoners, but Santa Anna, hearing of this demanded execution. On March 26th. The prisoners, including Fannin were taken out on the Victoria Road and executed by firing at point-bank range. Three hundred and fifty Texians were murdered that day in what has been called the "Massacre at Goliad".

So Houston was deprived of a total of five hundred trained soldiers so vital considering his small numbers, once again showing the near fatal, foolish division in effort within the Texas command. It did give them a further battle cry –'Remember Goliad'. Houston, now, had no option but to burn Gonzales, retreat eastwards crossing the Colorado River going towards the Brazos, intending to cross this, intent on making his own decision when, and where he would give battle with the Mexican Army. But others wanted immediate action.

President Burnet, furious at Houston's apparent lack of courage sent his Secretary of War, Thomas Rusk, to order him to give battle Burnet now panicked and evacuated his headquarters at Washington, on the upper Brazos, fleeing southward to Harrisburg believing he, and the government might escape by sea to the United States. Meanwhile Houston continued his retreat, reached San Felipe on the Brazos and still continued eastwards. Even his own command were now wondering what were their commanders intentions, as he had not communicated his attentions to them.

They believed he intended to reach the Sabine River where they knew a United States army was waiting to prevent the Mexicans invading Louisiana, possibly Houston might then receive American help. But they were wrong he turned south towards Harrisburg, knowing the government had travelled further to Galveston on the coast and that one of the three prongs of the Mexican Army, the one directed personally by Santa Anna was rushing towards that town. Houston knew he must make his stand somewhere near that town.

Eventually they were to meet on April 20th. on the San Jacinto River, between the Bayoo and the Bay on a stretch of land, heavily wooded and near water, but with open ground rising to towards a small hill on which Santa Anna's main force took up their position. There was a small action between Colonel Sherman's cavalry and Mexican infantry. A private named Mirabean Lamar, so distinguished himself, that Houston promoted him to the command of the cavalry. Houston had decided this was the moment of decision, The question was, whether on the following day they should stand and try that way to destroy the Mexican army. Or make an attack of their own on Santa Anna's position. It was late and Houston decided to make his choice the next day.

As they waited that evening both Victor and Hanz received some disquieting news, Evidently Elvira had alluded her restrainers and knew she had taken a surrey to Gonzales where, at that time Santa Anna was supposed to be heading. Immediately two of them had tried to follow but the Mexican Army was moving so quickly eastwards and found Houston retreating so they had to avoid the soldiers and using information from Mexicans still remaining in their homes, had been able to follow, and at last arrived at San Jacinto to bring the sad news.

They could not be sure what had happened to Elvira but feared she had carried out her desire to make contact with Santa Anna, probably to carry out her threat to find him, enter his quarters and then kill him. They had not been able to find any information about her. So they must assume she had either succeeded in her quest or been killed. Either alternative was disastrous, for they feared if not already dead, she would be, if she had killed the Mexican leader.

That night was the worse night of both their lives. Hanz, now, was unconcerned of what might happen to him the next day. If Elvira was dead, Hanz had no wish to go on living. He came and told Houston, that he was willing for him to order him to carryout the most dangerous manoeuvre, the next day, explaining why he no longer cared if he lived or died.

Houston had smiled but told him, "It seems, tomorrow all of us may die. – Just do your best to help us win. – If not let everyone know we tried to free this land from its oppressors." Little did they know that it was due to powers over which they had no control, something happened which would give them a real chance of succeeding .

2.

"No! We came here for we had heard of the beauty of California, and wished to see it for ourselves. – We came simply for pleasure. You see we belong to very rich families in West Virginia. Our parents own the Carroll/Marshall Steam Boat Company, which carries people and cargoes on the United States rivers and down the Mississippi to New Orleans."

Donald Read was speaking to the Military Commandante. Santiago Arguello, as the all enjoyed the hospitality of Juan Bandini. Bandini was of Italian extraction and his large family owned this large house and estate. Juan was renown for his social gatherings and Donald and Rachael, as new comers, had been invited. All guests that evening were from families who had settled in San Diego for sometime.

All was so peaceful and their evening was so like what might have happened on the Potomac. Although California was part of Mexico, none in that room were aware, that in another part of Mexico, at that time many persons were dying as they tried to win Independence from Mexico and that the President, Santa Anna, was certain, now, he could rid his land of these hated people.

But then the residents of San Diego, as in most of California, felt little loyalty to those ruling in Mexico City. They had been willing nationals of Spain, and forced, reluctantly, to raise the Mexican flag in 1823. So the cared little of what happened in the country of Mexico, giving lukewarm obedience to the capital.

It had been an interesting evening for both Donald and Rachael. Now settled in their new home. They had met for the first time Joaquin Carrillo, from whom they had purchased their new house. The Carrrillo family, like so many families here tonight had lived in San Diego for many years, and helped to establish this place as their home. In fact Juan's daughter, Josefa Carrillo had married Captain Fitch who was one of the first Americans to settle there and their new house was the one her father had given them when she married the captain. Now they lived in a much larger mansion.

This was necessary, for as Roman Catholics all their wives were prolific and dutifully presented their husbands with many children. In fact they learned that night that the Commandante, to whom they had just spoken, had sired at least twenty children. In fact it seemed their invitation that evening, had been to ascertain, the true reasons for them settling in the town, for the residents were very wary of Americans coming here.

Donald was amused when the Commandante seemed very pleased with the answer Donald had given him, stating his concern of such men as Jedediah Smith, a fur trader, who had recently descended on the town, being very pleased Smith had left, quickly, and that the Reid's had no connection with that man. Donald had smiled to himself, for he had no intention of telling him, that he had, in fact meet Jedediah Smith nine years before, and it was he who had first began Donald's determination to go to California.

Juan Bandini and has wife now came to join them as they spoke to the Commandante. "Have you now settled here amongst us and do you intend to stay, perhaps trade here?", Bandini asked, obviously following the inquiries Arguello had made. So Donald repeated what he had just said, "Yes! We do intend to stay for a time. At the moment we have no intention of starting a business, though, of course we may in the future."

Now more cautiously he continued, "No! My wife and I intend this to be our base, whilst we travel up the coast to see so many parts of your lovely country. Certainly we intend to sail to Los Angeles, and probably to San Francisco ." Now more to allay fears Donald added, "However we are not sure about the latter. Though we have heard of the wonderful bay and the beautiful surroundings, I am told that many wild men, both Americans and Russians sometimes descend on the town, coming from Oregon or British Canada. I fear we might not be made welcome there and I would not wish to endanger my wife's life."

The Commandante replied, "Oh! I don't think you have any need to fear that way. From what you have told us, it is simply your desire to see the whole of California is the reason you came here. It seems you have some wealth and therefore would not seem to come to seize this land for the United States or others. – In fact if you decide to travel around California, I will gladly give you a letter of introduction to the Commandante of San Francisco, which would allay any fears he might have."

Of course Donald was delighted at his offer. It seemed they had passed the test of why they came. However, he felt he should clarify a point or two. "That is very gracious of you, but as you say we are wealthy, we might wish to purchase another house in these places we visit.- Again, I assure you our objective is to give us pleasure and enjoy your magnificent scenery."

This did not seem to alarm Arguello in any way and he responded, "Of course. I understand. It is natural considering your own resources. I shall ensure the Commandante knows of these wishes and I'm certain he will welcome you to his town."

Of course both Donald and Rachael now circulated and entered into conversation with many of the other guests that evening. It seemed they had established their credentials and their coming, no longer, disturbed the established residents of the town. Eventually they made their departure and now, pleased, returned to their home.

As they sat together in bed, still too tired to sleep, although it was late. They were too tired to indulge in any serious intimacy, but they could both give each other comfort by stroking their bodies to enable them to relax. Donald asked Rachael if she had enjoyed that evening and did she now regret deciding to come to California.

"Don't be so silly, Donald," Rachael replied. "You had told me so much about California as I first stayed with you. Even then I knew, which ever way you decided to try to get here, I desperately wanted to come with you." Now she smiled, "But it seemed you considered it too dangerous for a woman. But when I stated how many men brought their wives or lovers with them on those trails, hoping you would see I wanted to be, at least, one of these, you gave me little hope."

Now Rachael kissed and hugged him to her virtually naked body. "Then amazingly, when I had given up hope, you thrilled me by not only embracing me in the way I had been wanting for so long. You immediately asked me to marry you. At that moment I would have been willing to walk with you though a building on fire, without any fear. – Darling, I wanted to come here. I would gladly have come as your mistress and given you satisfaction, but, instead you brought me here as your wife. Now I always want to be with you, where you go."

Donald now, lovingly, returned her embrace, "Dear Rachael, I was the fortunate one that you could accept me as your husband, and the intimacy, after the terrible way Sydney treated you. But it seems you now want to be with me as we explore this land I love so much. – I think you will be able to help me to somehow interest the United States in this land, in spite of their present reluctance, – and someday take possession of California then our country will stretch from the Atlantic to the Pacific."

Now after another gentle kiss he went on, "Now it seems we are accepted here, I believe very soon we should sail up the coast. I want to see Los Angeles. But I am far more intrigued with seeing, and even, sometime, settling in San Francisco. Somehow I feel in time, this will become a very vital part of the United States. – I know there are rumours, completely unsubstantiated, but I learned on that journey to the salt lake that some trappers, and even some going to Oregon, swore they have seen tiny grains of what seem to be gold floating in the waters near to San Francisco, in a creek some distance inland."

Now he paused before continuing, as thoughts were rushing through his mind. "If this could be confirmed, then however, much these people in California dislike us, hundreds of Americans will pour across the continent, just to try to become rich. A veritable flood of men and women will descend upon this land. The United States government, then would have no choice. They would have to try to win this land merely to save the lives of these prospectors. Darling, if you agree, I think we should soon try to visit San Francisco, though I doubt we shall be able to find gold. But just being there is reward enough." Rachael merely agreed with him and once again they embraced

3.

"Dear Sheila, it was so wonderful to meet you again yesterday. In fact it is a miracle I came here, - though I often do, - at the very time you came for a visit. Of course you must know that I will never forget those very happy days on the ship and then bringing you and your family to Cole County." For a moment he paused before continuing, "I must apologise and beg your forgiveness for not keeping my promise, the last time we parted, to come to see you again. – My only excuse is that I have been kept so busy, ensuring my own financial success and my duty to others who helped me to make this possible. - However, I think you should know, I've many times thought about you, and wondered if you had gained the happy life you deserved."

Gordon could hardly fail to notice how his remarks had effected Sheila, for her face coloured with shame. For a moment she was silent, confused in how she should reply. Perhaps he did not know of her need to flee from her husband for the sake of her life an her babies. So she took a safer route.

Hesitantly she said, "You have no need to apologise, not after the way I sent you away, so long ago. – My mother and I were delighted to learn, as we stayed with Dora Reid, of your success in your profession as an engineer. How much you had helped the Carroll/Marshall line whose boats we travelled on, and your recent interest in railways in Maryland and Pennsylvania. It seemed you have become very rich. I am so glad. Perhaps if I had asked you to stay, it might not have happened. – Please tell me have you married?"

Now Gordon smiled disarmingly, "No! - Perhaps, - It was I missed those wonderful days, for it still robbed me of the company of a delightful girl, whose company I had enjoyed for many weeks. Also, if you will allow me, robbed me of the company of a very beautiful girl, for Sheila, I can see you are, even more beautiful, than when we first met, and why I, so, enjoyed meeting you again, yesterday. No! Sheila, I have never married. The truth is I have never found a woman as wonderful as I knew you were."

Sheila could not decide how she should reply. For a moment her heart leaped knowing he was a free man – but then she remembered she was not a free woman Now they looked at each other in silence. Sheila not knowing how she should respond. Gordon paused, fearing his next remarks might destroy his plan to try to help her. At last he could not resist, and broke the spell.

Taking her hand in his, as he had done the day before, he stated, "Sheila, I feel you should know. Before you arrived and knowing you were coming I was fully informed of the present difficulties you are suffering in your marriage. I have been told, how cruelly, your husband has treated you – even your mother's fears for your life and your baby Neil. – perhaps if I had kept my promise I might have saved you from this. Now, like so many others here today, I want to try to help you."

This was too much for Sheila, her hands covered her face, and she broke down sobbing turning away. How much Gordon would have wanted to hold, embrace her and cover her tear stained face and lips with his kisses. He knew at that moment, somehow, he must in future make her his wife, and ensure she had a happy one, after what she had suffered and would probably suffer in future. All he dare do was to gently place his arms around her and press her lovely head against his chest, attempting to comfort her.

Then gently he said, "Please Sheila, don't cry. We want to help you. You must trust all of us, for only you can let us find that way of ensuring you suffer no more from your husband's brutal treatment."

Now he raised her head so they looked into each others face, as she still continued to sob out her heart, "Sheila, I, - and all of us - know, you feel so strongly and remember your marriage vows to Simon. But he has betrayed those vows. – But of greater importance is that for a time, you must be separated from him. Let him come to realise the terrible life he has given you. – We know if you return to him soon, neither you nor baby Neil, may have long to live. The truth is he is not in full control of his passions." Sheila did not answer and went on sobbing though she did feel safe in the arms of this man she knew she had rejected. So she let him continue.

Gordon went on, "You must not stay here long. If you do he will find you. Then he will exert his legal rights as your husband and make you return to live with again, at Cole County. In spite of the loyalty, I know you, as his wife, you must feel for him, in spite of his past treatment. You must not let it happen – at least not for a time – not until your family believe it is safe and, at last, he realises his own true duties as a husband to both you and Neil. No! You must leave here before he comes to claim you, for once he knows you are not in hospital in St. Louis, he knew of your visit here some months ago. It is the only possible place where you could have come."

Now a look of fear came into her eyes, "Oh! No! I can't. Are you suggesting I should run away with you. Though I do trust you, I am Simon's legal wife, I will not betray my marriage vows. I am his, however much I may now, not like him, and what he does to me. Worse you should know, I believe I am carrying another child by him. It is his as much as mine. No! If you are suggesting I leave and travel with you to Pittsburgh, I will not do it."

Now for the first time he dared gently kiss the side of her face. Then he smiled disarmingly, "Sheila, much as I can tell you I would like you to come away with me. That is not the answer and not what we are all suggesting you should do. – No! Just before you arrived and as Dora had told us what you were suffering, we have discussed another way we can help you, and for a time remove you from Simon, where he could never find you. Please, I beg you, let us try to free you, at least for a time from his attacks. We think we have a solution. Let Lilie Downey, who herself had to endure years of purgatory as the unmarried squaw of an indian captor, - she knows what you have been suffering --- let her tell you how this can be achieved. – Go to her now and let her explain. I will speak to you again latter."

Pohanna who had been, discretely, standing close by, was waiting, knowing what Gordon intended to say to Sheila, now came to join them. Now Sheila accepted Gordon's advice, left him, and let Pohanna lead her to where Lilie Downey was waiting. The three of them sat down and Lilie ordered refreshments before conversing with Sheila. She waited until they had finished and then took hold of her hands and came and kissed her, seeing her tear redden eyes.

"Sheila you must not cry. You are among friends. As Gordon has told you, you must leave here very quickly, as we are certain your husband will appear and demand you return to live with him. We would try to prevent this but the court in Lexington might force you to return. – But we can hide you away, where Simon could never find you. It will be with our friends, who will be pleased to give you, and Neil, a home, for as long as you would wish to stay. Only you must trust us, for we do believe, that at the moment, your life is in danger."

Sheila gave a wistful smile and said, "But I am Simon's wife. It is his right." Now Lilie kissed her again, "No! My dear, everyone in this country has the right to be free. It seems to all of us, that your husband does not accept this and demands absolute obedience to his desires. That is not only wrong, it is against the very constitution of this land., - and I say all of us, - implore you to listen to our advice. We have some very special friends, who long ago had to flee to this country to avoid being killed. Now they are rich like us and have told us they would love to help you."

Now smiling she continued, "They are Louisa and Anton Albrecht who are actually a 'prince and princess' of Austria, who if they stayed in Europe would now be dead. In the past they helped us as we have helped them, and now they live in Tennessee. We want them to take you there, hidden well away from Simon, until together we can ensure you have a happy future. You will be their guest and I know they will love to have you. But if so you must go there soon. Dora has discovered Simon has come to St. Louis and discovered you are not staying there. Soon he will come here. Please, we beg you to do as we suggest."

Now Sheila broke down again and started sobbing, "Oh! Dear! I do not know what is right. I am a married woman. I did truly love my husband. – It is only his recent treatment which has destroyed that love, yet I carry his child." Her sobbing became more violent and then she confessed. "But I now am a wicked woman – I'm frightened to return to live with my husband, and, Lilie, what is worse, I thought yesterday, but now today I know, - I still love Gordon Taylor. I know, now, that he is the man I should have married. You see how evil I have become. Now he is kind to me but I can not respond to him."

So Lilie kissed her again, "Sheila your mother has told us how she and your father sent Gordon away, and persuaded you to find a life with Simon. Now, they both regret this. No! You are not wicked, I'm certain you have always felt that way about Gordon, ever since you met him on the ship. It is only you felt, it was your duty, to accept your parents advice."

Now Lilie came and hugged her to herself and said, "I tell you in confidence, for Gordon is a wonderfully honest man, and feels it wrong to tell you. – But Sheila, I know Gordon is still, and always has been completely in love with you – almost since the first day he met you. That is why he has never married. He is still in love with you and though he fears a life with you may now be impossible he wants, desperately to help you, and persuade you to go, - please - if you have any thoughts of him, - do take our advice and go to Tennessee."

Just for a moment her face brightened, "You say, Gordon still likes me after the way I treated him." Lilie smiled back, "Yes! But he loves you, - not just likes you. Please, if only for his sake, agree to our advice." At last Sheila relaxed. Though very sad knowing the happy life she had lost. It made her heart lift to know he still could love her. She smiled at Lilie, "Thank you, for your kindness. I will talk to mother, then give you my answer."

This was what they all hoped might happen but Patricia, the night before had told Lilie she felt Sheila believed as his wife, she must return to live with Simon, no matter what happened afterwards. For that reason, whilst Lilie had been in conversation with Sheila, as agreed before hand, Gordon had gone to talk to her mother. He found Patricia sitting alone, obviously very sad, wondering how she could help her daughter.

As soon as she saw him, she smiled at him and disarmed him. "Gordon, it was wonderful to meet you again yesterday. I've often wondered what had happened to you. Now I've learned you are a very successful business man with some wealth. I am so pleased, for I remember the way you helped us when we arrived in America and but for you telling me I would never have come to know our friends here-----" Then she paused, silent for a moment, and then added, "Now I am ashamed, the way we sent you away, not considering you could make Sheila a good husband. – I know now how wrong we were. – We are responsible for Sheila's life of purgatory. It is amazing that you would even speak with us after the way we treated you."

Gordon came and held one of her hands, "Patricia, the miracle is that I gave you this Kentucky address, or we should not be here now. –

Now, I may make you feel bad of me but you should know. – I am still very much in love with your daughter and why I have never married. Of course Sheila has now chosen another as her husband, but it still does not destroy my love for her. "

He kissed her hand, "Patricia, that is why I have come to you. I want Sheila to live and she won't if she returns to Simon. All of us here want, to at least separate her from him for a time, and Lilie is, now, explaining to her how this might happen. I have come to you to beg you to do everything in your power to persuade Sheila, possibly against her own marriage vows, to accept what we offer. – I beg you to do this, for I love her so much and I do not want her to die, which I know will happen if she returns with you."

Now to his surprise Patricia used her hand to pulled him to her and kissed his lips. "Gordon, if only to try to absolve a little of the wrong we did you. I promise I will do everything I know to get Sheila to go away where you all want her to." - Finally she kissed him again, "And Gordon, if it should ever be possible, I know, now, I would want you as my son-in-law – and now, whatever you think – I know Neil - now feels the same."

So they all waited to see if Lilie had succeeded. Unknown to all of them, even Gordon, only Charlotte knew of the very private conversations she had enjoyed with Louisa and Anton, in how, together, with the help of some very important persons they might yet be able to arrange for a happy life of Sheila with Gordon. But that must await her acceptance of going to Tennessee.

4.

Antonio Lopez de Santa Anna was well pleased with the success of his campaign to subjugated the unruly state of Texas and rid it of these detested American settlers, who were the cause of the trouble. He had enjoyed unqualified success ever since he crossed the Rio Grande on February 16th., entering San Antonio a week later. He found his army had already surrounded a combined group of Mexican and Americans in the Alamo, which had previously been a Mexican base. Since they had, already, refused to surrender he had ordered it shelled declaring no prisoners would be taken alive.

He had stayed at San Antonio until his forces overran the fort on March 6th. Apart for one or two negro slaves and fifteen women and children, everyone in the Alamo were killed, many bayoneted to death, including Travis, Bowie and Crockett. During that time he held a council of war with his three generals deciding to split into three columns as they proceeded eastwards. General Urea immediately began his attacks defeating first William Ward then Colonel Fannin both near the town of Goliad. When Fannin and his militia surrended, acting under Santa Anna's orders, they were all taken out and shot creating the Goliad Massacre.

Santa Anna had insisted on this emphasising that there would be no mercy for anyone who stood against him. As expected this had caused panic, so when General Houston realising his force, as yet, was inadequate to give open battle had retreated from Gonzales eastwards, intending to only stand when he considered he might have a chance of success, - however unlikely. This was what caused the 'Runaway Scrape' of so many fleeing from the Mexican army as Houston, crossed the Colorado and then the Brazos Rivers heading for the Trinity River, probably heading for the United States border on the Sabine River.

All this was ensuring the success of Santa Anna's campaign. Unfortunately the speed of progress eastwards, also meant that Antonio Santa Anna had little opportunity of enjoying the bodies of local females. He had left his harem in Mexico City before her left for Texas. He had no opportunity for amorous pleasures until he reached San Antonio. Only then did he stay for any time and his aides were kept busy providing him with two local fifteen year old girls. However with the fast rate of travel he had no option but to leave these two unfortunate girls behind, dishonoured and possibly pregnant. Santa Anna now craved for nubile feminine company. He obtained it in an unusual way.

* * * * * * * * * * * * * * *

Elvira Eliot had succeeded in escaping from virtual imprisonment on her estate using the assistance of her lifelong friend, Raquel Garcia, now married to Karl Downey. Raquel felt the same as Elvira, that life under Santa Anna was not worth living. She also supported Elvira, to enable her to get her revenge for her raping and pregnancy, seven years before. They were both Spanish women who believed such actions should be revenged. Their plan was ingenious.

Raquel called, driving her own surrey, ostensively just to give Elvira company. After refreshments they walked together into the grounds and deliberately spent time apparently conversing and exploring the area. Once they felt all suspicions had been overcome, they both walked casually back to the mansion. The Raquel went inside asking the servant at the door, who had, up to now, been watching carefully, where they had been strolling, to bring Elvira's coat, as it was becoming cooler.

As soon as the servant left the door Elvira, as was their plan, jumped into the Raquel's surrey standing less than twenty yards from the front door. Within five minutes Elvira had driven though the gates of the estate, before they realised it was Elvira and not Raquel who was driving it. They had learned that Houston had left Gonzales and now Santa Anna had occupied the town. So Elvira destination was that town. She had to drive through the confusion, as so many families were leaving in panic travelling towards the United States border.

However when she arrived at Gonzales she discovered the main part of the Mexican Army had left for Columbus leaving a detachment in control of the town. Cleverly explaining she was an 'intimate friend' of the President, a statement well understood underlining their chief's sexual activities. Not only did they direct her in the direction he had gone, but gave her an imposing document endorsing Elvira's position, and demanding everyone co-operated in helping her to meet the President. In fact he had already left Columbus and had reached the Brazos River before Elvira, eventually, arrived at his camp.

The document ensured Elvira was rapidly lead to his headquarters. As the document addressed her as Elvira Luna, and as she had sent with it a short note addressed "To Antonio from your intimate and adoring companion, Elvira Luna, in remembrance of those wonder days at Vera Cruz, so long ago." It did the trick and Elvira was quickly lead into his presence and as he came to her and took hold of her hand to kiss it, Elvira, wasted no time and threw her arms around Santa Anna saying, "Antonio, surely our remembrance of the happy times we enjoyed together in the past, demands a far less formal greeting". She buried her lips on his.

Though a little embarrassed, he could easily overcome any such problems, and, eventually, separated from her asking her to dine with him that night and to wait in his suite whilst he was engaged in military matters. Elvira was well pleased with herself. She would try to ensure she stayed with him after dinner and entice him to invite her to join his bed. She thought tonight will be the end of this monster, for she had hidden intimately on her person a tiny phial of a strong digitalis poison, which, first, would slowly make him unconscious but then would within hours stop his heart, giving everyone the impression of a usual heart attack.

Elvira's hatred of this man made it difficult to engage with him in the sensuous conversation over dinner and afterwards. However after briefly outlining a completely erroneous account of her life since she left him at Vera Cruz, the birth of their daughter, Adela, and how she had for so long hoped to renew their happy weeks of the past. Santa Anna, denied feminine company now for many days, leapt at her offer to spend an interesting night with him in his bed. After several more drinks she allowed him to lead her into his boudoir and he had just commenced to undress her, when to her utter annoyance, they were interrupted as a servant brought him a message which demanded his immediate attention. It seemed that the Texan government had left Washington and appeared to be trying to reach the coast and possibly to flee to the United States.

So poor Elvira was robbed of her chance to kill Santa Anna, but relieved that before she left, he begged her to remain with him and said, "Dear Elvira, I promise tomorrow night their will be no interruptions."

Of course Elvira was very willing to stay. The next day she was given luxurious transport as his military train pursed Houston's army first to Harrisburg, and then to the small town of San Jacinto, where at last they made contact with the fleeing Texas army. It seemed at last, possibly the next day, Santa Anna would be able, to bring them to battle and destroy them with his numerical superiority. So Santa Anna was in a very good mood as he once again entertained Elvira to dinner, consuming considerable quantities of brandy. Elvira, desperately trying not to become drunk, but happy that he was already showing its effects.

She began to wonder how long he might remain in control of himself, but she did not know his excellent powers of recovery. Soon, possibly quite inebriated, he at last without warning picked up her light body carried her into his bedroom next door and quickly undressed her, following by becoming naked himself. There was no interruption like the previous night. Elvira, though it repulsed her, knew she must let him possess her, happy that as she was pregnant, so she could not conceive another of his children.

He was a very accomplished lover and in spite of the drink was able to achieve his climax. Only then as she arose and poured out two more glasses did she have the chance to administer the poison into his glass of brandy. She smiled as they both downed their drink, knowing now that it would not be long before this evil man breathed no more. She felt she had achieved her end and kept her promise. Everything appeared to be working, for fairly soon afterwards, although he did attempt further intercourse with him, exhaustion, or because of the poison, caused him to fall back and became unconscious. Satisfied with her work. After ensuring he was complexly unconscious, Elvira left his bedroom, after dressing again, came to his aids tent explaining that the President had drunk himself to unconsciousness, but not before ordering her out of his bedroom.

The Aide understood as this often happened after the President had enjoyed female company for a night, and allowed Elvira to leave to return to the tent allocated to her. This she did, but after waiting a little time, as the night was warm, tried to make her escape before anyone found what had happened to the president. Elvira made her way in the dark, though there was some moonlight, back up the hill behind the camp and into some sheltering trees. She had wrapped her body in an thick army trench coat, which kept her body from freezing. She knew as soon as it was light she must effect her escape drop down to San Jacinto Bay and make her escape by water, determined to place as much distance as possible between herself and the army camp. Perhaps a Mexican family on the coast might give her shelter, as she now feared for her life.

In fact things did not happen as she had hoped. It is true that when his aids came to his bedroom the next day they still found him fast asleep. Though they tried they could not arouse him, he still remained unconscious. Believing it was the liquor he had consumed, they had no option but to leave him to recover The ordered meeting for that morning to discuss their plans to attack and destroy the Texans could not take place. Though General Cos' division, which Santa Anna had ordered to join him arrived, swelling his force considerably. Now everyone had to wait for the President to awake.

Of course it was not the brandy which had made Santa Anna incapable, but Elvira's digitalis poison that was doing its work. It was the reason for his unconsciousness, however her brilliant plan appeared to fail, for Elvira did not know that the poison was only partially effective when it descended into a stomach flooded with strong alcohol which dispersed its effects. In spite of what Elvira had achieved, Santa Anna would not die.

Yet it seemed that her plan could still to be effective, though, to her disgust she would fail to kill him. It would lead to his disaster in a very different way. It simply meant that Santa Anna remained in an unconscious state until well after lunch, and without him, few precautions were taken, believing that the Texas Army was so inferior to them in numbers. Even when he did awake, he was hardly in a fit state to think coherently, for foolishly they underestimated their opponents, believing that once they decided to attack the Texan army, if it stood its ground, it would not take long to eliminate its presence.

So there was still a chance that Elvira's audacious and impossible plan may yet prove effective, even if it was not in the way she had wanted. It seemed that Santa Anna would still continue to live and continue his dictatorship of Mexico. Perhaps she might achieve her revenge in another way.

5.

Meantime in Maryland a series of love affaires were developing. Now it was quite normal for Freda Ibsen to travel from Washington, on a number of weekends to join Otto Fallen at his house in Annapolis. Freda had discussed with her mother her developing association with Otto, and it had been her mother who had suggested she should stay with Otto, and enjoy intimate embraces. This was the way her mother had behaved many years before, and believed it would give her daughter a better chance of discovering what were her true feelings for Otto. Many people now believed they had become lovers.

But also the love affairs of Edwin and Joan Palatine were developing satisfactory. Andrew Carroll had kept his promise and after little more than eight weeks Edwin Palatine had been appointed into the new post of Professor of the School of Mathematics in the University of Maryland. In fact the university authorities had welcomed the chance to appoint him, as few lecturers at present were so qualified in higher mathematics. Though it had not happened, Edwin hoped that before long he might be able to establish within his school, a Department of Astronomy.

Now with a guaranteed salary Edwin was able to develop further his association with a very willing Audrey Carroll. This had the blessing of both her father and mother, particularly as they realised Edwin's appointment would ensure they lived close by, should it lead to marriage. Already Edwin had taken Audrey to New York to meet their benefactor whose kindness after they landed in America and had enabled this liaison to occur.

There were similar developments between Joan Palatine and Keith Condorcet, which again seem to meet with approval from his grandmother, Sophia Chalmers, as well as his mother and father. So it seemed that the Palatines would continue to stay for long periods in the mansion of Rockville, though they both made frequent visits to New York and to the Chalmers estate in Virginia. It seemed that soon there would be a need for someone in the vicinity to arrange for two marriages.

Meantime Peter Vanderbilt and his wife Amy along with Cornelius Vanderbilt and his wife Sophia were achieving greater success in their combined development of ships driven by steam propeller propulsion, now that the Ibsen's and others were investing with themselves in its success. So it seemed, as so often had happened in the past, that Rockville and those who resided there, along with others who had come from that estate, was continuing to provide a base for so many happy relationships. There was no doubt but that the ghosts of Amelia and David Carroll still looked benevolently on anyone who dwelt for a time within those walls.

Amy Vanderbilt had continued the friendship began between her mother, Estelle, and Muriel Alexander. Like her mother, she was anxious to discover as much about her family as possible What had happened to Amelia's daughter, Blanche, had been, for too long, a mystery? Now her mother had discovered Blanche's descendents, the Backhouse family, living in Montreal. Amy was now, a frequent correspondent with both Muriel, and Rachael Backhouse in Montreal.

It seemed Rachael had heard from her son, David. He had told his mother of the terrible devastation by small pox and other diseases, less dangerous to American whites, but which had beset the indian population of the area. Previously their bodies had never met these ills. Ill prepared they died in their thousands. Anxious to avoid catching small pox he had left the Oregon country, riding to Vancouver, on the coast.

His last letter had arrived by a ship sailing around South America and bringing hides up the St. Lawrence to Montreal. In it he had told them he intended to use this same ship to travel down the coast to San Francisco. He had heard that in the port were many British and Russians, besides Americans. It seemed they were all attempting to take this important port from its present Mexican control. David hoped to get support from fellow British's compatriots, and help to add this area to British Canada.

Amy was not so sure she wanted this to happen. As a staunch supporter of the United States, she believed, it was for them to take this land from Mexico, just as they were attempting in Texas.

* * * * * * * * * * * * * * *

At the same time, now happily established in their home in San Diego. Donald and Rachael, having now explored the area surrounding the town, and finding it interesting but still very primitive, as it still depending largely on support from the mission stations, but which were gradually losing their control. In fact it was Rachael who said, "Donald, I think its time we explored further up the coast. – In fact, although it might be a little dangerous, I think we should, at least sample, what life might be like around San Francisco."

Donald was a little surprised for he too believed it might be a little dangerous, telling her so. Rachael had merely grabbed him to her in a long passionate embrace before replying, "Donald, as I told you so long ago in St. Louis, I shall never have any fear, so long as I'm near you. – Again, I know if you had not become saddled with me, you probably have already come to San Francisco, having driven along the Oregon Trail and across the mountains to get there. – I told you then and I repeat it today, - I do not want to become a hindrance. I, now, like adventure, just as much as you – provided you are always at my side. – Please let us sail north to see what the rest of California has to offer us."

Now action spoke louder than words, for Donald enjoyed intimately pressing his strong body against her soft flesh, completely forcing all her breath from her body. She was gasping for air when he realised her. Yet after few quick gasps she was embracing him again. There was no need for Donald to reply. Rachael knew Donald had accepted her advice and without speaking was telling her what a wonderful wife he believed he had married. Poor Rachael's only regret was that her suggestion must mean that she must still forgo her longing to conceive his child, for it might make him less willing to risk her life in more unsafe places. – and Rachael was longing to hold a young baby in the arms, having lost the one, Sydney had given her.

As a precaution they obtained a letter of introduction to the Commandante of San Francisco from Commandante Arguello, then paying for an indian girl to look after their house whilst they were away they waited for a ship to call at San Diego. At last the bark 'Louisa', Captain Bartlett, in command, arrived and they took passage along the coast, having ensured the ship was travelling as far as San Francisco.

Though they called at Los Angeles as the bark traded in the town, Rachael and Donald, only landed to see a little of the town whilst their captain went about his business. Once again on board they made their way northwards. The captain told them a little of the history of San Francisco, how in the past they had been forced to anchor off Black Point or Saualito, which was both unsafe and dangerous. Now however now, they had been allowed to anchor in Yerba Buena Cove, which had given its name to San Francisco.

It seemed that a Captain William Richardson arriving some years before, had become a naturalized Mexican and had now become captain of the port. The land was mainly inhabited by indians who worked as blacksmiths, carpenters and tailors. There were only about two hundred and fifty white men and women living near the anchorage. There were few houses, as up to two years ago most people lived in tents around the port. Now a mercantile businessman, John Leese and two partners had been building more permanent habitation along Clay Street and Grant Avenue. Only a short distance from the beach.

At least they learned that the Commandante was Captain Vallego, a Cavalry man, who was now married to an extremely beautiful Francesca Benicia Carrillo. So it would be to Captain Vallego they would give their letter of introduction. The question was where could they sleep after the bark left on its journey south. They were not particularly keen in living in tents, but this might be what they must do.

Rachael and Donald and smiled to themselves, besides any dangers, it seemed they might have to endure many other tribulations, however

Rachael had said, "Donald, if you had taken me along the Oregon Trail I believe we should have suffered far greater discomfort. – Let us see if we can buy one of these house that man Leese is building. – If not then we will set up home in a tent. – Donald, I do want to stay here for a time. From what the captain says it seems that San Francisco bays are very big and beautiful. In any case we must travel inland and see what the countryside has to offer us."

Donald readily agreed, "Yes! And since most of the mission stations are being forced to close, we might even buy land near to them and then build our own house. – You know we might even see if those rumours of gold dust in streams have any foundation. – However we shall have to conserve our expenditure, or our credit will be extinguished. Only by returning to Mexico can we obtain any more from the east, although I will write and send letters by the ships. – Of course – we might set up a business of our own! "

Soon the bark was sailing between two headlands into a wide bay, before turning south. The sight was magnificent, like nothing they had seen before. Then they were dropping anchor close to a quay in Yerba Buena Cove. The adventure they desired would soon be theirs.

6.

Sheila had come to her mother wondering if she should accept Lilie's offer and go away where Simon could not find her but she stated, "Mother, I am Simon's wife, I think I carry his child. – I know the risks but I believe I should return with him if he comes here to find me. – Surely you all can convince him he should treat me differently than in the past?"

Patricia pulled her down to sit beside her and placed her arms around her to comfort her. "No! Sheila you must go away, as they have suggested. It is not just your own life which is in danger, but Neil's and your unborn baby. – When he drinks Simon never knows what he is doing. Whatever he may promise us, he will never keep it. – Worse he does believe he owns you, and you have disobeyed him. For that reason he will demand punishment. For everyone knows you have run away."

Now she kissed the side of her face, "We are fortunate to be amongst such wonderful friends desperate to help us. – But there is another reason. – You know both father and I were very wicked when we sent Gordon Taylor away and made you tell him to leave. – We are responsible for your unhappy life. – I saw yesterday how much you still think of him. – Sheila, he still loves you. He has just come to me, begging me to persuade you to go away. – Sheila, he is still desperately in love with you, in spite of how we have all treated him. – Though he believes he could not hope for a life with you, he wants you to go on living."

Now she hugged her daughter, "We all owe Gordon an apology for sending him away. We can best repay him for you doing what he asks. It seems these friends who are coming for you, want to help and make you happy. – Please go with them for a time. Perhaps it may make Simon realise the terrible way he has treated you. Then when you return things may be different. – Please let me go to Lilie and tell her you will accept her offer."

Sheila at last made her decision after giving a long sigh replied, "Yes Mother, do this, I know now I must – if only to please so many persons who are trying to help me." Her mother kissed her and left to acquaint Lilie of Sheila's acceptance. After she left Sheila still could not believe what Lilie and now her mother had told her – that Gordon was still in love with her. It made her cry again., knowing she had thrown away a wonderful life with him, marvelling that after her treatment, he could still feel this way about her.

Then she stopped crying. Stopped feeling so sad for herself. She must go to him. Let him know she now knew he still loved her, if only to thank him and ask him to forgive her for the past. She found he was not in the house and had gone outside intending to go through the flower garden to the stables, intending to go for a ride. In fact he had only just left, and hurrying she caught up to him as he went behind some trees at the bottom of the garden. He stopped as he heard her coming.

She could not stop herself she ran to him, threw her arms around him and buried her lips on his to his complete surprise. However it only lasted a second before his arms were encircling her, and he was pressing his lips, even more firmly on his. It lasted for several minutes, before sanity prevailed.

Yet even then Sheila could not restrain herself, "Oh! Gordon! I love you! I love you! However wrong it may be I feel you ought to know. – Dearest, I simply cannot understand that both Mother and Lilie tells me you still love me, after the way I sent you away. – Now, whatever happens in the future. – However much I am unhappy, I shall remember there is one man in this world who really likes me. – You must know, if it were possible I would come to live with you if you wanted me. – But I'm not free – I still belong to Simon. However though I might not have a life with you, I will do what you have asked me. I will go away from here. I will do it, if only to repay you, a little, for your kindness. – And – Gordon – I do hope I will meet you again someday, for from now on you will always be in my heart."

Gordon still holding her kissed her lips again and then both her eyes as tears of sadness flooded from them. Then he said, "Sheila, I shall never marry anyone else. – I may have other women – I am a man with all the faults your mother must have told you. – but I will not place a ring on any girl's finger – unless it is on your third finger – left hand. Please go away as they have planned . – I promise someday I will come to you again – wherever you may go." Again they embraced and kissed, happy and sad at the same time. At least both knew now they truly loved each other, even if they might never have a future together.

The next day Louisa and Anton Albrecht arrived. Though both were over sixty years old, they were in good health. They had been friends of everyone on the Camargo estate, though Lilie and James Downey were their special ones, established many years ago when they arrived from the Potomac to test Bourbon Whiskey made by Doctor Crowe. Both of them had visited them many times. However their first desire was to meet both Sheila and her mother.

Once Sheila had accepted her proposal Lilie spent sometime explaining who were these mysterious couple who were coming to take them to live on their estate in Tennessee. When they learned that both had been born in Austria as a Prince and Princess, they felt their own upbringing was so inferior and wondered how they should behave. In fact it only took Louisa and Anton five minutes to place them completely at their ease. Louisa had seen at once their problem.

She took hold of Sheila's hands, pulled her to her and kissed her. "Sheila we are no better than you. But for this country which gave us sanctuary we both, would be dead. Like you we owe so much to the United States. We have been fortunate and now we are pleased to help others who have not had our advantages. – Sheila you will love our estate and remember you are our guest. We shall love showing you how wonderful is the land where we live."

Now Louisa spoke to her mother, "Mrs. McLean we should love for you to come back with us when we take Sheila, but that would not be wise. It is better that you stay here at Camargo and wait until Simon comes so that you can tell him that Sheila has flown and you have no idea where she has gone. – However, when things are not too difficult, we would like to invite all your family to come and stay with us. – You can be assured that Sheila will be complete safe whilst she stay with us. – In fact we have some very powerful friends who might, yet, make life much easier for your daughter."

Now Louisa asked both Patricia and Sheila to tell her everything that had happened in the past. Of course she had been introduced to Gordon on her arrival, now she learned of Sheila's past relationship with him. Again she took Sheila's hands, "You say you still love Gordon and miraculously, in spite of you sending him away, he has told you he still loves you and will not marry another."

She kissed Sheila's hands, "Please! Tell me truthfully. If you were free and he asked you to marry him would you accept?" Sheila looked Louisa in the face and replied, "I know now, whatever my family thought, if I were free, I would gladly go and live with him, married or not, and bear him any children he may desire. – But I am not free and I still believe my duty is to stay with Simon – although, now, I have lost, all my love for him."

Sheila saw that Louisa appeared pleased at her reply and then she said, "Then I believe it is up to me to try to provide a happy solution for your problem." Now she said they should leave as early as possible, perhaps the next day, as Simon might appear at anytime, and if so might be accompanied by someone in authority.

That night they all sat round the very large table enjoying a delicious meal with wines. Afterwards Gordon came to Sheila and suggested they went outside, as there was a very bright moonlight night. She gladly agreed. Once outside he stopped and stood facing her. However, not sure of how he should act he merely took hold of both her hands in his. Then Sheila smiled and used their combined hands to pull him close to her and as on the previous day buried her lips in his.

After a few minutes they broke apart, but it was Sheila who spoke, "Dearest Gordon, that was to show you that I love you with all my heart. If ever I become a free woman I will try to find you, and come to you. If so you must know then you can take me in any way – my body will be yours – you need not offer me marriage. For all I long for now is someday to have a life with you. – Would you accept me that way?"

Gordon simply hugged her close one again pressing his lips to hers. Then he replied, "No my dear. I would not." Seeing her startled look he smiled. "However if you would accept me I would want to make you my wife. Remember what I said yesterday. – I may enjoy pleasures with other women, but I shall never marry unless you find me and tell me you no longer want a life with me. This short time we've been together has been worth the waiting. I can tell you, now, I am willing to wait a long time, until we can be together. – Please remember that, whatever problems you face in the future."

Now they spent a full hour talking as lovers do. Each were finding it difficult to break away and go inside, knowing that after tonight it might be many years before they could enjoy a night such as this. Eventually they had no option but to return. The next day as Gordon stood by the side of her coach in which Louisa and Anton had brought to take her to Tennessee, Gordon leant over and kissed Sheila on the lips, not caring what anyone thought. Tears were rolling down both their faces as the coach moved forward on its journey to separate them possibly forever.

7.

On the morning of April 21ˢᵗ 1836. Houston held a council of war and all his officers favoured waiting for Santa Anna's attack being so inferior in numbers being, only, about eight hundred men. However Houston had other ideas. He discussed them with Thomas Rusk sent by the President Burnet to order the army to stand and fight. Rusk gladly agreed. Though it could not occur until the afternoon and by then Santa Anna might have further concentrated his army, and it already was in excess of one thousand four hundred men.

Houston's plan was exceedingly risky, particularly as it included an attack across open ground and, also, included reducing further his numbers using his cavalry to try to outflank the Mexicans. He then ordered his scout Deaf Smith to burn and destroy Vince Bridge, so neither the Texans or Mexicans could retreat from the field except by diving into the waters of the bay. The attack began at 4-20 p.m. with a fifer playing a favourite tune.

Houston led the infantry with Colonel Sherman, Hanz Eliot and Victor Luna on his left. In the centre was wheeled the 'Twin Sisters', two cannons donated by the citizens of Cincinnati. The Texas Army were completely exposed as they climbed the open ground to where the Mexicans were entranced expected to receive murderous fire. Two shouts strengthened their resolve – 'Remember the Alamo' – 'Remember Goliad' – yet amazingly not until they reached the walls of the encampment did they receive hostile fire. The reason was that no lookouts had been posted by the Mexicans.

There were two reasons. Firstly because the Mexican commanders foolishly under estimated their enemy, believing they were untrained volunteers. However the most important reason was the incapacity of their President Santa Anna, the failure of him being not well enough to give definite orders. Neither the Texans, Houston nor Hanz Eliot knew at that time that this was entirely due to Elvira's attempt the night before to poison and kill Santa Anna.

The Mexicans were unprepared. Excellent when standing in battle order they were incapable of independent action. Outflanked by the Texan Cavalry, unprepared for a frontal attack, they panicked as the Texans swept over them. Apart from General Castillo's vain attempt to mount resistance until he was killed, the rest of the Mexican army fled. Their escape blocked by the destroyed bridge, they threw themselves down the bank into the marshes and the waters of the bay, many drowning as they struggled to escape.

Santa Anna had vanished and soon General Almonte had no option but to surrender his last four hundred men. Santa Anna's army ceased to exist. Amazingly the actual battle contact time was less than eighteen minutes. In that short period Texas won its independence. Yet that amazing victory had only been possible because of a woman reeking her revenge. It was probably one of the most unusual and yet most important victories of any army, turning certain defeat into overwhelming victory.

However they had failed to capture Santa Ann. The next morning Houston sent James Sylvesta and three other to search for him. They discovered him now having removed his uniform. with several other escaped soldiers. However as he was led away, the others referred to him as 'El Presidente' and so he was taken to stand before Houston. Most Texans wanted to execute him for the atrocities made in his name but he pleaded for his life. Houston only wanted Texas to be independent and so negotiated with him.

Eventually Santa Anna on May 14th signed the Treaties of Velasco giving Texas independence with Santa Anna promising to withdraw his forces back to Mexico and obtain Congress' approval of what he had signed. In fact he remained their prisoner for six months before being sent to Washington, to obtain President Andrew Jackson's support. Meantime General Filisola, now commanding the remaining Mexican forces, over ruled General Urea, who still wished to fight. He accepted Santa Anna's signature on the treaty. However very soon Congress removed Santa Anna as president and for many years did not recognise the independence of Texas.

All this was in the future. With their victory Hanz and Victor spent the day after their battle questioning every important Mexican soldiers trying to discover the whereabouts of Elvira. Though they, now, feared she would be dead. Only then did they discover that she had spent the night before the battle in Santa Anna's bed. Yet it seemed she had left early and returned to her tent, through his aides, they were told she had vanished by the morning. They had no ides where she had gone.

At least this meant that Elvira appeared to be alive on April 21st.., but why had she left without carrying out her threat to kill the president? Little did they know then how, though she failed in her attempt to kill him, her action had possibly ensured victory when defeat was to be expected. Believing she may have escaped down to the Gulf both obtained Houston's sanction to leave the army and try to find her.

Both Victor and Hanz combined the entire coastal villages for three days, hoping she might have escaped there, but without any success. In fact the chaos following the battle meant no one would notice an unescorted woman travelling alone there. Reluctantly they returned to the army staying until the Treaty was signed before, in great sadness, after being demobilised, made their way back to San Machos.

* * * * * * * * * * * * * * *

In fact a very frightened and desperate Elvira Eliot had almost stumbled down the hill through the trees with only the weak light of an obscured moon to guide her. At least she had her purse, in which was a considerable amount of money, given her by a generous Santa Anna after her arrival on the first day. Eventually, her clothes torn, filthy and completely dispirited she arrived at the coast at the tiny village of Free Port. A fisher woman had taken pity on her and took her into her house, as her husband was at sea.

She was given a chance to bathe and then completely exhausted fell asleep. She slept for almost twenty four hours. When she awoke she learned that there had been a battle at San Jacinto. Though it was still to be confirmed it appeared the Texan Army had won and that it was said Santa Anna had been captured

Though if true Elvira was delighted that they had won, yet it seemed that Santa Anna was still alive, yet she knew he was unconscious when she had escaped. Why had the poison not killed him. She felt she had failed in exacting her revenge on this evil man. However there was nothing she could do. Perhaps, if he had been captured, the Texans would now execute him. If so, belatedly, she would have achieved her revenge. At last she was able to tell her hostess who she was, and the Luna name was well known throughout the land.

Telling the woman she had money and first wished to recompense her for seeing to her needs. However after explaining that both her father and husband had been pleased as others were fighting the president, the woman refused her offer, only too pleased that Elvira's family had helped to defeat, the person they both considered an evil man.

Although things were still chaotic Elvira wanted to return to San Machos as soon as possible. She knew the dangers but wished to accept them, just to return to her family and she was now suffering her advancing pregnancy. Her hostess took her into the village and with the money in her purse was able to hire, a not very new, and very dilapidated small coach. She could handle almost any horse driven vehicle, so, provided it stood up to the strain of the poor roads, she knew it would take her home. But it was a long journey and she had to avoid the area of the battle as it was still a dangerous area for any woman.

In fact she took her time and it took her five days before, at last, she drove into her estate to receive an over whelming welcome form everyone in San Machos, though no one knew anything of Hanz or her father. In fact they might have perished in the battle. So it was very unhappy Elvira who now waited in her mansion.

By now she had learned that Santa Anna was alive and a prisoner. It seemed she had failed. Now she feared she might have lost the two men she loved more than her own life. In any case what use was the Texas victory, if first Santa Anna still lived, yet either of her two loved ones had died. It seemed all her plans had failed. She would have no wish to go on living, except that as a mother she knew her duty to her two children, and the unborn baby of the husband she adored, inside her.

Both her mother and Julio and Gloria Garcia did their best to raise her spirits as did both Raquel and Karl Downey. For both Victor and Hanz were very close to them. Perhaps her seven year old daughter, Adela, was just as heart broken as Elvira, for never knowing the evil father who had sired her, she had believed Hanz was her true father. At least they had learned that the Texian losses at the battle had been very small in comparison to the Mexicans.

Then on May 19th. a miracle happened. Both Victor Luna and Hanz Eliot arrived in a large battle wagon they had taken, now their use was not necessary. Neither Elvira nor Hanz could believe their eyes. Both had believed the other dead . Now they were, at last facing each other again. Hanz simply jumped down from the coach, swept Elvira into his strong arms lifting her off the floor, caring little for her pregnant condition. There was no need to speak. They each buried their lips in each others, holding together until they both nearly fainted for lack of air.

Only then did they return to normality but it was Hanz who was the first to speak. "I was certain you were dead after learned you were in Santa Anna's bed the night before the battle and before you ran away. It matters not that you did not kill him, for we beat him complexly. He is finished and now Texas is independent. – Darling, at last we can plan our life together, without fear. I doubt the Mexicans will try again, not without their president to lead them. – But when we have time I must tell you how it happened. – I cannot understand it. They seemed so unprepared for our attack. It was so unlike that man for, however we hate him, he is a brilliant general. – Perhaps it was a miracle."

It was several days more before Hanz and Elvira realised what created this miracle. How Elvira's failure was possibly her greatest victory. – In any case did it now matter, for now Texas was an independent country, free from Mexico, and would remain so – until a few years later, its very existence, ensured war between Mexico and the United States.

8.

Gordon Taylor had arrived back from Kentucky and very soon Cherie Marshall had come to see him. "Did you meet your Sheila?" She smiled then continued, "Mother told me why you went there. It seems another woman is closer to your heart. I am no longer the girl you want."

Gordon was embarrassed. He felt conscious stricken. He had known he must face Cherie, though he had been dreading it. He had expected her to turn her venom on him declaring he had betrayed her. Yet she had done no such thing. Even as she had challenged him she had been smiling, not apparently criticizing him, merely stating a fact. He did not know how to reply.

It seemed Cherie was amused at his discomfort, enjoying it, but then took pity on him. "Gordon, mother told me why you went to Kentucky and all about your lost girl friend. – It seemed I never had a chance. I understand, - though I admit I'm sorry. I shall miss you."

Gordon could not understand why she was accepting it so easily and admitted he was sad. She had given him much pleasure, but then he realised he had, also, pleased her. He took comfort in this. "Cherie, I'm sorry, I did not want to hurt you. But we knew months ago, when both you and Frances started toying with my affections. It was not intended to become serious. – Please tell me, this was what it was. You see, whatever you think of me, I do like you very much. In fact you kept me sane when I first arrived here."

Now Cherie became more serious, "Yes! Gordon, you are right. That is how it began – er – but then – well I became more interested. I do like you – I did even come to believe I might love you. That was why I wanted us both to go, together, to England. – Perhaps then it would have developed further. – I can't complain – you have given me many hours of pleasure. – But I shall not be alone."

She saw he was puzzled and continued. "After you left, mother told me all about you and Sheila McLean and how you met on the ship coming here. Your prospering romance and then her rejection of you. However mother, told me she had no doubt but that you were still in love with Sheila, and how she had been trying to help you to see her again. I knew then I must look elsewhere. – I'm not sure, - I may have found another. I don't think you met him, he is Daniel Wilson. Although his father was English both his mother and grandmother were related to the French royal family, coming here many years ago. I think you may not have heard of the Scarron and Tencin families living along the Potomac."

There was no doubt but that Gordon was relieved, and begged her to tell him more, if only to absolve his conscience. Cheri was happy to oblige. "Actually you may have met him at Frances wedding to Henry Foyle last year. Well Henry's father, Hugh Foyle came with my father to Philadelphia to set up the first steam driven Cotton mill, and both father and Hugh came to know Donald and Kate Wilson long ago and even more knew his son, David who married Louise Scarron. Well Daniel Wilson is David and Louise grandson."

Gordon now took hold of her hands and asked, "Please tell me is it likely to become serious – I know you still do not want, yet, to settle down. – I can tell you, if it was to become more serious, I should feel a lot less ashamed then I do at this moment."

Now Cherie bent forward and kissed him lightly. "Gordon, you have no need to be. Neither of us committed ourselves very firmly to each other. – I admit, now, I would have liked it to develop further. – To answer you, all I can say is that it may develop as I hope. I know he likes me." Now she laughed, "And I confess I have found him as good a lover as I found you. – The truth is I'm now twenty five. Perhaps the birth of Frances baby daughter, altered things. I knew I wanted children. Once mother told me about you. I suddenly realised how foolish has been my past life. – Yes! Gordon, I will do my best to make Daniel like me, for I, now, know I like him very much."

Gordon could not help it. He took a willing Cheri into his arms and kissed her fully on the lips. Then smiling he replied, "That is to thank you for the many wonderful hours you have given me. – Dear, Cherie, I shall never forget you. – I could not, even if I wanted. – I do hope you find Daniel could become your partner. I shall feel forgiven, if you ask me to your wedding." So ended the somewhat passionate affair between Cherie Marshall and Gordon Taylor. It was fortunate that, in the end, they could part as friends.

Charlotte Marshall had just returned from New York after inspecting progress on the New Jersey to Trenton new railway line being laid and she came immediately to see Gordon, anxious to learn how his meeting with Sheila had developed. He was glad to tell her everything that had happened, and that they had persuaded her to go to Tennessee. However he saw how delighted she was when he told her Sheila admitted she still loved him, however, impossible might be a life with him.

Charlotte took hold of his hand. "Now I know it is what you both want, do not be so sure, it may end unhappily. I can't tell you more, at present, but now there are several persons trying to make it possible. – Meantime we need your help on our railways. Progress is too slow. I have done what I could but I'm more a draughts woman than a mechanic, I want you to come with Roy and me to try to expedite matters. Otherwise our investment will be extinguished before we can gain from its results."

Gordon was only too pleased. Firstly to get away from Cherie, still feeling guilty, but more to throw himself into work to stop him thinking of Sheila. However he was elated at what Charlotte had just told him. He could not see how they could help for Sheila was still married to Simon and she respected her marriage vows. Yet it seemed other people, ones he did not know, were trying to help both of them. So he gladly went with both Charlotte and Roy and very quickly reorganised the work program on the railway.

He was even surprised when Roy one evening told him that their consortium were all ready planning to invest further in other lines, and he had not forgotten their earliest idea of a line from Buffalo to Pittsburgh. A line which would help to retain their shipping route up the Hudson and along the Erie Canal. But before they left Pittsburgh Roy had doubled his salary, as Charlotte had promised weeks before. Still at night as he rested, he wondered how Sheila was responding to her new life in Tennessee.

He had managed to speak to Charlotte about Cherie telling her he still felt ashamed at concluding their affair. Charlotte had just smiled, "As I said before, I am sorry, for I believe you would have made a good son-in-law. But if anyone is to blame it is Cherie. If she had shown greater interest, or at least let you feel their was a chance of a future with her, - well you might not have needed to look for Sheila."

Again smiling she continued, "Don't feel any conscience, you have no need to do so. Cherie has behaved like I did when young. A really doubt if, in the long run, she would have chosen you, as a permanent mate. – No, as she has behaved in the past, she has, always, tried the field, and you were one of these. – Actually, I do believe, now, that she really believes she has found that man, in Daniel Wilson – I admit it may be just her maternal instincts and her desire for a baby – but Cherie is not a fool – I doubt if she would marry just to solve her desire for a baby. – No! I believe she is falling in love with Daniel. – The real question is, how strong is his real feeling for Cherie."

Laughing again, "You know you men take a long time in deciding who to marry. You all want to get your pleasure with us, but do not always then, want to repay us. It took Roy a long time before he asked me to marry him, though I lived with him for several years and bore him Charles before he proposed. I believe neither Roy nor Fay Bradbury, as she was then called, could decided if they should tie the not. You know they lived together as husband and wife for several years. I still thank my brother Francois for persuading Fay to marry him."

So Gordon learned a little of the early years when in Pittsburgh they were establishing their boat building business. He could only compare this with his own love life with both Sheila and Cherie. Suppose he could never gain a love life with Sheila, would he eventually decide, - in spite of what he had said to Sheila – would he eventually chose another to be his wife.

9.

Whilst Hanz and Elvira enjoyed the apparent miracle of their happy reunion, and Victor Luna was delighted to be once again reunited with his family, Sam Huston was dealing with the all matters resulting from their, almost impossible victory. He had to prevent, and stop, so many in his army who wished to see Santa Anna executed, for not only the massacres at the Alamo and Goliad, but also his continual attacks on the whole of Texas. However Houston realised that whilst Santa Anna was President, his signature on the Treaty guaranteed the Independence of Texas from Mexico. It was therefore imperative that Santa Anna left his camp as soon as possible.

Santa Anna realised how insecure was his position, so when Houston told him he was sending him away by sea, still as a prisoner, but to Washington, for him to explain his past and future intentions of Mexico in the United States, to President Andrew Jackson. Santa Anna readily agreed. Within a few days, Houston had been able to rid himself of the problem of the President of Mexico.

However Houston was not to know it, at least not at that time, for although the Mexican Army had eventually obeyed their commander's orders to leave Texas, it seemed that soon afterwards there would be unfavourable developments. The Mexican Congress, well pleased that, at least for a time, their dictatorial President had left their country, voted to remove him from office and by doing so nullified his Treaty giving Texas its Independence. Although the decimation of their army prevented them from quickly resuming hostilities, their Congress never did accept the fact.

Now Houston was able to devote his attention to increasing his own political power in Texas. The country was still extremely divided. David Burnet still claimed to be president, but then he had virtually been appointed in March and not elected. Houston had not forgotten how much Burnet had caused dissention at the height of the crisis. He wanted rid of this man. Again so many people realised how much they owed to Stephen Austin, believing him to be the father of the new Texas. With so much confusion Houston was able to persuade his congress the need for an election, where everyone in Texas could vote to elect the new President. It was agreed to be held in October.

Then again there was the question of the future of the new Republic of Texas. Should it continue as an independent country. Mirabeau

Lamar demanded this, even stating he wanted the Texas boundary extended westwards to the Pacific Ocean. On the other hand Houston, had always believed Texas should become another new state of the United States, and was he reason he had first come to Texas. Now his ideal could be achieved. But what would be the view of the people.

Hanz Eliot and Victor Luna, whilst realising how much Texas owed to Houston's military ability, were not sure if they wanted the country to become part of the Union. They also, also realised, how necessary it was to for Texas to gain, from the strengthening of the leadership of this man. It was essential that he did not emulate Santa Anna and become the dictator of Texas. Strangely if Texas gave up its independence and became a state, this would limit any dictatorial ambitions Houston may have. So, almost reluctantly they were being persuaded to accept Houston's ideas. Of course their strongest support was for Stephen Austin but had to admit he was not as strong as Houston, particularly should hostilities begin a again. It was agreed that if their was an election, they would stand, as representatives for San Machos and the surrounding areas and wished to be part of a future government.

So 1836 would always be known as the most important year in the history of Texas. However 1836 was to become a very important year for many others in America. Donald and Rachael had landed at San Francisco and quickly established themselves. Donald still had considerable wealth in the letters of credit he carried and during the journey on the ship, he had written a letter to his mother in St. Louis, asking her to send further letters of credit, from his own account. After they arrived at San Francisco, they had decided, rather than living in tents, they would to try to find a house for a home, in addition to the one they already held in San Diego.

However their first necessity was to ensure, as at San Diego, that their coming would be welcomed and not seen as an unwanted invasion, particularly if they intended to stay here. So they first must introduce themselves to the Commandante, Captain Vallesco, and give him their letters of introduction. In fact he was delighted to meet them, particularly as they had stated they wished to buy accommodation here, so they could in future divide their future between, both San Francisco, and San Diego, ensuring he knew they were quite rich. Donald told them they had no wish to live in tents.

Captain Vallesco assured them of his welcome, introducing them to John Leese, who was in the process of building homes in Yerba Buena, several of which were now for sale. Leese took them to see two possible purchases and they immediately fell in love with a small house on Grant Avenue with its beautiful view of San Francisco Bay. Leese promised to furnish it to their requirements and they passed the necessary letters of credit to him for this purchase.

Now Donald could at last finish his letter to his mother asking for further funds, sending this completed letter by boat to the Carroll/Marshall office in New Orleans, asking it to be forwarded to their office in St. Louis. Meantime, until everything was ready Vallesco graciously suggested they stayed with him, introducing them both to his delightful and very beautiful wife, Francesco. So it seemed that both Donald and Rachael were intending to spend some time in the town and explore the areas around, however undeveloped these might be.

That night as they retired to bed, extremely tired after their hectic day. As Donald took Rachel in his arms telling him how fortunate he was, to meet her on that boat going to St Louis, and to find such a wonderful woman to become his wife, it made her think again of her sister. Rachael gently kissed Donald, "Dearest, it is I who is so fortunate that you took pity on me. I fear what my sister, Constance will be suffering at the hands of that man who was our evil husband, Sydney Gilbert. – You know, maybe our marriage is illegal. Perhaps I am still married to him!"

Rachael did not know but that in Independence, her sister along with Nancy and another young girl, who Sydney had taken as a wife to replace her after she had fled with Donald, were at that moment being looked after by Donald's sister and her husband, Charles Marshall, after they had saved them from the mob which had descended on the Mormon settlement killing many, and driving them from Independence to escape further north to establish a new settlement in Caldwell County calling their new town Far West. Ever since 1833 the gentiles, from the first, were very concerned in so many Mormons descending on

Independence, realising their combined voting power would soon gain virtual control of the area and could impose their irreligious ideas on the whole community.

This had gradually escalated, and fear had driven them to open warfare. At first it had been uncoordinated attacks on their homes and particularly their shops and businesses. However during 1834, this had increased and finally the following year it had come to a head.

10.

Even whilst Donald stayed at St. Louis as Rachael recovered from her miscarriage, on Rachael's pleadings, he had written to his sister, Sharon, at Independence, begging her to try to discover the whereabouts of Rachael's sister, Constance. He begged her if she found her, to try to help to free her from her cruel and dominant husband, Sydney Gilbert. Donald had explained how Sydney treated his wives and how Rachael had suffered at his hands when married to him.

Donald continued to plead with his sister, telling her how Rachael feared for her sister's life. His last letter was sent from Rockville just before he went with the Carroll's to Mexico. Of course Sharon had accepted her task. Donald had told her everything of how Rachael had suffered, and she knew Constance would still be enduring Sydney's cruelness. With her husband, Charles' approval, as they increased the numbers of their own security men, now very necessary as the battles between Gentiles and Mormons increased during 1834. Necessary as more and more Mormons were arriving at what they called Zion The Marshall's, now, realised what might happen.

From what had happened elsewhere, it seemed Mormons always voted together, as one unit, receiving instruction from one of their elders. This meant that in any election, should their numbers become so great, they could ensure their men would be elected to civic positions. When this occurred they could impose their own religious beliefs, and multiple marriages, on the entire community. As most gentiles believe these views as wicked they knew they must do something to prevent it happening.

What at first was isolated attacks on Mormon buildings, and shops, by independent groups of gentiles, soon became more organised as it seemed the Mormons intended to stay and fully establish their Zion and its beliefs. During this period the Marshall's bodyguards needed to infiltrate Mormon communities, if only to obtain warning of the atrocities taking place and so be prepared should the Mormons retaliate.

In turn this gave them a chance to try to discover the whereabouts of Sydney Gilbert and his family. In fact by 1834 it became easy as it seemed this man Sydney Gilbert had become one of the most senior elders in their community. He seemed to be feared by others. Gradually both Sharon and Charles were informed of his families house and his wives. Of course Donald had told Sharon of his two wives, Constance and the elder, Nancy. Their men found that Nancy had now born Sydney two children, and Constance was pregnant for the second time.

However it seemed Sydney Gilbert had married again, taking another third wife, to replace Rachael, after her escape from him. She was Hilda Phelps who although barely sixteen was already, more advance in pregnancy than Constance. So she had conceived when only fifteen years of age. Only later did they discover how Sydney had used his exalted position an a church elder to obtain the young body of poor Hilda Phelps.

In 1835 Sharon even persuaded one of her very reliable servant women to call on the Gilberts, when their security men knew Sydney was away. She was able to speak in some privacy with Constance Gilbert telling her about her sister, Rachael, and that she had escaped and was now happy, even leaving St, Louis and travelling with Donald Reid towards Pittsburgh and the east. The servant offered Constance a chance to follow her sister and escape.

Even the servant was surprised at Constance's reply. "Go away at once. You are an evil woman. You would want to rid me of an everlasting life in paradise, and want me to leave my lord and husband. How dare you come to me to tell me of the evil life my sister has chosen. Her soul is damned to eternity, and will fall into hell fire. There she will earn her painful punishment for leaving her husband, to whom she had sworn to obey. Begone before my husband returns and uses his whip on you for the punishment you deserve." It was a very frightened servant who returned to inform Sharon of her failure.

So it seemed that the Marshall's would not separate Constance from her husband who believed her sister had committed blasphemy and would fall into purgatory. Sharon sent a letter to Donald at Rockville, but it arrived after both he and Rachel had left for Mexico. After this Sharon made no further attempts to communicate with Constance but still demanded that her security men continued to spy on the Gilbert family and report their findings.

As the attacks on the Mormons increased in early 1836 and many had now been driven out to flee to Far West in Caldwell County, Missouri. The gentiles were now determined to free Independence of any Mormons. It seemed, however, the Sydney Gilbert with several others, who had profited, greatly, financially, since they arrived here. Unlike the others they had no intention of leaving their prosperous businesses, so had recruited their own bunch of bodyguards, several not Mormons, but drifters being very well paid to ensure their loyalty. Sydney now virtually ruled the whole of the remaining Mormon flock, and had cleverly appeared to plan their resistance as piety to their Maker. So it had become a religious war.

What might have been the result, if the Governor of Missouri had not sent the militia to strengthen the gentile insurgents, determined to rid the area of all Mormons, is difficult to judge. Sydney Gilbert's group were better trained than the gentile mob, but they were no match for the efficient militia. Even to the end Sydney showed his true colours and cowardice. Realising they were losing the pitch battle, only concerned with saving his life, to the amazement of his three wives and their children, Sydney deserted them, to flee to the river, and to try to escape to Far West.

They were not there to see Sydney's end, but several gentiles had guessed some might try to escape that way and a group had waited in hiding for this possibility. The moment Sydney appeared, with two other men fleeing with him, the gentiles set upon them, virtually tearing the three of them apart. It was an agonising end for all of them. So his family were left destitute, but not for long.

Once the battle had begun Sharon had sent a group of the security men to where battles were in action. They had orders not to become engaged but try as soon as victory was assured to then enter and look for the Gilbert family, including Sydney if he was still alive. Of course when they arrived they found a number of Mormon women and children in desperate state with their menfolk killed or seriously injured. They found the three deserted Gilbert wives, Nancy, Constance and Hilda, sobbing in complete distress. They could not believe that the man they worshiped, and to whom they had been so pleased to obey as their husband, had deserted them and left them to fend for themselves now the battle was lost. It seemed to the security men that the Gilbert family were not the only one deserted by their husbands.

Now the security men obeying instructions virtually ordered the three women to accompany them. Believing these men had been sent by the authorities they had no option but to obey, now fearing that their own bodies may soon be attacked, as they were now, completely defenceless. So as ordered they followed them and were amazed when they were lead a long way on foot, pleased that the captors were willing to carry their young children, saving their own flagging resources, from complete disaster. Eventually they could not believe their eyes as they were lead up a steep path then through a large ornamental gate and along a long drive to the entrance of a large mansion.

This was no authority building but was obvious the private residence of a very prosperous family of some importance in the town of Independence. As they were lead through the large portals into a magnificent hall they were met by a woman about thirty years of age who introduced herself as Sharon Marshall.

Sharon explained, "Ladies you are all safe here. Please let my servants take you upstairs and bathe your bodies. I understand two of you are with child. I have arranged for a doctor to come to examine all of you and your delightful children. Then you must rest. I look forward to meeting you all tomorrow and will then explain our plans for all of you. – Please sleep peacefully tonight. You have nothing to fear."

This was the situation as Rachael lay with Donald in San Francisco, in Vallesco's house and wondering and fearing for her sister, Constance. She would have been very relieved if she had known they had just arrived at the home of Donald's sister in Independence, knowing if so Constance would be in good care. But they were thousands of miles from Independence and it would be a long time before they were to discover the good news.

So 1836 was a very important year for many people. Those in Mexico and California. Like those now in Independence, as well as Sheila Doyle now safely ensconce with the Albrecht's in Tennessee, wondering like Gordon Taylor, if they might one day have a future together. It had been a year of developments for everyone and a promise of even more happy developments in the future. In Maryland Edwin Palatine was now established as Professor of Mathematics in the University of Maryland and, now, with sufficient means, would soon be married to Audrey Carroll, who had already accepted his proposal of marriage.

Just as his sister Joan had become a very happy woman, when Keith Condorcet had asked her to marry him. It seemed both weddings would occur the next year. However there had been very encouraging signs from their investments in railways by the Marshall and Le Raye families. Also it was a very relieved Danton and Claudia Carroll in Mexico City, now that their compatriots in Texas had survived Santa Anna's attack and won their independence. For a time, at least, it meant they need not risk their own positions, and possible their lives, trying to win survival for the Texans. So pleased, they had written to Donald and Rachael, now, knowing their San Francisco's address. Telling them about events in Mexico and offering to become a post office for any letters they wished to send to the United States.

It did seem that their fears of the last few months had vanished, for they knew that the United States, through the meetings between President Jackson and Santa Anna would yield a more peaceful future for them in Mexico City. However they did wonder if Congress, by stripping Santa Anna of power might yet decide to unleash themselves, once again on the Texans. It truly had been a year of developments with the possibilities of a very much more settled, and happy future, in the next few years.

PART 7

CULIMINATION

LEBENSTRAUM PART 7
CULMINATION

CULMINATION

1.

After a restful nights sleep, awaking to realise their bedroom was a luxurious one, in the large mansion they had seen as they had walked along that drive the previous night. Servants had helped them undress and bathe and similarly bathed their young children, before dressing them all in cotton nightclothes. Before they were allowed the luxury of relaxing their tired and distraught bodies in those soft beds, they had all been examined by a doctor. His only fear was for Sydney's third wife, Hilda, now barely sixteen but very advanced in her pregnancy. The doctor feared she might miscarry, after what she had suffered so recently.

The next day servants had come with breakfast, encouraging them to eat and regain their strength. Then after bathing and dressing in new clothes provided, they all went downstairs wondering what would be their reception, though they had felt the lady of the house appeared to be a kind woman, and her words last night had helped them accommodate.

They were received by Sharon Marshall, the woman who had welcomed them the previous night, and she ensured they were all seated comfortably. "Since I want to speak freely with all of you and will beg you to answer, truthfully all my questions, please let my servants, who have children of their own, take your own children to play and be seen to. You need have no fear for them, they will be well looked after and you will soon be reunited with them again."

Seeing their first look of apprehension had vanished she continued, "First let me introduce myself. I am Sharon Marshall, the sister of Donald Reid, who rescued Rachael from the boat as you travelled to Independence years ago. I must inform you that, now, Rachael is my sister-in-law, and is legally married to Donald Reid. They are both now living in California, which is where my brother had wanted to go for some nine years. So Constance, whatever you now think of your sister, she is a very happily married woman."

Poor Constance hands flew to her face, "Oh! How could she, she was dear Sydney's wife – she cannot legally marry another man – she is living as a whore. God will never forgive her. He will force her, eventually, to return to her lord and master."

Sharon quietly placed a comforting hand on Constance's as she replied. "I'm sorry to tell you this, and to you both Nancy and Hilda. I'm afraid none of you will be able to return to your husband, - and in spite of your strong religious beliefs – The truth is he deserted you, caring little for your impossible positions, only trying to save himself. Well his treachery received its deserved end. Our security guards have discovered his mutilated body not far from the river where he hoped to escape. The mob found him, and two others, and quickly, and very painfully, ended their lives. – So ladies, I am sorry to be the bearer of this news – you are, now, all widows. You have no husband."

As expected the news caused the three wives to break down sobbing on each others shoulders wondering what was to become of them. Sharon let them cry. She knew they needed to do this. Eventually when their sobbing became less she explained. "Ladies, none of you or your children near fear for your future. As Rachael is my sister-in-law and as my brother, a long time ago asked me to help you – especially, you. Constance. My husband and I will see to all your futures. We are very rich. – Perhaps later you may be fit enough to help us with our work, here. – We shall see."

She could hardly fail to see the relief on all their faces, and happily continued, "First of all I must ask you to tell me of your past. I know your devotion to your husband, but eventually, you will see, he really was a very cruel man, who used you. – But that can wait. Rachael has told us of how you, Nancy, and you, Constance, came to marry Sydney. However Hilda, you are very young to be with child and our doctor fears your recent stress may cause you to lose your child." She saw the fear come into Hilda's eyes.

So quickly she went on, "Constance you should know that if my brother , Donald, had not persuaded Rachael to escape with him – she would be dead. She miscarried her baby within a couple of weeks of her landing at St. Louis. It would have happened on the boat before you got to Independence with no doctor to save her. She and her baby were starving to death, and it was your husband who had caused this. To punish her he had robbed her of food. We saved her life but her baby died – it was ill formed due to starvation. Eventually you will see that Sydney was a very wicked man. So tell me Hilda, how you, became Sydney's wife and conceive his child so early."

Once again as Rachael had told them, they saw how Sydney preyed on their religious fears, using them for his own pleasures. It seemed that Hilda's mother, Edna a third wife of Joseph Phelps, a blacksmith, had been unable to conceive a child unlike his two other wives. She was in danger of being divorced. It seemed Sydney as her religious elder, came to her aid, and by doing so practically brainwashed her young daughter, Hilda, who came to worship him, though only fifteen. Poor Hilda was so besotted with her love for Sydney that she believed he could persuade God to cure her mother's infertility.

Playing on their religious beliefs Hilda believed her mother went away, sometimes for days on end, ostensibly praying with Sydney to conceive a child. Hilda's innocence shocked Sharon, for what she described convinced Sharon that, in fact, her mother was a very passionate woman who desired intercourse with Sydney, as a much more handsome man than her husband. Her mother conceived. It seemed that God had intervened. In fact Sharon realised that both Edna and Sydney had enjoyed sexual liaison. Her pregnancy was by Sydney not by her husband.

Well this so pleased Edna's unknowing husband, Joseph, that he gladly agreed for Sydney to give his daughter, Hilda, religious instruction. Obviously, illegally, Sydney enjoyed her young body. Then when he found she had not been careful and she had conceived, he saved her from disgrace by marrying her, though only fifteen, replacing Rachael as his third wife. This then was why Hilda was soon to go into labour. Even then, though she tried, Sharon could not convince either Nancy nor Constance of Sydney's disgraceful actions. They still consider him their lord and master

Sharon now realised she would have a very difficult task of freeing their minds of the domination still present in spite of his death. During the next few days, both Nancy and Constance could not acknowledge that Rachael had not committed a terrible sin, by disserting her husband. However Sharon was determined, as the three of them lived with her, she would eventually, change their minds. But she would do this by kindness, not by any force, and by simple remarks, but made frequently.

At least the three of them knew now they all had a home, and readily agreed to help in the house in any way possible, extremely grateful for Sharon's kindness. Certainly the doctor was right. The stress had been too great for young Hilda and two days later went into labour. It was a difficult birth with some dangers at her young age but she survived, as so did her baby, a beautiful girl, she called Edna, after her mother.

Of course Constance was also seven months pregnant, but good food and a doctors attention, ensured her well being. Constance bore her third child by Sydney, a daughter, Elaine, two months after Hilda's birth. By then all three women were fully established in the household and were delighted to act as servants when Sharon asked anything of them. She knew they now believed that she was a Angel sent by God to look after them, and it seemed they must have been very virtuous women, to deserve such kindness. They knew they now loved Sharon, and would try to do whatever she wanted of them.

In early 1837, through the good offices of Danton and Claudia, now acting as a Post Office, Rachael was to learn at San Francisco, from Sharon, how her sister, as well as two other of Sydney's wives were now living with the Marshall's at Independence, in more comfort than they had enjoyed for many years. Further more Rachael's past evil husband was now dead. Her fear that her marriage to Donald was not legal, had now vanished. Now established in their new home on Grant Avenue, she was as anxious as Donald to see the surrounding areas and possibly set up, even a small estate, for their was plenty of, virtually, free land available. Now this was possible, for again due to the kindness of Danton and Claudia, Donald was now able to restore his financial position and had received several new letters of credit sent from the United States, from his growing fortune there.

However the news that her sister was now the mother of three children had re-awoken Rachel's mothering instincts. She was now determined to seduce Donald in giving her the child she had wanted for so long, to replace the one who had died in St. Louis. As it seemed they might make San Francisco a more permanent address than their house in San Diego and were now more settled, with Donald only wanting to explore the nearby countryside.

Rachael felt sure of her ability to overcome any doubts in Donald's mind. Rachael was in fact newly pregnant in early 1837 and sent Constance her third letter since she had learned of her whereabouts. Rachael was delighted, and proud, to tell her sister that, she soon would have either a nephew or niece for her own three children

2.

Houston was a very busy man throughout 1836. In fact the new Republic of Texas occupied three capitols that year. However there was a general appreciation of how much they owed to this man in obtaining their independence. A group had even established a small town, naming it as Houston. The fight was still between those like Mirabeau Lamar who wanted to keep Texas independent and those who supported Houston's belief they should join the United States as a new state.

So it was no surprise when in October, Houston, along with Lamar and Stephen Austin, stood for election as President. Houston won with an overwhelming majority but the new constitution demanded an election of President every two years and no man could severe as President for two consecutive years. Ensuring no President could become a dictator. Also during the next two years Texas suffered from indian wars. Houston, no doubt due to his past friendship with the Cherokee indians, enabled a short treaty. He also managed to obtain support from the Shawnees, though Lamar and many Texans opposed this, believing they should remove all indians from Texas territory. Fortunately as northern Texas was only being settled slowly, they did not, at present face outright war with the fierce some, Comanches.

Sadly Stephen Austin, regarded as the Father of Texas died in December. At least Houston's election enabled him to gain a vote to request annexation by the United States. However it reached Washington, too late in 1837. Andrew Jackson would most certainly have accepted this request but in 1837 he had completed his two terms of four years as President and now Martin Van Buren had been elected president. Van Buren was not anxious for trouble with Mexico and refused to consider the request. So Texas had to continue as an independent country.

Houston knew that for the present he would not achieve his ideal and, also, in two years, as he could not stand this time, so Lamar would become president and never consider annexation. This then was the situation whilst Rachael and Donald established themselves in San Francisco, and after a short exploration, even bought, with their new letters of credit, a strip of land in the interior, intending in future years to establish a ranch there possibly for cattle, or even fruit farms, which were being developed further south. Meantime Rachael had got her wish and was now happily pregnant by Donald, longing to become a mother again.

*   *   *   *   *   *   *   *   *   *   *   *   *   *   *

Meantime Gordon Taylor along with the Marshall and La Raye families were gaining much wealth from their investment in railway construction. Most of this was in property ownership but soon, if they wished they could, now, easily sell their assets and add considerably to their finances. Now his financial future was secure, Gordon had built himself a large house on land the Marshall's had given him near to their own estate

Of course Charlotte knew that Gordon's eagerness in their work was far less his desire to acquire wealth, than to stop him thinking about Sheila. He had at least received encouraging information from both Charlotte, and those in Kentucky, concerning the activities of the Albrecht families efforts to help Sheila.

At last Charlotte had explained their friends plans to help him. It seemed that due to their work years before in Tennessee in helping to establish Andrew Jackson. Firstly as Governor and then eventually to be elected President of the United States, they had hoped to bring Sheila's case before him and hoped he would either over rule as president, or use pressure, to allow Sheila to sue for divorce from Simon Doyle. At present the Missouri laws did not consider Simon's attacks on Sheila, sufficient to warrant her right to sue Simon for her freedom. Missouri still consider it was right for a husband to use force, if necessary, to control their wives behaviour. Even his savage attacks were not considered to be life threatening.

In fact the Albrecht's had made a passionate request to Andrew Jackson for his help. Unfortunately, though he had replied that he would have been glad to assist, he was leaving office and could only pass their request to his successor Van Buren giving it his support. Once again Van Buren took an easy course not wishing to interfere so early in his presidency in state matters, so he ignored the request. So there was no progress that way. Never-the-less Gordon was pleased that others were trying to help both Sheila and himself. At least he learned of what had happened in Kentucky after Sheila had flown, and he had left to return to Pittsburgh.

It seemed Simon Doyle had arrived at Camargo accompanied by a lawman from the Lexington Police Office, for Simon carried a writ given him in Missouri which gave him the right to demand his wife, Sheila, to return to their home in Missouri with him. Actually as the writ did not originate from Kentucky, it was not binding, but the lawman could demand that Sheila Doyle returned with him to Lexington, where the matter could be resolved. There was no doubt that Simon was furious to find her mother staying there.

After Sheila had left everyone had devised a planned reply should her husband appear and, now, this was what Patricia did. She said that after travelling to St. Louis with Sheila to stay with Dora and Andrew

Reid whilst Sheila went into the hospital for treatment. It seemed one morning Sheila had suddenly disappeared, She had left a note to say she was leaving Simon and going east to escape his brutality. As Patricia felt the only place she could have gone was to horse ranch at Camargo, Kentucky, where they both had spent time in the past, Patricia had left St. Louis and came here to the ranch.

However it seemed that Sheila had not done as her mother had expected. Now, nobody knew the whereabouts of her daughter, and wondered what she meant by going east. Had she continued on the boat to Pittsburgh or even further? Nobody knew. Accordingly Simon could not take possession of his wife and was furious. It seemed he became quite violent and would have attacked Patricia, claiming she had hated him for some time, and connived with her daughter to leave him. In the event, he had to be restrained.

Since Simon had no idea where his wife had flown, and receiving no help from the ranch he left with the lawman swearing to avenge himself on the McLean family. The threat was so real, that all asked Patricia to stay with them a little longer, and then one of the family would, eventually, accompany her back to Cole County. Patricia was extremely grateful for their continued help, but all they said was they were all one large family, and so must help. This then was what Gordon learned after his returned to Pittsburgh.

Gordon also learned in another letter of news of the two men he had met on the boat going to New Orleans so long ago. These were Steven Downey and Tony Brady, who had been travelling with a stock of horses to join relatives Hanz Eliot and Karl Downey on a horse ranch in Texas, all relatives of those families at Camargo.

Now Gordon was to learn that that the four man had not only settled in a large combined horse rearing ranch at San Marcos but all four had married. Three had married Mexican ladies and one a widow of a Texan settled there many years before. However Gordon, also learned of the recent hectic life they had lived as the Mexican President, Santa Anna, had made war on Texas intending to expel, or kill, all Americans.

It seemed that Hanz Eliot, who had married Elvira Luna, had fought with her father at the battle of San Jacinto where Santa Anna had been, decisively, defeated. However an intriguing extra point in that letter was, that in some way Hanz' wife, Elvira, had helped in trying to gain her revenge. It was her revenge for Santa Anna's sexual attacks on her body years before, which resulted in her bearing his illegitimate daughter.

Though she failed to kill him with poison the night before the battle, it had, never-the-less so incapacitated him, that he was unable to ensure his army was ready for the Texan attack. As a result he was defeated completely in just a few minutes. So Texas had become an independent country. Of course Gordon was intrigued with this news and well remembered his time on the boat with both Steven and Tony.

Still he was pleased for it seemed, that Simon Doyle had failed to find Sheila, now safely installed in Tennessee with the Albrecht's. Simon was still her husband and so Gordon, could not make her his own wife. Yet Charlotte kept telling him of her plans, and that someday, it would be possible, and must be patient.

Gordon was not to know, but very soon the situation might be resolved.

3.

Louisa Albrecht had just received one of her numerous letters from her daughter, Claudia Carroll, long since married to Mark Carroll, who was part of the United States Diplomatic Corps in Mexico, telling her mother of recent events since Texas had obtained their independence. It seemed Claudia was happily pregnant once again.

She was reading it to Sheila Doyle who had settled comfortably, but still very sadly, in the Albrecht country estate at La Falette, on the Cumberland plateau, in Tennessee. Louisa and Anton had made her very welcome and she had enjoyed riding around the estate with its beautiful vistas. They had, for a time, taken her into Nashville to their town house, were she learned of life in a large urban community, quite different from her childhood in Ireland, and very different from her married home in Missouri.

Still she preferred La Falette. It was here she had born Simon's second child a month before, a daughter, she named Georgina, named after the only man in her life she now loved, - Gordon Taylor. As she had just laid Georgina down to rest, having breast fed her, she wondered if she would ever meet Gordon again, let alone ever have a life with him. Still, he had promised her he would come and amazingly, after her past treatment of him, Gordon had declared his love for her. Then she wondered about her cruel and brutal husband, Simon Doyle.

She had learned from Louisa that he came to the Kentucky ranch, almost attacking her mother, before leaving swearing to seek revenge on her family. Since then they had received no further news of what had happened and for a time her mother had stayed, not returning to her father, fearing Simon's insane attacks. From Louisa she had learned of everyone's attempt to get first President Andrew Jackson, and later, - as he had finished his term as president, - President Van Bruen, to intervene with the State of Missouri, to get her marriage annulled.

But this had failed because the President did not want to be engaged in state matters, just as he had refused to accept the pleas of the new Texas Republic, to become a new state of the United States, as he did not want war with Mexico. So poor Sheila had resigned herself that in a few more months she must accept her married status and return for further unhappiness with her husband. She now sat listening patiently to Louisa as she read Claudia's letter to her.

"Sheila, you would like Claudia," Louisa said. "She has very strong principles. I know if she was here, she would fully support my views, that you should apply for a divorce from Simon. No husband in the United States, has the right to ill treat his wife as Simon so often treated you. Even the foolish laws of Missouri, should not allow him to make such viscous attacks on you. – Now, they must take into account the future safety of your two children."

Poor Sheila sighed, "I can't – I can't. I made my marriage vows to him. I have always believed a vow made to God must be upheld, otherwise I will not have right to a life hereafter. – In fact, though I hate the idea, and have loved staying with you – You have been so kind to me. – I know I should have asked you to take me back home. – It's only my fear of what Simon might do to Neil and Georgina. – I would accept anything he might do to me."

Again Louisa knew she had failed to change Sheila's mind, so she changed the subject, telling Sheila, how well she and her husband, knew Sam Houston. Now Sam had been elected President of the new Texas Republic. They knew Sam did not want Texas to remain a separate republic. He had always said, it should be part of the United States, and that was why Texas had asked the president to allow this. However the President wanted a peaceful life and refused the Texas plea, just as he had failed them concerning Sheila's divorce.

However neither Louisa nor Anton could alleviate poor Sheila's sadness. After dinner and a few drinks they retired to bed. But Sheila could not sleep. She knew, now, just how strong was her love – her desire for Gordon. Wanting him to come to her, crush her body to his and make unrestrained love. – Then her conscience told her, how wrong were these wishes. She was a wife, married to another man. She was committing a sin even to consider such terrible behaviour. She wondered if she should go on living.

Then she heard Georgina starting to cry. She got out of bed to attend to her. In spite of her sadness she began to smile. Now she knew she must somehow endure her torment, if only for her two lovely children. At least Simon had given her them. For their sakes she must go on living, and very soon she must return to him. They were his family as much as hers. Having comforted Georgina, sadly she returned to her bed. This time. exhausted, she finally fell asleep.

The next day she arose, attended to both Neil and Georgina, dressed and went down for breakfast. After last night she had decided that later that day she must tell Louisa she wanted to return to Simon, and ask her to make arrangements to take her back to Missouri within the next week..

Before she could speak to Louisa, Anton came and asked to take her and the children into the countryside. Louisa was very busy and so would not be coming with them. Sheila realised she must wait until evening to ask this favour of Louisa. Anton led her to the waiting carriage carrying a lunch box and food for Neil and Georgina, as they would be away all day. Almost without caring, she followed him holding Georgina in her arms as Anton led Neil to the carriage. It was a beautiful day, and Anton was very attentive, but poor Sheila's mind was far away, and she remembered little of the entire journey and the picnic, returning in time for late afternoon tea.

Anton helped them to dismount but suddenly Louisa came out of the mansion shouting. "Sheila, he's here, he's come for you." Sheila almost collapsed. So Simon had discovered her whereabouts and would demand they all returned with him. – It would not be necessary for Sheila to speak to Louisa. Resigned to her fate she reluctantly followed Louisa into the house. Then as she entered, her whole being trembled, she shouted, "it can't be", then sank to the floor in a faint.

When she recovered consciousness, she saw both Anton and Louisa looking down on her as she lay face upwards on the day-bed. But the other face gazing down on her was none other than Gordon Taylor. Sheila then realised it was not Simon but Gordon who had come for her. It had been this apparition which had caused her to faint.

She almost shouted as she lay, "Oh! Gordon, it is you. It's wonderful to see you, but why have you come." Not minding the others Gordon smiled, then bent down and kissed her, then replied, "I have a lot to tell you - some sad - but I feel certain there will be more you will like to hear. – But are you well enough to listen, or shall I wait and tell you later."

Sheila had now recovered, sat up, then pulled Gordon to her and kissed him passionately. "Please", she said, "tell me now. I want to know." Gordon now sat on the edge to the bed before taking both her hands in his. Then he smiled, "Firstly the sad news. Your husband Simon Doyle is dead, killed in a drunken fight in a St. Louis brothel. Sheila you are a widow – but it means you are free from Simon, forever.

– Now I hope you might accept my offer of marriage, as we discussed in Kentucky."

Without waiting for a reply Gordon continued to tell her everything that had happened since she came with Louisa to Tennessee. Sheila already knew of Simon's appearance, his attack on her mother, and his leaving, promising revenge on the entire McLean family, and why her mother had stayed for a time in Kentucky.

Gordon continued. Eventually Patricia had returned to Missouri accompanied by James Downey, who stayed until he was sure she was safe. Patricia found that Simon after returning from Kentucky, store a large sum of money from his father Kevin Doyle, left their farm and went to spend his life in St. Louis. He spent this money in drinking and frequenting brothels, determined to enjoy life. His resources were great and he indulged himself for several months. Evidently Dora Reid had kept everyone informed as Simon had become infamous in the town. Then just three weeks ago, he once again became involved in fighting when severely drunk, but this time his opponent thrust a knife into his heart and he fell down dead.

Of course the law intervened and Dora was able to inform everyone, very quickly of what had happened. Though at the time Gordon was away planning more rail routes, as soon as he returned Charlotte informed him and ensured he left quickly, to come to tell her the news, sailing on one of the boats down the Ohio river. Disembarking he took one of the smaller boats arriving at Nashville. Then, today, he had hired a coach and came to Le Falette to tell all of them the news, arriving whist Sheila was still out on her picnic with her children.

Of course Sheila was to learn far more about this in the days that followed but that evening, having recovered, - suddenly from desperation in the morning, - Sheila had become the happiest girl in the world. Of course she was sorry how Simon had died. However she knew from the past, his drunkenness would be both his and her sorrow. Now he had paid the price with his life. Even as she mourned him as a very religious girl, she could not stop her heart beating wildly knowing that Gordon had kept his promise and come for her.

After dinner Sheila, still in a dream, let Gordon lead her by the arm into the moonlit garden. The others did not follow. They knew the two of them wanted to be alone. Now Gordon placed his arm around her tiny waist and gently kissed the side of her face. Finally, some distance from the others, they stopped. Gordon took hold of her as Sheila let him press his body against hers, burying his lips on hers in along passionate kiss which sent thrills through her entire body.

At last they broke apart. Then he clasped her to him again saying, "My Dear, Dear, Sheila. I told you in Kentucky I would come for you. I've always loved you, even when I thought I had no future with you. – Now you are free – This means, I also am free. But I do not want to stay free for very long. – Dear Sheila, will you marry me. I want you to marry me soon. – Then, if you will allow me, I would want to adopt both Neil and Georgina as our children to bear our name of Taylor. – This time. I'm sure both your father and mother will approve."

She merely hugged him close again, once more burying her lips in his. Only then did she take her lips from his before saying, "Oh! Darling, wonderful, Gordon. Yes! I do want to marry you – Yes! And if it is your wish let you adopt my children. – But I must warn you, that very soon I shall want you to give me a replica of yourself – not one – but many. Please I do so want this."

Desperately in love they kissed again,. Gordon, only took a second to say, "I promise, - for you have just made me the happiest man in this world. – I also promise, that I will ensure the rest of your life is one of extreme happiness, after want you have had to endure in the past."

Though they lingered in their embrace for a little time. Eventually they had to return to the others. But as she walked besides Gordon, Sheila could not help thinking of her desperation, as she dressed and saw to the children that morning. Determined to ask Louisa to take her back to Simon. Then her sad picnic, even though Anton did everything to relieve her sadness. – Then that wonderful moment as she returned and saw Gordon standing there. – Now this wonderful evening – Gordon's proposal and her acceptance. It had all happened in a single day. Sheila now resolved to ensure that she gave Gordon all her love, her body, and everything he wanted of her. She knew she would have a happy future, but was more determined, that he, also, should have a wonderful future life.

4.

With Elvira and Hanz once again united, and desperately in love with each other, they were both delighted when Elvira gave birth to Hanz' second child in 1837. It was a happy event for the whole of the Luna family, - as it was for Karl and Raquel Downey, now Raquel was pregnant for the second time. In fact, now free from the terror of Mexican domination the new republic flourished. Though the Mexican Government had repudiated Santa Anna's treaty with Texas, they merely blustered and except for infrequent minor intrusions, Texas was never, seriously threatened.

In fact its greatest danger was the prevalence of indian attacks by the many tribes in this vast territory. In a single year in October 1836 and October, a year later, both Lt. Miles, who had captured Santa Ann and Moses Lapham, who had destroyed Vince's Bridge, preventing the Mexican army retreating, were killed by indians. Houston used wherever possible, his past friendship with the Cherokee indians to diffuse many such engagements, but indian attacks continued for many years.

The Luna and Garcia families, had always been very prosperous, except for punitive taxation by the government, Now with both Hanz and Victor elected to the new Congress, they became, even more, wealthy. However, the greatest effect was on Elvira. She had never been able to rid her mind of Santa Anna's raping. Her religious upbringing had made her feel a dishonoured woman. Hanz, ever since he began to court her, had tried hard to alleviate this but without success. Now with this man no longer powerful, and with her religious attitude, it had made her realise she should never have attempted to murder him. Now she felt he had truly paid for his attack on her body.

Freed now, from guilt, and so deliriously happy with Hanz and her new baby, She felt reborn. As they lay together one night she kissed Hanz, "Dearest, you know, that day when we first met in Stephen

Austin's office, was the beginning of a new life for me. It was you, not my dear father, who released me from purgatory. Only my religion, and my love for Adela, prevented me from committing suicide. Then you came – though even when you tried to please me – I still distrusted all men. – But heavenly, you persisted. Due to your patience I now feel I am living a new – a second life. – Now, all I want is to live long enough to repay you, for giving me this chance."

Hanz crushed her lovely body to him, "Elvira, remember, you too, have given a new life. One I never dreamed I might enjoy when I left Kentucky, merely wanting adventure. – My dearest, I thank you for this, just as much as anything you owe to me. We are one, large family, and it is Texas which has given us this chance."

Now, freed from ever present despairs of the past, they both wrote regularly to his family in Kentucky. Rich as they were, they could be spared from work on the ranches, and during 1838, both made a journey to Camargo and received a rapturous reception from everyone on the estate. As both were good riders, they enjoyed travelling around the estate. Elvira, saw that in Kentucky, the families methods of horse breading were, superior to their own, and was determined to improve matters when they returned.

But it was a long happy holiday, and the families not only accepted their new daughter-in-law, but ensured she knew how much they loved her. When Hanz and Karl had left them, so long before, they had never expected to see them again. Now Hanz had told them that Karl and Raquel would soon call upon them, not forgetting the other two who had followed them to Mexico. After a stay of three months, it was a happy Hanz and Elvira, who return to Mexico, only sad to be parted once again from these families. So the next two years were years of happiness, after the many years of fear of their lives, whilst Santa Anna ruled.

As the Texas constitution demanded that its president could only serve for two years, and then could not stand immediately for a second time, Houston's term as president ceased in December 1838. As President Van Buren had refused Texas' request to become a new state of the United States, Houston realised it was useless to try again for some time. In any case he was kept very busy dealing with the multiple problems besetting the new republic.

The new man elected as President was Mirabeau Lamar, who had always opposed Houston, believing in its independence, outside the United States. He violently advocated seizing more of Mexico, and extending the Texas boundaries as far as the Pacific Ocean He even altered the capitol from the new town of Houston, some of Sam's admirers had built, changing it and making a new town to be known as the town of Austin, built and named in remembrance of Stephen Austin, now regarded as the Father of Texas.

Houston retired temporary and in 1840 married again. This time to Margaret Lea. He was then 47 and Margaret only 21. In fact Houston lived long enough to sire no less than eight of their children. Now all the families in San Marcos supported Houston, believing that their new president would lead them once again into war with Mexico, even though they did believe Texas should remain independent. They did not want another war. They could now appreciate the ability of this man, Houston, even if he wanted union with America. They, rightly felt he was the only man capable of governing sensibly.

So they were delighted when December 1841, Houston stood again for president and was elected, this time holding this post for three years. He now had the difficult task of dealing with the many indian raids and an internal war, which became known as the Regulator-Moderator War.

By now hundreds of families were travelling to Texas from all parts of the United States, and some from Europe. Land was freely available to the north, which had been sparsely populated in the past. As explained during Donald Reid attempts to create a river passage to that area, it was the land of the Comanches. These indians tolerated the original small invasion, but now many families came to settle, they joined with the brother Comanches around Santa Fe, and what was to become New Mexico, and so decimated a number of homesteads.

Attempts for peace talks held in San Antonio turned into a battle and for a short time they ran amok, killing several people. However the militia eventually dealt with the uprising, and now ensured the majority of Comanche tribes were driven west, freeing large areas of north Texas, but providing further troubles for other settlers, in other areas, going west. Battles which continued for years.

At San Marcos everyone was enjoying their peaceful life, and all their wives were ensuring increases in their families. Of course, even these areas, were sometimes attacked by indians, but most attacks were to the north and the east. Victor Luna was now fifty years old but was very healthy. He was liked by everyone in the district, who remembered how he dared to stand up against Santa Anna, even at the risk of his life, long before there was any strong attempts by others to rectify the terrible situation. Both he and Hanz were respected members of the new Congress.

Besides the three children Elvira had born him, before Houston married Margaret Lea, Elvira's daughter, Adela, after her raping by Santa Anna, loved Hanz as her father, and she was rapidly growing into a beautiful girl nearly ten years old. It pleased Elvira that Hanz treated Adela, as his daughter, and continually showing his love for her, as much as for any of the children Elvira had born him. There was no doubt but that Texas was growing at a great rate, though large areas were now given over to cattle breeding.

Still the question was – should it remain independent – or should it become part of the United States.

5.

Donald and Rachael had now, firmly, settled in their new life in San Francisco. Besides their home on Grant Avenue, Donald had purchased a large strip of land across the bay, for future use. In February 1838, at the age of twenty five, Rachael had born their first child, a daughter, who at Rachael's request, they agreed to call Doris Reid, remembering the wonderful way his mother had comforted her after she had miscarriage Sidney's child. They were supremely happy.

Now that it seemed that he wished to make San Francisco his more permanent home, Donald realised he could not continue to exhaust, even his, now, considerable wealth. This was due, not only to, the profits from the fur trading endevours, but together with his income from the Steam boat company, of which he was a junior director. Donald knew he must establish a business venture in the town. With little knowledge of cattle breeding or fruit growing, he felt his estate across the bay, should remain, simply for future speculations. However his long association with steam boats on the rivers made him consider that the sea might provide a future. Not to sail on it, but derive financial benefits from it.

He, quickly, saw how the many small schooners and brigs sailing along the west coast and even those adventurous enough, to sail to Asia and China, were all reaping a very profitable income. The only drawback was that these same ships must travel nearly half a year, before they could reap their profits in eastern United States. The lengths of these journeys reduced, heavily, their profits. However what surprised Donald was that it took far less time for his letters to reach his families in the east and to receive their replies. He discovered the reason from Danton Carroll in Mexico.

Evidently there was now a much shorter route for passengers, and therefore mail, then on ships rounding Cape Horn. The route was by ship to Panama, across the short isthmus, to the Pacific side, then by another ship to San Francisco. Suppose Donald could establish a small shipping line on the West Coast, to trade, not only along the coast for hides and other things, but also use them to trade with the Far East, this route via Panama could become very profitable for trade to the eastern seaboard.

Of course this would require mule transport across the isthmus and another ship to sail north. Donald suddenly thought of what he had learned about Cornelius Vanderbilt, at the meeting at Rockville, who were deciding whether to invest in propeller driven ships. At that time he remembered that Cornelius, already, had several sailing ships trading along the East Coast and the Gulf of Mexico.

The Carroll Marshall Company had considerable experience, in not only building, but sailing river boats of some size. Suppose, as a minor director, he could persuade them to go into partnership with Vanderbilt, buy two schooners from him, or have built new ones. Then in association with Vanderbilt extend this trading to include goods obtained by Donald's ships, transported across Panama, and taken for quick sale in the east. It would be the quickest way goods from the Far East could reach the large populations of Eastern United States. He was fortunate that Rachael fully supported his idea.

He set out his ideas, immediately, in a letter, to outline his project, sending it to all his families there, and it seemed Roy Marshall became an enthusiast. Charlotte was involved in railways. Now Roy, who had done so much in years before, in establishing their boat company, now liked the idea of making a branch of it a Shipping company. However he realised that not only would it need other investors, but must require the full cooperation of Cornelius Vanderbilt, and his willingness to offer two schooners to sail to the Pacific and form the basis of Donald's seagoing fleet.

Roy had always been adapt at persuading investors to accept his ideas. Now he interested the other Carroll descendents of Sir David, to join the Carroll's of Pittsburgh, particularly, Peter and Amy Carroll, already with close family relationships with the Vanderbilt's. Together they persuaded the Ibsen family, it was a worthwhile idea. By 1840 a new company RMCV was established. The initials denoting its constituents, Reid, Marshall, Carroll and Vanderbilt. Very quickly Vanderbilt sent two fully crewed sailing schooners, round the Horn to San Francisco for Donald to establish a Western office in the town. Surprisingly he had no difficulty with the Mexican authorities, as they saw that it would add to the economic prosperity of the area.

By 1842 benefits were already accruing, and goods from the Far East, as well as all the products of the west coast were being taken by Donald's ships to Panama, transported to the Atlantic side, then taken by Cornelius ships to lucrative outlets throughout the whole of eastern United States. Likewise much need engineering and build parts, came the opposite way. However it now established a regular passenger route for those wishing to seek prosperity in California, without having to risk the dangerous overland routes, or suffer the discomfort of the stormy Cape Horn passage.

Donald's financial situation was now, firmly established, in San Francisco, and he used some of the profits to extend his land ownership away from, but near the eastern coast of San Francisco bay. He did this purely for speculation. Still believing this area must sometime become part of the United States, he knew, that then, future settlers would need to purchase this from him gaining even more wealth. However, though he had no wish to sail with his ships to China and Asia, he did use them for his own entertainment.

Rachael had presented him with a son, who they named Alan, after his father in 1841. Once recovered Donald took her and their two children on one of his ships, back to San Diego to visit and stay for a few weeks in his first house in the town, renewing his friendships with everyone there. Though it was not his wish, it seemed they, now, all regarded him as a Mexican. So it seemed his family were now accepted as prosperous business people, in both that town as well as San Francisco. Little did they know of his still strong desire for the whole of California to become another American State.

In San Francisco one of his greatest problems was to find well educated staff, to relieve him of the considerable demands on his time. He had employed some recent incomers, who had come overland from Independence along the Oregon trail. They were good workers but few could read or write. To the annoyance of the Mexican authorities, but accepted as they were cheap labour, were Chinese workers who came on his ships from the east, willing to do much needed manual work, dirty work, not liked by white settlers. However Donald desperately need a well educated Manager to take the strain from him.

He obtained this in a strange way and it was only possible, because so many years ago Sir David Carroll had discovered and eventually married his beloved Amelia on that little ship coming to America from Dublin. For it was one of Amelia's descendents who provided the solution.

David Backhouse, had fled from the Oregon country to the western coast once the smallpox epidemic hit that land, decimating whole indian tribes, and still attacking white settlers. Finding little work there he had worked his passage on a ship down the coast to land at San Francisco, penniless. David still believed all this area should become part of Canada. Though he found even persons of British descent, working and labouring there, but they were not interested in his views.

He managed to obtain work around the docks, but his upbringing was not suited to heavy labour, though he had to accept it or starve. It was sheer chance that desperately tired, after a heavy days work on a ship recently docked from China, that when drinking away his sorrow. Now regretting leaving Oregon, where he had held a good position He accompanied one of Donald Reid's foremen, a good worker but illiterate. That night the man discovered David's ability to write, read and could calculate the cost of their drinks.

Almost as a joke, he told David he must take him to his boss, who that day had told him how much he needed a man who understood money, being almost exhausted in overseeing the goods delivered from the ship that morning. The foreman told him to come to him the next morning and he would take him to his boss, who could see if David might be of help, for his boss was a strict but very good man to work for.

David, glad to have the chance, came with the foreman the next morning and shown into his bosses palatial office. Left him there after informing his boss, before going to do his own job. The boss was none other than Donald Reid. Almost an hour later Donald found David patiently waiting for him. Donald laughed, "Sorry to keep you waiting, I'm up to my neck in work. Come inside. Sam says you can both read and write." David confirmed he could do this and was well educated, having been trained as an accountant. Donald, simply, could not believe his ears, rapidly transferring him to his office.

Realising how very American was this boss, he felt he must state his views, "Sir. I can see you are an American. I think you should know I am proud to be a Canadian. I firmly believe this land belongs to Canada and Britain, and not to either the United States or Mexico."

Donald exploded, but not with anger, but with laughter. "Hardly the words I would expect from a man wanting a job in this office. – But I hold nothing against you – There is land here for all of us, though naturally my sentiments are not yours. Please tell me your name, where you are from, and what services you could offer me."

Now it was David's turn to laugh before replying, "Sir, I respect you for not taking umbrage at my remark. It certainly was not intended to insult you, merely that you might be prejudiced against any Britisher's, which I have found so entrenched in Oregon from which I have travelled."

The ice was broken, Donald obtained coffee and refreshments then asked David to tell him his past. David very proud of his ancestry, and well versed, as how one of his ancestors, though an American, had married, gone to New York, then after America rebelled, had to flee to Canada. By chance only that weekend Rachael had been reminding Donald of the many branches of the Carroll family and how proud she felt that in some way she was, now, a part of that history. She had even told him what she had learned from Estelle of the descendents of Blanche Carroll, who had married a Backhouse, and their life in New York before going to Montreal. Also that one of her descendents had travelled to the Oregon country.

Suddenly Donald realised the man had told him he was David Backhouse and one of his forebears had been an American, married and moved to New York. Could that person be Blanche Carroll. Donald asked David. Though astonished that this man knew that name, David proudly affirmed she was that woman, and was why he now proudly held the name of her illustrious father. Then even more astonished when Donald held out his hand to shake saying, "Then in a very long around way, I know all about Blanche Carroll. In fact we might even be very distant relatives."

Now it was left for Donald to explain his own position and why he knew so much about the Carroll families – Yes! And even the history of the Backhouse family. From that moment on it mattered not, what was the country in which they were born. They could, each, hold their own views on the ownership of this land. Donald discovered David was an accountant, just the man he needed. Two hours later he had appointed him as Junior Manager of the San Francisco branch of his firm, with a good salary, David knew he would be fortunate to attain in Montreal. That night Donald took David back to his home, knowing just how much Rachael would want to meet him. Donald, as well as Rachael, felt how fortunate they had been that day to discover this young David Backhouse. Once again it seemed that the ghost of Sir David and Amelia Carroll was to haunt them, even more pleased that, this man in the past had left England and come to Maryland.

However two years later, and after much correspondence using their schooners, Rachael was delighted to welcome her sister, Constance, and her children, but even more to welcome Constance's new husband, who again was to provide help to reduce the heavy workload, at present carried by Donald.

6.

There had been great sadness at Rockville in 1840, when both Andrew Carroll and his wife Angela had died within two months of each other, though it was expected as each were now over eighty years of age. So at last the two branches of Sir David and Amelia Carroll's, who had established ownership of Rockville over a hundred and fifty years before, once again became Master and Mistress of that great estate. The English and American branches once again owned this birthplace of their families. It was a sad time for both Adrian and Estelle. Long ago Estelle had come to love Angela, as much as she had loved her own mother.

But in those recent years there had been, equally, happy occasions, all celebrated at Rockville. Edwin Palatine had married Adrian and Estelle's daughter, Audrey Carroll, in the same year that Joan Palatine married Keith Condorcet. Edwin was now, firmly, established as Professor of Mathematics, at the University of Maryland. He had, already, expanded this Faculty, establishing a School of Astronomy, and this required the appointment of the Dean of this School.

Once again it seemed that events in the past were to resurface, for the man appointed to that post was none other than Neil Reeve, a lecturer in the Edwin's faculty. Now Neil was also the son of Anna and Andrew Reeve. Anna was the Austrian Princess who had eloped pregnant with Englishman, Andrew Reeve, fifty years before, escaping death, if they had stayed in Austria. Then established, first a little school, on a small stretch of land near Pittsburgh, but which had grown into a large Academy, preparing students for a University education.

Neil was Anna and Andrew's third child, a son named after Andrew's uncle, Neil Reeve, who had come with prostitute, Claire Collins, from England, settling for a time in the same area. It seemed he deserted her and lived for a time with Sophia Brookes, as she tried to assuage her despair at the loss of her loving husband, Keith Brookes, at such an early age. Well the younger Neil having graduated, had become a lecturer at the university. Now nearly forty, had been promoted to become Dean of the School of Astronomy.

Otto Fallen, had, so, proved his brilliance in advising on suitable investments, that, whilst retaining his Managership of the Annapolis Bank, had been promoted as a junior director of the Casimar/Wycks Banking Empire. Perhaps it was because Freda Ibsen, had, herself, been so involved in advising her father, Kanson Ibsen, that she appreciated Otto's equal brilliance in investment. However it is far more likely that she felt her extremely amorous and intimate relationship with Otto, was superior to a similar enjoyment with Pieter Wycks.

Whatever the reason in 1840, Freda, at last capitulated to one of the many proposals of marriage, Otto had offered her. Or again, was it that her maternal desires which had, at last, overcome her self imposed insistence in remaining a spinster. Never-the-less when she married Otto in New York she was, already, two months pregnant with his child. Again a happy ending to the short romance which had occurred as Otto fled to America on the same boat as the Ibsen family.

Louisa and Anton Albrecht, having so ably enabled the happy reunion of Gordon Taylor with his lovely Sheila McLean, had enjoyed another long vacation on their original estate in Florida, purchased, as a necessity when like the Reeve's, they had fled death in Austria. Long ago this estate, though divided, was now occupied by the their two eldest children, one of which Antonia conceived before marriage in Austria, and the reason for them to leave so quickly. But also by their eldest son Franz Albrecht.

It was memories of the past which made these visits so necessary, for but for this estate, and their neighbours, which had caused them to travel to New Orleans. Then to meet their American friends at a conference held there, before ensuring their safety. Afterwards becoming citizens of the United States and buying, first the small land near Pittsburgh, now generously given to the Reeves, enabling the establishment of the Academy. Only later did they establish themselves in Tennessee. Now there was no doubt it was this estate, with its wonderful vista, which ensured, in spite of their earlier memories of Florida, was where they wished to live and die.

* * * * * * * * * * * * * * *

It had been a deliriously happy Sheila McLean, after he came for her in Tennessee, who so gladly let Gordon Taylor take her and her two children back with him to Pittsburgh. They stayed, temporarily with Charlotte and Roy Marshall, whilst a delighted Charlotte arranged a superb wedding for the two love birds. Gordon, already owned his large mansion near the Marshall's, a home Sheila felt was more like a palace than a house, being for so long living in small wooden houses, first of her father's then that belonging to Simon Downey.

Before they married, as Gordon took her there, she turned and once again hugged Gordon. "Gordon you are so wonderful. I know now I have loved you, and no other, since we met on that ship coming to America. – You must believe me, on that ship I had never before come to know a boy friend. I know you scared me as you so, obviously, flirted with me. I did not know what to do. – I was afraid – yet – even then, wickedly, I even hoped you would seize and possess me. Perhaps it was because you were so kind to me, even disappointing me, by not being a villain. – Now I know I fell completely in love with you on that ship and as you took us to Pittsburgh."

Now after passionately kissing him she continued. "I was completely broken hearted when father told me I could not marry you. Perhaps it was because I found I could enjoy Simon's more amorous relationship with me, that I, eventually, capitulated to my parents pleadings and married Simon. Even as I gave my marriage vows, I wondered if I sinned, for as I stood beside him in church, I then, too late, knew I did not want to marry him. Perhaps these long years of purgatory are a punishment, for swearing my vows, when they were not what my heart desired. – But, by then, I had lost you. You never returned. I was not tempted to betray my vows."

She smiled after kissing him again. "Then my head swimmed as I saw you standing there at Camargo. I could not believe my eyes. You looked so handsome, - at that moment I knew I still was desperately in love with you. Again I was terrified, especially as you spoke to me in private. I was sure you would ask me to elope with you. – Much as I desired it – I knew it must not happen. Instead you amazed me by encouraging me to go to live with the Albrecht's. – Yes! In spite of your forgiveness for sending you away in Missouri. – Yet, you could tell me, you were still in love with me and never married."

Gordon delighted at her confessions, did not interrupt. "Then at my lowest ebb. Having that very day, - I had decided I must ask Louisa to take me back to Simon, - like Prince Charming – you came and released me from my prison. Again begging me to marry you. Now you have brought me here, shown me the palace in which we shall live. – Oh! –Dearest! – Wonderful! Gordon, it is the end of a fairy story. – like those tales, all I want to do is to live with you - give us both a family – and live ever after, with you. – just as everyone in those fairy stories do. Dearest, Darling, Gordon. - I love you. - I love you."

After that – there was only one possible conclusion. Sheila Doyle married Gordon Taylor in Pittsburgh in early 1838, as all from Camargo, Tennessee and her parents from Missouri, were their wedding guests in a wonderful marriage service and reception, held by, an equally delighted, Charlotte Marshall.

Perhaps Gordon, felt he was forgiven for his previous past relationship with Cherie Marshall, for Cherie, gladly, came with her new husband,

Daniel Wilson, great grandson of Donald and Kate Wilson, who like Michelle Carroll had come to America together a hundred years before. There was no doubt but that Cherie was now an extremely happy mother of their son, George Wilson. At the reception in front of Sheila, Cherie came and embraced an embarrassed Gordon saying, "Dear Gordon, may you now have as happy life as I am now enjoying, but still thank you for your kindness to me in the past."

Sheila did not mind this event. In fact Gordon, had long since confessed his affair with Cherie. Sheila fully approved. She knew it was this liaison, which not only took away Gordon's great sorrow, but ensured Gordon was still a bachelor and thus able to marry her that day.

It was hardly surprising that nine months later Sheila presented Gordon with their first child, a son, Gerry Taylor. However, even though this was Shelia's third child, Sheila knew she wanted to bear many more children by her wonderful husband. After so many years of desperation, both Sheila and Gordon, had at last found happiness

7.

Meanwhile since 1837 Mexico had been in chaos. The national government was in disarray. Local bosses controlled their own regions. In 1838 France invaded Vera Cruz to collect debts, the so called 'Pastry War'. Before they withdrew, Santa Anna lost his left leg by a cannon ball. This made him a hero and so three years later he became President of Mexico again, holding this post, as dictator until 1845. This was his most disastrous presidency, though he married another fifteen year old girl, after his first wife died, who become his second wife, though he still retained many others as his mistresses. Then for misgovernment, he was sent again into exile, but was recalled due to conflict with the United States.

After Sam Houston gave up office, Anson Jones became the last president of independent Texas, for by then, Houston had once again asked the United States to make it a new state. This was granted, and Texas entered the Union in December 1845 as the twenty-eight state. A border incident the next April signalled the beginning of the American-Mexican War.

However this had been brewing for some time. After President Harrison replaced Van Buren as President in March 1841, and then died of pneumonia a month later, his vice-president John Tyler became president. He was a weak man and not liked publicably. Desperate for re-election, he not only supported Texas becoming a state, he almost declared war on Mexico, knowing it was in disarray. This was his vain attempt to regain popularity. But his bill was defeated in Congress. He then was dismissed, and James K. Polk, a Democrat was elected.

In fact there was no stopping the wish of all in America to make both Texas and California part of the United States. What is called her 'Magnificent Destiny'. All Americans believed Mexico had no right to its territories. Already thousands of Americans were pouring into Texas and many more into California. This provided even greater wealth for Donald Reid and its new company of RMCV Holdings. As their quicker, and less arduous journey, was the route preferred by many coming to the rich promise of California. Like Donald these came to acquire land, Mexican land, believing this must become part of the United States. Then they could profit by selling their holdings. The Mexican rulers, were too few, and without the resources, to any longer suppress this illegal invasion.

A border incident near the Rio Grande began the American-Mexican War, which lasted until Mexico surrendered in February 1848 with the Treaty of Guadalupe Hidalgo. Though Santa Anna, manfully resisted, as numerous separate invasions of Mexico and California occurred, resulting in fifteen battles, mainly won by the United States on normal Mexican soil, as well as the invasion from Santa Fe to capture San Diego, Monterey, then on to occupy San Francisco, eventually arriving at Sutter's Fort, where one year later, gold was found, producing the Californian Gold Rush, bringing many thousand more Americans, and others, to populate California.

The brilliant invasions of Generals, Scott. Kearny, and Freemont, not forgetting the parts played by the Missouri Volunteers in north Texas and Mexico, would provide an interesting book in itself. The final death knell of Mexico as it then existed, was assured when General Scott landed at Vera Cruz. Fought his way westward into the mountains, taking Pueblo and finally, after five battles, eventually entered Mexico City, forcing the Mexican surrender

In that three year war the United States won nearly as much land as they had bought in the 'Louisiana Purchase'. Not only Texas and western California, but land which eventually gave rise to many more states such as New Mexico, Colorado and Nevada. However to Donald Reid living in luxury in San Francisco, his greatest moment was when American troops arrived there, to occupy the town and the surrounding area, virtually without opposition. For twenty years Donald had firmly believed California belonged to the United States, - ever since his trek to Salt Lake City, collecting furs.

Now his wish had been granted. But he had not needed to fight to achieve this, and more important during that time, by circumstances beyond his control, he had found, courted and married the beautiful and wonderful Rachael, who not only had supported him all the years, since he took her off that steam boat at St. Louis. A woman he loved more than life, knowing she loved him just the same. Her only wish was to make him happy and bear their family, and live together. Also, with Rachael's help he had acquired a fortune, and an enormous area of new rich land, around, and near the town. They were now, quite as rich as any of his families in the east. He knew this would never have been possible without a loving wife to assist him.

Now the United States stretched from the Atlantic ocean, westward over the eastern mountains, across the great plains, over the Rocky mountains, now to reach the Pacific ocean. A country, almost a continent, stretching from the Atlantic to the Pacific ocean. Donald had a vision of this as he sat listening, at the Great Salt Lake, to the tales of Jedediah Smith, Mountain Man, learning of the wonderful Pacific coast in the land of California, and how then, it had determined him to go there.

Though he had vowed to do everything possible to make this part of his country, his action had not been necessary. Here he was, - now a rich man, living in this growing town next to that ocean. He had, merely, had to wait. Circumstances had forced the United States into this war with Mexico, and it had happened. However, Donald was now more than ever determined to live, here, enjoying a happy life with his beloved Rachael, and the four lovely children she had born him.

* * * * * * * * * * * * * * *

At San Marcos Hanz Eliot sat with his two year old daughter, Carlotta Eliot on his knee, the fifth child his darling Elvira had born him. His other four children stood in front of him as he sat with one arm around this wife. His beautiful sixteen year old step daughter, Adela, who Hanz loved just as much, perhaps even more than those Elvira had given him, was sitting close by with the arm of her finance, Tomas Cirilo, around her waist. They all knew that Adela would soon marry Tomas,. Elvira knew this happy event might never had happened but for meeting Hanz so many years before.

They had just heard the wonderful news that Santa Anna's army had been completely beaten, Mexico had surrendered and the peace treaty had been signed. Of course when the war had started Hanz and many Texans wanted to take part and help. Elvira had protested, saying he had risked his life too much in the past, gaining Texas' independence. Even, in spite of her pleading, he would have joined the United States army. However, very politely, he had been told this was a new, modern war, and frankly he was not been trained to fight in this way.

This did not seem too big an insult, for Sam Houston, had come to him, telling him, he had already done enough, in the past. As a past member of Congress he had enabled Texas to become part of the United States. Now it was for their country to ensure that Texas remained that way.

It was very relieved Elvira who had comforted him. Once again she had told him that she owed her life to him for giving her a purpose to live after her dishonouring by Santa Anna. She told him her life was his, for ever, and would not have live long if he had been killed. Their horse breeding ranch had prospered and gained considerably due to the war, as the forces had needed many horses in their campaign. Like their neighbours they were very rich, However Elvira was more delighted that once again Santa Anna had been sent into exile.

Now she told him she wanted all their family to go to Kentucky again, and live several weeks there. In fact, she intended to persuade all four of the families, who had come to Texas, married and established families, to accompany them. Her desire was for them all to all travel together, to meet their families in Kentucky. Elvira was a very determined woman. In 1849 they all travelled, together, to New Orleans and then took a steam boat to Cincinnati. Then by coaches to Camargo, to receive a an ecstatic welcome, and spent over a month meeting everyone, but travelling to Pittsburgh to meet the other families they all knew. This included Gordon and Sheila Taylor and their young family. It was a journey they would never forget.

So by the end of the war, it had established the United States as one of the largest countries in the world. What would Sir David and Amelia Carroll had thought if they had known this, as with their arms around each others waist, they gazed out of that large window in Rockville, with its many panes. looking at those distant hills, never dreaming that someday, that country would extend thousands of miles, until it reached another ocean.

8.

Gordon Taylor was a very happy man, having at last married his beloved Sheila. As he sat with her in his large mansion, now extended, to house his growing family. Sheila had blessed him already, with four children and he, equally, loved her two children born to Simon Doyle. Neil and Georgina, who he had adopted, and now were teenagers. Neither could remember their cruel and drunken father. Gordon was the only father they knew.

With ever growing wealth, he had never neglected his uncle Silas Taylor and his wife Gloria. But for Silas' invitation, he would never have sailed to America. Gordon had ensured Silas' early retirement, persuading Roy Marshall to buy his steam boats, ensuring he had a comfortable retirement. But he knew he owed so much to Roy's wife, Charlotte, and her faith in him when he first settled in Pittsburgh.

Charlotte though now nearly seventy, was just as fascinated in railway construction as was Gordon. She was, still, at heart an engineer, or more correctly an engineering designer. Her father had instilled in her, her love for design. Neither did she lose the friendship of her sister-in-law, Fay, essential now that Fay's husband and her brother, Frances Le Raye, had died. Neither wanted to forget the close intimate relationships they had enjoyed with their two men. They, virtually, had always been one large family.

Although Gordon knew how much he owed to Charlotte's faith in him, she also knew it was Gordon who had rekindled her love in engineering, teaching her the mysteries of railway construction. Her husband, Roy, was an innovator, always wanting to discover new ideas. Though never trained that way, he was capable of assimilating many engineering ideas, just as he had started in building his first cotton mill and attaching steam power to make it profitable. Likewise he had the ability to immediately see the chances open to him by investing wisely, just as he had seen it, in the few moments when he met Gordon, with Silas at his workshop.

Perhaps it was remarkable because of the circumstances which had forced Fay and himself, Charlotte and Francis, and later Gordon to come from England and France, and land in America. It had been essential they left and came here. Fay and Roy escaping possible transportation to Australia after burning down Grimshaw's cotton mill. Charlotte and Francis, escaping death during the French Revolution. Whilst money shortages had been what had made Gordon come to meet his uncle Silas. Yet it had been America that had provided them with the opportunity to become rich.

Railway construction, as well as river steam boats, now after, even, forming a shipping company, - this was the basis of all their wealth. Yet in doing this they had helped to increase the wealth of both the Reid and Vanderbilt families. Still again, Roy knew how much they all owed to the many divisions of the vast Carroll descendents, not only of Sir David and Amelia Carroll, but the original Roman Catholic families

---

Lebenstraum

who later had become protestants. It had been the Pittsburgh Carroll's who had given Roy his first employment when he landed with Fay, and with Hugh Foyle and his sister, Linda.

Sheila had just received a letter from her mother, Patricia. Her family now lived in Kentucky on land purchased by Gordon Taylor for them, near Camargo. It had been essential after Simon Doyle's death. The memories of both the Doyle and McLean families were too recent. Gordon and Sheila persuaded them to sell their Missouri estate, move to Kentucky where Neil could raise both cattle and horses, ensured of easy sales to the families at Camargo. Though not rich, they were quite prosperous. Both could not fail to see the irony, that it was Gordon Taylor, now married to their daughter, the man they had felt unfitted for her to marry, who now had provided this happy new life for them.

Gordon had kept in touch with his family in Manchester, ever since he arrived at Pittsburgh. It seemed they too had progressed and acquired some wealth, due to their involvement in the many railway lines being driven through the country. So much so, that the entire family had moved into the rapidly growing and very upmarket area of Moss Side, with its many green fields and large houses. For in the mid nineteen century, this was a very desirable area in which to live. Each family including, Gordon's, were pleased that they could write frequently to each other.

Sheila was telling Gordon how happy were her family and once again thanked their wonderful son-in-law for his kindness. Naturally he was pleased, however he replied, "You know my position in the firm now gives me an opportunity to take a rest. All my foremen are capable of seeing to our railway development for many months without my supervision. Really I now only act as overseer, and I know Charlotte would enjoy substituting for me whilst I am away."

He placed his arm around a very willing Sheila. "Sheila, though I know all your family, - you have never met mine. It pleases me that you have established a regular communication with both James' wife and sister Elizabeth. It's high time you met them. Sally is two years old and able to travel, as is all our family. We must all go to New York in the New Year, and take a ship to Liverpool. My family can meet us there and take us on the railway to Manchester."

Sheila turned and kissed the side of Gordon's face, "Dearest, I'd love that, and so would the children. I can never forget that it was on board a ship I discovered this wonderful Prince Charming who has given me already nearly thirteen years of paradise. Perhaps if we stayed there you could take me to London on the railway they have built. It's a place I always wanted to see, but never thought it would be possible."

Gordon pulled her close to him and smoothed her lips in a profusion of kisses. "Yes! We will do that. We can show our children, Buckingham Palace, the Tower of London, and of course, the Houses of Parliament, and we can go there on the railway. You know it is these wonderful railways, that has ensured all our fortunes, both in America and in Britain. Yet, it was my families growing so rapidly, with so many children, that I had to come to Uncle Silas. You know I worked by hand, my truck on the railway line to get to Liverpool to come here. Then I met you on that ship. So even then a railway played its part."

As so often happened when either of them relived in the minds the happy moments of the past, for ever excluding that terrible period they lived separate lives, it was the beginning of yet another period of intimate love making. To Sheila's delight, with the children playing outside or away from the house, she was thrilled, for she knew what was to happen.

Now Gordon picked up her tiny body in his arms and carried her upstairs to their bedroom, just as on that wonderful day, after their marriage and honeymoon, he had done as he made her mistress of this palace. Like then, Sheila now believed he had turned her, his Cinderella, into a princess. But unlike those lovely stories, her story never ended

However as he laid beside her on the bed wanting much, what she knew was about to happen, and which she so desperately desired, she said, "Much as I want you, you must wait a minute. If we are soon to got to England, you will have to forego – at least for a few months, - letting me add to our family."

But it was only a temporary pause, and soon Gordon was ensuring once again, that her desires, rose into the paradise of their intimate embrace as her Prince Charming made his Princess a very happy woman.

Afterwards as they lay, a little exhausted, Sheila, again remembered how Gordon, on that ship coming to America had placed his arm around her waist, scaring her, yet, even then, wanting it to go further. Now they could enjoy this until the end of their lives.

Yes! She knew she would enjoy repeating this on a new ship going to England, - repeating those wonderful moments – only this time – there would be no reason for stopping them achieving, what in the past she dare not do. She thought, 'Perhaps in England I may add to our family. I could conceive a baby there. It would be both English as well as American, but I know it is America where I will always want to live'.

9.

Over two thousand miles to the west on the Pacific coast, Donald, Rachael, David, and now Constance and her husband, Jack were celebrating the possible entry of California into the Union. Although it was not yet decided, they all felt it would not be long before, it entered the Union as a new state. If so Donald was determined to stand for election to the State legislature, for he was already one of the wealthiest business men in San Francisco, and very well accepted by everyone in the town. In time he might stand to become a Congressman.

Since by 1840 Donald and Rachael had built a large mansion with their newly acquired riches, on one portion of the land they had bought for future speculation. It was just across the bay in what was being called the San Leandro region of sparsely populated Oakland, but with his boats, there was a very easy access.

From his mansion, there were magnificent views of the bay both, westwards and northwards, and now with his ever growing, reasonably educated staff, Donald was only required to attend at his offices, a few times each week, when important decisions were needed. David Backhouse had been a boon, quickly relieving Donald of, at first, mainly, purely financial, matters, however very soon, recruiting men with book-keeping experience arriving on his own ships, David had quickly been appointed full manager of the entire office.

Then after Rachael had persuaded her sister to come with her family to live with them. Constance coming with her new husband, Jack Manners, who had been in charge of stores at the Carroll/Marshall Independence Steamer port. So his coming provided Donald with a man to manage the off loading and loading of all their ships when they landed at San Francisco. However much had happened at Independence since Sharon Marshall had befriended and brought, deceased Sidney Gilbert's three wives, to live with them.

It had been the loving patience of Sharon, - pleased to help her brother and his wife, to gradually convince Nancy, Constance and Hilda that their late husband had really been a very wicked and lecherous man, who had spent his life in misusing them, as he had to several other Mormon women. It had been a slow process. It fact it was probably helped by nineteen year old Hilda eloping with twenty one year old Stanley Bruen, a Mormon son, left an orphan after his mother and father had been killed in the fighting.

It seemed Stanley had long since had his eyes on Hilda's delightful figure, but then she was married to Sidney. Knowing Sydney was dead, Stanley quickly found where Hilda had gone. Now Hilda was a realist. It is true she had worshipped Sidney, and being very amorous, gladly gave herself to him. However when her mother, left her when her father had died, and gone away with another Mormon man, without even telling her. Hilda was more receptive to Sharon's persuasion then the others.

Easily excited, Hilda was quickly seduced by Stanley, conceived by him, then fearful to tell the others, she was delighted to accompany Stanley when he asked to take her westwards into Kansas, and there, set up a homestead. In fact years later they discovered the liaison had worked and eventually Hilda had married Stanley, not caring that she had to share him with another woman, as they were still Mormons..

This did help Constance and Nancy to reconsider their positions. Nancy had gone to help as a servant in Sharon's daughter Elizabeth's small estate, where she lived after marrying in 1833. There she had met Elizabeth's butler, a man six years older than Nancy, but whose wife had recently died in childbirth. It was he who persuaded Nancy how wrong she had been to accept Sidney's domination. Both having lost a partner, they fell in love, each, already with families, married and Nancy continued to help her husband eventually become Housekeeper for Elizabeth.

Now only Constance was left living with Sharon and she meet frequently Jack Manners when he came to report to Charles Marshall, Sharon's husband, as Jack was Storekeeper, and Manager of the Steam Boat workshops in Independence. Like Nancy, he persuaded Constance that Sidney Gilbert had been a wicked man. Again having lost his wife with pneumonia they were, very quickly, attracted to each other.

It was Jack who, eventually convinced Constance that her sister, Rachael, was not a wicked, but a very good woman, who had helped her husband, Donald, to establish this successful shipping line at San Francisco. Soon after Nancy married, they married, Sharon gladly giving them a wonderful wedding. However in her letter, even before Constance became engaged to Jack, Rachel had begged Constance to travel to San Francisco and live with her. Once Rachel learned about her coming marriage, and told Donald, who was desperately trying to find a suitable manager for their far more vast storehouses.

Donald asked Rachael to write to Constance offering to pay for Constance and Jack's honeymoon by coming on his ships to enjoy the Pacific. He, added, if so, if they liked San Francisco, and wanted to stay, he could offer Jack, the position as Full Manager of the Storehouses, at a salary, far in excess of the what he received in Independence, as those storehouses had been much smaller.

This was the deciding matter. Jack told Constance, not only did he want to accept Donald's offer of a paid-for honeymoon, but would like to accept Donald's managerial position. In fact, in spite of her previous fear that Rachael had sinned, she had always loved her sister. It was the fear her sister would fall into hell after she died which had so entrenched her attitude. Now after Sharon's continued assistance, Jack's insistence that Rachael had done no wrong, and was a very good wife to Donald. Now after this offer, Constance knew she wanted to be near Rachael again.

So in 1842 Constance with her new husband and with all their families, sailed on the Marshall boat to New Orleans, taken by Cornelius Vanderbilt's ship to Panama, crossed the isthmus, then sailed on Donald's schooner to land at San Francisco. They discovered that Rachael had persuaded Donald to give their Grant Avenue house to the Manners, as their home, as Donald and Rachael moved to Oakland. Very quickly Jack accepted his new position, with a salary which in time, would make him quite wealthy, in spite of their many children. But for Rachael the most important fact was that she was once again united with her sister, Constance. All their past differences had been forgotten.

By then David Backhouse had met, fallen in love and married a local girl his own age, and set up his own house in the town. He had written many times to his parents, using Donald's ships, telling them everything that had happened since he left Montreal. Now married he told them he intended to stay at San Francisco, but added, in a few years he would bring his wife and his family, to visit them in Canada. Though still believing all this area should become part of Canada, he was grateful for the new life Donald had given him, and the chance to find and marry a woman he could love.

He accepted that now, there were many more families settling there, who had come from the United States than from Canada. At least he was pleased it would not be taken by the fewer Russians living there. Then in 1848 the United States army landed and took possession of San Francisco and the whole of California, making it part of their American continent. David had no option but accept this, knowing, in due course he would have to become a United States citizen, if he, and his family wished to stay there.

However this was far less serious than the fact that gold was discovered at Sutter's Fort and the 1849 the Californian Gold Rush had begun. Soon thousands of people of many nationalities were landing at the port, anxious to stake their claim. Unfortunately, as always happens on these occasions, it attracted many lawless men, as anxious to commit strife and robbery, as they prospected for gold. Soon it would become unsafe for many people living there.

10.

This had necessitating Donald, David, Jack employing a virtual army of male defenders to ensure the security of their homes, as well as their offices and storehouses. This protected them from attacks, but many Mexican haciendas, who had lived in California for some years suffered. These evil men found such places easy to plunder, often killing the owners, sometimes sparing the females to enjoy sexually.

Donald's security men, whilst protecting one of their store houses in the centre of town, fought a group who were celebrating the results of their evil plundering. After a gun fight, having killed the looters, they discovered a pretty nineteen year old daughter, from a recently ransacked hacienda, with her maid. The only survivors of their murderous attack. Both had been raped many times.

Donald had the two of them taken to his Oakland estate, gave them medical attention, ensuring they survived and recovered. However traumatised by their experience and pregnant, it took them a long time to recover, their sanity saved by the kind and understanding consideration of Rachael Reid. In fact Alicia Recio and her maid stayed indefinitely with the Reid's, delivering their babies, and in a year or two each found men friends, who wanted to marry them and adopt their babies. There was another Mexican woman torn and raped by evil men who murdered her family on the hacienda they owned. A woman who Donald and Rachael came to know very well. Her name was Anita Madero

Never-the less, the gold prospectors added astronomically to Donald's wealth. Cornelius Vanderbilt had discovered a much quicker route from east coast America to the gold fields than the Panama route. Sailing to San Juan del Norje, on the east coast of Nicaragua, by boat up the San Juan river, across Lake Nicaragua, then a short overland journey to San Juan Del Sur, on the Pacific coast. Finally on Donald's schooners to San Francisco. This route was both cheaper and quicker, and speed was essential if the prospectors were to stake their claims. It gave the RMCV Holdings very rich dividends by 1850.

So all the families on each side of the United States accumulated even greater wealth. Roy Marshall and Charlotte at Pittsburgh, as well as Gordon and Sheila Taylor, were some of the recipients of this rich takings. As Roy lay with his beloved Charlotte they mused at the successes which had begun with the setting up of that small factory near the river in Ohio, building small boats to take the influx of settlers heading west, over fifty years before

As he lay with his arm around Charlotte he kissed her and said, "You know this was the start of our empire, with Fay and Francis helping and later Manon and Jack Eliot. Then we started the building of bigger boats, steam driven, even using them setting up the Carroll/Marshall Company, dominating the river traffic –"

Charlotte interrupted, "Yes! Then Gordon came and we started building railways, now we have even become involved in shipping. You know we have helped to secure, almost, every type of transport throughout this country. We have grown big as the United States extended its boundaries - ever westward." Yet even at that time they feared their country might be torn asunder on the question of slavery.

Gordon and Sheila were thinking the same way as they had paid a visit to Estelle and Adrian Carroll at Rockville. Both Estelle and Adrian were proud of their ancestry. She had been pleased to extend the magnificent work of Manon Eliot. Estelle was now pleased that Blanche Carroll's decedent David Backhouse had settled, prosperously, on the Pacific coast.

Proudly as the enjoyed their after dinner drinks in that large retiring room next to where they had just eaten Estelle remarked. "You know this country owes a lot to the two branches of the Carroll families who came to Maryland so many years ago. Certainly I am proud to be descended, like you Adrian, from that wonderful pair, Sir David and Amelia. However we would not be sitting here now, but for Edgar Carroll, the Roman Catholic Carroll's, bringing David here on the boat where he met dear Amelia."

She continued, "Now their descendents have multiplied so greatly that the Carroll families still enjoy a significant part of all Maryland,

Pittsburgh and the Potomac valleys. They are the proud owners of so many large estates and have played, even recently, a prominent part in the government of these lands. Though we can be equally proud of our industrial legacies."

Adrian came and kissed her as Gordon and Sheila were delighted at her musing. Then Adrian added, "Yes! But we must never forget the important part Daniel and Michelle Carroll, and Racoonsville, played in this. Gordon, but for him there would be no Carroll/Marshall Company, though, also, Edgar's descendent, Edgar Carroll, played his part. Again Donald and Rachael Reid would not be, now, wealthy owners of estates on the Pacific. – Gordon, it was the two of them who befriended the Reid's and the Hobbs, ensuring they married Erin and Mary, otherwise Donald Reid, would never have been born."

Again Estelle mused, "You know I hated Daniel Carroll believing he had robbed me and my family of this wonderful house of Rockville. Yet! When I learned the truth and how he saved my father from a debtors prison in England, I came to love him, as much as you know I loved my wonderful mother-in-law and father-in-law. Yes! It is this wonderful estate of Rockville which has, for so long, been the basis of our success."

She sighed, "At times, as I look out of the vast window in our bedroom, I feel as though David and Amelia are standing beside me. I know the many times they had stood there looking at those distant hills, wondering what lay behind them."

Now it was Gordon who added to this story. "You may be right, - but it also needed many other persons, not just those coming from Britain. Michelle was a French woman. Then later those French families fleeing from death in France during the revolution. Manon would never have been able to write her book, if the Eliot's and Brady's, had not rescued them, and brought them to America. I was told their history. and the part they played, as I went to Camargo to find and comfort dear Sheila."

Perhaps it was essential, that everyone learned the part so many persons had played in making the United States, what is was that day. Almost like a giant jigsaw, the parts, eventually, fitting together. Many had come from Europe to escape persecution, from revolution, or religion. Many were British, and quite a number French, but then some came from Germany, Poland and Sweden, some even bringing riches, but still needing to find a more safer future.

In fact the present position was the inevitable culmination, of the efforts of so many different people – so many different families – so many different nationalities, who had landed in America. Above all else, their was no doubt how much this land owed to those two different Carroll families. One Roman Catholics – one Protestant – yet together they had played their part.

Together as the four sat drinking, it was Estelle who asserted convincingly, "Yes! I must admit, many people have contributed to our present success." Now looking lovingly at her husband Adrian, she concluded, "But I still feel – Rockville – and above all the Carroll family, - of which I am so proud to be a part. – is the vital reason. I firmly believe it is *the Carroll Family Saga* – those two families who came from Yorkshire, Gloucester and Somerset so long ago, - which have contributed the most to making this country, the refuge for so many persecuted families, and with their help made this United States of America."

None disagreed. However Estelle thought, perhaps at that moment Sir David and Amelia Carroll might be amongst them, listening intently to what they had said. If so she knew David would take his Amelia in his arms, and lovingly embrace her, as he had done so many times in the past. Just as on that fateful day on that little ship, he had caught Amelia, and prevented her throwing her starving, pregnant body into the Atlantic Ocean. If he had not, instinctively, done this, - Estelle realised, - neither she nor Adrian would be sitting so happily in this haven of Rockville

But it seemed the Happy – even if involved - Saga of these Carroll Families would continue for many more years – perhaps forever..

The End

OTHER BOOKS BY ROYSTON MOORE

ALL PRINTED AND PUBLISHED BY TRAFFORD PUBLISHING

MAKERE – THE FEMALE PHARAOH – QUEEN OF SHEBA

Makere Hatshepsut was the only Female Pharaoh of Egypt who wore the Double Crown , destined to be worn by a man, for 25 Years – the last 10 Years as Sole Pharaoh

This book is her life written as fiction but it is her true story. It is her own love story with the two men in her life.- Web Priest Senmut – who she raised to high office – and King Solomon, the King of All Israel. Although she bore each of them a child, she was never allowed to marry them. – Enjoy lovers living for each other three thousand years ago.

The Carroll family sagas

Five books concerning Love life in America covering the period 1687 to 1850

MARYLAND – A Rags to Riches Story – Amelia Eliot sent as an indentured servant, already raped pregnant, and to conceive and bear three more children within five years by men chosen for her. Amelia became his Cinderella when she met aristocratic David Carroll on the small ship sailing to America. How he became her Prince Charming by later marrying her and giving her a title.

OHIO – five couples both French and English meet during the Seven Years War. Enemies who became friends. – Extending the Carroll Family Saga with now, Daniel Carroll, the grandson of Amelia and David Carroll. Introducing many new persons who fell in love as Britain fights France in America

LIBERTY - Daniel Carroll helping his friend George Washington during the American War of Independence. – Introducing other Carroll descendents and many others fleeing from persecution in Europe – Yet it is a series of Romantic tales still possible in spite of the war with Britain, Civil and Indian Wars

GENESIS - The United States a new country, ruled by an elected President not a King. Struggling to stay neutral whilst Europe descends into chaos during the French Revolution. Carroll descendents and many new persons finding refuge and love in this new country – Then in a day the Louisiana Purchase doubles it.

LEBENSTRAUM - Further Carroll descendents along with others continue the expansion West. Mexico, and Texas and California are acquired. The growing industrial might and both River and Sea Transport. Now Railways to take new immigrants to new lands to the West and to the Pacific which is now reached.

MAKERE – THE FEMALE PHAROAH –
QUEEN OF SHEBA

The passionate love story of Makere Hatshepsut – the only Female Pharaoh of Egypt – with lowly peasant Web-Priest Senmut – and Solomon, King of all Israel

Makere was a very beautiful, intelligent and courageous woman in a man's world. Yet who established herself and was to wear the Double Crown of Egypt for 25 Years, ruling as Sole Pharaoh, The Living God, for the last 10 Years.

Although Fiction, it definitely portrays her true life story 3,000 Years ago.

Made Joint Pharaoh by her beloved father, forced after his death to marry her perverted and evil step-brother, meeting and receiving the love of this Web Priest Senmut who gave her the desire to live. Raising him to positions of supreme importance but, though she tried, was never allow to marry him.

After enduring years of hell she eventually becomes Sole Female Pharaoh of Egypt. Then invited by King Solomon, as his 'Queen Shwa – or Sheba', -now because of the proven 500 Years error in the chronology of Egypt – Makere is therefore the legendary 'Queen of Sheba" who travels to Israel.

A story of love and intrigue, though written as fiction, but accurately portrays life and events, in Ancient Egypt over three thousand years ago. Today her two Obelisks stand in the Temple at Karnak, her Magnificent Mortuary Temple now called Deir el Bahri, and is available for all to see and visit on the banks of the Nile near Luxor, as is the engravings on the cliff walls at Syene, placed there by her lover Senmut over three thousand years ago

ROYSTON MOORE

SEE – www.shebamakere.com

MARYLAND

MARYLAND

A RAGS TO RICHES STORY OF
A MAN & A WOMAN'S
TRUE LOVE FOR EACH OTHER
IN 17TH. CENTURY
AMERICA
A CARROL
FAMILY SAGA

ROYSTON MOORE

This is the story of how the aristocrat David Carroll met and came to love, peasant girl and indentured servant, Amelia Eliot, condemned by an Irish Court to a life of virtually sexual slavery in Maryland, the British colony of Charles Calvert, Lord Baltimore, at the end of the 17th. Century.

It is set in the time when first King James II and then King William III and Queen Mary ruled Britain. It is a Rags to Riches story.

There is no doubt but that Amelia Eliot, was indeed 'Cinderella' and that David Carroll was to become her 'Prince Charming' turning her into his own 'Princess', though it took some time before the fairy tale took shape.

It is the first of five books which form the family sagas of the two Carroll families and their descendents. David Carroll is a young member of the Protestant Carroll family from Somerset going to America for the first time, where the Roman Catholic Carroll family from Yorkshire, have lived for sometime.

Every attempt has been made to ensure the historical accuracy of events at that time introducing into it the lives of several well known historical personages. John Washington was the grandfather of George Washington,. Sir Winston Churchill, was the forerunner of the World

311

War II Prime Minister, and his son, John, was to become the Duke of Marlborough. Charles Calvert was the third Lord Baltimore, and did own not only Maryland but lands in Ireland granted to his predecessor by King Charles I, when he once again became a Roman Catholic and had to retire as a Privy Counsellor.

However enjoy this love story whilst Britain and France continue their wars which have lasted centuries.

ROYSTON MOORE

OHIO

This book is the second book continuing the family sagas of the Roman Catholic and Protestant Carroll's began in book one – '*Maryland*'

The story of five couples, five men and women, born in England and France, who find love for each other. Who in spite of the war between their countries, which forces them apart, finding solace with others, go to America, to eventually find each other again.

Set in Maryland and Ohio in the 18th. Century at the time of the 'Seven Years War'. Introducing Daniel Carroll, grandson of Sir David and Amelia Carroll, with his boyhood friend George Washington exploring the region of Ohio, where France and Britain go to war to decide who owns it.

It may shock you but it is a fact. It accurately describes the true lives of several white woman sentenced for a crime in England, to endure both domestic and sexual slavery, to men without marriage, for several years. Desperately trying to limit the number of children they may bear them.

It accurately describes the licentious life at the court of Versailles and the salons where titled ladies bestowed their favours on men for benefit.

The love stories of men and women, torn apart, though of different nationalities, virtual enemies, meet, come to know and understand each other, becoming friends. Overcoming their differences helping them to meet again the women they love.

Made possible, only, because of this region called 'Ohio'.

Though a fiction story, and including many families introduced in the previous book, every event is historically accurate, including the lives of George Washington, as are the many actual governors of the colonies and military persons. Enjoy the love stories and enjoy living in those far off days.

ROYSTON MOORE

LIBERTY

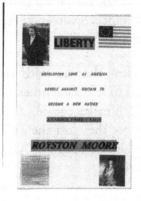

It is the third book written as part of five books, following my books, 'Maryland' and 'Ohio', before Books "Genesis" and "Lebenstraum"

It continues the saga of the Carroll family. Daniel Carroll, the grandson of Sir David and Amelia Carroll, now happily married to his French wife, Michelle. Daniel now helps the friend of his youth, George Washington, married to Martha, living on his estate of Mount Vernon. Daniel having promised to stand 'side by side' with George, when war breaks out, having previously been trying to keep peace in Maryland, Virginia and West Virginia, now with help of his friends, ensures they all support the rebellion.

The main characters are fictitious and includes many families from the previous books. Yet it is' essentially. a love story based on the lives of people living in America, just before and during, the American Revolution However it introduces many new persons fleeing from Europe. Some quite rich like the Casimir's from Poland, and the Holsteins from Sweden, buying estates near the Potomac and land in the Wilderness, but others such as the Scott's, Reeves' and Collins escaping from England, devastated, that the land they were given is covered in Hardwood trees and not suitable for farming, until helped by Michael Casimir for personal reasons, concerning his first love, Carla who committed suicide when Michael was forbidden to marry her, her likeness to Claire Collins.

However there are other couples brought together due to the war, and who discover love. This was not only a war with Britain, but a Civil war, and an Indian war. How France, Spain and people from Europe helped, in achieving, eventual, victory.

It is a romantic story. How the war with Britain brought together many people, who learned to love each other, leading to the creation of land of West Virginia, with exiles coming from England, France and other parts of Europe. How they lost their nationalities, and became Americans, creating the United States of America, when victory was assured in the Treaty of Paris.

ROYSTON MOORE

GENESIS

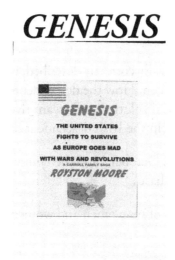

A romantic story of love triumphing during the Genesis of the birth of a new United States, as it fights to survive, as Europe goes mad with wars and revolutions. This the fourth book in the five book saga of continuing the lives of the two Carroll families descendents of protestant David Carroll and Roman Catholic Edgar Carroll. Following the previous three books, 'Maryland', 'Ohio', and 'Liberty'.

The first country with a democratically elected President, instead of a King. Having won its independence, trying to survive and prosper, attempting neutrality as the world lapses into chaos.

The saviour for many men and women escaping from war torn Europe to settle and expand this new country. Including the aristocratic Hapsburg Prince and Princesses whose scandal threatens them with death, to those exiles escaping death by the guillotine in France, and the many settlers beset and in danger from indian attacks.

Yet it is essentially a story of romantic love and lovers, new emigrants and those resident here for many years. How, in their own way they endeavoured to establish this new country, providing a refuge from many new families coming from England, Ireland, France and Austria, forgetting their previous nationalities and becoming Americans.

All events are all historically correctly described, including the despicable treatment of many women. How the descendents of Edgar Carroll help establish the industrial revolution and steam river boats, whilst Daniel Carroll continues to help the Irish descendent of his grandmother.

Then on a single day in October 1803 the United States doubled its size by the 'Louisiana Purchase'.

Enjoy this story of love of many men and women in America at the end of the 18th. Century.

ROYSTON MOORE